SWEET
AFTER
DEATH

Also by Valentina Giambanco
The Gift of Darkness
The Dark
Blood and Bone

SWEET
AFTER
DEATH

VALENTINA
GIAMBANCO

Quercus

New York • London

Quercus

New York • London

© 2017 by Valentina Giambanco
First published in the United States by Quercus in 2018
First paperback 2019

ISBN 978-1-63506-062-1
eISBN 978-1-63506-063-8

Library of Congress Cataloging-in-Publication Data

Names: Giambanco, V. M., author.
Title: Sweet after death / Valentina Giambanco.
Description: First edition. | New York : Quercus, 2018. | Series: A Detective Alice Madison novel ; 4
Identifiers: LCCN 2017047344 (print) | LCCN 2017057231 (ebook) | ISBN 9781635060638 (ebook) | ISBN 9781635060645 (library ebook edition) | ISBN 9781635060614 (hardcover) | ISBN 9781635060621 (softcover)
Subjects: LCSH: Women detectives–Fiction. | Policewomen–Fiction. | GSAFD: Suspense fiction. | Mystery fiction.
Classification: LCC PR6107.I22 (ebook) | LCC PR6107.I22 S94 2018 (print) | DDC 823/.92—dc23
LC record available at https://lccn.loc.gov/2017047344

Distributed in the United States and Canada by
Hachette Book Group
1290 Avenue of the Americas
New York, NY 10104

Printed and bound in Great Britain by Clays Ltd, Elcograf S.p.A.

10 9 8 7 6 5 4 3 2 1

www.quercus.com

For my mother

Prologue

The woods pressed into the town from all sides. The bite of land that had been scooped out of the wilderness by the original residents was barely visible from above during the day, and at night—when the only lights were a few scattered street lamps—it was all but gone.

The deer raised its nose, sniffed the cold night air, and took a couple of steps. It paused by the line of trees and waited.

Somewhere much higher up on the mountain the winds howled and shook the firs for what they were worth, but in the hollow of the valley the town of Ludlow lay silent and still.

The deer ambled into the middle of the empty road, and three others followed it out of the shadows. They made no sound as they padded on the veil of snow and their reflections crossed the windows of the shuttered stores on Main Street.

The town stirred in its sleep but did not wake: a dog barked from inside a house, a porch light—triggered by a faulty motion sensor—came on and went off in one of the timber-frame homes, and one of the town's three traffic lights ticked and flickered from red to green to marshal the nonexistent 3 a.m. traffic. And yet, tucked away in an alley, a thin shadow tracked the progress of the deer and matched them step for step. They didn't pick up its scent because it smelled of forest and dead leaves, and they didn't hear any footsteps because it made no sound as it wove between the houses.

The deer followed a familiar route that would lead them to the woods at the other end of Main Street, and it wasn't until they had almost reached their destination that they caught the ugly scent. It was a few hundred yards away, yet sharp enough to startle them. For an instant they froze, and then, one after another, they bounded out of sight. The acrid smoke spread through Main Street, reaching into the alleys and the backstreets, under the doors and into the gaps of the old window frames. But the car burning bright by the crossroads would not be discovered until morning, and by then the thin shadow was long gone.

A few miles away Samuel shifted his weight on the thin mattress and listened for birdsong: he couldn't hear any, and it could only mean that it was still pitch black outside. He sighed and tried to grasp the tail of a half-remembered dream. Something had woken him up, though, and it took him a moment for the notion to sink small, keen teeth into his mind—dulled as it was by sleep and the warm cocoon of his blankets. Then a rough hand grabbed his shoulder and Samuel flinched and understood. He sat up without a sound, eyes peering through the gloom.

The bedroom—such as it was—was plain, with pallets for beds and a wooden stove in the corner. Embers from last night's fire lit the bundles of blankets lying on the other pallets, and a cold draft found Samuel as soon as he threw off the covers.

He didn't have much time and he knew it. His heart had begun to race and his mouth was a tight line as he pulled on his boots and snatched his satchel from the side of the bed. The tip of the boy's finger brushed against his good-luck charm, hidden in the folds of the satchel, and he felt a crackle of pleasure.

Two minutes later, Samuel walked out into the night and the door closed softly behind him. He looked up: the sky was low with heavy clouds, and he could almost taste the snow that was about to fall. He ran across the clearing and straight into the forest. He knew each tree and boulder and rock, and the dusting of white on the ground showed him the way.

They had always called him "Mouse" because he was small for his age—fifteen years old the previous November—small and fast. He needed all the speed and cunning he could muster now.

Speed, cunning, and the spirit of the mountain on his side.

He was three hundred yards away when the bell clanged and shattered the silence. They would be waking up then, rushing and scrambling after their things, and when the door opened to the night they would fall out and come after him. And God forbid they should catch him. The black raven feather in the boy's satchel would have to work hard to keep him safe.

Chapter 1

The small plane flew into a cloud and for a moment there was nothing but hazy gray. Then, faster than it would seem possible, they came out on the other side and sudden rain streaked the windows and blurred the view of the Cascade Mountains way down below.

The pilot had not spoken since his last attempt at conversation had been met by a polite but economical response, and after that, turbulence had demanded his complete attention while the three passengers had kept to themselves.

George Goyer had held his license for nineteen years and flown the red Cessna U260A for the last seven. He carried supplies in the winter and tourists in the summer, and he knew this unscheduled journey on a chilly February morning was not about cargo or recreation.

It was still early and the sun was barely a smudge on the horizon. On the tarmac of Boeing Field, George had removed two seats from the lineup to make more room and had helped the passengers load and secure their luggage inside the cabin—three smallish bags and some surprisingly heavy boxes—while making calculations about gross weight, fuel, and distance. Although there had been formal introductions, by the time he had shaken their hands George had promptly forgotten his passengers' names. When they were all strapped in and cleared by the tower for departure, the Cessna had taken off and George had allowed himself one wide, smooth turn over the flat, glassy waters of Elliott Bay and the shimmering skyscrapers of downtown Seattle before he had curved east toward the mountains. The way he saw it, they might as well begin the flight with something pretty since they were heading straight for some moderate to heavy chop.

"It'll be short and sweet," he had said through the headset, trying to sound reassuring.

"The shorter, the better," the man behind him had replied. He was in his early fifties, with red hair turning silver, and sat in his leather seat as if he'd rather be somewhere else—anywhere else.

The two women seemed to fare better: the redhead in her forties sitting next to the man had closed her eyes and possibly already fallen asleep. She had been particularly fastidious about the loading and securing of the cases, but George didn't mind being told what to do by a pretty lady who knew her mind. The other woman was the only one of the three wearing a mountain jacket and hiking boots that looked like they had seen actual hiking—George was quick to spot and scorn brand-new gear bought by city folk who wouldn't know a moose from a whip snake. The woman, younger than her companions, had helped him load their cargo and barely said a word. The rain had stopped and he caught himself watching her as she gazed at the landscape rolling and changing and at the dark mountains drawing near. The towns had disappeared and the plains had become forests: an expanse of deep green that covered valleys and peaks, except for stretches of bare rock and occasional snow. Slivers of lakes reflected the clouds above, and most roads—where there were roads—were hidden under the canopy. It was relentlessly beautiful and it never got old. After that brief moment the clouds had closed in and the rain had started again, harder than before. George glanced at the woman. She hadn't asked him silly questions and had known not to spoil the moment. He liked her already.

The Cessna bumped through a hard crosswind, and George spoke into the headset.

"I know we're getting slapped around some, but don't you worry, I see this and worse every day." He added a little chuckle for good measure.

None of the passengers ventured a reply. Though he didn't remember their names, George Goyer knew who they were and why the call the previous day had come from Chief Sangster himself. Maybe, he thought, they could have done with a little more of the pretty at the beginning of the trip because, Lord knows, where they were going there was going to be nothing but ugly.

Chapter 2

Twenty-four hours earlier, in downtown Seattle, the weather had been overcast with a chance of aggravated assault. Alice Madison's feet hit the ground hard and slipped as she felt the crunch of glass. She swore under her breath. Bottles, perhaps shards from the broken windows in the alley. Maybe so, but she didn't have time to care. The figure ahead of her flying toward the mouth of the alley was going at full tilt and Madison was going to catch up and grab the runner if it was the last thing she ever did. She righted herself and kept going. Behind her she heard someone scramble over the same chain-link fence she had just climbed.

"Watch the glass!" she yelled over her shoulder. She heard Andy Dunne land heavily, slip in the glass, and swear under his breath, then a moment later his steps were thundering behind hers.

Ten minutes ago they were on their lunch break, sitting at the Grand Central Bakery in Occidental Square, talking about mortgages and the Seahawks. Then the call came in, the worst call possible: one officer down, another in need of assistance, two attackers on the run.

Detective Alice Madison and her partner, Detective Sergeant Kevin Brown, were in the car and driving in less than thirty seconds; Detectives Andy Dunne and his partner, Kyle Spencer, were close behind them. They were all Homicide, but that was the kind of call that got everybody to come running.

The radio in their car squawked and crackled with the back-and-forth between dispatch and the different responding units, while every officer in the area converged on the same place, wondering about one thing: Who had been hurt and how badly?

The International District sat a stone's throw away from the more picturesque Pioneer Square area with its new art galleries and expensive restaurants, but it held none of the charm: boxy concrete warehouses followed grocery stores and shuttered businesses under the shadow of the interstate.

They saw him streak out of the back of a Chinese store and they gave chase. The kid—how old could he be?—was white, skinny, wore jeans and a black hoodie, and probably right about then had realized the magnitude of the trouble he was in. His partner was already sitting in a patrol car with a bloody nose because he had had the good sense to stop when four uniformed officers with their weapons out had told him to. He had dropped the metal pipe and stretched out on the ground in the middle of the road. The nosebleed was courtesy of the small envelope of white powder in his back pocket.

"Let me out here," Madison had urged Brown. The alley was too narrow for a car, anyway—never mind the chain-link fence—so Madison and Dunne had continued on foot while Brown and Spencer tried to cut off the attacker from the other side.

Madison ran almost every day; however, the guy was fast. She wondered briefly what kind of drugs he was on, and what had happened with the officer who had been hurt, and then she pushed the thought away. She could run and catch the guy, or she could examine the intricacies of the drug war in downtown Seattle, but she really could not do both at the same time.

The alley was covered in litter, and the two buildings on either side were tall enough to cut out most of the sky except for a strip of gray above them. Madison tried to avoid the flattened cardboard boxes and the empty food cartons and worked through a mental checklist. *Is he armed? Is he injured? Is he on drugs? How far does he want to take this?* She could see his hands, and there was no weapon there—just clenched fists and arms pumping to get speed.

The alley opened into a street and the runner rushed across the sudden glare, ignoring the horns from the cars driving in both directions. Madison blinked. The man dived into another alley and disappeared. Madison crossed the road and followed as Brown and Spencer's cars shrieked to a halt beside her, five seconds too late.

The alley was as narrow as the previous one and just as long and, Madison noticed, completely empty. She stopped abruptly and Dunne almost bumped into her back.

"He couldn't have made it to the end. He was out of my sight for no more than a few seconds. He's still here." A part of her was pleased that she could speak almost normally.

Dunne, gulping air, nodded. Somewhere in the background sirens were approaching.

They each took a side and proceeded slowly. There was a dumpster at the other end, but aside from that there was nothing but fire escapes and boarded windows. Madison's heartbeat was slowing down after the run and the adrenaline was already kicking in: there were no hiding places before them, which could only mean that the runner had managed to break into one of the buildings. Soft steps behind her told her that Brown and Spencer had joined them.

A dank, earthy smell permeated the alley and occasionally a puff of white steam was released by a grid a few feet above their heads—somewhere on the other side of the building a Chinese restaurant was serving lunch, and the air was thick with garlic and spices.

They were about a third of the way up the alley when they saw it: a broken pane on a door, big enough for a person to squeeze through.

"What is this place?" Spencer whispered.

"Warehouse," Brown replied. "Been empty for years."

Well, Madison thought, *at least he didn't run into the restaurant*. She bent and looked into the darkness behind the broken pane: nothing but a murky glow.

"No time like the present," Brown said, then unholstered his weapon and edged himself into the opening.

Brown and Madison had worked together in the Homicide Unit for just over two years, since she had joined it, and he had never lost the chance to be on point—one of those times, early in their partnership, it had almost cost him his life. She reached out to stop him and go first, but he was already inside.

The small room was dim, with paint coming off the walls, and it stank of dead rat. The only light came from narrow horizontal windows way up near the ceiling. Whatever had been stored here was long gone and the place had been taken over by the gods of dust. Even the sounds from the street only a few yards away didn't seem to reach it.

An open door in the corner led to a cavernous space, and in the distance, somewhere in the heart of the building, metal clanked against metal. As the detectives went deeper into the warehouse four thin beams from their flashlights crossed and parted on the concrete.

Spencer pointed. Someone had been coming and going and had left a number of tracks on the floor.

Madison examined her surroundings: it might have been the middle of the day outside, but inside the empty warehouse the world existed in a state of perennial gritty dusk. Time had stopped the day the workers had left, and it wasn't by chance that the young man had ended up in that alley and found that broken pane. He had intentionally gone back there. The notion that this desolate, abandoned building might be somebody's "safe" place was more than a little troubling.

Madison's train of thought was interrupted because they had reached the other side. The only way forward was through a single door, and a stairway that led to the floor above. Natural light flooded in through frosted windows. They put away their flashlights and peeked: the tall shaft that went all the way up to the building's roof was deserted.

Madison and Brown started climbing the metal stairs, with Spencer and Dunne bringing up the rear. Their weapons were unholstered and pointing at the ground. *Let him come easy*, Madison pleaded silently, *let him come without fuss*. Behind them and back in the alley Madison heard the crackle of police radios.

Let him come easy.

They reached the landing and something moved beyond the door into the main room. Madison made sure she took the first step inside and her piece was half raised.

"Seattle Police Department," she said, loud and clear. "Come on out now."

Spencer and Dunne were on her left, Brown on her right. Madison's eyes were slowly adjusting to the gloom when a timid cough rang out from the other side of the room.

"It's okay," a soft voice said from inside the dimness. "It's okay." Feet shuffled toward them and a woman appeared with her gloved hands raised. "It's okay," she repeated.

She was wearing layer upon layer of clothing, and her graying hair was shorn close to the scalp. And then it hit them: the scent of stale sweat and unwashed human beings. The woman's skin was flushed pink and her bright-blue eyes were the only points of light. Even bundled up, as she was, she was tiny compared with the detectives. Madison instinctively put her Glock away and tied the safety strip. She raised her hands so that the woman could see them, so that she could see she meant her no harm.

"Where is he, ma'am?" Madison said.

"He's a good boy," the woman said.

I'm sure he is.

"Where is he?" Madison repeated. She was aware that the others had lowered their pieces but had not put them away.

"Come," the woman said, and she turned.

They followed her into a room that a long time ago had been an open-plan office—some desks and chairs were still piled in the middle, some had been broken up, and Madison could see the evidence of small fires that had been lit to keep out the worst of the cold. They crossed the wide room all the way to the opposite side of the building.

"Oh boy," Dunne whispered.

The group had huddled against the far wall and created a kind of fort with the discarded furniture, the sort a child might make out of sofa cushions. Ten, maybe twelve, figures reclined and sat on the vinyl flooring; some were bundled up in clothing, others wore cheap shelter blankets wrapped around their shoulders. They all looked at the detectives with fearful, startled eyes. Someone had pushed discarded food wrappers, empty bottles, and cups into a corner in an attempt at straightening up.

The woman pointed and, behind an upturned table, the young man they had followed lay with his arms around his knees, rolled up into a ball and covered with an old coat. His eyes were squeezed shut. *I don't see you, you don't see me.*

There were loud steps behind them and four uniformed officers flanked the detectives. The two groups eyed each other.

"Tommy, is that you, man?" one of the officers said, and headed straight for a shape sitting against the wall.

At first, bundled up as they were, Madison couldn't even tell their gender, let alone their age.

"I haven't seen you around in months," the officer continued, crouching next to the man. "Where have you been?"

"On vacation," the man croaked, and he chuckled. "On the Riviera."

"Who got hurt?" Brown asked the patrol officer next to him.

"Scott Clarke from downtown, broken collarbone. He was checking out a public disturbance call and his student officer took his eyes off the ball for a second. Told us enough before going to the Emergency Room, though, and he," the officer pointed at the young runner on the ground, "didn't do anything except look scared and scamper when his pal went nuts."

"It's okay," the woman said to no one in particular.

No, Madison thought, *it's really not.*

Chapter 3

Madison edged herself out of the broken door and was grateful for the rush of fresh air. She had been a uniformed officer in the downtown precinct at the beginning of her career in the Seattle PD, and she was familiar with the drill. Fifty percent of the day-to-day calls the patrol officers in the warehouse dealt with were more social work than policing. Someone had already called the Mobile Crisis Unit, and they would come and help with temporary accommodation and whatever ongoing medical treatment each homeless person might need. Her own field-training officer, Monica Vincent, had known the name of every down-and-out on her beat, their histories, and their conditions, and Madison was glad that at least one of the police officers at the scene had been able to put a name to a face.

At the time, Officer Monica Vincent had been everything Madison had wanted to be as a cop. She was capable, kind, and compassionate; she had *chosen* to stay downtown, *chosen* to deal—day in and day out—with the realities of homelessness, shelters, mental illness, and the plight of the conveniently forgotten. It was an unremitting tide of misery, and the joys it brought were subtle and elusive. After a while Madison had moved on, but the frontline work was still there—if anything, the front line had become visible at almost every corner.

Only a few minutes from the warehouse, Kobe Terrace stretched its green walkways over a hill with a view of the city. Monica Vincent had taken Madison there the first day they were working together. It was March and the cherry trees were in bloom, heavy with pale-pink petals on their curved branches. Madison had gone back at least once every year to sit under those trees. As they left the alley she looked up, but a few buildings were in the way—and it was too early in the season, anyway. It felt as if winter had decided to dig in and bring its friends. Madison made a mental note to call Monica that night; she couldn't remember the last time they had spoken.

"No rest for the wicked," Spencer said to the group, tucking his portable radio back in his inside pocket. "The boss wants us all back, ASAP."

"Do we have time to go back and pick up our lunch from Grand Central?" Dunne asked him.

"Sure, the boss said to take the scenic route and stop to pick up wildflowers too."

Their boss, Lieutenant Fynn, was in charge of the Homicide Unit, and when he said *ASAP*, he meant *Teleport yourselves back to the precinct this instant*.

They drove, barely stopping for red lights, and once there, they found Fynn angry enough to chew glass.

"Go wait for me in the conference room, please," he said, the last word clearly meant to reassure them they were not the reason for his foul mood.

Madison was glad of a couple of minutes' reprieve as she was still metabolizing what she had seen in the warehouse. She looked around the conference room—a pale-green spartan space that would never win any prizes from Martha Stewart. It seemed that the whole shift was sitting around the table: Detectives Spencer and Dunne, Kelly and Rosario, and Brown and herself.

Spencer and Dunne spoke quietly among themselves, and Dunne let out a snigger like a teenager before class. He was Irish red and the complete opposite of Spencer, who was second-generation Japanese and the calm core at the center of their long partnership. Both men had welcomed Madison into the team when she had joined just over two years earlier; since then they had been through enough that she considered them more than good friends, and when Dunne had gotten married three months previously, Madison had been the only woman at his bachelor party.

Detective Chris Kelly studied his nails and scowled at the world in general: he was not a friend, any kind of friend, and never had been. Madison and Kelly worked together because they had to, but it was painful for both. Their dislike had been immediate and had not improved on further acquaintance: at first Madison thought that Kelly might be an old-style cop who was wary of newbies, but she soon realized that he was merely a bully with a streak of aggression a mile wide and the social skills of a skunk.

As an unfortunate consequence of their mutual loathing she had not had a chance to exchange more than a few words with Tony Rosario, Kelly's partner, and had no idea what kind of person he was—aside from the fact that he was mostly mute, often on medical leave, and his usual color seemed to be an unearthly pallor. He was leaning back in his chair now, utterly still, with his eyes closed; Madison was relieved to see his chest rise and fall.

Brown passed her a bottle of water and she nodded thanks. Madison's partner, Detective Sergeant Kevin Brown, had been the shining light of her time in Homicide. He ran a hand through his red-silver hair, pushed up his glasses, and looked over the front page of the *Seattle Times* spread on the table. He was in his early fifties—twenty years older than Madison—and liked to get his news on paper. She could take a thousand Kellys as long as she had one Brown.

The door opened and Lieutenant Fynn hurried inside, followed by four detectives from another precinct Madison had never met, two investigators from the Crime Scene Unit, and a tall, dark man in an immaculate suit who drew the gaze of all the police officers in the room.

"Let me get straight to it," Fynn said as they took their seats. "I presume you all know each other. If you don't—quite frankly—I don't care, let's deal with that later. Right now time is of the essence. I need to have an answer for the chief within the hour. Mr. Quinn . . ."

The tall man looked around the room and Madison noted that two of the detectives from the other precinct were giving him the classic cop stare that is supposed to make regular people break into a sweat and trip over their feet. Nathan Quinn was not a regular person, and he ignored them. His voice was quiet because he knew he didn't have to shout.

"In case we haven't met before, my name is Nathan Quinn and I work for the US Attorney for the Western District of Washington."

Quinn had been a criminal defense attorney for many years before taking up this latest post, and chances were the detectives who were looking daggers at him had met him in court and come out the worse for it. Madison knew the feeling. Quinn had been lethal when he was working for the defense and had made many enemies.

"I was contacted this morning by the Office of the Governor regarding a situation in Colville County," Quinn said.

Fynn sighed at the blank stares around the table. "Anyone who can find me Colville County on the map gets a cookie," he said.

"Somewhere northeast?" Dunne ventured.

"Somewhere northeast," Fynn conceded.

"Between Stevens and Pend Oreille County, squashed against Canada," Brown said softly, to save the day.

"Teacher's pet," Dunne whispered.

Quinn continued: "Colville is a small—very small—county in a mountainous area with more deer than people, and their law enforcement is not equipped to deal with the present situation. Generally a case could be turned over to the state police or the county sheriff, but in this particular instance they need the skills represented by the people in this room. The state police are up to their necks and cannot take the time needed to deal with it properly."

"And *we* can?" Kelly said.

"Deal with what exactly?" Brown asked.

"Murder," Quinn replied. "The first murder ever recorded in Colville County."

There was silence around the table. *The first murder ever.* Madison found it almost impossible to get her mind around that simple point. How could it be possible? The statistics for Seattle were what they were, and still they were better than many other larger urban areas in the country. *More deer than people*, she thought. *That figures.*

"They need help," Quinn said simply. "They need a team of Homicide investigators to support their local force, and they need a crime scene officer with extensive experience of murder scenes to examine their evidence and help them collect, preserve, and analyze."

"How many do they have working it?" Spencer asked.

"The whole force," Quinn replied. "That is to say, one person. One full-time police officer, two part-time."

Seattle, Madison knew, had over one thousand officers.

"I need volunteers, people," Fynn said before Quinn's words could sink in, "and I need them fast. Because you're going to have to leave tomorrow morning, early—before the crime scene is blown away to all hell."

"The Eastern District has Spokane and Yakima," said one of the detectives Madison hadn't met before—a skinny man with eyes like a bloodhound. "They have police departments. It's their district. Why don't they help out?"

"Yes, they have departments. And yes, they deal with major crimes," Fynn said.

Madison knew that Spokane had a pretty healthy crime rate—in many ways higher than Seattle, which had three times the population.

"But," Fynn continued, "right now Spokane PD has got its hands full and can't offer the necessary support. There's no point in sending somebody over to Colville County next month when they need warm bodies on the ground tomorrow. The next time, it might be Spokane's or Yakima's turn."

It was Brown who picked up on that particular turn of phrase. "The *next time*?" he said.

"The next time a murder happens in a town with a police department of one, yes," Quinn replied. "There are nearly eighteen thousand law enforcement agencies in the US, and half have fewer than ten officers; three-quarters have fewer than twenty-five. Small-town police departments are closing down all over the place, and policing is being kicked up to state and county level. This is a nationwide initiative to create a core of investigators who can support and train the officers of the smaller agencies, if and when the need arises."

"Would save the state and county a bunch of time and taxpayers' dollars if they didn't have to get involved," Spencer said.

"You want us to go and *train* them?" Kelly snorted and, in spite of her feelings about him, Madison could see that he had a point: how could they teach someone in a matter of days what it took them years to learn on the street, and what kind of standards of training were they going to find?

"You behind this, Boss?" Dunne asked Fynn.

Fynn looked beyond frustrated. "I'm behind getting some help over to Colville County right now, this minute, before any chance of catching the murderer is completely lost. The rest I'm still thinking about."

"The issue of jurisdiction—" Madison started.

"We're still working on that," Quinn said.

Their eyes met for an instant, and he looked away.

"What about warrants?" Spencer said.

"The first set for home and place of employment are already in the works. They will be delivered to the investigators on-site."

"What about the *evidence*?"

Madison turned and smiled. Amy Sorensen was one of the Crime Scene Unit's chief investigators, a redhead in her forties with a dirty laugh and the skills to break into any car in under twenty seconds. In all the years they had worked together Madison had been able to appreciate both.

"By that I mean, whose signature and whose responsibility *in court* is it going to be when this little learn-on-the-job experiment goes spectacularly wrong and blows up in everyone's face?"

"We're still working on that too," Quinn replied, unperturbed. "The idea is that those of you who go will take the local officers through the investigation as you would do it here, and the next time something similar happens they will do better because they will know more."

"They're going to love us, for sure," Kelly said. "Who wouldn't want a complete stranger to travel across the state just to tell them they've been doing their job all wrong?"

Nathan Quinn's black eyes glowed with little warmth as he regarded Kelly. "Detective Kelly," Quinn said, and Madison noticed that the detective had no idea that Quinn knew his name, "a man was killed and his body burned inside his car. There was enough blood on the snow to show that he might have been tortured before being killed. At this stage we have no witnesses, no motive, and no clear cause of death. What we do know is that he lived in a place where the most violent crime their police department had to investigate was a bar brawl two years ago when someone got a broken nose in front of fifteen bystanders. Would you like me to tell the man's wife and children that the murderer will, in all probability, never be found because you just do not have the time today to look over the file?"

Kelly opened his mouth but no words came out.

"I'll go," Sorensen said, and sat back in her chair with her arms crossed. "Madison, how many extra units in criminalistics have you taken? Four or five? I forget."

Sorensen was often joking that Madison, who believed in *evidence as truth* as fervently as she did—and had taken extra courses in the subject for the sheer pleasure of it—should drop the whole Homicide Unit gig and come to work with her instead, where the real investigating was done.

"Five," Madison replied, sensing trouble.

"Perfect," Fynn declared. "Madison, you could help out with the evidence too."

Madison knew a trap when she saw one, and this one had already snapped shut around her ankle. Never mind that she was going to volunteer anyway. If she was going, though, she wouldn't be going alone; she turned to Brown and he straightened his newspaper, sighed, and nodded once.

"Excellent." Fynn stood up. "Thank you all for coming, and have a great day. Brown, Madison, and Sorensen, I'm calling the chief now and will speak with you in my office when I'm done."

Nathan Quinn was already out of the door with neither thanks nor good-byes.

One of the detectives from the other precinct nodded in his direction and muttered to Madison and Brown, "Once a shit, always a shit."

Madison was about to reply, but Sorensen cut in. "I'm going to give you a list of personal equipment to pack," she said. "We have no idea what we're going to find when we get there. I mean gloves, evidence bags, everything you normally keep in the trunk of your car, extra batteries, the whole thing."

"Batteries? Colville County is still mainland USA."

"Wanna bet?"

Fynn had lucked out, and he knew it. He couldn't force any of the detectives to volunteer for the assignment and the fact that he had ended up with the most senior of his investigators and two bright stars meant that, for once, his midafternoon ulcer wasn't burning as red-hot as usual.

"If we are going to do our jobs fast before things get lost or—worse—contaminated, we won't always be able to worry about stepping on people's toes," Sorensen said.

They were having the conversation standing up because Fynn wanted to keep it short and to the point.

"You do what you can to make it as easy as possible for everybody involved," Fynn replied. "The last thing we need is for the whole project to implode because of a personality conflict."

"What conflict?" said Sorensen, who, as Madison was well aware, was technically not under Fynn's command. "I'm delightful, as long as people do what I ask them to do."

Brown, however, had heard what Fynn had meant. "This thing has been in the air for a while and Colville County is the trial run?"

"Yes, we didn't know when the right case would come along, and now it has."

Madison didn't need to look at Brown to know what he was thinking: the powers that be had just been waiting for that poor sonofabitch to get himself killed in a manner that was sufficiently exotic and mysterious to satisfy the criteria of the trial and get the ball rolling.

"How do the local police feel about us going over?" Madison asked Fynn.

"It was the mayor who called us, and he made a point of saying that the local officers are absolutely on board. Looking forward to meeting you."

Madison smiled. They all needed a good joke, and it was the funniest thing Fynn had said all day.

Madison finished her paperwork, filed it, and turned off her computer. She wouldn't be at her desk tomorrow, she wouldn't be at her desk for a number of days. Madison had only been a police officer in Seattle; she had applied to the academy right after her degree in psychology and criminology from Chicago, because being a cop was all that she had ever wanted—and being in the Homicide Unit had been the ultimate goal. Madison wondered about the life of the part-time officers she was about to meet and how they could be *part-time* when being a cop had imbued every aspect of her life for years. She knew the answer, though: a small town that couldn't afford more than one full-time officer, and a community with low rates of nonviolent crime.

Until now.

"Pack for a week," Fynn had said. "We're going to have to play this by ear, but I'm going to need a report every day. And pack for cold weather: they have ice rinks in July in Colville County."

"See you in the morning," Madison said to Brown as she shrugged on her coat. "Bright and shockingly early."

"Are you all right?" he said.

"Sure, why?"

"You seemed pretty mad after the meeting. I thought maybe you changed your mind about going."

Madison had been plenty ticked off after the meeting, but it was not something that she could explain to Brown. She shrugged. "Nah, just a moment of . . . whatever," she said, and hoped that he would buy it.

"You realize we might be back in twenty-four hours," he replied.

A dead man in a burned-out car with the real possibility of torture, and no witnesses.

"Do you really think so?"

"Nope. Do you?"

"Not for a second."

He nodded. "See you at the airport."

Madison left and Brown went back to his report. Whatever had been on her mind was not something he could pry out of her, and yet something had shifted in his partner in the last couple of months, something had changed. Brown had seen it in Madison like you see a sail catching a new wind.

Chapter 4

Traffic was slow coming out of downtown, and Madison got stuck with everyone else who was traveling southwest. Rush hour in Seattle was ten lanes of headlights inching toward a release that might possibly never come.

By the time she had reached Alki Beach the sun had set, and across Elliott Bay the city was a box of lights over the black waters of Puget Sound. It always surprised Madison how traffic seen from across the bay was almost soothing, like a distant stream of fireflies, as opposed to the exasperating experience of actually being one of the fireflies.

Madison parked her Land Rover Freelander in the usual place; she had changed in the locker room at the precinct and her Glock and the backup piece were locked inside a metal box in the trunk. It was such a relief, after the day she'd had, to feel the sand under her feet, to let the briny air fill her lungs and the clean cold seep into her bones.

After graduating Madison could have gone anywhere and done anything, and yet this city by the water had already claimed her:

at college Madison had badly missed the line of blue mountains in the distance and the silver water at dawn; she had missed the wide sky and the changing colors in the seasons. And so she had come back to become a cop and hunt the worst that humankind had to offer.

Two men in their twenties were packing up their kites and their harnesses, and they stared as Madison bounced on the spot and got the blood flowing.

Don't you go stretching first thing when you're as cold as death and twice as ugly, her high school coach used to say. Madison rolled her shoulders a couple of times and then took off.

Madison ran at the end of a good day and at the end of a bad one—and working in Homicide, the difference between them was stark. She ran because, somehow, the constrained energy in her body needed the air and the salt and the water. And that long, slow burn in her muscles helped her process whatever was going on in her life. Running on a treadmill in a gym—surrounded by tiny screens on mute and sealed in by concrete walls—would have been unthinkable.

Brown had been right: Madison had been angry—no, she had been furious—but she couldn't talk about it with him yet, and even turning the tight ball of rage around in her mind was not going to help. She sprinted and slowed down, sprinted and slowed down until her breath was coming out in puffs of white and her lungs burned.

Alki Beach—a strip of sand wrapped around West Seattle and Duwamish Head—had been part of Madison's life since she arrived in Seattle, age twelve, to live with her grandparents. The life of the neighborhood was an intricate mosaic, and Madison added to her knowledge of it with every run. She wiped the perspiration off her face with a sleeve: there it was, the old bungalow decorated with floats and shells, getting more and more decrepit every week; and the café next to the bicycle-rental place, the owners chatting on the pavement; and two dog walkers with their odd, tiny charges. She ran past them and the little dogs yapped their annoyance. Madison didn't have a problem with dogs, but she thought that they should, at the very least, be as big as cats—otherwise the world made no sense.

The sharp edges of her day softened with every step, and by the time Madison returned to her car she was already working through a list of what she needed to pack and which bag to use. Sorensen was right: they didn't know what they were going to need once they got there. All they had was the certainty that something awful had happened and people expected them to find the truth. She climbed back into her car and cranked up the heat.

No pressure then.

"No, that's not what I said." Amy Sorensen passed her cell phone to her left hand and with her right she picked up a pack of latex gloves from a pile on the table and put it in a large box.

It was getting late, but her regular duties at the Crime Scene Unit had not been put on hold just because she had to prepare for the trip, which is why she was having an argument with her younger daughter on the phone instead of having it face-to-face in the kitchen as she fixed dinner.

"No, I never said you could go. What I said was that we would think about it." Sorensen picked up another pack of gloves and then moved on to the brushes. How many would they need and how could she cover every base? Her daughter's voice was rising in pitch according to her displeasure.

"What I meant was that your dad and I needed to think about it because it's a party with college kids—which you're not—and they will have the legally validated freedom to do what they please, including drinking—a freedom that you don't as yet have—and they will exercise their prerogative to its natural consequences."

Five regular powder brushes, two fiberglass latent print brushes.

"Of course we trust you."

One white feather duster, one black feather duster.

"That's not true: you went to Katie's party, and you went camping with the Campbell kids."

Black latent powder, white latent powder.

"It's not you, honey, it's the situation. It's very easy for things to get out of hand when there's a big group of you and—"

Her daughter had cut in. Sorensen remembered having variations of the same conversation with her two older children—more than once.

"I know you don't, but others do, and it's tricky when you're all together and you don't want to be the only one who says no to the beer or the punch or the wine."

Black magnetic powder, white magnetic powder.

Sorensen sighed. "Can we talk about this when I get home?"

She surveyed the table and counters covered in all the equipment she still had to pack.

"Soon, honey, soon . . . I hope."

Detective Sergeant Kevin Brown lived alone in a town house in Ballard. When he got home, he called his sister in Vancouver to say that he wouldn't be able to make it there for the weekend as planned, and then he packed a neat suitcase as per Sorensen's instructions. He was taking some socks out of a drawer when he paused, his mind flashing back to the moment he had squeezed into the opening in the alley to get into the empty warehouse. Something in him wished that things had played out differently. He paused, closed his eyes for a second, and then went back to his socks and Sorensen's warnings.

As few clothes as you can get away with. They have washer-dryers in Colville County, and we need payload weight for the equipment, not for your fashion choices.

Brown grilled some salmon and threw some rice from the day before in the pan with it. He ate dinner with a glass of Riesling and a book propped open on the table, but his thoughts kept finding their way back to the job and all its unknowns.

Were they going to be the harbingers of all that was to follow? Now that the county had had its first murder, how quickly would it catch up with the rest of the state in its darkest statistics? Perhaps they could draw a line under it. Perhaps they could take that number and freeze it, as it was, for all time.

One murder. Surely that was enough for such a small county.

After dinner, Brown made sure he had watered every plant in the house.

Alice Madison lived in Three Oaks, a green neighborhood on the southwestern edge of Seattle. She lived in her grandparents' home, the home where she had grown up, and even though they had passed away a few years earlier—and it was her name on the deeds—it was still, and always would be, her grandparents' home.

The stone-and-wood house sat on a lawn that rolled into the water, edged by a narrow beach and across from Vashon Island. Madison went into the kitchen and dropped the bag of groceries on the counter: dinner would have to be simple—steak and salad—and would take only minutes to put together. She had stopped by Trader Joe's in Burien and stocked up on food that wouldn't turn to mush while she was away. She didn't know how long that would be—and that not-knowing was like a tiny cut that kept catching, whatever she did. And yet, in spite of that, Madison was curious. She had wanted to go, had wanted to put her name forward, and was relieved when Brown had agreed. Madison didn't care for advancement and promotions: the best cop she knew had been a sergeant for years and didn't care about becoming a lieutenant or a captain. If it was good enough for Brown, it was good enough for her—no offense to Lieutenant Fynn. Still, this was an opportunity Madison didn't want to miss.

She opened the French doors and walked out onto the deck. She could hear the waves lapping at the beach, even though she could not see them, and the tall firs on either side of the lawn murmured in the breeze. Would the darkness be different where they were going? *Where you're going, the darkness has teeth*, a small, reedy voice whispered. *Just because it is the first murder, it does not mean that creatures don't kill and get killed every day there, and that's as it should be.*

Madison went back inside and lit a fire in the hearth. She grabbed a backpack from the utility room and packed quickly. She knew Sorensen well enough to know that she was not above asking—no, demanding—that she and Brown ditch part of their luggage on the tarmac if they had brought too much.

Then Madison peeled off her sweats, stuffed them into the laundry hamper, and took a long, hot shower.

The fire in the living room was crackling when Madison came back with her hair still damp and wearing a terry cloth robe. She checked her cell for messages—a smile came and went—and then proceeded to set the table for two.

Chapter 5

Samuel looked up. The clouds were rolling in and the air smelled like rain. He frowned: he might just have enough time to do what he had set out to do before the heavens opened wide, right over his head, and he got soaked to the skin. He didn't like to be wet in the freezing cold, but a job was a job. He was on wolf duty—looking for fresh scat and tracks, in case the pack had wandered too close to the homestead. For Samuel it meant time alone on the mountain, following streams and trails and getting pleasantly, willingly lost for a few hours. Sometimes those hours of freedom ran away from him and he returned to the farm later than expected. *No problem*, he'd say to himself, *they were worth the occasional hiding*.

Samuel left the clearing and took the path that would lead him north, toward the denser forest, and soon the sounds from the cabin where he lived were behind him. Next to the barn and at the edge of the clearing stood a hut, a small structure with a tin roof and worn planks nailed together for walls. Samuel had skirted it and hurried to the path without looking. No one liked to walk too close to the little hut: in the winter it was the promise of nightmares to come, and in the summer it carried the scent of rotting meat and fear.

Samuel quickened his step. He had already fed the chickens, collected the eggs, and done his share of milking. Someone else was on firewood duty, and the others had their own chores to attend to. *No one gets a free ride, not in this world.*

He wouldn't have minded tracking the wolf pack for a while. Three times he had seen them in the far distance, and each event was scorched into his memory: scattered gray-and-white shapes moving gracefully behind the trees; skinny legs and long muzzles. Each time he had been with his brother Caleb, and now Cal had left the farm and Samuel hadn't seen the wolves for a long time. Maybe the wolves would leave too, maybe he would never see them again either. Finding droppings felt too much like a tease. He knew they were there, he could hear them sometimes, and yet that was all he got from them—a dried-up piece of scat full of animal fur.

Samuel had always lived on the farm and he knew to be wary of wolves, but Cal had told him how smart they were, how they protected one another and cared for their wolf family. And since he had nothing left of his older brother, he clung to those memories and looked for scat. One day, as soon as he was old enough, Samuel would leave too. He would find Cal and forget about everything else.

The boy's eyes scanned the ground: the spots where shade had lingered the longest were still covered by a skin of snow. He crouched and pulled off a glove; his hand was a boy's hand, with a grown-up's thickened skin and nails bitten to the quick. He broke off the end of a fallen branch with a snap and poked a dark object that looked like a curved cigar half covered by dry grass. It crumbled under his stick and the boy let out a breath. *Frozen dirt. It figures.* Samuel put his glove back on, shifted the rifle on a strap around his shoulder, and kept walking. These excursions were as good as it got. The mountain was his home: the cabin was just the place where he slept and ate and where, night after night, he listened to the fire in the stove crack and hiss.

On the mountain, ravines and gullies lurked under the thick vegetation and a distracted walker could get lost, or much worse. For Samuel, though, everything above him and around him was alive and he never felt truly lost: when his step faltered, he would just wait for the mountain to find him and put him back on the right path.

After almost an hour of meandering, the light around Samuel changed and a sharp wind picked up. The boy stilled. He was nearly there. He lengthened his stride and fought his way through thick shrubs to reach a small glade that backed against a rock face. He paused for a moment and listened. The notion that one of the others might have followed him was too awful to contemplate; he could hear only his own ragged breathing.

Samuel hurried across the clearing and reached for a bundle inside his pocket as the first drops of rain tapped on the brim of his hat. He opened the square of white cloth, and in it lay a small piece of bone carved in the shape of a snake's head, a chunk of cooked meat, and a slice of cornbread from last night. He had survived the previous day's dawn run with nothing more than a few scratches, and the mountain deserved his thanks. His most treasured possession—a single lustrous raven feather—was his talisman, and the one thing he could not give. His offering—the foodstuff, at least—would be gone in minutes.

He placed the objects in the deep hollow of a fallen maple and then made to leave. The drone of an engine cut through the air and Samuel looked up: a small red plane had appeared out of the clouds. The boy watched it as it dropped altitude—the red so bright against the clouds behind it.

Once it had disappeared beyond the trees, and the hum of the engine had been whipped away by the wind, Samuel turned and bolted back into the forest.

Madison had lost track of time. They had been flying through cloud cover for a while, most of it in turbulent air. She was glad to be sitting up front, next to the pilot—glad that he was busy and didn't seem inclined to chitchat.

The world was a stream of gray. Behind her, Brown sat with his eyes closed and his hands folded politely in his lap. He would have seemed perfectly relaxed to most people, but Madison was not most people. She knew the thin frown between his brows for what it was.

"You okay, Sarge?" she said.

Brown nodded without opening his eyes. Next to him, Amy Sorensen slept with her head against the window and a gentle snore that was lost in the engine noise.

"Here we go!" The pilot shifted the control column and the plane dropped out of the clouds.

"Oh—" Madison said.

A valley had opened below them: tall, blue-green mountains around them everywhere she looked—the peaks still covered in snow—and a thin ribbon of a river catching the light from above. It was eerie. Madison felt as if she could reach out to every tree and every rock. They flew over a lake, and the reflection of the plane glided on the water below.

"Nearly there," the pilot said.

And yet Madison hadn't spotted a landing strip or control tower—or a town, for that matter.

"Reason why we needed to start off early is that I need to be sure I can eyeball the landing strip, otherwise we'll end up in the woods like so much kindling," he chuckled. "None of those fancy control towers up here. No landing at night either. We do it old school."

The plane followed the bend of the valley and just then, tucked at the foot of a mountain, Madison spotted a smattering of white timber-frame houses among the trees.

"Welcome to Ludlow," the pilot said.

Polly had been standing by the window for the last hour, or so it seemed. It was probably only ten minutes, but to Will Sangster it felt as if she had been standing there forever, sipping from the travel mug she brought from home and peering at the sky as if it was going to start raining snakes any second. It made him nervous, but then again he was already nervous, and it wasn't Polly's fault. She was his secretary, part-time and poorly paid, and he was thankful for her presence in the office—more a benevolent great-aunt than a secretary—thankful for the homemade cookies she brought in every Monday, and even more grateful for the town gossip that was, after all, his best source of information on the goings-on in the territory he was supposed to police.

He had tried to occupy himself with paperwork, but his attention kept going back to Polly at the window. It was almost a relief when she turned and said, "They're here, Chief."

Chief Will Sangster picked up the radio on his desk. "They're here, guys."

Through the crackle two voices responded and acknowledged his message.

He stood, sat his hat on his head with a well-practiced gesture, and grabbed his heavy coat off the back of the chair. "All right, Polly, you know what to do," he said as he left.

The woman nodded.

Sangster climbed into the cruiser parked in front of the small building that housed the Ludlow Police Department and started the engine. They were guests in his town, he thought. *His* town. As he drove to the landing strip he reached for the glove compartment, took out a half-full bottle of Tums, and popped two into his mouth. The bodywork of the white cruiser was spattered with mud, and for a brief, surreal moment Sangster mused whether he should have washed it off.

Chapter 6

The landing turned out to be no more pleasant than the journey, with a tall line of firs right by the end of the strip just waiting for the pilot to lose control. However, George Goyer knew every bump on the tarmac, and the Cessna found its footing on the ground with an almost delicate thump. The plane turned around and taxied toward the only visible building, a modest hangar that doubled as passenger and freight terminal. The pilot engaged the brake and Madison took off her headset.

"Here we are," Goyer said, as if it had been no more than a quick cab ride downtown.

"Thank you," Madison said.

"Anytime," he replied.

Three cars had pulled up as the Cessna came to a full stop. Madison unbuckled her safety harness and glimpsed two police cruisers and a pickup. Behind her, Sorensen was stretching in the tight confines of her seat and Brown looked ready to gnaw his way out of the plane if someone didn't let him out quickly enough.

The pilot opened the door and Madison jumped onto the runway, her legs stiff after the cramped seat. It had been cold inside the plane, but the chilly air on the landing strip was cool resin mixed with something green, clean, and mulchy. City cold was different, *this* was something else. They zipped up their coats and fastened the Velcro straps.

Brown stepped forward with his right hand out. "Chief Sangster?" he said, addressing the middle-aged man flanked by two twenty-somethings.

There was a fluster of introductions and a crossing of handshakes while everyone was trying to get the measure of everyone else, then Deputy Hockley backed the truck right up to the plane and opened the covered back.

Deputies Hockley and Kupitz would have been the kind of kids that high school coaches grab as freshmen and never really let go. It could have been football, or hockey, or basketball—it didn't matter. They were tall and wide. Hockley called Sorensen *ma'am* three times in one minute, and Madison saw her biting her tongue. They made short work of unloading the plane and Sorensen's cases were handled as if made of spun glass.

"What kind of weather have you had in the last twenty-four hours?" Sorensen asked.

Madison could almost hear her brain calculating the damage that the crime scene would have suffered out in the elements.

"Pretty nice for this time of year," Kupitz replied.

"Some rain, temperature in the mid-thirties during the day," Sangster said, ignoring his deputy. "Last night it dropped to the low twenties. It probably snowed higher up."

Kupitz blushed.

Before Sorensen could reply, Sangster added, "We put a tent up around the car yesterday morning to get it out of the weather. By then it had already snowed and rained on it, and God knows what the wind had blown onto it."

Sorensen nodded. "Thank you."

Madison had had a chance to look the chief over while they were unloading the plane. He was about the same age as Brown, and very tanned for a guy who lived in northeastern Washington State—maybe a recent vacation, definitely not a tanning-bed type. She saw livid shadows under his eyes and wondered if he had managed to get any sleep the previous night.

Brown was the senior investigator among them, and though that distinction wouldn't have mattered when he was alone with Madison and Sorensen, he was aware that the three strangers before them would have picked up on it.

Brown spoke to Sangster. "How do you want us to proceed, Chief?"

Sorensen shifted her weight and Madison could feel her itching to get to the crime scene. Nevertheless, those first few minutes on the tarmac, establishing boundaries and civility, were going to pay off—wherever the investigation might lead. Sangster was old enough and smart enough to understand that.

"What did *you* have in mind?" he replied.

Brown turned to Sorensen.

"The crime scene first," she said. "We're going to work it step by step. Where's the body?"

"In the medical center. The county ME is going to meet us there, and he'll take Bobby to Sherman Falls later tonight."

"*Bobby?*"

"Robert Dennen," he replied. "The victim."

They knew the dead man, and *that*, Madison reflected as they piled into the cruisers, was the main difference between small-town policing and everywhere else. Chances were Chief Sangster personally knew not only the victim but also the killer, his family, his wife, and his kids. And they would all still be there after the killer had been found, arrested, and hauled off to jail by him.

"The car was found on the other side of town," Sangster said. "A couple of miles from here. We'll be there in no time."

They left the landing strip and the pilot began to guide the plane into a section of the hangar just as it started to rain.

* * *

"How much do you know about Ludlow?" Sangster asked.

Sorensen was sitting in front while Madison and Brown were in the back.

"Not much, I bet," the man continued. "We're pretty much lost somewhere between Canada and Idaho and other counties most people don't know about anyway. Let me fill you in a little."

The road out of the airport was lined by firs that grew so thick that even the air between them was green and the ground around their roots had been scrubbed clean of grass by perennial shade.

"The town was founded around 1897, and back then it was all about mining and timber. Right now we have six hundred and forty-seven registered residents plus some regular visitors, like the folk from the Department of Fish and Wildlife or the geology department from UW. We have Jackknife up near the pass; the travel books call it a ghost town. It's where one of the mines used to be, and there's still buildings and all kinds of things from when the miners left. Tourists love it. Summer dollars are important: tourists come to visit the old mines and the farms in the valleys; they camp by the lake and fish to their heart's content. This is a quiet place, a safe place."

The cruiser rounded a bend, and as the road opened they reached what seemed to be the main artery of the town. Madison was born in Los Angeles and the smallest town she had lived in was Friday Harbor on San Juan Island when she was a little girl, and even there she could have counted the residents in the thousands. Madison could hardly imagine life in a place where everybody knew who you were and what you did, and their parents had known your parents going back generations.

"Were you born here?" she asked Sangster.

"Me? Nah, I'm from Boise. Came over from Idaho fifteen years ago with my wife and kids. The kids have left for college but we're still here. I was in Boise PD for four years before Ludlow. Patrol."

And *that* was the heart of the conversation, Madison thought: the chief wanted them to know that he had been a cop in a place with more than three traffic lights. *Fair enough.* Even so, he had also told them that, having been in Patrol, he would never have been in charge of a murder investigation.

"This is Main Street," Sangster said.

It was a combination of red brick and wood: the timber-frame houses were freshly painted, and if there was a town council they had made darn sure everything looked as pretty as a picture for those summer dollars. She glimpsed other streets and narrow houses with peaked roofs close together, huddling for warmth.

"Right, this is what we know," Sangster said. "Yesterday morning, around 6:30 a.m., Buck Ahlberg was driving into town and found the burned-out car—still smoking. He called me, and it was clear that someone was inside, but whoever it was had died in the fire, or before it."

"Are there pictures?" Brown asked.

"Every which way," Sangster replied.

"How did you know it was Robert Dennen?" Sorensen said.

"Car plate. I called his wife and it turns out Bobby had been called out sometime after midnight by the Jacobsens because their baby has asthma and she was having an attack—he was a doctor. I spoke to the Jacobsens, and Bobby left them after 3 a.m., but he never made it home. We'll get DNA confirmation with a sample from his toothbrush after the autopsy."

"What made you think it was murder?" Madison said.

"The car had been parked on the side of the road—it wasn't a crash or anything like that. It was driven into a turnout. There was blood on the snow a few yards away."

"Pictures?"

"Yup."

"Any chance it was a suicide?"

"Set himself on fire while quietly sitting in his car?"

"Could have shot himself before the fire caught on."

"No weapon recovered—and it wouldn't have fallen far."

"Snow could give us footprints, if there's still any."

"Some are still there, some were melted by the heat of the fire. And they got rained on quite a bit."

"There was more to it, though, wasn't there?" Brown asked Sangster.

The chief found his eyes in the rearview mirror. "Yes," he replied. "The victim was in the passenger seat and his hands had been tied."

"How?" Sorensen said.

"Not sure—whatever it was, it burned away in the fire."

The procession of police cruisers and a pickup had attracted a few stares as they drove along Main Street. How quickly had the town grapevine spread the news of the body in the car? Madison was ready to bet that everybody knew why they were there.

Including the killer.

Deputy Hockley rubbed his jaw with the back of his hand and made sure he stayed no more than ten yards behind the bumper of Kupitz's cruiser. He had wanted to drive Ludlow's second cruiser himself, but Koop's silly Toyota was never going to be big enough to carry the load the Seattle cops had brought, and so he was stuck driving his own pickup—even if, technically speaking, he had been on the force four months longer than Koop and was, therefore, a senior officer.

Hockley was twenty-three, worked part-time on his father's farm, and had been hunting since he could hold a rifle. He had seen life and death from all angles on the farm and in the forest, but he never again wanted to see anything like what was in the body bag in the medical center. He had helped the chief to extract it from the car, and his eyes had stung for hours afterward.

Hockley hawked and spat out the window. More than twenty-four hours later and he still couldn't get rid of the taste of smoke in his mouth.

He thought about the two women in the car with the chief—especially the younger one, who couldn't be much older than he was. Even the shitty situation they were in had a silver lining.

"That's it," Sangster said, and he pulled in on the side of the road.

The green tent was not Crime Scene Unit issue: it was a green tent that in its regular life would be protecting merry hikers from the Pacific Northwest weather. It sat as an ungainly lump under the canopy of firs, without guard, and the admonition of the yellow crime scene tape around it seemed too mild a warning to keep anybody away. If there were teenagers anywhere in the vicinity they would have already uploaded more pictures online than Sangster had ever thought to take. A few bunches of flowers had been left against the roots of a tree nearby; a few envelopes and cards had been tacked to the rough bark.

Hockley and Kupitz held back while the others went ahead.

The chief unzipped the entrance to the tent and lifted the flap. The scent found them as if it were a live thing. Acrid, cloying, and repulsive. Madison inhaled—the sooner she got used to it the better. Human beings are animals—even if they often try to forget it—and their reactions on a purely instinctive level are still based on survival. This, Madison reflected, was the stench of a violent death, and it said: *Go away, you don't want any part of this, do you?* Madison felt the small hairs on her arms rise against her shirt. *Did you die of smoke inhalation? Did you see the first flames licking at your feet?*

The red Chevy was a husk of blackened metal: the upper part of the bodywork had been almost completely destroyed—the windows must have blown out when the fire had started. It had eaten through the upholstery and devoured the body of Robert Dennen, and Madison could only hope that he was already dead when it happened. They would find out soon enough. There was barely any space around the car, and they stood by the tent opening.

"Have you called an arson investigator from State?" Sorensen said as her eyes took in the scene.

"Yes, and they don't have one to send for at least a week," Sangster replied. "Today, ma'am, you're it."

Sorensen and Madison exchanged a look: this was going to be the point where things might start to go south with Chief Sangster.

"We need a larger tent, Chief. Much, much larger. Big enough for at least two people to work around the car without bumping into it," Madison said. "And we need to close this road right now."

"Close the whole road?"

Sorensen pointed at some brown patches near the ditch. "That's the victim's blood, right? Or maybe it's the killer's. We don't know that yet and we need time to find out. We need time to create a perimeter and search this road inch by inch, and we can't do that while we're dodging SUVs."

Strike one. They'd barely set foot on the ground and they were already telling him how he should have done his job. Madison noticed Hockley and Kupitz were standing very still and scrutinizing something in the opposite direction. An engine rumbled from around a bend and a truck drove straight through their crime scene—the driver slowing down long enough to nod hello to the chief and get a good eyeful of the strangers.

Sangster hesitated, then turned to Deputy Kupitz. "Koop, here's what I need you to do . . ."

His words were lost in the background as Madison turned around, her gaze sweeping the gloom of the woods on both sides of the road, and she wondered whether the killer was already watching them, gauging them, assessing the kind of threat they posed. Something shifted in the murk and a raven croaked twice. *I bet you are.*

George Goyer made sure the Cessna was safely tucked inside the hangar. He was Ludlow's main pilot, and his runs to Spokane and Seattle supplied whatever the town could not produce and whatever eighteen-wheelers could not deliver. The little red Cessna was his baby, and it had never let him down. *You take care of me and I take care of you.*

George had left his car in the parking lot behind the hangar the previous night and spent a night in Seattle on Ludlow's dime to be ready to set out early from Boeing Field. The hotel had cable and he had fallen asleep with a room-service tray on the bed and Jimmy Kimmel on the screen.

Now his eyes were gritty and he felt the familiar postflight energy crash: it hadn't been as choppy as three weeks earlier—when he'd had brief, frantic thoughts of emergency landings and calling his mother in Florida to say good-bye—but, nevertheless, it had taken a chunk out of his natural reserves. All he wanted from the day at that point was coffee and pie, and possibly a little conversation too. He was a man with fresh news in a town that couldn't wait to hear.

The moment he walked into the Magpie Diner on Main Street he knew he was good for an extra slice of pie on the house. Joyce Cartwell, the owner, waved him over to the counter and poured him coffee from a pot even before he had settled on the red leather stool. Some customers turned and looked; a couple of them stood and joined him at the counter.

"So?" Joyce said as she reached for George's favorite—key lime pie.

"Three. One man, two women," the pilot replied. "The guy looks like he could be in charge—he's, what, fifties?—but it's hard to tell. They had some heavy cases. Brought all sorts of fancy equipment, I bet." George took a bite of pie.

"I saw them drive past."

Everyone had seen them drive past.

"Yeah, I heard them say they were going to the car first."

"Did you see it—the car? Before they covered it up?"

George nodded. A crowd had gathered around the burned-out wreck. Thank the Lord, the body had already been moved to the medical center.

Joyce leaned forward on the bar. "I have seen car wrecks before, and that's not what we're talking about here," she said quietly.

Buck Ahlberg, who had found the car and had seen the body in it, had not stinted on the details: the whole town knew Robert Dennen had been sitting in the passenger seat and it looked like his hands had been tied. No one thought it was anything other than murder.

The pilot was quizzed in detail about the Seattle detectives, their conversation during the flight, and any scraps of information that might be gleaned about what kind of people they were and what they thought about the case. He enjoyed the attention, and he didn't turn down a second slice of pie when it materialized on his plate as he did his best to satisfy their curiosity.

New customers came into the diner; the same questions were asked, and the same answers duly repeated. Still, nothing could change the fact that George knew much about the weight of the detectives' luggage and little of the substance of their minds.

Chapter 7

Madison looked up at the sky and saw nothing but waves of sheet-metal gray hurrying purposefully toward them. The chief had explained that Ludlow's inclement weather was due to its position at the bottom of a long, narrow valley surrounded by mountains, which acted as a funnel for the icy winds coming from Canada.

"Things can change quickly around here—generally not for the better."

"How long do we have?" Madison asked.

Sangster's eyes measured the heavy blacks and grays at the mouth of the valley. "Ten, fifteen minutes, tops."

"Pictures in a grid," Sorensen said, and she pressed a camera into Madison's hands. "Snap one and move on. No art, I beg you."

Madison nodded and started.

"I know you've already covered the scene, Chief," Sorensen said. "But this way we'll know if anything was significantly altered in the last twenty-four hours."

And we'll catch whatever you missed. Madison adjusted the aperture and the focus on the Nikon.

The car was under the relative protection of the tent. If a storm was about to hit, the most vulnerable area was going to be the perimeter around it. Madison scrutinized the ground: the killer had walked through it, stood on it, shed epithelials and other DNA material; perhaps he had even gifted them a nice chunk of fabric that could be matched to his blood-spattered clothing. Madison smiled behind the camera. *A Crime Scene Unit officer is an optimist trapped inside the body of a pessimist*, Sorensen had told her once.

While Madison was taking pictures, Sorensen bent over the blood stains and scraped the substance into various containers, labeling them in her neat script.

Brown took Chief Sangster to one side to speak to him in private and, more important, to get him out of Madison's way without seeming to be doing so.

If Robert Dennen had been murdered in Seattle, if Brown had been working the case from his own desk at the precinct instead of out in God-knows-wheresville, he would have put in motion the SPD machine many hours earlier. Instead, he had to hope that Chief Sangster had remembered what he had been taught at the academy.

"So," Brown started, "on a regular homicide investigation—not that such a thing exists, but bear with me—we would have started a canvass straightaway to find potential witnesses and would have taken statements from whoever was the last person to see the victim alive. We would have spoken to the spouse and worked a time line for the last hours of the victim's life. Considering that you had to deal with everything yourself—as well as organizing our visit—how far along are we?"

"I've spoken with Betty Dennen and with the Jacobsens, and their accounts match."

"Did they sign their statements?"

"No, they'll be coming to the station later." Sangster gave Brown a crooked smile. "I thought you'd want a pass at them, anyway. The time lines make sense: the victim had dinner with his wife, everything was A-okay, and they went to bed after *The Late Show*. Then the call wakes them up, and it's not the first time—the Jacobsens' little girl gets these attacks once a month or so. The victim drives straight there—departure and arrival time checked—stays with them, takes care of the baby, and leaves after 3 a.m. Then . . . nothing. This," Sangster waved his gloved hand, "is not the way home, and there's no reason why he would come by here instead of taking Dutton Road back to his place. It makes no sense why he would be here."

"Nobody called him while he was with the Jacobsens?"

"No."

"And—"

"Yes, I checked his cell, and there were no calls at all since late afternoon, when he called his wife to tell her he was going home."

Brown pondered the question of Dr. Robert Dennen's state of mind. What does a man think about at 3 a.m., after trying to get a baby to breathe? Something occurred to him. "Do you have CCTV in Ludlow?" he asked.

"Not in the streets. In the stores, sure, some do have it, but not in the streets."

"It can be useful."

"Maybe, but you'll find people around here don't like the idea of surveillance quite as much as city folk seem to."

Brown smiled. "Doesn't surprise me one bit." Then the smile faded. "Is someone staying with Mrs. Dennen?"

"Her sister drove up from Republic."

"Good," and he added, "how did Mrs. Dennen take it?"

"What do you mean?"

"You know what I mean, Chief."

The statistics of spousal homicide were unforgiving, and every cop knew it.

Sangster zipped up his coat to the collar with more vigor than needed. "She was devastated. She was in shock. She puked up her coffee right in front of me."

Brown nodded. He was going to meet everyone and speak to everybody again anyway—he didn't care how many witnesses would throw up on his shoes.

He had not formed an opinion about Chief Sangster yet, and his next words were more about the officer than the victim. "Did *you* know Robert Dennen?"

Sangster took so long to reply that Brown thought he had not heard him. At length, the chief met Brown's eyes. "A little. The way you can know people in a town like this without being close friends. Once, when Dr. Foster was away, he prescribed some antibiotics for me for a throat infection and we chatted for a while. He was active in the community, knew most people's business around town, and was a volunteer firefighter. Last week, if you had asked me the same question, yes, I'd have said I knew him as well as anybody in town, and he was a good man. Today, if you're asking me if some part of his life people don't talk about at PTA meetings suddenly turned up and left him in that burned-out car . . . maybe, I don't know, and I sure couldn't tell you."

Madison worked fast and it wasn't until she had been taking pictures for a few minutes that she realized just how much she was enjoying it. Her bare fingers were numb in the chill and her back ached from crouching over the ground, and yet there was something satisfying in the repetitive movements and the utter focus the job demanded.

The dirt ran in shades of brown and gray streaked with snow, and Madison's world shrank to the height and breadth of the camera frame as she took a picture, advanced one step, and took another picture. The Nikon D7100 was a good camera, much better than the one she had learned on—Madison wasn't entirely sure the Nikon was not Sorensen's own. However, as it had been drilled into her, a tool was only as good as the person using it. *A fair warning*, she thought as she scanned the edges of the frame to make sure she was following the grid pattern, and then moved forward.

Suddenly the light changed and the drizzle became icy needles on her cheeks. *Damn.*

Deputy Kupitz's cruiser rumbled around the bend and stopped on the side of the road. The young officer jumped out and hollered to his colleague, who ran to help him. Together the deputies quickly assembled a tent that went over and around the burned-out car and its current meager covering. No one offered to help them, as it was obvious they were much more efficient working by themselves. Judging by the grim set of their expressions, it seemed that putting up that tent under the worsening rain was their one contribution to the progress of the investigation and it would not be wrested away from them without a fight.

After the first was dealt with, a second tent—smaller but still sizable—was set up near the cruisers and everybody took shelter. The inside of it smelled of warm rubber and cotton candy. Madison shook the rain off her coat and a few drops found their way inside her collar. One thing remained to be done to mark their territory.

After a moment, Madison took the CRIME SCENE—DO NOT CROSS tape from her coat pocket and went back out into the rain. Hockley and Kupitz followed her.

Madison hurried down the road, and they kept up in long strides. Once she felt she had created a wide enough perimeter around the tents she knotted one end of the tape around the trunk of a fir and unrolled it at waist height as she crossed the street. She took out her folding knife from her back pocket, sliced the tape off clean, and tied the other end around a portable STOP sign. The blade caught the light. Stepping through the trees in a wide circle with the car at its center, they taped off the crime scene section by section: the wilderness owned every shadow in the forest, but the small island within the boundaries of the tape was theirs. The deputies scrambled after Madison under the lashing rain as she worked without speaking.

That night, when Hockley was tucked up in his bed and warm under the comforter, he would remember how the Seattle detective had handled that knife and how her hands had moved easily around the patterned steel blade.

Chapter 8

In the time it took for the small procession to leave the crime scene and reach the medical center—a squat redbrick building at the end of Main Street—the rain had turned to sleet, the mountains had all but disappeared, and the sky hung low. Even the wind had picked up, and Madison tried not to think about landing a puny little plane in those conditions—the red Cessna as slight as a child's toy against the rocky crags.

The room where the remains of Robert Dennen had been kept was at the back of the center, past the cheery waiting room with the kids' drawings tacked on the corkboard. Madison wondered what it would be like to live a life meted out in this building: to come for croup as a baby, for a skinned knee from a skateboard fall as a teenager. It was a gentle place where residents took care of lesser injuries because nothing bigger than a bloody nose had ever been inflicted in Ludlow and adults could get a lollipop from the nurse if they asked nicely.

A pretty young woman with her arm in a sling was leafing through a magazine as they filed past; she looked up and Deputy

Kupitz nodded to her. He might have winked too—Madison wasn't sure.

The nearest funeral home was in Sherman Falls, and the medical center had the facility to keep two bodies; it was a recent addition to the doctors' offices and very useful, especially in winter when the snow might block the roads for days and the odd, unexpected natural death had to be dealt with. Chief Sangster explained this as he unlocked the door, led them into the room, and closed the door behind him. "Bobby's office is across the hall," he said.

They would go through it, by and by, and no one missed the absurdity of it.

There was nothing left to say. Madison had seen a few arson deaths and she knew what to expect—that is to say, she knew that knowledge would not help her one bit in the face of what lay inside the fridge locker.

"All right then," the chief said, and he pulled out the drawer.

Samuel took off his boots: his socks were as cold and damp as the rest of him, and the wood stove was all the way on the other side of the room. He would have gladly climbed inside it to warm up just then—even at the cost of turning into kindling. The weather had shifted too quickly for him to make it back to the farm before getting soaked and, since he wore third-generation hand-me-downs, nothing he owned would keep him warm or dry quite as well as it was supposed to. He peeled off his socks and rubbed his feet with a thin towel.

"Where did you go today?" The man's voice cut through Samuel's musings.

The boy started, as if ice water had been poured down his back. "Up toward the creek, sir, all the way to the pass and back around the old mine trail."

"And?"

"Nothing, sir. They're keeping away."

"They'd better," he said.

Samuel did not reply.

The man walked off and the boy went back to trying to get some warmth into his feet. He hadn't told him that he had seen the town plane—and on a day he did not expect to see it. More important, he hadn't told him about the beautifully clear paw print he had seen up near the pass. It had been pressed into clean dirt—four and a half inches long, three and a half wide—the claws peeking out, and enough weight behind it to have been an adult male. *So pretty*. Samuel turned the image around in his mind. The pass was far enough from the farm that it didn't matter—and if the pack stayed put, there was no reason to tell anybody where they were. Samuel had run his fingertip inside the indentation—four wide toes and a central pad—and he could still feel the packed earth against his skin.

The detectives had looked at the body for as long as it was useful and were happy to pull up the zipper on the black bag and return Robert Dennen's remains to the fridge locker once they were done.

Madison had seen more dead bodies than most people ever would in their lives, and that was understandable and the way it should be, she considered, because she had chosen to be in that line of business—the business of hunting killers. And yet there was something particularly awful about arson, about someone setting a fire that would consume a human being. It spoke of the complete destruction of the victim, and there was something repulsive about it that struck everybody who investigated those cases—officers who were, if not used to, at least prepared to witness the worst human beings did to one another. In other times, in times of savagery of the mind and of the heart, human beings had been burned at the stake for their sins, both real and imagined. In Madison's times, fire was still seen as the force that would purify a body in death, and inevitably it would also obliterate every trace of the killer on the victim. Why had the killer set fire to the car? Why had he or she made sure that Robert Dennen would be almost totally obliterated inside it? Was it purely to conceal the circumstances of the murder, or was there a deeper meaning behind it?

Even with the victim back in the locker the stench still permeated the room, and they were all eager to leave.

"We have a space where you can set up," Chief Sangster said. "I'm afraid the police station is too small, but the community hall across the road should be all right. Usually it's used by seniors to visit and do their art classes—this week they'll be using one room in the elementary school. And Polly, my secretary, has been preparing the guesthouse for you."

"The guesthouse?" Madison asked.

"We have a few motels about a ten-minute drive out of town, but they're closed for the winter. The guesthouse is around the corner from Main Street and a short walk from the hall. Edna Miller, the owner, is in Florida until March; I called and she said, sure, to go ahead and use it since we kept a set of keys. Polly has turned on the furnace in the basement this morning because the house has been empty and cold since November. It's not the Hilton, but it's the best we could manage."

The detectives were quick to assure him that it would be fine, and in the flurry of thanks and necessary courtesies they left the medical center. The deputies, Madison noticed, had kept quiet; however, their eyes had never left Sorensen while she had taken samples from the body, and—as pale as the young men had been—neither had turned away.

The senior center was a bright, wide room with the scent of dried flowers and freshly sharpened pencils. It smelled like the first day at school, minus the teenage perspiration. Dried lavender sat on the shelves next to how-to books that ranged from watercolors to whittling your own buttons. It was spotless, and the linoleum floor had been recently swept. Madison knew without checking that one of the doors in the back would lead to an orderly cupboard with cleaning products and detergents, and there would be a roster on the wall so that everyone would be aware of their day to make sure the place was left clean for the next class.

The chief and the deputies had helped the detectives to unload their cases and then had left them to arrange the makeshift incident room as they wished. Madison suspected, correctly, that the chief knew they all needed a little space from one another and had dispatched his men on errands around town to get them out from under the detectives' feet.

A kitchenette stood in a corner with a microwave oven and a coffee percolator; Madison approached it warily. She'd had coffee in Seattle what seemed like days earlier and nothing to eat since then. Madison found the coffee—Equal Exchange Colombian— and measured it in the filter, adding a bit more than was strictly necessary, and then left it to brew. The machine was ancient, and so was the carafe; however, the coffee inside the pack seemed fresh, and that was all that mattered.

The pavement was deserted, but Brown dropped the blinds anyway for a degree of privacy and turned on the neon overhead lighting. It flickered and then caught. They pushed three tables— which would serve as desks—toward the middle, and Sorensen appropriated a smaller room with a bench by the back wall as her own lab and evidence work surface.

"Do you have enough power outlets?" Madison asked her.

"I *never* have enough power outlets," Sorensen replied. "But this will do."

The chief had given them the password for the Wi-Fi and as Brown turned on his laptop and connected to the Seattle PD site, the hall began to look a little more like home.

Madison poured the coffee. They sat at their desks and looked at one another. It was their job to talk about the things no one wanted to talk about. About the body in the fridge locker. And which one of the merry villagers had put him there.

"Darn fire took everything," Madison said. "No obvious sign of injury."

Brown dug into his bag and produced a package of Oreos; Madison almost hugged him.

"No," Sorensen said. "And the ME will have to look very carefully to find any kind of wound that predates the fire. It would have been good to have Fellman onboard."

Dr. Fellman was the King County medical examiner, and if there had been a clue as to cause of death hidden in the folds of charred skin he would have found it. They didn't know anything about the Colville County ME except that he was late, had missed them at the medical center, and had never worked a local murder.

"Well, Fellman isn't here. Where does that leave us?" Madison said.

"In a dangerous place," Brown replied. "In all probability the ME will find heat fractures and he won't be able to confirm they're the work of the killer unless they bear a particular shape from the weapon that caused them."

"Then we have to hope for a bullet still inside the body," Madison said.

"Could have melted in the fire." Sorensen sipped the coffee and picked up a cookie.

"Not necessarily," Madison said. "The internal organs could have shielded it from the worst of the heat."

"Are you thinking of—?"

"Yes, the Bellevue case from a year ago."

"I remember." Sorensen nodded. "A bullet would be nice."

"How are you going to deal with contamination?" Madison waved a hand around the room.

It might be a lovely place for senior citizens to gather and for cops to discuss murder, but it was far from being the sterile environment needed for court-approved evidence analysis.

"I'm doubling up every sample I take. One I seal for the Seattle lab, and the other I work on here. If anything holds any results, they will repeat the process there so that it can stand up in court. Fingerprints and DNA I can handle here."

"What do you think of the hands?" Brown asked her.

After the ME, Sorensen was the one among them who would have examined the largest number of homicide victims as she found, collected, and preserved the evidence around their bodies.

Sorensen didn't want to think about Robert Dennen's hands. "Almost completely consumed by the heat. And, even considering the contraction of the muscles, the way the arms rested seems to indicate they were tied by something that disappeared in the flames."

"Plastic cuffs," Madison said.

"Probably," Sorensen concluded.

"Then we have a problem," Brown said. "Why did the killer need the cuffs?"

Madison sat back in her chair. Her thoughts had been circling around the same idea.

Brown's eyes were blue and sharp. "We don't know *how* the killer and the victim met and—for that matter—we don't know *where* they met. If they met by chance on that stretch of road and the killer murdered Dennen and set fire to the car—"

"He wouldn't have needed to restrain the victim, unless he was going to spend some time with him." Madison finished Brown's thought: plastic cuffs meant premeditation.

"Dennen was sitting in the passenger seat," Sorensen reminded them.

Robert Dennen had been intercepted between the Jacobsens' home and his own, and someone had held him hostage for a while, somewhere nearby. And then the killer had driven him to the place where they had found him.

Madison stood up. "We need a map," she said.

Deputy Kupitz sat forward on his chair to get a better view of the senior center across the road through the sleet. The blinds were drawn and the light escaped in thin strips.

"What do you think they're talking about?" he asked Deputy Hockley, who was doing the paperwork for a parking violation.

They had gone to school together, and their families had known each other for a long time; because of this Hockley could swear, hand on his heart, that Jay Kupitz had all the sense of a bag of jam nuts.

"What do *you* think, Koop?" Hockley replied.

Kupitz shrugged. "Did you see how the redhead worked the body?"

"I'd like to see you call her that in front of her."

"Don't start. You know I'm no good with names. I only know yours 'cause you wear a tag. I meant to say that she did the whole thing like they do on TV, and she knew what she was doing."

"Yes, she sure did."

"Did you hear? The nurses at the medical center are making a banner for the vigil with signatures from all his patients."

"I heard."

The door of the senior center burst open and a figure ran across the road and into the police station. Alice Madison wiped the dampness off her hair with the palm of her hand. Her eyes were bright and her cheeks were rosy with the cold.

The deputies froze.

"Hi," Madison said. "Do you have a map of the town we could borrow? We're going to need all the major and minor roads, any hiking trails, and all the houses, farms, huts, and shacks within three miles of Ludlow."

Hockley and Kupitz stood up at the same time but the latter was closer to the bookshelf and quickly grabbed a folded map from the stack that was inches thick.

"Here you go," Kupitz said.

"Thank you," Madison replied, and she was gone before he had the chance to say anything more.

Kupitz's gaze followed her back across the road, and when he looked away he saw Hockley's grin. "What?"

"Never gonna happen," Hockley said.

The map was spread out and tacked to a corkboard. Madison took a couple of steps back: most of the map was taken up by swathes of green and brown.

Chief Sangster had left them copies of the notes he had taken, with details of the witnesses. They were not printed statements; his writing was small and cramped, his turn of phrase precise and to the point. She consulted the notes, then stuck a pin on the Jacobsens' residence, one on the victim's, and one where the car had been found.

There was only one thoroughfare in and out of town, and the other roads radiated from Main Street into the forest. Beyond the town there were miles of nothing—aside from the odd farm and homestead—until Canada.

"There are no houses immediately close to the crime scene. However, I bet a gunshot in the middle of the night would have been a very loud, sharp crack," Madison said. "Too loud for the killer to risk it, unless he was using a silencer."

"If he was using plastic cuffs and a silencer, we're going to be looking for a particular kind of fellow," Brown said. "I'm inclined to say probably not a farmer."

"Nope."

"I want to meet the wife," Brown said. "When did the chief say he'd be back?"

"Soon, I think. Amy, what are you going to do?" Madison said.

"I'm going back to the car," Sorensen replied and turned her attention to something that looked like a large printer set up on her workbench.

"Anything useful in the samples they took yesterday at the scene?"

"Possibly," Sorensen replied. "I don't know yet. I want to get to work on the blood as soon as I can, and I need my bag of tricks for that."

Madison followed the line on the map that was Main Street with the tip of her finger. "I wonder if the chief has realized—if anyone here has realized yet—what kind of a mess this sort of case makes in a community this small."

"They don't know," Brown said. "They have no idea. Our best hope is that the killer has come from outside."

If he has come from outside, Madison mused, *he's come ready with cuffs and a silencer.*

Chapter 9

Alice Madison walked through the unlocked back door of Robert Dennen's home, into the large kitchen/dining room with the country-style cabinets, and she saw the casserole dishes covered with foil placed on all the available surfaces, the freshly baked bread in a basket, and the plain cakes in plastic containers. Such were the signs of a home marked by grief: neighbors came with sympathy and food. A blue ribbon looped through the handles held the fridge doors closed.

"This way," Chief Sangster said as he led Brown and Madison into the house.

Robert Dennen's wife sat on a sofa with a baby on her lap, surrounded by a small group. The woman's bare face was pale and her dark eyes shone. The baby, asleep in the folds of a pink blanket, had the same long lashes.

"Betty," the chief said.

Betty nodded, and an older woman stood up from her side and ushered the people present into the next room. Madison checked them out automatically: three women and one man the same age as the wife; one older man. Their clothing said local, their manners said close friends or family.

"Betty," Sangster said. "These are Detective Sergeant Kevin Brown and Detective Alice Madison from Seattle Homicide."

"Thank you for coming," Betty Dennen said as she rocked the baby.

The notes said that she was forty-two years old and a schoolteacher. Betty and her husband had three children—a boy and a girl in middle school, and the baby.

Madison spied a blonde girl watching them from the hallway. She wore jeans and bunny slippers and leaned against the wall with her arms crossed, listening. There were livid smudges under her eyes. The older woman found her, put her arm around her shoulders, and led her into the kitchen.

Madison knew about losing a parent when you're that age, about the kindness of neighbors and school friends and the awful, awful silence when everybody goes back to their own homes and you are left alone with your pain and a father who doesn't understand that your heart is only beating because you're willing it to with each breath.

"I don't understand what happened," Betty Dennen was saying—not for the first time in the last twenty-four hours, Madison suspected.

She was still in shock, but ran through the time line of events exactly as Sangster had reported and then answered their questions as best she could. No, nothing remarkable had happened in the last few weeks, and she hadn't noticed any strangers around the house or around town. No, Bobby had never argued with anyone in the community, not about so much as a parking place.

"Did he suffer?" she asked Brown, as if he had been in possession of information the chief had not.

"We'll know more in the next few days," he replied.

"I just don't understand," Betty Dennen said. "Why did this happen?"

She kept rocking the baby absentmindedly, as if understanding the reason why her husband was dead would somehow bring him back to her.

They could not give her an answer, and the longer they stayed the more obvious it seemed that they knew nothing yet of any relevance and could offer very little comfort. Their presence there—all the way from a place that had an actual murder rate and the clearance statistics that went with it—was all the comfort that was to be had. As if they had received training in some kind of advanced magic that was not allowed in Ludlow, where people didn't kill each other.

They were offered coffee and cake and knew to accept both. Madison sat with the older woman, who turned out to be Betty Dennen's sister and lived in Ferry County, while Brown sat with one of the neighbors. At the kitchen table the woman gave Madison a picture of Betty and Robert's life in Ludlow, which was not far from *The Waltons*—a close community where people had to work hard for every dollar the state didn't take away in taxes, but a good place to bring up a family.

"They don't have gangs here," she said. "And everybody's American." The woman's eyes were washed-out blue and her blonde hair was tied up in a ponytail.

Madison didn't want to get into the demographics of murder. *Lots of Americans kill each other*, she wanted to say, but she didn't. She also didn't say that the numbers for spousal homicide would make her eyes bug out. Still, Betty Dennen had looked devastated. And reading her body language, Madison had seen nothing except a wife in shock.

The house wore the details of the Dennens' life: children's drawings under fridge magnets and school pictures framed on the walls. The Dennens had been high school sweethearts in Spokane and had moved to Ludlow before their oldest child was born.

Madison and Brown spoke in turn to all the neighbors, and while they drank their coffees and listened to their stories about what a wonderful doctor Bobby was and how important he had been in the community, they quietly looked for the breadcrumb trail of lies, pretense, and deceit.

Amy Sorensen adjusted her disposable coveralls and slipped on a pair of heavy-duty rubber gloves. Her arson toolkit was packed in a metal box by her feet and she picked up nine-inch stainless-steel tongs. She turned to Deputy Kupitz, who lurked by the aperture of the tent that housed the burned-out car, and said, "Glove up and come in."

Sorensen had been vaguely disappointed to be assigned Kupitz instead of Hockley, as his gaze seemed rather vacant compared with his colleague's. However, to complain would have felt churlish and mean; and since they were there to investigate and train, she was going to try her best in both.

Amy Sorensen was not an arson investigator. Arson was a sinister combination of chemistry, opportunity, and intent, and it was studied and investigated by a particular branch of criminalistics. The fire in the car had not been the killer's main objective, though. This, Sorensen reflected as she walked around the blackened metal body, was a kidnap, hidden inside a murder and wrapped in an arson investigation. And kidnap and murder she understood all too well.

Sorensen stood next to the LED floodlight she had brought from Seattle and shifted the stand a couple of inches so that the 180-degree beam would hit exactly the area that she needed covered. Once she was satisfied she took a step back, and her eyes traveled over the destruction that the heat had caused.

A couple of minutes went by.

"Powerful lamp," Kupitz said. He had spoken because Sorensen made him nervous, and he wasn't very good with silences anyway.

Sorensen had almost forgotten about him.

"At middle strength it gives us twenty-three-hundred lumens for six and a half hours," she said. "And we can stretch it to ten hours if we go down to fourteen hundred. Fully portable at 2.85 pounds."

Sorensen regarded the young man. "So, Crime Scene Investigation 101, Deputy Kupitz: On the scene of a fire, what's the first job of a fire investigator?"

Kupitz's mouth opened and closed and opened again. He had hated school and felt a blush rising to his cheeks. "To find out who set the fire?" he managed to get out.

"That's on the list, for sure," Sorensen replied. "But it's not the first item. A fire can be accidental, natural, or deliberate. Until we know which, we don't have a case." Sorensen remembered that she was teaching someone who had not chosen to be in her class and, given the chance, would probably opt out of any class. "What do you think we have here?" she said, hoping that he'd rise to the challenge of a conversation.

"Looks deliberate to me."

"Yes, it sure does."

Sorensen approached the side where the victim had been found and peered in. "See that pattern of burns on the seat?"

"Driver's side?" he said, taking a step closer as if expecting an ambush.

"Yes, after we decide that a fire looks deliberate we look for *origin* and *cause*. And by that I mean, where did it start and was an accelerant involved?"

Kupitz nodded. "Like gasoline?"

"A chemist would say that gasoline is fuel for the combustion process—and I agree—but if some numbnut sprayed it on a sofa on the side of the road and then lit a match to watch it burn, he would be using it as an accelerant."

Kupitz smiled—she had said *numbnut*.

Sorensen paused. She didn't know what kind of training Kupitz had had, and there was a strong chance that anything she was going to say today would be forgotten in a week—or that he'd leave the force and take a job as a waiter in Milwaukee. Then again, something she said today might stick and, Lord knows, might even be useful to him and to the town of Ludlow one day.

"I don't know what kind of training you've had," Sorensen said. "So I'm going to start from the beginning and whip through it."

The deputy was only a few years older than her own son, and Sorensen recognized the startled look in his eyes—the "Please don't ask me any more questions" look.

"The crime scene," she continued, "is your best chance to identify and locate the offender you're looking for, and as such, you protect it all costs. That's why your chief covered the car as soon as he could. That's why we closed the road and built a perimeter around it. Four things you need to remember: first, protect the scene, then recognize, collect, and preserve the evidence. Okay?"

"Okay," Kupitz said.

"Good. Do you know why offenders love fire?"

"Because it destroys evidence?"

"Because it destroys evidence. Because fire consumes the evidence of its own origin. But we are not fools, we were not born yesterday, and—most important—we live in the age of mass spectrometry."

Kupitz didn't know what *mass spectrometry* was and made a mental note to look it up later.

Sorensen picked up a steel-blade spatula from her equipment. "Every contact leaves a trace," she said. "It might be burned-out, charred, and damaged beyond all recognition, but it's still a trace. And I'm the—" Sorensen cut herself off before the profanity, as if she had been speaking in front of one of her children. "And I'm just the person who'll find it."

Outside the tent the rain and the sleet had stopped and the clouds were moving on briskly, as if called elsewhere. A car stopped by the bottom of the street—where the chief had stuck his ROAD CLOSED sign into the ground—and paused there.

In the gloom of the deserted road the tent shone bright orange, and two shadows were visible moving inside it. The driver watched them: the tent seemed so fragile in the blowing wind, like a Chinese flying paper lantern. A hard gust could just lift it and carry it off with its precious, delicate cargo, off into the black forever.

The driver counted sixty slow heartbeats and then drove on.

Chapter 10

Madison lifted her eyes from the witness notes she was typing;
on the other side of the desk Brown was lost in thought. Their
canvass had yielded little or no results. They had spoken to the
visitors at the Dennens' home; then the chief had driven them
around to the houses in the vicinity and those close to where the
car had been found. The people of Ludlow were hospitable and
eager to help, and not a single person had had anything useful to
contribute to the day. Brown and Madison still had no idea why
the car had been found there, instead of on its way home. And the
only conclusion they had reached was that the less people knew,
the keener they were to talk at length to them about it.

There was another issue, one that this precarious scheme
from the US Attorney's Office had not considered—or maybe
they had considered it and simply flapped it away like a gnat—
namely, the flesh and blood of a homicide investigation was held
together by more than the detectives' experience in the process.
It was supported by intimate knowledge of a specific place, its
history, the tides of people who had gone through it. The map

on the wall, with its colorful pins, was at best a reminder of how much they didn't know and at worst an omen of failure.

Sleet was lashing the windowpane and Brown seemed to come back to himself.

"We can work with *unusual*," he said out of the blue.

"We can?" Madison said, not entirely sure where he was heading.

He nodded. "We don't know the ways of this town, but *they* do." Brown pointed at the police station across the road. "Something happened here that led to this, and they might very well know a lot more about it than they think they do."

Madison thought of Chief Sangster: when they returned to the police station after the canvass, the chief had been ambushed by one of his citizens who wanted to report that her dog was missing. The woman had been waiting for the chief because talking to Deputy Hockley about her dog was clearly not enough: Tucker, her poodle, deserved the chief's attention.

"I've been telling you, Chief, this town has changed. Someone took Tucker."

Sangster had been conciliatory and understanding, and finally the woman had left.

"Sure, someone took Tucker, and it's *her* fault," Hockley said once the woman was out of earshot. "Around here that kind of dog is eagle bait. Little Tucker is probably in some nest up by the pass about to become bird food and wondering how the heck he got there."

A missing dog was only one thread in the fabric of lives Sangster dealt with every day, and he did so with grace. It had not escaped Madison's notice how kindly he had spoken to the woman—as if her concern mattered and he wasn't cold and tired and hadn't spent the day as little more than a chauffeur to two big-city cops.

Tomorrow there would be more people to interview. And late morning, the town council had planned a vigil for Robert Dennen in the main square. There would be speeches; there would be an appeal for information; there would be flowers and candles. Madison eyed Sorensen's camera; it could take photos and video, and she planned to take plenty of both. Madison loved vigils—more often than not they were irresistible to the killer. All that genuine sentiment, all that sorrow. A vigil was the best kind of party, thrown in honor of the killer's work. How could he stay away?

Brown pushed his glasses up on his nose and slapped his notebook shut. Madison smiled. Between them on the desk the package of Oreos lay crushed and empty.

"Hungry?" she said.

"Starving," he replied.

Sorensen pushed the door open with her elbow and walked in carrying a boxful of samples. She was still wearing the disposable jumpsuit and looked like the end of a forty-eight-hour day. She set the box on her workbench next door, then slumped at her desk next to Brown and Madison. Her red hair was pulled back in a messy ponytail and there was a dirt smudge on her brow.

"The bad news is that anything we collect we can't keep here, because this place is as open as a bus shelter," she said. "Every night we'll have to put the evidence under lock and key across the road."

"What's the good news?" Madison said.

"I'll have to get back to you on that."

"How do you feel about mac 'n' cheese?" Brown asked Sorensen.

"Is it a trick question?" she said.

Madison pointed at the table where some of the seniors' craft work had been stacked. Two large covered casseroles sat next to the wicker baskets.

"Betty Dennen wouldn't let us leave without taking them. She said she had so much food that it would spoil before they could eat it all, and she'd heard we were staying in Edna Miller's place."

"People around here know where we're staying?" Sorensen said after a beat.

"Only a handful," Madison said. "The chief's assistant and a couple of volunteers opened up the house for us today, and one of the volunteers was a friend of the Dennens. They're not broadcasting it on the local radio."

"They *have* a local radio?"

"Yup," Madison consulted her notes. "KCVW, broadcasts from 6:40 a.m. to midnight. Hits, news, and the schedule for the charter flights to Spokane, Wenatchee, and Seattle. They also read out weather alerts, emergency notices, and supermarket offers."

"That's how they let everybody know about the vigil tomorrow?"

"I think so, yes, and we're going to record an appeal for information early in the morning so that they can come find us at the vigil."

"Anybody been speaking to you yet?" Sorensen asked the others, and her tone implied she believed that no such thing was possible.

Brown and Madison exchanged a glance.

"They speak," he replied. "But they don't say much."

"Except how awful this whole affair is, and how it couldn't have happened to a nicer guy," Madison continued.

"Don't worry," Sorensen said. "Give them a day or two to get to know you and the down-and-dirty will come out. It always does."

"You're a cynic, Amy," Madison said. "I didn't know that about you."

"I'm not, but I was born in a town barely bigger than this where nothing, *nothing*, ever happened. You, and the murder, are the big news. Give 'em a minute to compose themselves and you'll be beating them off with a stick."

In the heyday of mining in Colville County—when around two thousand miners had been crawling deep inside the surrounding mountains for zinc, copper, lead, iron, and silver—the town of Ludlow had flourished, and some of the original buildings still stood to bear testimony to those times long gone. Edna Miller's house belonged to that period. Edna's grandfather had bought it for a handful of dollars from a mine owner who'd gone bust, and there it still stood in all its glory. So Chief Sangster had explained as he unlocked the front door.

The house was four floors of Victorian gable trim, with bay windows wrapped around every corner and a porch that would become useful in the brief hot summers. Snow had dusted the peaked roof and decades of harsh Canadian winds and sleet had turned the sapphire blue of the sides into washed-out slate that suited its age and shape. It sat only a few yards from the main street in a road of similar if smaller houses, watching over them like a dowager and her subjects.

It had been mutually agreed that they were old enough and capable enough to find their own way to the Magpie Diner or the Tavern, if they so wished. Thus the chief ran through the basics— the furnace in the basement, the fireplaces scattered around the house, the fuse board—and then left them to themselves.

Some of the beds had been made up for them; the rest they could work out as they went along. Madison looked around the living room with its wide stone fireplace, old-fashioned squashy chairs, and doilies covering almost every table, sideboard, and armrest. It was *country* with no sign of irony, as if Edna Miller had purposefully kept the place in the early 1900s. She was relieved to see that the kitchen was more modern, and when Brown turned the oven on it purred without a glitch.

Madison claimed the smallest bedroom, on the top floor right under the eaves. The wallpaper was daisies and bluebells, and even though the heating had been hard at work for hours, she could see her breath in the frigid air.

The bed was a single brass frame on a bare wooden floor, with a handmade quilt in shades of cerulean over a thick comforter. There was a small desk under the sloping roof, with a padded stool the same color as the quilt and an armchair—with doilies—in the corner. Overall, Madison reflected, it was like a child's room in a doll's house—only life size, and the doll's house had been plunked in a freezer for a few days.

She reached for her cell and dialed. It went to voice-mail. She gazed at the deserted street below through the round window as she listened to the familiar voice. She knew that voice like she knew her own—better, in fact—she knew the color of it, the warmth of it, in spite of the clipped, almost brusque tone of the message. She took a breath. "Hi," she said. "We're in Ludlow. I just wanted to say goodnight. Well . . . goodnight, then."

Madison finished the call, astonished by her own awkwardness. It was unlike her—except that it was totally like her, these days. She dug her phone charger out of her pack and left the cell with its dying battery plugged into the wall under the round window.

The bedroom had a fireplace and—God bless Edna—there was a basket with logs next to it. Madison imagined watching the embers of the fire, growing drowsy, the warmth spreading through the cold room, which in turn reminded her of her fireplace at home in Seattle and how she had fallen asleep on the sofa in front of it the previous night.

Last night was last night, Madison told herself as she climbed down three floors to the kitchen and the smell of mac 'n' cheese.

Sorensen had found some dishes and Brown was checking the casserole in the oven. There was a touch of the surreal about it. This was work, they had come here on the darkest of errands, and yet it also felt unnervingly like camp.

They sat around the wide table, surrounded by the life Edna Miller had built for herself, and ate their first proper food of the day. Madison felt a rush of gratitude for whoever had taken the time to cook that dish for the Dennen family. It was comfort food and reassuring. It was so much better than anything they could have ordered in a restaurant and—at least for that first night—she was glad to be in a private place, sheltered from the looks of the locals and from their wary curiosity.

"Check the fridge," Sorensen said.

Madison leaned back and opened the fridge door without getting up: the shelves had been stacked with eggs, cheese, milk, and bacon. A plate of homemade cookies had been left on the sideboard covered with plastic wrap, next to a loaf of bread. *Polly, the chief's assistant, and her volunteers.* It couldn't have felt more different if they had been dropped in the local Motel 6 with its free morning coffee and a hot-breakfast voucher.

"How's your apprentice?" Brown asked Sorensen between mouthfuls.

"Valiantly struggling on his way to enlightenment," she replied.

"How big of a struggle?"

"To the death," she said. "He has a smattering of common sense but no science at all. It's not his fault. There's no budget for it. I'm just glad I could get my hands on this one," she pointed at Madison, "when she was fresh out of the academy and before she could be corrupted by all of you."

"You win some, you lose some," Brown shrugged.

Madison ignored them. *I hope Kupitz realizes just how lucky he is.*

They got through the whole casserole and Brown washed up while Madison built a fire in the living room.

"I'm going to the Tavern for a drink," he said, as the first flames flickered in the hearth. "Any takers?"

"Early night," Madison replied.

Sorensen was on the sofa reading her notes and had no intention of moving away from the fragile heat. They heard the door close, and the house fell into a comfortable silence. However welcoming, Edna Miller's home was still uncharted territory, and Madison listened to the unfamiliar ticks and clicks; the furnace and the pipes had their own individual language, and their voices grumbled on from room to room. Upstairs the windowpanes in one of the unmade rooms rattled in the wind—possibly they were becoming loose in the frame—something else for Edna to check when she returned, before the spring and summer visitors flocked back and filled the large house with noise.

Madison picked up a book from the shelves and settled close to the fire as Sorensen's cell rang. She stood to take the call in the kitchen. Madison couldn't hear the words but she certainly understood the tone. When Sorensen came back, she arranged herself on the sofa but didn't go back to her notebook.

"Trouble at the homestead," she said after a minute. "Lisa wants to go to a party with college kids and we said no. And since I'm not there, she's trying to charm/bully/swindle/wheedle her dad into letting her go."

Lisa was Sorensen's younger daughter. Madison had never met her; she imagined a teenage version of Sorensen, a prospect that should panic any parent.

"Why don't you want her to go?"

"I imagine you were quite the paragon of virtue at fifteen— straight-A student, running track and volunteering with the homeless. Never drank a beer before you were twenty-one, never rolled a doobie in your life."

Madison had never spoken to Sorensen about her background. "I wasn't exactly trouble free," she said.

"Did you party with college boys when you were fifteen?"

"Nope."

"Did you raid the fridge for beer when your parents were out shopping for your birthday present?"

"Nope."

"Did you steal your older sister's ID to get into a club?"

"Nope."

"There you go, that's why she's not going to the party."

"She did all that?"

"No, she's a good kid. I did all that when I was a teenager, and I'm just trying to keep her out of harm's way."

"I see: the glory of hindsight."

"What did you do?"

Madison sighed. Too much history to tell in a stranger's home at the end of a tough day. Sorensen would have to make do with the bullet points.

"I ran away from home when I was twelve. My mom had died a few months earlier and . . . well, there was stuff going on with my dad. Anyway, I ran away and they didn't find me for a week."

Sorensen gaped. "A week?"

"Yeah, I was . . . sort of hiking."

"Alone?"

"Mostly."

"Well . . ." Sorensen was uncharacteristically dumbstruck. "And you were okay? You were safe?" she said, her mind still thinking like a parent, traveling in ten different upsetting directions.

"Mostly," Madison replied.

"But not the whole time?"

Have you ever skinned a rabbit?

The house creaked, as if someone had rested a great weight on its Victorian gable roof. They both looked at the ceiling.

"Cookie?" Madison said, stretching and standing up.

Outside the wind was still blowing hard, even if the sleet had called it a day. The street was quiet and lined by shadows; there was darkness between the houses and behind the thick bare shrubs, through the alleys and on the edge of the front gardens. It would have been easy for someone to watch the Miller place, the guesthouse where the Seattle cops were staying. It would have been easy to do so unobserved in a town where nothing bad ever happened.

Chapter 11

Joyce Cartwell, owner of the Magpie Diner, had finished work early and, on a rare night off, had left the keys for her cook to lock up at 8 p.m. and headed home.

She lived only a few minutes away and, as much as she would have wished for a small farm and a few acres to play with, that close proximity was a blessing in the long winter months when the diner's doors opened at 7 a.m. whatever the weather. Joyce knew what the town looked like before dawn in every season, and she knew which windows would be bright in which houses. At that time of day her town—and the world—felt pristine and somehow uncomplicated.

After a few hours at home she had met a couple of girl-friends at the Tavern for dinner and, over a beer, they had enjoyed a long session picking at whatever gossip they'd heard about the murder of Robert Dennen. None of them knew him as a close friend, but all of them had said hello to him at least a few times in the last year. Joyce had served him breakfast three weeks earlier.

The Tavern was a country-style combination of bar and restaurant with a pool table in the back. Customers could bring their kids if they wanted something different from the diner's fare. They had Italian Night once a week and it was rumored that the chef had once used truffle oil in the mashed potatoes. They opened for lunch at noon, stayed open until late, and there was a pleasant overlap of business, which meant Joyce often talked shop with the owner. Their competition was a pizza joint on the highway and plenty of choice in Sherman Falls; however, as the only two establishments of the kind in Ludlow, the Magpie and the Tavern fought the same battles and suffered the same pains.

Joyce was about to return her glass and bottle to the counter and take her leave when one of the Seattle detectives walked in and made his way to the bar. He was an average-looking guy with graying red hair and an expensive parka. He sat on a stool, ordered a drink, and looked around. One quick look to take the measure of the place and the customers before he turned to his drink and the television in the corner. One quick look with sharp eyes, clever eyes, that Joyce had noticed from her booth on the other side of the room while everyone else had been busy with their evening.

No, she said to herself, *maybe not an average kind of guy at all.*

Detective Sergeant Kevin Brown had left the Miller house reluctantly, but glad that Madison and Sorensen had chosen not to venture out with him into the bright lights of Ludlow's nightlife.

He only meant to have a beer and then return to what might hopefully be a marginally warmer bedroom. Going to the Tavern was about giving someone who might be hesitant to approach him officially during the day a chance to strike up a casual conversation—a conversation that might lead to something useful.

After the brief, chilly walk the Tavern was warm and welcoming with a hint of chili and wet fries in the air. It was also busy, which was a good thing for Brown's purpose. He suspected pretty much everyone there had worked out who he was within the first five minutes.

Brown ordered a draft beer from a local microbrewery—something pale with an instantly forgettable name—and let his eyes fall on the television screen in the corner above the counter. Two pundits were discussing a vintage football game with the sound muted. He watched without any interest.

The bartender—a young man with a goatee—wiped the counter with a cloth.

"Here's the menu, if you'd like something to eat. The kitchen closes in half an hour—after that it's only subs and snacks."

"Thanks, I'm fine."

"Here, Darryl," a woman's voice said, and someone passed a glass and a bottle to the young man.

"Thanks . . ." The bottle ended up in a recycling bin and the glass in a sink.

Brown turned. The woman was zipping up her coat and lifting her hood.

"Could you tell Norman that I have some extra boxes of those tomatoes he likes?" she said.

"Sure thing."

She was small and there was something appealing in her manner and the way she smiled at Brown just because he was sitting there and it would have been rude to exclude him from the exchange.

"Hello," he said.

"Hello . . ."

She was small, with very dark hair and freckles—the kind of coloring his mother used to call *Irish*.

"How was your first day in town, Detective?"

"Is it obvious?"

"Yes, it is."

Brown took a sip of the beer. "It was a tough day. Did you know Mr. Dennen?"

"A little."

"I'm sorry for your loss."

"Joyce Cartwell—I own the Magpie Diner around the corner. Robert would come by sometimes. He seemed like a nice man."

Brown did not reply at first. Whether Dennen had been a *nice* man or not, they would find out in due time. Or maybe not at all. "Would you join me for a drink?" he said.

She smiled again, and it was a lovely smile. "I'd love to, but I can't. I'm opening up tomorrow morning. Then again, we're the only ones doing breakfast in this town so I'll probably see you at the Magpie at some point."

The woman left and Darryl slid a bowl of nuts near Brown's glass.

"Technically speaking, the Stone Bakery does breakfast too," he said, as if he was sharing a great truth. "But only rolls and cakes. If you want *cooked*, the Magpie is all there is."

"Thanks."

"No problem."

"I'm Kevin Brown from Seattle PD." He offered his hand, and the young man shook it.

"I know," the bartender said with a shy grin.

"Do you live in town, Darryl?"

"Yes, I'm staying in the apartment on the top floor." He pointed at the ceiling. "Comes with the job."

"Has the Tavern been busy in the last few weeks?"

"About the usual."

"Any new faces? Any strangers?"

Darryl stopped wiping the counter. He thought about it for a minute and then shook his head. "Sorry."

Brown finished his beer and thought of the bottle of Jura Prophecy whiskey he had left on the sideboard at home in Ballard. He could have done with a tumbler right about then. Instead he put a few bills on the counter and left.

Darryl watched him go. It was on the tip of his tongue to tell Brown about seeing Robert Dennen having an argument with a woman in a car about ten days earlier. Darryl had driven past and barely caught a flash of two people fighting in a parked car by the bridge. He hadn't seen the woman properly, but he could have sworn the man was Dennen.

He watched Brown go and didn't say anything. The woman could have been his wife, could have been anybody at all. It didn't have to mean anything—even if the man was dead, and his car was a shell of charred metal.

In his bed, after an evening recounting every detail of the day to his parents and his younger sister, Jay Kupitz sighed. He really liked the red-headed detective and was also a little afraid of her. It was a heady, intoxicating combination. When the case was wrapped up and they returned to Seattle, maybe he would fly out there and visit her, take her out for dinner.

Why not? Weirder shit happened all the time.

Kupitz closed his eyes and spelled the word he had looked up in the online dictionary.

s-p-e-c-t-r-o-m-e-t-r-y.

He would definitely use it on Hockley the following day.

Sorensen had gone to bed and Madison found herself wandering from the ground floor upward toward her attic room, checking the windows on all the floors and making sure the locks were in place. The wind was doing its best against the house and Madison thought of the inside of a tall ship in rough seas. She hoped Brown would be back soon. It would have seemed strange to tell him to be careful when he was only a few minutes away; nevertheless, Madison worried. They had not had a chance yet to get a sense of this isolated town and its community. Did they want them there in the first place? Had Brown left his duty weapon in his bedroom? What about his backup piece?

Madison lit a fire in the hearth of her daisies-and-bluebells room. A small fire that would consume the log quickly but would keep her company as she undressed and slid between the cool sheets.

Her cell was still charging, but she didn't find any new messages. She was disappointed, though not surprised. To be honest, she didn't know what to expect, how to behave, what she should say or do: she was seeing a man, except that she was not really seeing him. They were spending most of their nights together, but it always appeared to happen as a spontaneous, last-minute decision and not by plan. It had been going on for a couple of months, and most people would call it a relationship—except that they were specifically not in a relationship.

"We're not in a relationship," she had said to him only the previous week, waking up on Sunday with the anticipation of a long, delightfully empty day ahead.

"Of course not," he had replied, his head on the pillow next to hers.

And that had been that. Nonetheless, now that they were apart, there was no manual for how to behave with a man who was explicitly not her boyfriend. And yet she missed him. If there was etiquette for that kind of situation, she was not aware of it. She had wanted to hear his voice at the end of the day, and yet that was not who they were—or was it?

Madison heard the door downstairs open and close and a key turn in the lock. Brown's steps, so familiar, climbed the stairs, and she was glad. He was there, he was fine. Maybe the citizens of Ludlow had been captivated by his understated charm and decided to reveal all their secrets; maybe they'd solve the case tomorrow, arrest the killer, and fly home in time for dinner.

The fire crackled and the quivering light played on the walls while the tiny flowers bloomed and faded. Madison wrapped herself in the comforter and watched the log hiss and spit until she fell into a deep sleep. She did not hear the ping of the message when it arrived a few minutes later.

The wind kept her company as it swept away the clouds and left a starry sky in their place. A family of deer crossed Main Street, as was their habit, unhurried and unafraid. The business of the town and its people was of no consequence to them: sooner or later the mountain would claim back the land, and it would be like Ludlow had never existed.

Chapter 12

It had been eight hours since Alice Madison, twelve years old, had left her home in Friday Harbor on San Juan Island; seven hours since she had taken a ferry to the mainland and cut off most of her hair in the locked restroom using her scissors with the pink handles.

She had left behind everything, except for the small backpack resting on her shoulders as she pedaled her red bike, and her baseball bat tied to the pack. *Good*, she thought, *this is all I need and this is all I want.* The tree-lined, winding road would lead her from the town to her friend Jessica's empty home a few minutes away, soon to be her refuge. Jessica's family was visiting her grandparents in San Diego, and Alice knew the vacation home because they had been there together only weeks earlier.

The forest around her was in full summer glory and the light shone gold through the trees. It was a perfect summer day, and Alice inhaled the fresh, spicy scent of pines with relief. She was okay; she had made it. No one passing her would have thought she was anything other than a kid on a bike ride through the neighborhood. Her long hair had been cropped at the jawline, and with her baseball cap low on her head—and if she didn't speak too much, or say anything too dumb—she could probably, maybe, hopefully, pass for a boy. That would go a long way to keeping her hidden, and *hidden* meant *safe*. She couldn't go back—she wouldn't go back—not after what she had almost done.

The day had started with rage, fear, and despair. It had been too much for her pink, girly bedroom to contain, and she had run.

Once at Jessica's house she would regroup and decide what to do. She had stuffed a couple of ham rolls and a bag of Cheetos she had bought in a convenience store near the bus stop into her pack, and she was hungry.

The bus journey from Anacortes on Interstate 5 in the August heat had been long and sticky, and Alice reveled in the cool shade along the road. She would have to shop for food once she was settled in the house, but that was fine; in fact, she was looking forward to it. It was a mark of her independence.

She would get in—the key was behind the fourth pot by the hedge—she would eat and then she would sit down at the table, where she had played Monopoly with Jessica's family, and figure out her life. She had three fat rolls of banknotes held together by elastic bands in the bottom of her pack—her savings—and a few ten-dollar bills in her back pocket for immediate expenses. There was no reason to panic.

Her father wouldn't start looking for her properly until sunset—in the last few months, rocked by her grief, Alice had occasionally gone hiking alone in the lush, green interior of San Juan Island. After one of their arguments she often spent the day by the lighthouse at Lime Kiln Point, peering at the sea and hoping to spot the resident pod of killer whales. No one, she thought, no one in the whole wide world would think of looking for her in Jessica's house.

The mountains rose around the valley, and even from miles away Alice saw the dark trim of woods; wild woods that led farther and farther away from the small community and into nothing.

Around Alice life flowed as she remembered it—a quiet place where families came to spend weekends and summers. The houses were as big as the ones in Friday Harbor but somehow felt more rural. Most were cabins with porches and terraces that jutted out onto the lake. There would have been fireworks on the water on the Fourth of July, and the smell of barbecues. Sure, she would have to be careful not to be seen, but Jessica's house sat in a copse far back from the main road and off a dirt path; the only living creatures who would conceivably see her were woodpeckers and squirrels.

Alice reached the turnoff and took it. In one minute she would be able to—

A metal-gray SUV was parked in front of the house and all the windows and doors were open. A tall man was unloading a couple of suitcases from the trunk, and three little kids were streaking back and forth between his legs and the front door. A woman's voice called out from inside and the man replied.

Alice had frozen, her bike stopping into a skid. *What? How?*

She watched them for a minute, and it was only when one of the children noticed her that the father turned around.

"Hi," he said.

"Hi," Alice replied, and her heart was beating so fast she could hear it in her voice. *Think, think quickly.* "I was looking for the Palmers' place," she said. "I thought they were coming this weekend."

"This is the Palmers' place," the man said. "They've rented it out to us for two weeks."

"Oh," Alice said.

The man lowered the cases.

"You a friend of the Palmer kids?"

"Yes. No. I mean, yes, I know them. That's great, okay, thank you."

Alice turned the bike and flew away.

It was only once she reached the turn onto the main road and stopped that she realized she had no place to go.

Chapter 13

Alice Madison woke up with a start and black fear clutching her by the throat. She didn't remember the details of the dream, and she didn't need to, because she knew where the dream had come from, where it had been hiding: a memory from another time had been waiting for her between the ridges and the grooves of the mountains around Ludlow.

The dream—a vague shape of jagged feelings—was gone but the panic had been real. Madison breathed in and out, and the sense of oppression slowly began to dissipate. She was not a child: reality was a small attic room with old-fashioned wallpaper and glowing ashes in the hearth; reality was a grown-up with gunmetal and a gold shield on her bedside table.

Madison shook off her blankets and stood up. If she had been at home, she would have made herself some warm milk and walked around until the lingering weight of the dream had left her. There was no reason why it shouldn't work here too.

The Miller house was quiet, except for the wind outside. Tree branches brushed the side of the house from time to time, making a rasping sound against the wood. In their darkened rooms Brown and Sorensen were fast asleep and warm in their beds.

Madison tiptoed down the stairs and turned on the light in the kitchen. The round clock over the fridge told her it was 1:15 a.m. She poured a little milk into a saucepan and stood by the stove rubbing her eyes as it warmed up.

Those everyday gestures chased away the nightmare and left her with the bare facts. Seven days she had been alone and on the run; some of those days had been good, some had not. Some had been terrible. All of those days—the good ones and the bad ones—belonged in another part of her life, and there they would remain. Madison—with a degree in psychology—knew how to talk herself out of bad dreams, and yet she wiped her hand unconsciously on her pajama bottoms to wipe away the tacky, hideous warmth of rabbit blood that had not been there for twenty years.

Just before the milk boiled Madison poured it into a mug, rinsed the pan in the sink, and turned off the light to return to her bedroom. She was at the bottom of the stairs when she heard the crack of splintering wood, and in the gloom of the hallway Madison froze. It could have been many things, all innocent and perfectly safe. Then again, it could have been the sound of a boot stepping on a stick in the dark, someone creeping around a house surrounded by tall trees.

Madison, off balance and at a disadvantage in the unfamiliar building, peered into the living room, where she had been sitting with Sorensen. There wasn't enough light to see clearly inside it, but one thing was sure: if a window had been forced open, the sharp night air and the chilling breeze would have found her very quickly. Madison stepped forward and turned on the light.

The room was just as they had left it. She sighed. The wind was still keeping busy, and that was probably all there was to it.

Madison turned off the light in the living room and sat on the bottom steps of the stairway. The heat from the mug was pleasant under her chilled fingers. She sipped the milk and waited.

Anxiety from the dream had stayed with her, and she had heard zebras instead of horses. The crack had been close but not too close, and definitely not upstairs. If anybody was interested in getting up close and personal with the Seattle detectives—especially the two fast asleep upstairs—they'd have to go through her, and she was ready and armed with a mug, scalding hot liquid, and the will to use both.

Madison sipped the milk and for the next ten minutes heard nothing more worrying than the rattle of windowpanes that Edna Miller would have to fix in the spring. Ever since she had been little, she had had trouble sleeping through the night. Occasionally, she would wake up in her bed after a dream, but often she would just wake up and blink in the darkness. Not crying, not afraid, just awake and watching the shadows on the ceiling above her.

Madison finished her drink and returned to the attic room.

The following morning Madison woke up and gazed at the daisies and the bluebells slowly coming into focus around her. The nip in the air confirmed where she was, and Madison dragged herself out from under the covers and shivered with her bare feet on the wooden floor. A peek behind the heavy drapes revealed a murky street with blurred edges.

She unplugged her phone from the charger. One voice mail. She remembered her awkward message from the previous night, cringed, and pressed PLAY. A pause after the beep and then only two words in a whisper. *Goodnight, Madison.* She could hear the smile in his voice. Twenty-four hours ago she had kissed him good-bye in her bed.

Madison dressed quickly and left a message for the others on the kitchen table. Outside, the air was frosty and the ground crunched underfoot.

She had spent more than ten years in the Seattle Police Department and she knew the city as a patrol officer knows it—square foot by square foot. There was no way around it: she needed to walk the length and breadth of Ludlow to get a feel of the place. The map on the wall of the senior center told her little more than the lay of the land, when what she needed was to make sense of its core.

Madison had not packed her running things—all too aware of Sorensen's peremptory instructions—but a good, hard run would have been a perfect way to become familiar with the neighborhood. Of course, she considered, it was only a diversion from the fact that she felt far from her home ground, playing on a foreign field.

There was a fabric of relationships here—of acquaintances and friendships and loves and enmities—so much more powerful than any in a city the size of Seattle. And the three of them had been dumped right in the middle of it—blind and grasping at clues.

Madison emerged onto Main Street: at one end, in the distance, she could see the red glow of the diner's sign, almost the only brightness in the half gloom. She began to walk in the opposite direction.

She passed Larsson's Meat Market, Greg's Pet Supply and Feed Store, Ludlow Sweets, and Garner's Pharmacy. Paula's Gift Shop doubled as an office supply store, and should Madison wish to go hunting or fishing, Mike's Hunting World could outfit her in a minute. Somewhere nearby a bakery was already at work. The buildings had kept the style of western frontier commercial architecture and clearly had enough business to keep them going, if not busy, through the winter months. The flat, wood-lined fronts and sloped roofs had been well maintained and left in the timber's natural colors.

It reminded Madison of Friday Harbor on San Juan Island, where she had lived briefly when she was a little girl. She had loved it there; she had learned to kayak and explored the little inlets with her friends. She had camped out in the fields under the buffer of a fragile happiness that had shattered when her mother became ill and Madison's life changed.

The street was deserted, and Madison wondered whether the events of the previous days were keeping people in their homes.

Halfway up, Main Street opened on one side into a large square—a neat lawn made scruffy by the weather, with a gazebo at her end and benches all around the edges. A good place for a vigil, Madison thought, as she worked out where the best place to take pictures and a video of the crowd would be.

It was very likely that the whole town would turn up, which was good, but there were merely six of them to keep an eye on the event—and that was only if both deputies were on duty. She didn't know what to expect, but it would be a useful way to feel the pulse of the community. It always was.

The mist was lifting and a pale-blue sky seemed to promise a better day for Sorensen and all the work to be done outside the tent. It would be cold but dry.

A thin stream bordered the opposite end of the square, with a footpath alongside it. The water ran fast between rocks and boulders; it felt icy just watching it rush past.

Madison was turning away when a voice called her back.

"Detective!"

A short man in a bright red mountain parka was half running on the footpath toward her, with an Alsatian on a leash. The dog could easily have outrun the man but politeness made it keep the pace.

"Sorry to startle you," the man said, drawing level with Madison. "I believe you're Detective Madison."

"Yes, I believe I am."

"I'm Randall Gibson," he said as he caught his breath. "I'm the mayor of Ludlow."

"Good to meet you, sir."

"I wanted to be at the airport when you arrived yesterday but I had to spend all day in Sherman Falls. This is . . . this is a terrible, terrible business. I was the one who called the US Attorney's Office, you know. I mean, it was the county sheriff who mentioned it, but I was the one who put in the call."

"Yes, we were told."

"I hope you can help," he said. He had graying hair and large eyes, like a child's, behind round glasses. Randall Gibson was a couple of inches shorter than Madison and spoke in quick bursts, as if he couldn't help the words coming out.

"I hope you can work with Chief Sangster and get to the bottom of it. He's a good man, he's been great for the town."

"He's been very supportive, and we'll do our best."

Gibson patted the dog absentmindedly. "Good, good. If there's anything you need, anything at all . . ."

"Thank you, sir, I'll bear it in mind."

"I'm not from around here, Detective. I moved to Ludlow a few years ago—like many others, like Chief Sangster himself. And this town has been good to me. It's been hard, with the economy being what it is—people are spending less and don't go on vacation so much—but Ludlow is pulling through. I want to do everything I can to make sure we catch whoever did this. For Robert Dennen's family and for the town."

He didn't seem to require a response, and looked beyond the stream and toward the woods.

"I don't know if you know, but it was the first murder in Colville County," he said.

"We were told, yes."

"This is a special place, a beautiful place, and it's worth protecting."

His eyes came to rest on Madison.

"Did you know the victim, Mr. Gibson?" she said.

"Yes, Robert was my doctor."

"Would you mind if I asked you a couple of questions? We're trying to get a picture of the kind of person he was, the kind of life he led."

"Sure, ask away, Detective."

"How long have you known Mr. Dennen?"

"Since I moved to Ludlow, about ten years ago."

"Did you know him socially as well?"

"It's hard not to around here. We were on some of the same committees together, had a beer in the Tavern after a meeting every so often."

"When was the last time you saw him alive?"

"Will Sangster called me when they found him . . . I . . . I saw him in the car." Gibson had paled and two pink spots had appeared high on his cheeks. "Before then, I don't know, a couple of weeks ago in the grocery store, I think."

"Did you have a sense that anything was different? That anything was troubling him?"

The long eyelashes blinked a couple of times. "No, nothing. He was with Betty, they were shopping. There was nothing odd, nothing out of place."

Madison nodded, and somewhere in her mind she made a note of the man's every word.

"As the mayor you must hear about everybody's business," she said. "Has there ever been any trouble? Maybe a professional complaint against Mr. Dennen? Maybe someone who was upset because he wouldn't prescribe the medication someone wanted?"

"No, never."

"Are you sure?"

"Yes. You've seen this place. If someone—" Gibson caught himself, "sneezes in the morning, the whole town has a cold by lunchtime."

"What about the medical practice?"

"What about it?"

"How many doctors does it employ?"

Madison knew it only employed two doctors but would rather Gibson gave her a complete picture in his own words.

"There are two doctors . . . there were two. One was Robert and the other is Eric Lynch. We managed to hire Dr. Lynch four years ago, after Dr. Foster retired. It's not always easy to find someone willing to move their family to Ludlow." His smile came and went. "Lord knows why."

"Was there ever any trouble between them? Between Dennen and Lynch?"

"No, of course not. What kind of trouble could there be?"

"I don't know, Mr. Gibson. It's what we're here to find out."

The Alsatian had begun to pull his owner toward Main Street, and Madison walked back with him.

"Have you . . . have you found any evidence?" Gibson said.

"What kind of evidence?"

"Any kind of evidence. I mean, the fire was awful but I thought maybe you would find something. I hope you'll keep me posted on what you discover."

"We're still looking."

"That's why I had hoped you could get here as soon as possible. That's why I made the call. I've heard that the first two days are the most important in an investigation."

"Yes, they are." Madison would not say more than that.

Gibson had to content himself with walking quietly through the empty square. His eyes went to the gazebo: in a few hours they would be back there.

They parted on Main Street. Gibson went into the bakery and Madison continued her reconnaissance, glad to be by herself. Her first impression of the mayor of Ludlow was that he was well meaning—a little pompous, but well meaning.

At the end of Main Street a stone bridge crossed a river—the Bow, Madison remembered, from the map in their makeshift office. It was fifty, maybe sixty yards wide and flowed, freezing and fast, from the mountains above. Just on the other side stood a three-story log building in the rustic style of the early 1900s. Madison could just about read the sign: LUDLOW & COLVILLE COUNTY NATURAL HISTORY MUSEUM.

Maybe another day, she thought, and her cell phone rang.

Chapter 14

"I met the mayor," Madison said, and took a sip of blessedly strong coffee.

They had taken a booth in the corner—Brown and Sorensen on one of the red leather banquettes and Madison on the other. The diner was busy and agreeably warm after Madison's long walk.

The Magpie was the kind of diner Norman Rockwell would design, Madison thought—if he had been alive and inclined to design diners. A long chrome-topped counter with stools on one side and a line of booths on the other. The black-and-white floor tiles were spotless; ketchup and mustard came in immaculate red and yellow plastic bottles.

Nothing would have mattered, though, if the coffee was less than nuclear strength, since Madison had left the Miller house with nothing more than a glass of milk in her system.

She had ordered French toast and bacon, and it came with a cinnamon smiley on the top. Sorensen was steadily demolishing a "Farmhand's Favorite," which seemed to include every item on the menu piled high on a single plate. She had told Brown that he was letting the side down when he ordered his oatmeal and toast, and he had replied that he would very much like to live to see sixty.

"What's the mayor like?" Sorensen said.

"A little pompous, a little annoying, means well," Madison said quietly, even though no one was close enough to overhear them. "He's very interested in the details of the case. Wanted to know about any evidence we recovered."

Brown was quick to spot the signs that something troubled Madison. "What's on your mind?"

"You know how every single person we met here, the first thing they told us when we asked them about the victim was what a good guy he was?"

"Yes."

"Not the mayor. Also, he used certain words when he was talking about the last time he saw him alive. He said 'nothing odd, nothing out of place.' He didn't say the doc was fine, the words meant the *situation* appeared fine."

Sorensen was used to playing devil's advocate. "You don't think you're being picky about language?"

"Possibly. But he asked me to keep him posted about what we *discover* not about what we *find*."

"He knows there is something for us to discover as opposed to the eventuality of us finding something?" Brown said.

"That's what I'm thinking," Madison said.

"Be careful," Sorensen said, and when she knew she had the others' full attention she leaned forward. "We have nothing to go on: no motive, no suspects, and barely a clear cause of death. If we start to weigh people by their casual words, without any evidence, we're going to be left flapping in the wind—and it won't look pretty."

"All I'm saying is that the guy used some peculiar turns of phrase, and I'm going to keep an eye on him—"

"He doesn't have a record, this much we know," Brown interjected.

"How . . . ?"

"I put in a request yesterday to find out if there were any warrants out or any felony arrests for the whole town." When Madison blinked, he continued, "It's not like I asked them to run the New York City phone book. Anyway, unfortunately for us—though kudos to Ludlow—there isn't one citizen with a felony arrest of any kind. The closest we got was a record for assault in Sherman Falls—and anyway the guy was drunk when he hit his brother-in-law. This town is mercifully free of ex-cons and felons."

"Good to hear," Madison said, and she did not want to consider that something as dark as murder with a side of arson could be the first fledgling step of an offender. If it was, what could possibly follow?

"Do you need me at the vigil?" Sorensen said.

"Yes," Brown and Madison replied in unison.

"We'll be stretched as it is," Brown continued.

"Thought so." Sorensen finished her last bite of egg. "Do you have your own camera?" she asked Madison in a tone that implied that Madison was in fact one of the investigators in her unit and only temporarily seconded to Homicide.

"Yup, ready and waiting."

"If the killer is coming to the vigil," Brown said, "he might want to have a real front seat for the show."

"Be close to the family," Madison agreed.

"Yes," Brown said. "There might be a few hundred people there, and he's going to be in a place where he can see and hear well."

"There will be speeches?" Sorensen said.

"I'm reasonably sure Mayor Gibson will want to say something," Madison replied.

"One of us should speak," Brown said, tactful as always about his seniority in a situation where he was not the primary detective.

"You have fun with that," Madison said. "I'm going to be eyes on the crowd."

"We should update the boss and Nathan Quinn. We'll need warrants in the near future," Brown said. "Okay if I take Fynn?"

"Sure," Madison replied. "I'll call Quinn on my way to KCVW."

They paid and left for their separate tasks: Brown to interview the Jacobsens—the last known people to see the victim alive— Madison to record an appeal for information at the local radio station—after the bakery, before the bank—and Sorensen back to the car crime scene—taking advantage of the clear, dry morning.

The woman behind the counter gave them a smile as they left, and Madison was grateful that she had let them get on with their business without joining them for a chat. Then she instantly felt guilty about that notion. *You have a cold, big-city heart*, she told herself.

She hadn't failed to notice, however, that the woman's smile had been mostly directed at Brown.

Joyce Cartwell watched the detectives as they left her diner. Every customer in the place had been staring. Stare they might, but the investigators had specifically chosen the last booth against the wall, the one without neighbors, and she didn't think they wanted to chitchat. She wondered what kind of person they were looking for, what kind of trial had befallen her town. Had it been the end of a terrible sequence of chance events? Or was it the beginning of a different kind of darkness?

Under the diner's uniform, under her garments, a three-inch scar traveled over her ribs. Not all crimes in Ludlow ended up in a report.

Unheard by Joyce, or by the detectives, one of the customers told her elderly mother that she must have imagined the face she had glimpsed outside the kitchen window in the middle of the night. They didn't have those kinds of perverts in Ludlow.

Chapter 15

Alice Madison strode toward the building that housed KCVW, fished out her cell from her bag, and dialed the number for Nathan Quinn, the senior counsel to the US Attorney for the Western District of Washington State.

"It's Detective Madison," she said when he picked up.

"Detective," he replied, and there was another voice in the background. Quinn disappeared for a moment and then came back. "The US attorney is in my office. I assume you wanted to brief me about Ludlow. I'll put you on speaker."

Madison had not expected to speak to the US attorney. She had never met her, and it felt somewhat uncouth to start their acquaintance while she was rushing down the street. Nevertheless, that's how it was going to be. *Use five words where you would use ten, and don't leave too many pauses,* she told herself. *Pauses make you sound dumb on a speaker.*

Madison briefed Nathan Quinn and Judy Campbell: she was to the point and left no pauses. As they both soon realized, Madison had more of a status report than a progress report. The detectives had been on the ground for just about twenty-four hours. Progress would come. So they all hoped.

Quinn took Madison off speaker. "Thank you for calling, Detective. Keep me posted."

Madison shoved her cell into her bag and almost bumped into a woman who was leaving the pharmacy. She apologized and kept going. They had worked out the radio appeal in the diner and it was written on a napkin crumpled in Madison's pocket.

The radio station turned out to be the size of a small store with a glass front from which the DJ could wave to the passersby. Ben Taylor had long hair in a ponytail and a fake diamond stud in his left ear—at least, Madison assumed that it was fake.

They did three takes because he was trying to "get to the truth of the words." After the third take Madison told him without uncertainty that she was happy with what they had.

Madison's voice, Taylor explained, was very appealing and, when he listened back to the recording on headphones, he found there was an *earnest* quality to it that the listeners would find extremely attractive. He would run the appeal every couple of hours and after each news bulletin.

Madison thanked him and left, grateful that Brown and Sorensen hadn't been there to witness the *earnest* quality of her speech, and even more so that Spencer and Dunne, her colleagues in Seattle—who would have never let her forget about it—would never know.

Betty Dennen sat on an upturned basket in her laundry room and wept. She had been weeping, on and off, since Chief Sangster had knocked on her back door early in the morning a couple of days before. She was crying again now in her utility room with the smell of soap and fabric conditioner, crying because she was going to the vigil for her husband and she didn't know what to wear.

Everything was surreal: from the constant flood of people streaming through her home to the conversations with funeral directors. And then there were her babies, her little children who had been told but couldn't quite grasp the finality of it. And they too would have to be dressed for the vigil.

It was too much. Everything was too much.

Betty Dennen wiped her face with her hand and loaded a wash into the machine. She was mixing whites and colors and jeans, and she just didn't care. At the last minute, mustering more energy than she thought she possessed, she emptied the washer, sorted the laundry, and put on a white wash. As it began to tumble and the suds started to foam, she paused and gazed at it, at the rhythm and the movement inside the drum. It was a soothing, empty nothing.

She slumped back on the upturned basket and remained there until her sister's voice found her a few minutes later.

The roster had been drawn up two weeks earlier. Deputy Hockley knew in advance that he would be on duty on Saturday, while Deputy Kupitz's day off had been hurriedly canceled only on Thursday. It meant that Hockley would be driving the second cruiser and Kupitz would be riding shotgun with the chief. It was a trivial thing, sure, but that's what life was made of, and even though he was going to a ceremony in memory of a man he had known and who had died in horrendous circumstances, a part of Hockley was excited by the day's events and his own part in them. He had never been to a vigil—he had only seen them on TV—and the town, as he drove in, had felt restless, not just deflated but a little on edge.

It was more than he remembered ever happening, and he was going to enjoy every little bit of it. He caught that thought as it popped into his mind and he flashed back to helping the chief with the body in the car.

As penance he offered to make coffee for Kupitz, and even laughed at his silly joke.

"Are you all right, Chief?" Polly asked Will Sangster as she stood by the door of his office.

"As all right as I can be," he replied to his secretary.

In truth, he felt brittle—as if his mind hurt, whatever thought passed through it. He would have to speak in front of the town; he would speak, and yet he could offer neither facts nor comfort.

He hoped that it would rain; no, that it would snow. That the wind would rise and bring black clouds heavy with all kinds of weather and the ceremony would have to be canceled. It was his fault: he had managed to keep the town safe for a number of years, and yet in the end he had failed. Robert Dennen had left a message on his private cell the morning of the day he had died. It might have been something, it might have been nothing: *Please call me, Chief, there's something we need to talk about.*

He had never gotten around to returning the call and had felt too ashamed to mention it to Detective Brown.

Outside his window the sky was a delicate blue, cloudless and pure.

Chapter 16

Samuel's day had started in full darkness and it seemed that, one way or the other, it would continue in the same manner. A heavy hand had shaken the boy awake and the game had started. Except that it wasn't a game—and he had, yet again, drawn the short straw.

Samuel had stumbled out of the cabin and started running because there was no time to lose, there never was. If he made a mistake, if he was caught, there would be painful, drawn-out consequences. There would be dreadful hours in the lonely place and no food for one whole day. He was already slighter and smaller than the others, and he could not afford to be weak.

Weakness on the mountain was the harbinger of death, and he had to survive long enough to leave and find Cal. Three more years. During the hardest days and the coldest nights Samuel knew he wouldn't survive that long, and the thought of not ever seeing his brother again, of leaving the little ones alone to fend for themselves, made him howl with grief.

So Samuel ran.

And even with his advantage, he could hear three sets of rushing steps tracking him through the forest.

He ran and remembered the first time: he had been twelve and his father had woken him up before dawn, his hand gripping his shoulder in a way that would become terrifyingly familiar.

"If your brothers catch you, you know where you'll end up. But if you manage to escape, *they* will get punished."

Samuel had six older brothers—taller, heavier, stronger, and swift with their hands and their temper.

"But . . . why?" he said.

"Because we are alone in the world, son, and I want to make sure that my boys grow up to be able to take care of themselves. Out there, beyond the boundaries of our land, there's nothing but beggars, killers, and thieves. You cannot trust anybody, you cannot rely on anybody. One day they'll come for us and, when they do, we'll be ready and they'd better bring body bags. Do you understand?"

Samuel understood. He was twelve and had never left the farm, never seen a school or spoken to another child who was not a sibling. He could read short words and had been shooting squirrels since he was eleven, but he had never seen a television set or listened to a pop song.

The boy took his father's truth, put it in his heart, and when the man opened the door that first time, Samuel ran as fast as he could. Cal caught him in the first ten minutes, put his hand on his younger brother's mouth so that he wouldn't make a sound and dragged him off, deep into the forest, farther and farther away from the others.

The cave's entrance was hidden by heavy shrubbery, and in the summer it was completely invisible. Cal pushed through the foliage and Samuel found himself in a low, narrow tunnel that disappeared into the gloom. Cal sniffed the air and, apparently satisfied, took his brother's hand and led him forward.

"Bears and wolves stink—you'd better remember that," he said. "If you smell bear when you put your head in the cave, you might want to think twice about going in. The worst hiding would be better than getting whupped by a mama bear."

Samuel had nodded. Cal was a few years older and mostly he was busy with the farm's daily chores. He didn't remember ever being alone with his brother like this: the older kids had their routines and seemed to work like a tight, efficient army unit, and Samuel—ten years younger than the oldest boy, Luke—was still collecting eggs from the coop while they went hunting.

The tunnel opened into a larger space. Eight feet or so above them a slim fissure allowed enough light for the boys to see each other and the stone walls around them. It was an ugly, misshapen room dug by time and pressure into the mountain and, as he looked around, Samuel saw a threadbare blanket thrown in a corner and a small pile of dry kindling. They sat with their backs against the cool stone. It smelled of damp earth.

"I'll teach you how to light a fire without smoke," Cal said quietly.

"Okay," Samuel replied, still unsure about what had happened and why his brother was helping him. Didn't it mean that Cal would be punished?

It had been a shock that day to realize that his brother was kind. Cal had found the cave when his father had started to wake him up at dawn for the others to chase. Sometimes you were the hunter, sometimes you were the prey.

"The trick," Cal said, passing Samuel a hunk of bread he had hidden in his coat pocket, "is to let yourself be caught every four or five times. Otherwise they'll know something's up."

Samuel nodded.

"You'll have to get yourself caught today," Cal said.

"But—"

"It's your first run, it would be strange if you weren't caught, wouldn't it?"

"Yes," Samuel said, after he'd thought about it for a while.

"Don't worry. I'll teach you."

"What?"

"Everything," Cal said. "Here, for luck."

The long raven feather was glossy-black and shone in the light.

At fifteen, Samuel—who everybody, including his younger siblings, called "Mouse"—knew more about the mountain, about tracking and stalking and trapping, than any of his older brothers. He could shoot too, though he did not much care for it.

Now Samuel ran. And he was convinced that his father wanted to punish him for something—he knew not what—because it was the second time in a handful of days that he was the prey, and that just wasn't fair.

Samuel knew a lot about discipline and little about fairness. *I'm not getting caught today*, he said to himself. The mountain was his home, after all, and it was on his side. Cal had always said so.

Chapter 17

Detective Sergeant Kevin Brown sat back in his chair at his desk in the senior center as the door closed behind Mr. and Mrs. Jacobsen. They had come into town to see him and had left their baby, Bella—named after a character in a book her mother loved—with her aunt.

They had arrived at the appointed time, given their statements, and signed on the dotted line, but—in essence—they had not told Brown anything he didn't already know, and it vexed him.

Somehow, he had hoped that the mere fact of his presence would release previously forgotten details and they would remember something that would help him understand why, if Robert Dennen had left A to go back to B, he was in fact found near X. He knew it had been a crazy hope; nevertheless, he couldn't help his disappointment.

The Jacobsens had been very clear: the night, and the nightmare it had been, was seared into their memory. Dennen had arrived as quickly as he could and had stayed with them for a while, even after Bella had begun to breathe normally, to make sure that her recovery would continue.

When a young child has an attack there is always the question of what to do, how to proceed. As their doctor, Dennen had written an "asthma attack plan" for them to follow to the letter whenever it seemed that Bella was in trouble. The nearest hospital was almost an hour away, and it was crucial to give her prompt medical care—if they had taken her to the hospital, her condition might have worsened during the drive, and the unthinkable might have happened.

Brown had noticed the couple pale as they recounted the events of that night and how fiercely Dennen had fought to get the baby to breathe. And he had succeeded.

"He saved her life," Mr. Jacobsen had said. "And not for the first time."

"He was constantly looking for better ways to do things, for better meds," his wife said. "He mentioned he'd heard that day that there had been an article in a journal about a new trial, and he would look it up for us. That's the kind of guy he was."

"Will you be seeing Dr. Lynch now?" Brown said, feeling tasteless for mentioning it.

"Yes, we will," the woman replied. "He can use Robert's notes for Bella. He's been taking notes since she was born. It won't be the same, but at least he'll be able to follow Robert's work."

Brown sipped the coffee—now cold—that he had brought over from the diner. One of the questions that bothered him was whether the killer had crossed Dennen's path by accident or whether he had been lying in wait for him. And if—for whatever reason—the killer had meant to harm the doctor specifically, weren't there easier ways to accomplish that task than to brave the midnight freeze on the off chance the doctor might be called out?

Brown stood up and grabbed his coat. He had all this to think about, mull over, and analyze. And somewhere in the back of his mind the ember of the diner woman's smile still glowed.

Madison was just coming through the door as he was leaving. "How did the appeal go?" he said.

"It went," she replied. "They'll broadcast it often enough that people will start to hate it, but that's the way it goes."

"Look . . ." Brown pointed.

An outside broadcast van had parked on the corner where Main Street opened into the town square; the back doors were open and an operator with a camera on his shoulder was filming a reporter. They couldn't hear the words, but the young woman was wearing black and speaking into the lens with what Madison called *practiced television sorrow*.

"Took them long enough," Madison said.

In Seattle they were used to the press arriving at a murder crime scene at the same time as the medical examiner, sometimes at the same time as the detectives.

Dr. Eric Lynch was in his late thirties, fair, and clean shaven to the point of pinkness. He regarded Brown and Madison from behind his desk with owlish eyes. His office was a large, comfortable room with a degree-and-diplomas wall and some colorful children's health posters.

"Yes," he said, "Robert and I talked about patients all the time."

"What in particular about the patients?" Madison said.

"We're the only doctors in the practice. We talked about issues with medication, insurance, everything. Any problem either one of us was having. He was very supportive when I moved to Ludlow. It wasn't easy for the patients, because most of them had known the previous doctor since they were kids."

"What did you talk about in the last few weeks?"

"I'm sure you understand about patient confidentiality."

"I'm not asking about the specifics, Doctor. I'm asking you if there were any particular issues, serious issues, that concerned Dr. Dennen."

"How serious?"

"Serious enough that someone might want to hurt him."

"One of the patients?"

"We're looking into every possibility."

Eric Lynch looked at the wall cabinet of drawers and files for a long, quiet minute. His thoughts seemed to have snagged on something. Brown and Madison's job was not to distract him while he worked out what it was that had caught his attention.

At length he turned to them. "I can't believe what I'm about to tell you has any relevance to Robert's murder." He leaned forward in his chair. "The only person Robert has ever argued with is Jeb Tanner—if you can call it arguing, and everybody in town has had words with Jeb Tanner at some point. It started even before I moved here. Tanner's a farmer. Robert wanted to make sure Tanner's kids were all right. He's got a bunch of them—he's one of those eccentric types you find away from the big cities. Eccentric, sure, but harmless. The kids' mother left him some time ago. His children are homeschooled and don't mix with other farming families—or with anybody else, for that matter. We never see them. I'm not even sure we know exactly how many he has. Robert wanted to make sure they were okay. He went to visit them a few weeks ago, but Tanner didn't let him see them. We talked about him calling Children's Services, getting an inspector up to Tanner's place."

"Did he call Children's Services?" Madison said.

"I don't know. We had disagreed about it. I told him we should give Tanner another chance. Once Social Services gets involved, any kind of relationship you have with the patients is shot to heck."

"We need to find out if he did."

"There'll be no one there. It's Saturday."

"For some people maybe. What number would you have called?"

Once Madison had the number, it took her fifteen minutes to find out who would have received Dennen's call and another five to get the social worker's home number.

* * *

"Who did you say you are?" The woman's voice crackled down the phone line.

There were children's voices in the background and a television blaring. Madison paced the empty medical center waiting room and repeated her name, title, and her badge number too—in case the civil servant wanted to check her credentials.

"Can't this wait until Monday?"

"I'm sorry, ma'am, but it can't."

"Look, for emergencies—"

"It's not that kind of emergency. We're investigating a homicide and your help would be appreciated."

Madison's voice was as polite as she could make it while being clear that a negative reply was not acceptable.

"How can I help you?" The woman's tone was far from cooperative, but at least she had moved to a quieter spot in her home.

Madison explained that a doctor who might have contacted her office had been murdered, and she needed to know whether he had been in touch. Hopefully, the social worker would tell her, even though—like everything else in Dr. Dennen's life, it seemed—there was the issue of privacy and confidentiality.

"Dr. Robert Dennen?" the woman said.

"Yes."

"From Colville County?"

How many Robert Dennens does the woman know?

"Yes, ma'am, the very same."

The social worker was quiet for a moment. Madison was about to make sure that she was still on the line when the woman spoke, and her voice was different.

"Yes," she said. "Yes, he wrote to us and I picked up the case and started a file."

"What does that involve?"

"It means that he sent us the details of a potential child abuse situation, and I investigated."

"You *investigated*? You visited the Tanner farm?"

"I cannot give you the name of the family in question."

Madison's mind raced to find a way to make the conversation work; somehow, she sensed that the woman wanted to tell her something. "I completely understand and I value your ethics, ma'am. Let me just rephrase it . . . and you only need to say yes or no . . . am I on the right track here?"

A beat of silence. "Yes, you are."

"Thank you. Without compromising anybody's rights, what can you tell me about the letter and about your visit?"

The woman sighed. "The e-mail mentioned a local resident and his children. It was not unusual in any way. That's how we find out about most cases."

"When did the e-mail arrive?"

"About two weeks ago, and the implications were extremely serious. I scheduled a visit as soon as I could."

"You called the family?"

"They don't have a telephone. I drove up to the home of the family in question."

Suddenly Madison wanted to hug the woman. "You just went?"

There was a grim chuckle. "Yes, I just went."

"Did you see the kids?"

"No, I saw a few young men and women—in their twenties—but no minors."

"Did you speak with Jeb Tanner—I mean, with the father?"

"Oh yes, we spoke all right. He told me that his children were not the state's business, that he had all the paperwork for the school testing in order, and that he didn't welcome the government's interference in his family's life."

"That's it?"

"No, he also told me to leave and never, ever come back."

"What's next?"

"I've started a file on the family and I've sent a report to my line manager. The man didn't threaten me—he didn't need to, and wasn't stupid enough to. I can't force him to let me meet his kids, because there's no proof of abuse or neglect. And there is no proof, because no one has ever seen them. Lord knows if they even exist. Even the doctor's letter could only say that he *feared* for the kids. Between you and me, I think there was something more, but he wouldn't tell me."

"Another reason to contact you?"

"Yes, but he didn't explain. If he'd had any kind of evidence—if he'd seen a child himself, or someone else had—he would have told me."

"Something had pushed Dennen to seek help for the kids," Madison said, after she had briefed Brown and Lynch. "Something happened, but we don't know what—or when."

"We need to see his office," Brown said.

Lynch stood up. "Sure, but you cannot have access to his files—his patients' files."

Brown—ever the diplomat—nodded. "Of course, at this stage we're just trying to understand the big picture."

Forget the big picture, thought Madison, who was inclined to get right into the meat of the files first and comply with the relevant warrants later—warrants that would inevitably require a conversation with Nathan Quinn, and possibly another chat with the US attorney.

Robert Dennen's office was identical to his colleague's. His remains had lain only yards away, and when Madison crossed the threshold she could not help thinking about the body bag and what had been inside it.

There was a desk, one chair behind it, and two more for the patients. An examining bed stood in a corner and posters covered the walls.

"The last time Dr. Dennen was here, it would have been on Wednesday. Is that correct?" Brown said.

"Yes," Lynch said. "On Wednesday we finish at 7 p.m." He hovered by the door and appeared reluctant to leave them alone in the room.

The whole place was a gigantic patient confidentiality trap: from the doctor's planner on the desk, to the drawers that might contain any kind of medical test result, to the brand-new computer crammed full of information that Brown and Madison were not intended ever to see.

In the meeting with Lieutenant Fynn in Seattle, Nathan Quinn had told them that he was working on the warrants that would allow them enough access to do their job without tramping over the Hippocratic Oath. However, without a signed warrant in their hands, they couldn't so much as open the first page of the diary. Anything they found and any progress in the investigation that was not backed up by a warrant would be considered *fruit of the poisoned tree* and would get them kicked out of court. But not before the defense attorney and the judge had a good laugh.

They couldn't touch, but they could observe. Brown turned to Eric Lynch.

"Doctor, take a look around. Is there anything that feels out of place to you?"

The room had been sealed off first thing on Thursday morning, after the body had been found. Chief Sangster had sent Deputy Hockley to stick a length of crime scene tape over the door, and no one had been inside it since then.

Lynch took a cautious step into the room. Madison could see that he did not want to be there. It wasn't about confidentiality and it wasn't about sorrow. One step inside the room was one step closer to whatever had killed his friend.

He looked around and his gaze trailed over the objects, the furniture, and the oatmeal carpet.

"Take your time," Madison said. "You know this room. You know what's normal for this room. Has anything been moved from its usual place? Has anything been removed or added?"

Lynch frowned with the effort of finding something. To Brown and Madison, Robert Dennen's office looked neat but not obsessively so. It was the workplace of someone who thought he'd get back to it the following day, to his orange Post-its on the edges of the computer monitor and his pens in a desk organizer.

Lynch looked all the way around the room, then stopped suddenly and took a step forward.

"That," he said, and pointed.

Brown and Madison followed his eyes. At first, neither could see what he had noticed.

"What is it?" Brown said.

"The wastebasket."

All three stood over the plain metal-mesh basket with a single paper tissue scrunched up in it. The tissue was white and looked clean.

Lynch looked at Brown and Madison, as if it were obvious. "The cleaner comes in around 8 p.m. and empties all the baskets. I remember thinking how sad it was that he had wiped away all traces of Robert from this room before we knew he'd never come back to it."

The tissue lay in a wastebasket that had been empty at 8 p.m. the night Dennen had been murdered.

"We need the cleaner's name and phone number," Brown said.

"We need the warrants," Madison muttered. Without the warrant the tissue would, for the rest of eternity, remain in the basket.

She left the room and for the second time that morning dialed Nathan Quinn's number in Seattle. It went to voice mail. "It's Detective Madison. We need those warrants. We might have found something, but Sorensen isn't going to be able to do anything about it without the warrants. If they have to be signed by the pope, could someone please tell His Holiness to shake a tail feather and get a move on?"

Madison ended the call. She was still annoyed that she'd had to brief the US attorney on the hoof, and in an oblique way she blamed Quinn.

Keep me posted . . . those had been his parting words.

Sure thing, Counselor, I'll keep you posted when you get me my warrants.

"Brown just checked and the cleaner had emptied the basket, as always, at around 8 p.m.," Madison told Sorensen on their way back to the town center.

"Someone was in the victim's office in the middle of the night?" Sorensen was still at the car crime scene.

"That's what it looks like."

"Where are my warrants, Madison?"

"I know, I know. I'm chasing them."

"Tell your friend to hurry up, he's the one who sent us up here."

"Quinn is—"

"You know what I mean. You worked with him on enough cases to push him when needed and, believe me, it's needed."

"I got it."

"Madison?"

"Still here."

"The ME called me. He recovered a bullet. The body shielded it from the heat. Someone will drop it off at the station."

"Good news."

"I'll see you in the square. My homeboy Kupitz here is going to drive me."

Chapter 18

Traffic in town was definitely busier than it had been since the detectives arrived the previous day. People walked down Main Street with a definite purpose, almost hurrying toward the square. They were coming with candles and flowers. Some carried small stuffed animals. *Children, he had taken care of children.*

Madison was surprised by how familiar the place felt after having been there for barely twenty-four hours. Some of the faces she had seen in the diner, others she had walked past once or twice. In a group she recognized the woman she had bumped into at the pharmacy earlier that morning.

The weather was on their side: cold but clear, the sun as high as it would get on that late February day, and the air was still.

It was a vigil and it would also be another occasion for an appeal for information—it had been decided that Chief Sangster would do it. Madison felt a rush of unease without knowing why; she watched as the crowd gathered in the open space, and something inside her bristled.

* * *

Lee Edwards stepped out into her backyard. It was time to go to the square, but she wanted to try one more time.

She took a deep breath and hollered. "Tucker!" She waited a few seconds. "Tuckeeeeeeer! Here, boy!"

There was no movement around the shrubs or by the trees, and it was the darndest thing. Tucker would never leave; he just wasn't that kind of dog. He wasn't one of those fancy huskies who—soon as you let them off the leash—run off to join the wild packs and you never see them again. No, her Tucker was a sweet dog who stayed close to home.

She called out again, but there was no answer, and Lee Edwards felt that the weight on her heart, not knowing where her darling boy was, would never lift. She was in her late sixties, her grand-kids lived in South Carolina, and that little dog meant the world to her.

She went back inside and her husband, Ty, gave her a brief hug. They left the house for the short drive and all along the road she looked out for the poodle.

When Madison and Sorensen widened the perimeter around the car crime scene, they had made it difficult for the locals to have a place where they could leave their tokens of remembrance and sadness in the mourning of their doctor. The gazebo in the town square had filled that need, and since Madison had walked past it that morning, flowers, candles, and notes had been left on the gazebo's steps and all around it. A trestle table had been set up on one side and volunteers were handing out coffee and hot chocolate to the milling crowd from large metal pots. The mood was muted, the talk was hushed.

Chief Sangster had briefed his deputies and the Seattle inves-tigators in his office and they all knew what they were doing: six of them in all to keep an eye on a crowd of a few hundred, and people kept arriving.

Brown and the chief would be by the gazebo, with the mayor and the family, while Madison, Sorensen, and the deputies would mix with the crowd. Both Madison and Sorensen had checked their cameras and were already taking discreet pictures.

"Do you think *he* will come?" Kupitz asked Sorensen.

"I think it's likely. Not a certainty, but a definite possibility."

"What . . . what do *you* want me to look out for?" he whispered, as if Sorensen was now the highest authority in his own private hierarchy and the chief's instructions were important but secondary to hers.

Sorensen hadn't missed this. "Do what the chief said," she replied. "Look out for anything that feels wrong to you, and especially if you see any lone strangers."

Kupitz nodded and went off.

Sorensen looked around: too many people and too few warm bodies to cover them. Just then the crowd parted and she saw a woman with a baby in her arms and two young children by her side. They walked by the flowers without seeing them; there was no question about who they were.

Randall Gibson, the mayor of Ludlow, had replaced his bright red parka for a subdued smart black coat. When he tapped on the microphone that had been set up in the gazebo, the crowd moved closer. *They want to hear, sure,* Madison thought—unlike the deputies this was not her first vigil—*but they want to look just as much.*

She stepped to the side, out of the main body of the crowd, sweeping her eyes over the faces turned to the mayor: four hundred people, maybe more. As Randall Gibson began to speak, the silence in the square was a heavy, tangible object pressing down on all of them. She saw Dr. Lynch with someone who could have been his wife; she saw the lady from the diner; and Polly, the chief's secretary, her gray hair tightly permed and her hands busy with a handkerchief.

"*We are here today. . . ,*" Gibson started.

But Madison was not listening to him. She was looking for something, anything, that would catch her attention, and she knew that Sorensen, on the other side of the crowd, was doing the same.

Kevin Brown didn't really want to listen to the mayor, and he sensed that the small, dapper man in the black coat would have been quite happy to do all of the talking during the event.

Brown's main concern was the crowd: How many of them were there? Three, no, at least four hundred. Inside the gazebo they were a few feet higher than the ground, and as much as Brown hated being on show, it gave him a far better view of the square. He went into a sequence: his eyes searched for Madison and then Sorensen, then he scanned the first few rows of watchers, checked the position of the deputies, scanned the back rows of onlookers, and went back to Madison.

Brown hoped for something unequivocal, like a crazy stranger who would begin to rant about doctors and medical insurance—someone they could cuff on the spot and interview at leisure in the police station. Then again, he doubted they—or the town—would be that lucky.

Alice Madison was vaguely aware that the mayor was talking about Robert Dennen and how much the town owed him. And yet, like a hunter, her attention stayed fixed on the mourners. A look, a gesture, a smile at an inappropriate moment, body language that spoke of unease, of repressed anger: the list went on and on—though when it came down to it, it meant that Madison had to follow her gut and question anything that felt out of step with the event.

Her gut, Madison considered, was clenched hard, and as the crowd stepped forward to hear the mayor's words more clearly, she understood why: if there were 450 people at the vigil, it was more than two-thirds of the whole town's population in one place at the same time. She wasn't sure why this should be a concern, but there it was. Nothing like this ever happened in Seattle, where even CenturyLink Field could seat only 67,000 in a town with ten times that number of residents.

Madison observed and took note. Most of the people present had dressed in similar fashion: a lot of dark colors, coats, baseball caps, and woolen hats, many hooded tops under jackets, and boots. The age range covered all generations. It made for a homogeneous mass that Madison was finding difficult to keep distinct.

Some stared at her, some glanced and looked away. Her Seattle PD gold badge was on a thin chain around her neck. They knew who she was and it was a good thing. She wanted to be visible. If anybody was nervous about Madison watching the crowd, she wanted to see it in their eyes.

The mayor had moved on to *the values held dear in the heart of our community*, and Madison moved down the side of the throng, taking pictures on a small camera that fit neatly in one hand. A woman with a toddler in her arms was weeping silently as she bounced the little girl. A couple of teenage boys in the back pushed each other and giggled. Someone threw them a harsh look and they fell silent.

Betty Dennen was not going to speak. Madison had seen the lost, haunted look of someone still deeply in shock too many times to count, and she was pleased to see that the widow had her family and friends around her. She would have found it hard to breathe, let alone to speak coherently, in front of a crowd. Mostly she just sat—thank God someone had organized chairs— and nodded.

The crowd stirred, and from the front a group of teenagers stepped out and lined up by the bunches of flowers. It was the Ludlow Goldfinch Choir and their voices rang out in the square. They sang John Lennon's "Imagine" a cappella, and they sang it with more emotion than talent. Though they wouldn't make it onto *Glee*, Madison felt a knot in her throat: they were singing for a man who had lived and died among them.

A movement to her right and Madison was suddenly aware of the camera operator filming. No prizes for guessing who'd end up in the news—the dull mayor or the cute kids singing.

"What's going on?" a voice said to her, and she turned.

An older man fixed her with a piercing glare and repeated his question. "What's going on? You're one of the Seattle detectives, right?"

"Yes, sir, I am."

"Nobody's telling us anything. The local news is useless and all we know is that there was a fire and the doctor was found dead in his car."

"Yes, he was." Madison's eyes shifted between the man in front of her and the people behind him. The last thing she wanted was to talk to him.

"Well?" He was getting into his stride. "It's been two days already. What's going on? The chief is usually really up front and straight up, and that's why we like him around here, but he's told us diddly-squat about this and the community is feeling . . ."

Madison would never find out what the community was feeling. The song was coming to an end and Chief Sangster moved to the microphone to speak.

"Here you go," she told the man. "I think you should listen to the chief, sir. Pardon me," and she moved off.

A small crackle in her earpiece and Deputy Kupitz's voice whispered, "I see someone."

"Where are you, Koop?" Hockley replied through the static.

Madison stood on tiptoes to look around.

"*I'm Chief Will Sangster, y'all know me, and I have the privilege to serve this town . . .*"

"I'm at the back of the crowd," Kupitz said, "and I'm looking at a guy I've never seen before—"

"Details, Koop," Sorensen cut in.

"About late teens, early twenties. Five ten. Dark clothes, black hood, and a baseball cap. I've never seen him before, and he looks real squirrelly."

"Where is he?" Madison said as she turned left and right.

"Edge of the crowd, by the TV station's van."

"*When something like this happens,*" Chief Sangster said, "*you need to know that we are doing everything possible . . .*"

"I see him," Hockley said.

It occurred to Madison that she could have been standing right next to the guy and she wouldn't have known: she could very well spot a liar and a crook, but she didn't know the faces of all the town's residents like the deputies did. There was no point in trying to push her way through, so she rushed around on the outside of the crowd to get to Hockley. A few turned but most were listening to the chief—the mayor had given them the *values held dear,* but the chief was a decent man and they might finally get some facts instead of all the rumors that had been flying around in the Tavern and the Magpie Diner.

Brown had heard the exchange in his earpiece and noticed Madison was on the move. He kept his gaze on the van and on the young deputy near it. He stayed where he was, even if he'd rather be among them. *Slowly, approach him slowly and carefully. Be polite but watch his hands.*

Madison saw the van and headed for it. She spotted Sorensen and Kupitz with Hockley, arriving from the other side. They all converged on the side of the truck. The lettering on the doors read "KSKD IS THE NEWS," which, even in the urgency of the moment, Madison thought made no sense.

Kupitz nodded toward a group. There he was: a young man, his eyes fixed on the family in the gazebo. His hands were in the pockets of his hooded top and he was balancing on the balls of his feet. A second later he took his cell phone out, checked the screen, and then the hand went back into the pocket. He did that every few seconds. His hood was up and his narrow eyes searched the crowd.

"You don't know him?" Sorensen said.

"Never seen him before," Kupitz replied. "You?"

Hockley shook his head.

They had agreed on a procedure at the briefing: the deputies wore the local uniform and represented the local law enforcement agency . . . *they* would approach any individual they wanted to check out. And Madison and Sorensen would back them up.

Hockley stepped forward. "Sir?" he said to the young man. "May I have a word?"

The young man turned. "What?"

"I'd like a word, sir."

He had stubble on his chin and his eyes were red rimmed. Madison could smell the stale cigarette stench of his clothes from where she was standing. There might have been some marijuana in that reek too.

"What?" he repeated.

He didn't seem any more dangerous than a campus kid after a really long night with a keg. They were looking for a murderer and the worst this kid had likely ever done was some drunk texting after too many shots. Madison's main focus went back to the crowd.

"Would you—?"

But Hockley was cut short by a large man in a parka who had stepped up to the young man and eyed Hockley with mock suspicion. "What's he done now, Hock?" he said.

"Hey, Walt," Hockley said. "Do you know this young man? We're keeping an eye out for strangers. You know how it is."

"I know how it is. He's my nephew. Got here last night from Spokane for a visit."

The young man nodded.

"Thanks, Walt." Then he added to the nephew, "Thanks for your cooperation, sir."

"Walt's my neighbor," the deputy said as the two men walked away. "If he says the guy's his nephew, he's his nephew."

"His nephew stinks of pot," Kupitz said, embarrassed for his bad call.

* * *

Brown saw the young man being led away by a larger man and the deputies' frowns. To Brown the guy looked like a stoner who had turned up at the wrong party.

Chief Sangster was still talking, and Brown tuned in for a moment.

"... *this is a safe town and we're going to keep it that way* ..."

He tuned out again.

In a few minutes the mob would disperse and the Tavern and the diner would reap good business. Maybe even the bakery. The sky was still clear, and there was nothing like a morning pastry after a brush with someone else's grief.

Madison caught the last words of Chief Sangster's speech—something about the police station's telephone number and his own private line. In the middle of the crowd a child let out a shriek and Madison flinched.

The choir started a new song, something uplifting that Madison didn't know and didn't much care about. She was eager for the vigil to end, for the crowd to break up, and for everybody to go back home. Madison, who had never been claustrophobic in her life, for some reason couldn't wait to get the hell away.

She was moving back toward her previous position as she watched people take pictures of the singers, but a sound kept intruding into her consciousness. The child shrieked again and Madison flinched. It was a sharp wail and it cut through everything else—except for that sound, still there, still tugging at her attention.

What now?

It was a dog. A dog was barking, somewhere behind them—close by, but out of sight. It had been barking for a few minutes and it was becoming more and more upset—a small dog by the sound of it. Others had noticed it and had turned away from the choir, craning their necks. A couple were walking fast toward the other end of the square and Madison picked up something in their gait, something in their hurrying that felt like panic, and she followed.

The footpath lined the end of the square, and beyond it rushed the stream that Madison had seen that morning. On the other side a steep bank rose to the forest, the firs so close that hardly any light filtered to the ground.

Madison caught up with the couple on the footpath. They were somewhere in their late sixties, and the woman was leaning forward against the railing.

"It's Tucker! That's our dog!"

A small brown poodle was on a leash, tied to a tree on the top of the bank, on the other side of the stream. The dog had seen them and was dancing in a frenzy of happiness, yapping and whimpering and straining against the collar.

"That's my dog," the woman said to Madison, as if that explained everything. And Madison remembered her in the police station the previous night. *Eagle bait.*

"Stay here, hon," the husband said. "I'll go to the bridge."

"We had lost him, see?" the woman said. "And I told the chief."

"It's okay, sweetheart, I'll go get him."

Madison looked at the dog, and from somewhere the image of a goat on a tether came to her. *Eagle bait.*

A handful of people had joined them and Madison heard someone behind her say, "We can't cross here, we need to—"

The first pop was like a firecracker, and it hissed close to her ear.

The second found its target next to her.

A muzzle flash flared between the trees, and the third pop flew above her head as Madison grabbed the woman and dropped to the ground on top of her.

"Shots fired! Shots fired!" she yelled into her radio as the fourth pop landed somewhere to her right.

The railing was metal bars screwed into the ground and afforded no protection at all: the shooter was in the woods above them, and they had nowhere to run.

A shooter?

Madison struggled to understand what was happening, but her training kicked in. She was crouching and shooting before she even realized what she was doing. She had seen the muzzle flash in the gloom under the trees and that's where she aimed, sweeping the area around it, covering anybody who was trying to run away from the sniper and emptying her magazine into the woods. Her chest had been punched by the adrenaline spike and it was hard to draw breath and think straight.

Let them get away, let them get away.

Her ears rang and buzzed and her hands automatically ejected the spent mag—quickly, without thinking, because thinking makes you slower and slower makes you dead—body memory at work, she reached for the new mag in her belt, clicked it into place and was about to start shooting again when she stilled and breathed. Breathed and listened. All around her the square was quiet and only the elderly couple remained next to her; everyone else who had been near them had vanished.

Madison lifted her Glock toward the woods—her hands were shaking. The woman lay curled up at her feet. Madison kept her eyes on the line of trees. "Ma'am, are you shot? Are you shot, ma'am?" she said.

The lady shook her head. Next to her on the ground her husband lay on his back: he had been shot four times in the chest, a tight grouping that would make any sniper proud.

Across the bank the dog was barking, struggling to free itself, miraculously unhurt.

Brown watched Madison veer away and hurry in the opposite direction from the gazebo. He narrowed his eyes. She had definitely seen something and two people ahead of her were in a serious rush.

Brown saw them arrive at the bottom of the square, and saw the woman point at something. Others had joined them now.

The first crack was a distant pop that didn't mean much to the crowd in front of him. He heard the second and the third, and he knew it—even before Madison's voice burst through his earpiece. He bit his lip and tasted blood.

"Shots fired! Shots fired!"

The choir kids were still singing as Brown grabbed Sangster's arm. "Clear the square. Now!" he said. And then he ran.

How long was the square? How long would it take him to cross it?

There was an explosion of noise on the radio as the chief issued his orders.

Chapter 19

Alice Madison felt a slick of something on her cheekbone and didn't wipe it off because she didn't want to see the red on her hand. Sounds seemed to find her with difficulty: she could hear the dog, she could hear the exchanges on the radio; nevertheless, she was in a bubble of half silence. And reality—even the reality within the reach of her arm—seemed very far away. She saw more than heard the woman scream as she knelt by her fallen husband.

Without realizing that she was doing it, she checked herself for injuries and found none. How could it be? She had been standing right next to the man. Somehow, she had not been hit. And as Madison looked around—standing with her piece still trained on the trees—it seemed that no one but the man had been shot. Some people were cowering behind the benches nearby, others were running toward Main Street. Those still at the gazebo end were also moving off, she registered.

There was no movement in the trees aside from the jumping little dog. After a minute Madison allowed herself to look down:

the man was obviously dead but she reached for the spot under his jaw and felt for his carotid pulse anyway. There was none.

"Madison? Are you hit?" Sorensen's voice came through the radio.

"I'm okay," Madison replied. "We need a bus. Zero-one-zero, two-nine-one."

It was the Seattle Police Department code for *homicide* and *person with gun*. Madison had used it without thinking—Colville County was probably using a different code. Another damn thing that wasn't working in this crazy setup. She was angry. She was furious.

Madison looked up and Brown was there, his eyes taking in the situation. Two people on the ground—one fatality, one witness—Madison standing over them, and a dozen spent shells around her feet.

"He was over there," Madison pointed.

"One shooter?" he said.

"He stayed put. Didn't change position. I only saw one muzzle flash."

"Where exactly?"

"Four feet to the left of the dog."

Brown looked at the man on the ground and his eyes met Madison's. The sniper had been interested in only one person out of the hundreds in the square, only one person out of the group right there by the railing. He could have picked them out, one by one.

"I'm going to pursue," Madison said.

"No," Brown laid his hand on her forearm. "You can't. Your hearing is compromised. You would be a target, and you would make me vulnerable too."

Madison opened her mouth to argue, but Brown was right. His voice—what she could hear of it—was muffled and reaching her as if she were inside a box. She tried to object anyway, but he had already climbed over the railing and down the bank to the stream.

"Officer in pursuit," Madison called into the radio. Forty-eight hours earlier they had been chasing one unarmed kid down the alleys in Seattle's International District with the support of the whole department. Here, Madison considered, they had a shooter and not enough cruisers for the whole department.

The water was freezing but Brown had to cross the stream and get to the other side. He was glad the dog would be a marker for where the sniper had lain in wait, because there was no way to cross where he was. The water was ten feet wide. *And who knows how deep?*

Was it worth getting himself wet if it slowed him down? If it made him more vulnerable?

Twenty yards to his right he noticed that the stream was narrower, and he headed there. Six feet wide, with a protruding rock on one side and a stuck log on the other that might—maybe, hopefully—carry his weight. He took a couple of steps backward and launched himself forward. One of his boots skipped in and out of the water, but somehow he made it across.

The dog greeted him enthusiastically, and Brown was glad that the little thing was tied to a tree—even though he wished it would shut up. It must have been terrified by the shooting. Brown was about to pet it and then stopped himself. There might be DNA or other trace evidence from the sniper on the dog.

Even with the sun still high in the sky there was a distinct murkiness in the forest that felt damp and mulchy, because daylight didn't often make it all the way to the ground—and when it did, it was too drained after its struggle to matter. And Brown saw it: a spot where the dirt had been disturbed, where a long form had lain in wait, where metal casings from the shells glinted in the shade. Metal casings that the shooter had not bothered to take with him.

Brown—his weapon out in front of him and moving with the sweep of his eyes—progressed yard after yard, from one tree to the next, looking for someone who had probably already left.

Or who might still be there, ready and waiting for the cops who would inevitably follow.

There was something rank in the air and it spoke to Brown's natural instinct: it was the scent of death, recent death, like a shrill warning drifting all around him.

His footsteps were muted on the dirt and Brown was glad that Madison was not there: anybody could have snuck up on her on the needle-covered ground with the odd patch of snow. Everything on the forest floor was decaying and covered in moss: rotten wood and fallen logs, fluff from the fur of a small animal, and feathers from another animal's prey.

Once he was out of sight of the dog it felt as if the view in every direction was nothing but the same repetition of trunks, low branches, and heavy, silent murk. He paused and listened. Birds rustled above him, high in the trees and close to the light. And yet, where he was, there was no sound except for the thunder of his heart. He should have been the one being shot at, not Madison. He pushed away that notion, the cool lump it brought to his stomach, and pushed on.

The putrid smell was becoming stronger and a sudden thought froze Brown where he was: Could it be a distraction? Could it be something the shooter had devised to sidetrack the attention of his pursuers? It would have been easy to hunt and kill something and leave the carcass as a disturbance to the focus of any other person who would come after him.

Brown breathed in the foul smell, trying in vain to become desensitized to it. His eyes swept his surroundings and caught a movement—barely a flicker of movement—on his left. He aimed his piece. He breathed in. He directed every ounce of perception to that point in space.

Nothing moved, nothing shifted.

He was exposed and unprotected, but no gunshots rang out.

He progressed again, and there it was: the fox had been killed recently by something bigger, faster, and stronger. The injury that had killed it had not been made by a knife or a bullet.

Whatever had taken its life had probably been disturbed by the shooting and left it there—in death, as in life, part of the life cycle of the forest floor that would claim it back. The words of a poem found Brown like a startling gift from his school days, and he shuddered: the woods might have been dark and deep, but they sure as heck were not lovely.

After a few minutes trying to move ahead in a straight line, he felt the warmth of the sun on his face, the firs opened to the sky, and Brown walked onto a paved road that sliced the forest in two.

Shit.

The road was deserted on either side. If the shooter had left a car parked and ready for him—and why would he have not?—he could have been anywhere by then. Brown looked to the left and to the right. The shooter could have been gone forever, or, if he so wished, he could have gone to Ludlow and checked in person on the aftermath of his work.

The lack of noise made Brown uneasy: by then, in Seattle, the air would have been rent by sirens, while in Ludlow there was only a swish of wings as he turned and went back into the shadows.

Colville County was already catching up with the rest of the state.

Madison watched Brown cross the stream and stand where the shooter had been. She lost sight of him after that and unconsciously pressed the earpiece into her ear to make sure she would hear anything that might pass. The square was the size of a football field, and Brown had covered it at record speed to get to her.

She wanted at the very least to join the other officers evacuating the mourners, but she could not leave the woman still crumpled by her husband on the ground.

She knelt by her. "What's your name, ma'am?" she said. "I'm Detective Madison, Alice Madison." She used her title because her training told her that it would be reassuring under the circumstances. The circumstances, though, were pretty fucked up, Madison thought.

The woman turned, startled—as if she had forgotten that the officer was there.

"Lee Edwards," she replied.

"Lee? May I call you Lee? Can I just make sure you're not injured?"

The woman nodded vaguely.

Madison took stock: there was blood on the woman's green coat, but it was not hers. She needed to get her somewhere warm, or she'd go into shock right there next to her dead husband.

"Madison . . ."

A hand touched her shoulder and Madison recoiled—she had not heard the steps approaching behind her. Sorensen had brought Dr. Lynch and a woman they had never met, who turned out to be one of the nurses at the medical center. Together they persuaded Mrs. Edwards to leave her husband, Ty, and guided her toward cover, where the doctor would examine her and—Madison had no doubt—prescribe her a mild sedative.

"What the hell is going on?" Sorensen blurted out when they were alone, putting into words the question that had been in Madison's mind since the first muzzle flash.

Madison shook her head. She wanted Brown back out of the forest: something in her partner's tone when he'd intimated she should stay behind had bothered her, and she wouldn't be capable of any in-depth appreciation of the predicament they were in until he was back safe.

"His name is Ty Edwards. The woman is his wife, Lee, and that," Madison pointed, "is their poodle, Tucker."

"She was the one who waited for the chief at the station yesterday."

"Yes. Hockley called the dog *eagle bait*. He was right, though not about the eagle part."

"More than ever, then," Sorensen said as she crouched by the body and started her examination, "see my previous and as yet unanswered question."

What the hell is going on?

Brown emerged from the line of trees and shook his head. Madison nodded and only then replaced the Glock in its holster.

It took three attempts to fit the key in the front-door lock of the Miller house. Madison shut it behind her, ran up to the bathroom next to her attic room, and closed the door.

Her hands were shaking and in the mirror she saw a pale face with a smudge of red. Her eyes were wide with shock and upset. It was not fear—she was not afraid then, and she had not been afraid before—but the life of a man who had been within the reach of her hand had been stolen away in an instant, and it was a body blow.

She didn't know him. She barely knew his name. Ty Edwards, married to Lee. What was he saying to his wife just before the first shot? *It's okay, sweetheart, I'll go get him.* How much life together, how much love and days and years were in those words?

One moment he was with her, and then he was not.

Madison reached for a tissue and wiped off the blood. *It's okay, sweetheart.* She felt the tear rolling down her cheek and wiped that off too.

She sat on the edge of the bath and waited until her hands had stopped shaking. There was work to do, the work that no one else but they could do. Madison splashed her face with cold water and returned to the empty square.

Chapter 20

Miles from Ludlow, a boy crouched in a small cave. A fire—without smoke, because the boy knew better than that—warmed the air up a little and the boy's outstretched hands craved the waning heat. Samuel had wrapped the old blanket around his shoulders and his back rested against the stone.

The sun had come out, and the deep indigo he had rushed through when he had left the cabin earlier that morning had turned into washed-out blue. A shard of light cut through the cave's shadows and fell on the rough walls.

In the last three years he had spent time in the cave in every season and in every weather, and he had seen the light change as the months progressed. Samuel did not have a word for the streak of warm color—a lighter shade than blood, but more intense and darker than yellow—that sliced through the grayish wall. He only knew that it looked prettier in winter.

It had started out of boredom one day while he was waiting to hear the shots that signaled the end of the game: he had cut his hand on a broken branch in his run to get there; it was a small scratch but a few drops of blood still bubbled up on his palm. Samuel had smeared it on the flat of his hand and pressed it against the stone. The handprint was still there. Over the months he had used a twig and charcoal from the fire, spit, and occasionally blood: there were more handprints, which had grown larger as Samuel had grown taller; however, scattered around the ochre stripe there were, mostly, tiny stick figures with four legs and a tail and a long thin muzzle. They chased one another and ran together, in and out of the crevices in the stone. One minute, perfectly formed wolf for each time Samuel had been in the cave; for months now he had been the only living soul visiting it, and the stories that Cal had told him about watching the wolves on the mountains lived only on the stone.

Two shots rang out in rapid succession. They signified the end of the game; the hunters would be returning to the cabin. Samuel stood up. The game could last hours or, maybe, just give him enough time to get to the cave; they might play it out twice in a week or once in a month. That day it had gone on for hours and hours, so long that Samuel had fallen asleep twice. It depended on his father's whim, and Samuel did not know the source of his father's wisdom. They had a Bible in the cabin, and his father read to them, but Samuel didn't remember anything about teaching your sons to hunt one another. Maybe it was in a chapter they hadn't read yet.

Another set of two shots told him he could return safely home. There would be a pat on the back and extra food on his plate. Samuel dropped the blanket on the floor and stomped out the remains of the fire. His victory would be sweeter if he didn't have the suspicion that his father would prefer him to fail.

The boy peeked around the hidden mouth of the cave. When he was content that the trail was clear, he started to make his way back. The light told him that it was midafternoon, and his stomach felt hollow with hunger.

He had been walking maybe ten minutes when something lifted him off the ground, turned him around in the air, and slammed his back against a tree.

His brother Luke held him by his coat and shirt, and Samuel's feet struggled to find the ground.

"Here you are," Luke said. "I've been looking for you everywhere."

At twenty-five Luke was taller than their father and made out of bare muscle over bone. His face had never held the softness of youth but had seemed to pass from child to old man. His hands on Samuel felt as if the boy was gripped by the roots of a tree.

"I heard the shots," the boy said. "I'm clear to go back."

"I heard the shots *after* I grabbed you, little mouse."

"No, I *heard* the shots . . ."

"Where do you go, little mouse, when you hide in the woods?"

Samuel clamped his mouth shut.

"Where do you hide? Under a rock? In a hole in the dirt?"

Samuel didn't reply. Luke's eyes were level with his and they were a hard bright blue.

"Tell me where you hide, little mouse, and I'll let you go. If you don't, you know what's waiting for you."

The punishment was harsher for the prey who got caught than for the hunters who had let him escape; and Samuel had always thought that this made sense, because their father was trying to teach them how to run when the enemy came for them. He thought of his punishment—it was winter, and it would be particularly tough. And he was already hungry. He thought of the cave, of the wolves in the cave waiting for him to go back. The decision was surprisingly easy.

"I heard the shots," he said. "You *have* to let me go."

Luke swung him away from the tree and began to march him back toward the cabin. "I've caught you and I'm keeping you," he said.

Samuel didn't speak. There was no point in arguing when you were being propelled forward and your feet barely touched the ground. He would tell his father, he thought, and even though a tiny voice told him which way his father would cast his vote, he had to believe he could convince him.

"Father won't believe you, if that's what you're thinking," Luke said. "Like he never believed that little liar you followed around like a puppy."

Samuel went rigid. "What do you mean?"

"What do you think I mean?"

Their father had forbidden them from talking about Cal, because his older brother had abandoned them and chosen to live his life among beggars and thieves.

Luke shook Samuel as if he were nothing but empty clothes and whispered, "That little liar."

The boy's mind staggered as he looked for Luke's meaning.

"What do you mean?" he repeated, and his voice cracked.

Luke smiled a nasty slash of a smile. He knew then that he had Samuel just where he wanted him. "Liar," he whispered, and he said no more.

After a short walk they emerged from the forest into the open ground where the compound had been built. Samuel looked around. Some of the others had already returned: Jonah, the fourth son, who hardly ever spoke, and when he did was slow and hesitant; and Jesse, two years older than he was, Luke's shadow. Were they going to be Samuel's allies?

His father came out of the barn and the boy's heart contracted when he saw the man's eyes glitter at the sight of Luke holding him by the neck.

"Got him," Luke said.

"You got me *after* the second shots," Samuel bit back.

"Are you calling me a liar?"

"Only if you say you caught me."

"I did catch you."

"Then I guess you are a liar."

"Don't ever—"

"Let him go, Luke," the father said.

Samuel found himself dumped on the ground, and he struggled to his feet.

"Why would Luke lie, Samuel?"

It was a question with a dozen answers, but the words danced in front of the boy's eyes and he couldn't get them out. "He's lying," he said.

His father seemed to think about it for a minute or two. Samuel noticed a couple of his younger sisters had come out of the cabin to watch—eyes wide, sensing danger in the air like rabbits.

"You are very good at this, Samuel," his father said, and for a moment the boy dared to hope. "You are hardly ever caught. It is stubborn and disrespectful to deny your brother his victory. And to call him a liar, why, that's worst of all."

Samuel looked at his brothers: Jesse was almost giddy with the anticipation of his punishment, and Jonah was entirely blank. And yet, even in the moment when his fate hung in the balance, it was Luke's words that upset him the most. *That little liar.*

Chapter 21

Jay Kupitz pressed the hat down on his head and pulled up his leather gloves. The screen that had been hastily erected around the body of Ty Edwards shivered in the breeze, and the deputy was ready to grab it and stop it from flying away. His eyes scanned the open space, lingering over the shadows and checking every movement in the distance. He had been left to guard the body and it was a weight that made him tight around the shoulders.

From time to time he stole a glance—more than anything to convince himself that what seemed to have happened had in fact happened. He had bought something in Mr. Edwards's shop only a couple of weeks earlier—he couldn't remember what now—and he couldn't look away from the dark slick on the man's chest and the white whiskers he had missed with the razor that morning. He wouldn't have stared if anybody else was there. But he was alone, and so he looked.

A car engine rumbled on in the distance and the young man turned around quickly, looking away only when he saw it was a familiar pickup; soon Dr. Lynch would come with the chief in a different truck, and they would take Mr. Edwards away.

Jay Kupitz placed one hand on the butt of the weapon by his side and the other on the screen to hold it in place. That's how they found him a few minutes later, and if they had been delayed a couple of hours he would have been there still.

When Chief Sangster had received Brown's orders he had not paused to wonder at the cheek of the man who presumed to supersede him in his own town. He had merely gotten on with the task of moving a large group of people, who didn't particularly want to be moved, out of harm's way without causing panic—because a stampede would have been as lethal as a bullet.

At the other end of the open field Detective Madison's shots had been sufficiently distant for the mourners to believe the dangerous-animal rumor, and the vigil had been cut short without too much fuss. After all, they'd had a cougar on Main Street the previous year.

Sangster's instructions had been clear: go home, drive carefully, and keep your eyes open.

Most people had done just that; others had found solace in the Tavern and in the diner, while the ones who had been close enough to see the victim being shot were doing their level best to spread the news.

Still, the chief's only concern had been to protect his people in the moment of danger; he had needed to get them away from the square and had managed it without so much as a sprained ankle.

He wasn't looking forward to going to the radio station and making a statement. He didn't know what he would say, really; the idea that a sniper had taken out old Ty Edwards who ran the hardware store seemed absurd. Nevertheless, that's exactly what Detective Madison had seemed to imply. Sangster had stood over the victim, peered at the bullet shots, and even in his limited experience of homicides he couldn't think that the grouping of the shots had been accidental.

The body—shit, the *new* body—was in the medical center and the whole dance with the medical examiner and the autopsy report was going to start all over again.

Sangster ran cold water in the sink and put his wrists under it. The neon lighting strip in the restroom of the police station flickered. He dried his hands with a paper towel. His face in the mirror looked sunken, which, as luck would have it, matched exactly how he was feeling, he thought. This was not why he had moved his family to Ludlow, this was not it at all.

The chief's message was broadcast in the middle of the Saturday afternoon *Golden Hits* hour and was caught by everyone within reach of a radio. It would be repeated at regular intervals throughout the day and cut into the television news reports.

"*A serious police incident has occurred in Ludlow's main square during the vigil for Dr. Robert Dennen. It seems that an unbalanced person with a high-powered rifle has taken shots into the crowd from a hill above the town. There was one fatality. At this time we ask for the residents of Ludlow to shelter in place. Stay in your home, lock your doors, and contact the police department if you see or hear anything unusual. We do not have a description of the shooter at this time. We suggest that you make sure everyone you know is safe in their home and aware of what has happened. Local, county, and state law enforcement agencies are working together to find the shooter and we appreciate your collaboration.*"

The words had felt empty on his lips, but the DJ had given him the thumbs-up after the first recording.

The line of cruisers had already left Sherman Falls by the time the chief's message had been broadcast, sandwiched between Frankie Goes to Hollywood's "The Power of Love" and Tears for Fears' "Everybody Wants to Rule the World."

None of the troopers in the state vehicles or the deputies in the sheriff's cruisers were saying it, but they all thought the same thing: there was one main thoroughfare out of Ludlow and into the world—Highway 395—however, if the shooter had decided to go hiking instead of conveniently coming to meet them, well, there was nothing but forest behind and around Ludlow all the way to Canada. And if a person wanted to enjoy quiet solitude and his own company, chances were he would not be found.

Madison stuck close to Sorensen: they had a crime scene that had not been charred to all hell, and they needed to work it before they lost the light. There were casings to pick up and trace evidence to look for on the ground where the shooter had lain. There was a small chance that the shells recovered near the victim's body might tell Ballistics something about the weapon used. IBIS, the Integrated Ballistic Identification System, might help them to connect the rifle—Madison had no doubt that that kind of precision shooting had come from a rifle and not a handgun—to a previous crime, but her instincts told her that they would draw a blank on IBIS. The best they could do was put it in the system and hopefully find it in the suspect's right hand when they went to question him—whoever he might be.

Madison picked up another casing and studied it as she slid it into a clear plastic evidence bag. It looked like a .300 WSM. It was the kind of cartridge everybody would be using for hunting deer or moose or any of the lovely creatures wandering through the woods. Madison was not a hunter—she understood hunting in terms of eating and survival, but not for pleasure. Her day job had somewhat inoculated her against killing anything for fun.

Madison's hearing was back to normal, but she felt jittery. Evidence recovery and collection was an art and a craft, and Madison felt too frazzled for the rigors of Sorensen's discipline.

"Don't anybody touch the dog," Sorensen had decreed, and nobody had—aside from bringing it food and water.

"This little mutt here is the only living creature who knows exactly who the shooter is, and he is going to tell us—one way or the other."

Sorensen brushed the poodle's coat and ran a hand vac over the curly brown fur. She detached the collar and the leash, and even looked under the dog's paws and between the pads. Throughout the examination the animal stood stiff and slightly cowed, and when it was over it lay on the ground, exhausted.

"You can take him back to Mrs. Edwards," Sorensen said to Deputy Hockley. "She'll want to have him back as soon as possible."

From their vantage point the rows of homes and storefronts were framed by the mountains behind them. The white trim of the roofs was sharp against the blue green of the forest and the umber of the naked earth. Smoke from the chimneys rose in thin coils. It was a model train's toy town, and Madison tracked the line of lights until they were swallowed up by the shadows. Above them birds of prey were gliding high, high above the town, watching and waiting.

"The state patrol put roadblocks on the highway within minutes of the call," Madison said, looking away from the sweeping birds and picking up a cigarette butt that could have been left two hours earlier by the shooter or six hours earlier by a dog walker.

"Do you think he hightailed it outta here as soon as he was done shooting?" Sorensen replied.

"Nope, I think he's in town—possibly in the Tavern—yakking it up with the other locals like he didn't just kill a man he'd known all his life."

Sorensen paused. "That's cold."

"You don't really think that one or two strangers decided to stop by and start killing locals?"

Madison's cell started vibrating and she reached for it inside her coveralls.

"Oh, shoot . . . oh, boy."

"What's wrong?"

"I have to take this . . . ," Madison said, and walked a little way from the crime scene. "I'm sorry," she said quickly into the cell when she was far enough away from Sorensen. "Honestly."

Chapter 22

Two days earlier, in Seattle, Alice Madison had returned home after the meeting with Lieutenant Fynn and her run on Alki Beach. She had peeled off her sweats, stuffed them into the laundry hamper, and taken a shower. The logs in the fire were hissing when Madison came back with her hair still damp and wearing a terry cloth robe. It was a peaceful, elemental sound and it soothed away the worst of her day.

Madison checked her cell and set the table for two. What she wanted was a quiet evening before the early flight, with the warmth of the fire on her skin, a glass of red wine, and the crackle of the logs to send her to sleep.

She heard the car pull into her driveway and the door slam, and she opened the door. Nathan Quinn—tall, dark, still in his immaculate suit with the maroon tie perfectly knotted—looked exactly as he had hours earlier.

"Counselor," Madison said.

"Detective," he replied. "I heard you'd had a tough day and I thought you might like company."

"Where did you hear it?" Madison said, and she leaned against the door frame. He was so much more than handsome—behind the finely drawn features lived the heart of the bravest man she had ever known, as hidden as it had been unexpected.

Quinn shrugged. "I have my ways."

"You sure do."

"I heard that some sonofabitch from the US Attorney's Office is sending you across the state on a stupid scheme that a bureaucrat thought up in his lunch hour."

"No one is sending me anywhere. I volunteered."

"But he *is* a sonofabitch."

"Only when needed."

He was close now and his black eyes held Madison's. She laid her hand on his cool cheek in a familiar gesture. He looked the same as hours earlier and yet completely different: he looked the way he looked when they were alone.

They had met on Madison's first case in Homicide, when Quinn had been the prime suspect's attorney. The case, and their acquaintance, had become more complex, and alliances had shifted and changed. Nathan Quinn had saved the life of her godson, and Alice Madison had found the man who had ordered the death of Quinn's younger brother when he was a child. They had been together and they had been apart, and together was much, much better.

At the time their loyalties had been incompatible, and Madison had taken a step back before they could be irrevocably questioned. Two months earlier, though, Quinn had arrived on her doorstep and she'd asked him to stay for dinner; he had stayed the night, and almost every night since. Occasionally they would spend a few evenings each in their own home, because it just wouldn't do to always be together—not when they were careful not to admit to each other and to themselves what was happening, what had already happened.

Nathan Quinn had grown up in the kitchen of the restaurant his father had owned and passed on to him, and he cooked with pleasure. The glow of the fire was quite enough as they picked at their steaks, sitting on the rug with their backs against the sofa and the plates on their laps. Quinn's jacket and tie had been swiftly removed and his shirt was unbuttoned. In the half-light Madison could not see the thin, silvery scars that twisted around his chest but she knew they were there—almost invisible after two years, and still the mark of his courage and his strength.

Madison took the plates into the kitchen and returned with two glasses of wine. She pulled his shirttails out and settled with her arms around him under the fabric and against his bare skin.

When he had called himself a sonofabitch it had hurt her in a way she could not begin to tell him. He knew his own reputation in the police department, he knew he had enemies because he had been a brilliant and ruthless defense attorney. Madison would have gladly punched the detective at today's meeting who didn't know, or didn't care about, this man's heart, about his honor and his spirit. The fact that she couldn't was the price she paid for their silence: no one knew about them, not even Madison's best friend, Rachel, whose son Quinn had saved; not even Brown, whom she trusted with her life every day. Their silence made her days sometimes harder to navigate, and yet it kept it— whatever *it* was—safe and private. His arms around her and the warmth of his skin in the quiet room were worth it.

"I have accidentally discovered the nickname my staff have bestowed on me," Quinn said.

"Do tell," Madison said.

Quinn sighed. "Loki."

"The Norse god?"

"He was a maleficent shape shifter who changed sides."

"I'm sure they mean it as a compliment."

"I work them to the bone. I suppose they've earned the right to call me what they want behind my back."

For a few minutes there was only the fire and the wind shaking the trees outside.

"Do you really think it's going to work? Sending strangers into a situation, into a place they know nothing about?" Madison said.

"The best chance we have of helping the town is sending them the best we have. And that's you, and Brown, and Sorensen."

"Thank you for the endorsement, but I'm not sure it's the way to go. The state should make sure the town has a larger police unit, better trained, better equipped."

"I agree, but that's not going to happen. The town funds the department and they just don't have the money to spend on it. It's happening everywhere."

Madison turned to look at him. "Everywhere?"

"It's a pilot scheme and we're the guinea pigs. If it works here they'll roll it out nationwide."

"What's your place in it?"

"I answer to the US attorney and to the governor."

"That's tricky."

Quinn held her closer. "No more than usual."

Madison smiled.

"What?" he said softly.

"I guess this is our version of pillow talk."

"*Pillow talk* is supposed to happen after, while *dirty talk* happens before."

"A subtle and possibly confusing distinction."

"I sense a challenge."

The log was little more than embers in the hearth by then, but she could feel his smile. "Try me," she said.

"As you wish," he replied.

Quinn woke up hours later on the sofa, disentangled himself from Madison's arms, and went into her bedroom. He returned with her comforter and lay back down next to her, making sure she was tucked in.

In the morning—so early it was still night—they had coffee together and then Madison left for Boeing Field to catch a small red plane that would take her across mountains and fields and water to the other end of the state. Quinn drove back to his home in Seward Park, changed his clothes, and went to work.

The day felt empty, and an unfamiliar heavy kind of hollowness dogged his steps.

Sometime on Saturday he would see on the news the footage from Colville County: a Seattle detective being shot at while protecting a woman on the ground, and the same detective returning fire. In spite of the distance and the poor quality of the images there was really no doubt in his mind.

Madison.

Chapter 23

"I'm sorry," Madison said into her cell when she was far enough away from Sorensen. "Honestly."

"Were you hit?" Quinn's voice was dark with worry.

"No, I'm fine."

"Have you been checked?"

"Yes," she replied a tad too quickly. "I have."

Quinn sighed. "No, you haven't. Just make sure that you're okay. Sometimes the adrenaline and the shock can mask an injury."

There was no point in arguing. "I'll make sure."

"Madison," his voice was low and tense. "I found out watching the news."

"I know, and I'm so sorry. In the middle of it I didn't realize you would . . . that the camera guy was there and . . ."

How would she have felt had she found out on the one o'clock news?

"What happened?" Quinn said after a moment.

She told him, and the horror of it and the woman's screams came back to her. What was her name? Lee. Lee Edwards.

"It was a hit," she said, and she knew it without question. "The sniper had made sure that they would come close, that they would be exposed. And he wanted to do it in front of the whole town."

"That's—"

"Insane?"

"I was going to say *organized*."

"That too."

"Two murders in three days?"

"Yes."

"What are the chances that they're unrelated?"

"Completely different MOs, but, yes, it would be a nasty kind of coincidence, and I really don't believe in those. The town is on lockdown."

A beat of silence.

"Are you wearing your vest?" Quinn said.

Madison rolled her eyes—it made her feel childish, but she couldn't help it. He meant her Seattle Police Department ballistic vest, and there was no point in lying. "No, I'm not."

"Would you mind stopping your crime scene work for a moment and putting the damn vest on?"

Madison's memory flashed back to two years earlier, to a black night in the woods and forcing Quinn to wear her own Kevlar vest for protection.

"I'll put it on," she conceded, and couldn't help adding, "The kind of distance we were, the way he grouped the hits—if he wanted to shoot me too, he'd have done it there and then."

"Well, give him a chance to get to know you."

"Thanks. By the way, we need those warrants."

"A trooper is on his way to deliver them as we speak."

"At last."

"Look, I just wanted to make sure you weren't hurt, and I wanted to apologize."

"Apologize?"

"I wasn't expecting Judy—the US attorney—to be in the office today, and when you called—"

"It's all right. It happens."

"We'll speak later. Yes?"

"Yes."

"Good."

"Good."

They said good-bye—a tiny light at the end of their day—and Madison returned to Sorensen. The crime scene investigator didn't ask what the call had been about, because she wasn't that kind of person, and Madison didn't volunteer the information.

Two minutes later, Brown called her: the warrants had arrived.

The door of Robert Dennen's office in the Medical Center was made of plain blond wood, and Madison had been staring at the patterns on the grain for twenty seconds, reflecting that she must have been crazy to think that five courses in criminalistics taken—how long ago was it?—qualified her for what she was about to do.

"We're here because there's no one else, and I—in spite of all my magical powers—can't be in two places at once," Sorensen had said, and that had been that.

Deputy Hockley had driven Madison and her toolbox to the clinic, and the rest was up to her. She wasn't going to do any of the actual analysis and identification, of course, but she was capable enough for collection and preservation—if she was careful and followed her training to the letter.

The drive had been quick—the streets were deserted—and Dr. Lynch was in his office waiting for the medical examiner. Thank God it was Saturday and the clinic would have been closed anyway.

"Don't think like a detective," Sorensen had told her in a less than helpful manner. "However hard it might be, try to rise above the badge and just *see*. Don't push a narrative onto the scene, just observe the scene. Let it talk to you."

"Detectives don't *push narratives*, Sorensen."

"Rise above the badge and let the scene talk to you."

Madison had muttered a reply. Given half a chance everyone turned into Yoda, it seemed.

"You okay, Hockley?" Madison had said, skipping over the "Deputy" part and deciding to address him as she would any SPD officer. Especially any young officer who had witnessed something that would stay with him for a very long time.

"Yes," the young man had replied, looking at the road ahead.

She'd wanted to say that it was normal to be shaken by what had happened, but he was gripping the wheel pretty tight. Maybe it wasn't the right moment.

"You did good in the square," she'd said simply.

Hockley had nodded, still looking ahead.

Madison now twisted the key in the lock, without touching the handle, and pushed in.

The room was just as they had left it earlier that day, which meant just as it had been left by the night visitor after the cleaner had done his work.

Begin at the beginning, Madison told herself, and examined the lock. There were no signs of forced entry, and the window looked similarly untouched: whoever had come in after the cleaner had done so with a key. Madison took pictures of both sides of the lock and moved on. She photographed the whole room, including the walls and the different points of entry and exit—one door and one window that opened onto a scrubby yard—wide-angle shots and close-ups.

After placing a "number 1" card next to the wastebasket, Madison took a picture with the tissue still in it. Only when she was satisfied that every inch of the office had been documented did she put the camera away.

Her nerves were still humming under her skin; nevertheless, the repetitive nature of the work had calmed her. She was doing what she had been taught to do, and there was something peculiarly satisfying about that—especially considering that she would never have been given the opportunity in Seattle, where

Sorensen's highly experienced army would have run the scene with military precision.

The tissue—white paper, three-ply—could possibly have come from the box on the windowsill behind the desk, a common brand bought almost certainly locally in bulk. It had been scrunched up, but only slightly, and when Madison lifted it from the basket with her tweezers, it seemed entirely clean. She placed it in a paper bag, and for the sake of chain of custody, she wrote the name, description, date, and location of the tissue on a tag and signed it with her own name, title, and badge number. The tissue box followed into another bag, with the same procedure, for comparison purposes. Both items were entered into a log sheet.

The office—as they had noticed earlier—did not look as if someone had ransacked it, and if the only trace of the night visitor's presence was a single tissue, it begged the question of why anyone had broken into the clinic in the first place. Sorensen had been clear about not creating a story where evidence hadn't given her one; however, as Madison knelt by the door to fingerprint the lock and the area around it, it was impossible not to wonder.

Evidence as truth. Maybe the burglar had removed something that was not immediately obvious to Dr. Lynch. Madison surveyed the wood and decided to use black latent print powder with a regular fiber brush.

It didn't take her long to pick up a few prints on the lock—smudged ones—and a number of tiny prints a couple of feet up from the floor where young patients had pushed against the door. She worked both sides, though nothing seemed unusual about the location or the type of the latents.

Madison dusted the shelves and the desk for prints—and proved only the excellent standard of work of the clinic's cleaner.

Next, she walked the rectangular room in an outward spiral from where the wastebasket had been found, looking for anything that might be of significance. *Let the scene talk to you.*

Madison was torn between the street cop's natural reaction to BS and the belief that scenes do in fact talk—if you know how to listen.

Step after step, she walked the spiral. And yet there was nothing on the floor, on the shelves, or on the furniture that caught her eye. The examining bed with its paper cover looked freshly prepared, and a closer look with a magnifying lens gave up no secrets.

Madison turned her attention to the desk: the warrants had been particular about searching the doctor's place of work. Areas that were generally accessible were allowed, but anything relevant to doctor-patient confidentiality was excluded. *No surprises there*, Madison thought.

She sat at the doctor's desk. The chair was comfortable and she sat back, gazing at the surface before her with her gloved hands on the armrests. What was the scene telling her? There was the door—not forced. The shelves and the bed—seemingly untouched. The desk—as tidy as Dennen had left it. Madison closed her eyes; the view of the room was imprinted like a negative. Someone had come into the room in the middle of the night and they had known how to acquire the object of their interest without making a mess. They had known what, where, and how.

Had they taken prescription pads? Madison instinctively reached for the desk drawer and pulled it open. It should have been locked, as doctors' drawers often are, and yet it was not. And just inside it there was a small pile of brand-new prescription pads. Next to them lay a folded piece of cloth, too grubby to be a handkerchief, and Madison's hand reached for it and was about to pick it up when she froze: she had not photographed the interior of the drawer.

Swearing under her breath, she took a few quick pictures and, with her tweezers, lifted the cloth and placed it on the desk. There was something about the fabric, something rough and unwashed, that had no place in the spotless, well-organized doctor's office.

Madison picked up one corner and gently unfolded the frayed square of white cotton. Inside, written with charcoal in uneven capital letters, were only two words:

HELP US

It was a young child's handwriting. A memory flickered, and Madison went cold. Who was *us*? Who had reached out to the doctor? What would it take for someone to grab the first thing they could lay their hands on and scribble out that kind of plea? Madison knew exactly what it would take.

She was turning in the swivel chair to get up when her eyes caught the dark blur on the glass, which had been invisible up to that point. She looked at the blur; she looked at the desk and at what was on the desk. She thought of Dr. Robert Dennen, found somewhere far from where he should have been, and she thought of his neat office, where the burglar had not disturbed a single Post-it and had not been interested in the precious prescription pads. The map in the senior center had been detailed, but Madison remembered the lines of intersecting roads and the colored pins stuck in them. She reached for her cell.

"What if Robert Dennen himself was the burglar?" she asked Brown when he picked up.

"What do you mean?"

"What if someone intercepted Dennen on his way back home from the Jacobsens? What if this person forced Dennen to come here, to his office, in the middle of the night, because it was the only way to get access to his computer and the files in it?"

"The patients' files?"

"Yes. That's why the door wasn't forced and nothing was touched in the room. They came in with Dennen's key. The only thing the killer was interested in was in the hard drive. And there's blood on the window just behind the chair, the kind of blood spatter pattern you would see if someone was sitting at the desk and someone else hit him with enough force."

"And you think the only thing of any value on the desk is the computer."

"Sarge, I think I've found what pushed the doctor to call Child Protection Services. There's a note . . . someone was pretty serious about asking the doctor for help. Someone who could barely write. Looks like a young kid."

Brown was quiet for a moment. "The killer didn't take the note?"

"No." Madison's eyes searched the fabric for any clue of its provenance. "He didn't, maybe he didn't even know about it. I found it tucked away next to the prescription pads, but in plain sight if anyone opened the drawer. Dennen wasn't trying to hide it, and the killer wasn't trying to find it."

"We need to get the note and the blood DNA tested ASAP."

"I know, I'm about to take samples."

"You're doubling everything?"

"As per my instructions."

"Madison . . ."

"Yes?"

"You need a drink tonight, I'm buying."

Madison smiled. "I'm okay. I need to be sober in case the son-ofabitch tries to go three-for-three with me."

"You think it's the same guy?"

"Do you? I don't know what to think. Where are you now?"

"Still talking to Lee Edwards."

"How is she holding up?"

"As you would expect. Never thought anything like this could happen in Ludlow."

"Sounds familiar." Madison felt black humor seep into her voice—the only shield cops ever have against tragedy.

"Sure does."

The blood had dried on the glass and Madison's immediate task was to get it to Sorensen. Taking the photograph of the blood spatter in situ was difficult because of the dark background; once she had a few clear views and perspectives relating to the chair,

Madison used a stainless-steel spatula to scrape the stain into a square of folded paper, and then placed it into an envelope. She did it twice to make sure of a clean sample for the Seattle lab.

Her eyes kept glancing at the cryptic appeal. *Help us.* An appeal, maybe even a warning of danger. Madison focused on the task at hand, but her heart beat faster.

When she turned around, Eric Lynch was standing by the door. "The medical examiner has just taken the body," he said.

"Good." Madison sealed the second envelope. "Dr. Lynch, do you have the password for this computer?"

"We already talked about—"

"We have the warrants."

"I know, but—"

"There's a possibility the killer was in this room and forced Dr. Dennen to access patients' files. Do you have the password for this computer?"

Lynch blinked and looked around the room as if the revelation would lead to the killer materializing in front of them, right there and then.

"The password," Madison repeated, not unkindly.

"I do . . . it's just that there's nothing personal on the computers. We all work out of the same server and our appointment calendars are shared."

"I need to see what's there, and I need to know what files the killer looked at."

"You can't."

"I don't need to read the files." Madison already knew that Dr. Lynch had an alibi—and in any case, he wouldn't have needed Dennen to get inside the server. "You'll be my eyes. You can look at the files for me and tell me what you see. Okay? Okay. Now please, Doctor."

Dr. Lynch stumbled slightly as he came in, and his cheeks were flushed. He sat down at the desk as if he were being strapped to a bomb. Madison gave him a pair of gloves. He turned on the computer.

"I need you to check which files or documents were the last to be accessed."

Lynch looked at the screen for a full minute, his eyes zigzagging on the clinic's home page.

"Yes," he said.

"How many patients are registered with the clinic?"

"Eight hundred and thirty-two," he replied automatically.

"Eight hun—But you only have six hundred-odd residents. How . . . ?"

"The clinic covers a larger area than just the town." Dr. Lynch worked the keyboard, moving the cursor, and opening and closing windows in rapid succession.

Madison wanted to speak, but she bit her tongue; she wanted Lynch to concentrate on what he was doing, because there was no one else who could look at the entire contents of that computer without getting whipped by the Bill of Rights.

Lynch's mouth opened and closed and opened again. He turned to Madison with a mortified look. "I can't do it."

"What do you mean *you can't do it*?" The words were out of her mouth before she could stop them. It was a dumb question. "I meant," she said "*why* can you not do it?"

"This system is quite old, it's not built for that kind of thing. It's not—how can I put it?—it's not one of the search criteria. I need a name first."

"We don't have a name."

"We can look for patients' ages, addresses, their last appointment. We can look for who has been classified at risk from flu or which new babies need vaccinations. But I can't ask the system to look for the last files Robert accessed and . . . see . . . the last document he opened was a letter to a pharmaceutical rep last Monday, nothing on Wednesday night. Nothing." He looked back at the screen and again at Madison. "Nothing."

"Can you check if Jeb Tanner is registered?"

Lynch tapped on the keyboard, waited, tapped again. "No, he's not."

No surprise there. If Tanner didn't like mixing with the towns-folk, he was hardly going to get himself—or his family—registered. Dennen must have gone out there on his own initiative.

"What we need is in there, sir, and we'll get it out one way or the other—even if it will take a crowbar to do it," Madison said, and after a moment she added, "Dr. Lynch, when was the last time Ty Edwards's file was accessed?"

Chapter 24

Lee and Ty Edwards's home bore the marks of the family life of a couple who had been together for a long time. Brown busied himself looking at the photographs on the mantel and let Chief Sangster take the woman's statement. They already had Madison's statement on record and there was, of course, the issue of a police officer discharging her weapon—which, in Seattle, would mean a review of the situation leading to said discharge, and for the officer to be on administrative leave. In Ludlow, it meant that a cop had been shot at by a sniper and now she just needed to get on with her job, thank you very much.

Brown was ready to jump in, if necessary; however, for the moment he preferred listening to Sangster, who, in spite of his lack of experience interviewing victims' family members, seemed to be doing well enough. It came from knowing the person, Brown considered, and treating them like an individual and not like a form to be filled in.

Lee Edwards sat on her sofa with her poodle curled up next to her. The dog's head was in her lap and her hand rested against it, as if to make sure it was there.

A friend had come to stay with the widow and had made coffee for the police officers and lemon tea for Mrs. Edwards before retiring to the kitchen to give them privacy.

Brown had stood over the body of Lee Edwards's husband and had drawn the same conclusions as Madison: the man had been targeted. And whether the reason was personal, entirely random, or because the sniper had believed Ty Edwards was the reincarnation of a demon who was about to destroy humanity and civilization as they knew it—and Kevin Brown had had a few of those, courtesy of the cuts in mental health provision—the key was how the target had been chosen.

You understand the victim, you understand the killer.

Chief Sangster shifted on the chair and it creaked under his weight. "Lee," he said, "tell me a little about Ty's work at the store. It seems weird, I know, but I'm trying to get a picture of how things stand, to make sense of something that doesn't seem to make sense."

The woman wiped her eyes and nodded. "The store is doing all right," she said, and to Brown she added, "We own the hardware store on Main Street."

Brown met her shiny, red-rimmed eyes.

"We're never going to be millionaires," she continued. "But that was never the point. A town needs a hardware store, and we kept on with it. It wasn't going too badly, you know. We even had the March specials out already, made a promo for the radio only last week, and it went out county-wide on Monday."

Brown thought of the radio commercial from the tiny town like a pebble thrown into a huge black lake.

"I know I've never had a problem with anything Ty sold me," Sangster said. "I know you sell quality, not dime-store, but did Ty have words with anybody? An unhappy customer perhaps? Someone who wanted to make trouble?"

What a world it would be if the right to bear arms meant the opportunity to address customer service matters with such finality, Brown thought—and immediately realized that, yes, that was exactly the world he seemed to be living in from time to time.

Lee Edwards had not replied. She was frowning and thinking in a manner that seemed almost painful, as if the question had produced an answer too distressing to conceive.

"Jeb Tanner," she said after a moment. "Two weeks ago, Jeb Tanner came to the shop to exchange something—what was it?—and Ty told him he couldn't, because he had broken the thing after he'd bought it and there had been nothing wrong with it in the store. And Tanner was very nice about it and he kind of smiled and told Ty he'd cancel his account with us if Ty didn't."

"What did Ty say?"

"Ty didn't want to cancel the account. Tanner is a farmer—we know how hard life is for farmers around here. Tanner's not like most people: he can be real charming one minute and he can be . . ." Lee couldn't find a word that would work in polite company. "Well, the way it ended he told my husband that he should have known better than that. He was courteous, you know, and very civil. But he canceled the account and left. There was something about him . . . I don't care how well mannered he is."

"He paid what he owed?"

"No, and we didn't expect him to. We thought he'd come back in a few weeks, pretend it had never happened, pay a little toward the account, and buy something else. He runs his farm like it's the 1920s, you know. It's his family we felt sorry for. You don't think he could have . . . ?"

Jeb Tanner. Brown turned the name around in his mind. A farmer certainly has the opportunity, sometimes even the reason, to become a very good shot. And Ty Edwards's killer had been a very good shot indeed.

The woman stroked the dog's head. "I can't even remember what it was that he wanted to exchange. I told you last night, didn't I, Chief? This town is not what it used to be."

They sat in the cruiser with the heating on full blast, still parked in front of the Edwards residence. The chief's hands rested on the steering wheel and his thoughts were elsewhere. Brown was jotting down some notes in his pad: he preferred doing it right after the interview, when the memories were fresh, without interrupting the flow of words at the time. They had a name, they had a potential suspect. He looked up after a couple of minutes and Sangster was staring into the middle distance; his eyes were on something only he could see, and his face was set hard.

"Jeb Tanner . . . ," Brown began to say, and he stopped when the chief turned toward him.

"There's something I need to tell you. I didn't mention it before. I didn't want to . . ."

Brown sat back and shut up. He was good at that, good at letting people talk when they needed to, and he certainly had no idea where the conversation was heading, only that the chief looked stricken.

"The day before Robert Dennen was killed he called me on my cell, he left a message on the voice mail. He said there was something important he needed to talk to me about. I never got back to him, because it was a busy day and I thought I'd catch him in the clinic on Thursday. Robert had never called my personal cell phone before. Never. I didn't call him back, and he was dead by the morning."

Will Sangster looked Brown in the eye and waited for the cutting remark, for the jibe and the criticism that never came. His face was flushed in shame and regret and he was rigid on the seat, expecting a verbal blow of some kind, of any kind.

"You couldn't have known," Brown said. "You could not possibly have known what was going to happen or the nature of what the doctor wanted to talk to you about. You still don't. We still don't. It means only that there was something on Robert Dennen's mind, and he was serious enough about it to call you on your cell."

Sangster blinked and the big man sort of wilted against his seat.

"You couldn't have known," Brown repeated.

"What if it was something that could have saved his life?"

"You can't work on what-ifs," Brown replied. "How many calls a day do you get about something-or-other that someone wants to talk to you about?"

"It's not the same."

"How many? Not just calls for assistance but anything from the state, the county, the sheriff's department, locals, and anybody who's passing by and needs something from the police department."

Sangster sighed. "A few dozen calls."

"Exactly. You couldn't have known." Brown gave him a second to absorb what he'd said, because he liked the chief and wanted—needed—to be able to work with him at his best. If he needed support about this, he'd give it to him. In his heart, though, born out of the experience of years on the force and mistakes that had cost the lives of innocent people, Brown knew that sometimes *what-ifs* are all that fate has left us. In the myriad of possibilities, of alternative worlds, there might be a world where the chief had acted on Dennen's call and the doctor was still alive, perhaps even Ty Edwards was still alive, but the moment where the right path could be taken had passed. And Brown ached for the man who would have to live with it.

"Tell me about Tanner," he said.

Earlier in the day, as soon as Brown had confirmed that the patch of wood that had hidden the sniper was deserted, the ponderous machine of law enforcement on the county and state level had swung into action and roadblocks had been established on Highway 395. They didn't know what the shooter looked like, or whether he would be inclined to leave the town at all; however—in moments where not much else could be done—a roadblock was always a good idea. At least, that was how the troopers waiting on the side of the road looked at it.

They were cold, they had run out of coffee, and their shift was about to end. All they had to show for it were five stops, all very early in the day—all local residents who lived out of town and had not gone to the vigil because they had other engagements. All were driving to Sherman Falls without a clue that anything had happened.

The troopers had been in position fifteen minutes after receiving the call from dispatch—in plenty of time to meet anyone who was coming from the other direction—and yet, after those early stops, too early for the driver to have shot the victim and then driven onto the Interstate, no one had been through. The residents of Ludlow had gone back to their homes, or wherever they had decided to hunker down, and no one had driven past the troopers.

"How long should we stay out here for?" one trooper asked the other as he slapped his gloved hands against his thighs.

"Should have worn your tights."

"It's not my legs I'm worried about."

"Like that would be such a loss for humanity," his colleague replied. "Let me check with dispatch."

They were parked in an open stretch of road that seemed to reach the end of the horizon on both sides. Behind them the glow from Sherman Falls was too distant to be visible, and ahead of them the blank road seemed to lose itself in the mountains. The beams from the cruiser were the only lights for miles, and they fought a losing battle against the approaching nightfall.

Chapter 25

The darkness could be hard to deal with, especially in winter, when it appeared to come suddenly and so completely that it felt like a hood had been pushed down over your face. Still, the darkness was little compared with the cold. The long summer evenings, with their soft light filtering through the gaps in the planks, were a relief when they came after the torture of the sunny days, which transformed the tin-roof shed into a small hell for anyone who deserved it—and many did, it seemed, on a regular basis.

The cold in winter, though—the numbing cold that drained all the life out of one's body—that was the worst of all, and it was reserved for those particular days when the offense had been of outstanding malice and thus needed the cold to purge it out of the sinner. Samuel sat in the lonely place—he could only sit or stand because the hut was too small for any other kind of physical exertion. He couldn't remember how it came to be named *the lonely place*. It was what everybody had always called it—even his younger brothers and sisters—and for a reason he couldn't explain, it made him achingly sad when they did.

The punishment had come, as he knew it would, and he had been inside the hut for hours. Incapable of stirring to keep himself warm, except for the most basic of movements, the boy opened and closed his hands and shifted his feet against the dirt floor.

He had not eaten all day, he had not drunk since noon, and he had on his back only what he had been wearing when his father had woken him up and sent him out into the forest for the hunter-and-prey practice.

The offense had been serious because not only had Samuel been caught by his brother Luke, but he had also lied about the circumstances of his capture. He had been hunted and captured and had tried to escape the consequences of his mistakes. *No one*, his father had said, *escapes the consequences of their mistakes.* And he was there to teach them that some mistakes were more serious than others, and lying was the worst.

Samuel had understood too late that his fate had been sealed the moment his father had seen him in Luke's grip, that nothing he could say would have changed the man's mind. He wondered what lesson his father was trying to teach him. What was the good in being stuck in the lonely place for a lie he had not told? Samuel wiped his nose on his sleeve.

Cold and hungry and weak as the boy felt, Samuel thought of Cal, and the mere notion of his brother being free somewhere out there in the world was a warm spot in his chest, under all the layers of chill. Cal had explained to him that the best way to get through the lonely place was to make sure his body didn't become too rigid in the winter and too parched in the summer.

He always had to be prepared for a stint in the hut and must keep himself strong in order to withstand it. "There will be hours when there's nothing but the cold trying to hurt you. So you forget about the lonely place and think about walking in the forest, think about going for a walk in the woods with me. What we would see, where we would go. Can you do that?"

Samuel had been twelve at the time—the age when grown-up punishments had begun—and he had nodded. His first stay in the hut had been a nightmare: ten hours one April. He had come out at the end with shaky legs and hollow eyes.

Though Samuel's body was bound to the inside of the hut, his mind was not, and it kept traveling back to Luke's words and the leer in his voice. What had he meant? Cal had run away one night after their father had put him in the hut for a particularly long spell. It had been months earlier: last spring, just before the thaw. When his father had gone to release him at dawn, he found that Cal had disappeared. And from that day on, the boy's name could not be uttered in his presence. Something uncoiled in the back of Samuel's gut, a nameless dread that he could not and would not face. He stood up suddenly, feeling a bite of damp, freezing air deep inside each breath and reaching into the middle of his chest.

There was a rustle close by and Samuel stood still. Hardly any light filtered through the heavy drapes in the main cabin across the clearing and Samuel's eyes blinked in the gloom. Had his father come to let him out? No one else was allowed to come close or even talk to someone when they were in the lonely place.

A soft step creaked behind him and the boy whipped around. Something scraped at the wood, at the planks that had been hastily nailed together. It could have been an animal, it could have been anything. Samuel backed away from the wall as far as he could, flattening himself against the door.

"Samuel . . ."

It was barely a whisper and he leaned into it, praying it would come again.

"Samuel . . ."

The boy reached forward. His hands were on the rough, plain surface, on the gaps between the planks. He felt it immediately, and his numb fingers caught hold of it. Bread. A slice of bread first and then a hunk of cheese. The smell of both flooding the darkness of his senses.

Samuel held both in one hand and waited with his head leaning against the wall, afraid to make the smallest sound in case anyone in the cabin heard him.

Nothing more came for him through the gap, and after a few minutes the boy sat back down and devoured the food. He honestly tried to eat slowly and make it last, but it was entirely beyond him. He was famished, and the fresh bread and tangy cheese tasted wonderful.

Who could have done such a thing? He himself had never dared. As far back as he could remember no one had ever dared to bring food to someone in the lonely place. The food made him giddy. That's why it was called the lonely place, silly, because no one could talk or give food or water to anybody in it. Could it have been one of his younger sisters? Would any of them have been so brave, so reckless? What would it take to go against his father's will? Only a strong heart would dare, only someone who was not afraid. Samuel shivered in the shed as the icy breeze found all the openings and the slits in the walls around him.

He was not entirely alone, he thought, someone out there was on his side. It was the first spark of hope in months, and it made him feel all lit up inside: he could get through the night, he could survive being hunted and Luke's clasp around his neck, because he was not alone. In a way, he had always known that Cal would not leave him—not entirely—and he would be watching over him, somehow.

Samuel stood, stamped his feet, and ran his hands over his wiry arms. His head felt warm now, like his chest. When his father came to let him out—hours and hours later—Samuel wobbled his way back into the cabin and curled up in front of the wood stove without a word. None of his siblings looked at him and he didn't even try to meet their eyes.

The boy bolted down the half bowl of stew he was given, but it didn't taste as good as the bread and cheese had. What a strange day it had been: so dreadful and yet so good. There was the wolf pack out on the mountain and the wolf pack on the wall of his cave—and he had managed to protect both.

The mouse had saved the wolf.

Chapter 26

Joyce Cartwell had decided that the Magpie Diner should stay open. The doors would be locked, but she would be inside should anyone decide that the comfort of company was preferable to being at home, possibly alone, waiting for news of what to do next. She had made a fresh pot of coffee, hung her apron in the back-room closet, and now sat behind the counter reading the next book in her book club—something funny and snappy set in New York that she just couldn't get into—while the local news burbled quietly in the background.

People had come: a single man first, then a couple, then a woman who lived alone nearby. Within ten minutes of the "shelter in place" instruction—or was it an order? Joyce wondered, almost as if they were at war—about ten people occupied the booths of the diner. There had been a lot of talk at the beginning, but since no one could contribute more than conjectures and guesses, the chat had died down and mostly they were just waiting to see what would happen next. Even George Goyer, the pilot who had flown in the Seattle detectives only the previous day, had had very little to add to the conversation and had sat in silence, working on a slice of key lime pie.

When the state police cruisers and the county sheriff's cars drove onto Main Street, most of Joyce's customers stood up to watch them pass. Before long the streets were awash with blue uniforms and khaki uniforms, the hurrying shapes blurred behind the frosted glass. And for the first time that day, watching the scurrying and rushing, Joyce was afraid.

Darryl, the bartender at the Tavern, had locked the doors and turned off the outside lights as soon as he had made it back from the vigil. He had told the other staff to go back to their homes and had retired to his flat above the restaurant. It had a good view of Main Street, and if he stood on tiptoes he could see the bright lights of the investigators still at work on the hill behind the square. He went online and posted a short piece on his blog, titled "Inside the Ludlow shooting." It received fifty likes in three minutes, which pleased him more than he'd care to admit.

Darryl popped open a bottle of his lightest ale—he needed his wits about him—and dragged a chair close to the window. Some of the troopers and the deputies wore body armor, and even Darryl—who was a country kid and had grown up around firearms—was impressed by the display of gunmetal.

After a brief conversation with Chief Sangster, Fred Cherevka, the sheriff of Colville County, directed his men to work through the town in a grid sweep, and he posted lookouts on the back roads that led out into the wilderness. They had no description of their quarry and no idea as yet about what kind of rifle had been used.

Sheriff Cherevka had not asked to speak with any of the Seattle detectives: he had a manhunt on his hands and no time to waste.

Chapter 27

"Ty Edwards's medical file was accessed at 3:37 a.m. on Dennen's computer the morning he was killed," Alice Madison said.

"That's our link." Brown gave Madison a tiny nod. It was a "Brown gold star," and Madison pinned it on her imaginary board.

Sorensen looked up from the evidence bags that Madison had brought back from the clinic. She had twigs in her hair, and in spite of a good shake at the door, her boots had trailed dirt all over the senior center floor.

"Log sheets?" Sorensen asked.

Madison passed her the pages where she had noted each item she'd recovered. She also placed a cup of coffee on Sorensen's table, because the woman had just come back after hours on the hill and she looked like she could do with warming up.

"Well, are we all agreed that—if the blood on the window matches the doctor's—the killer met Dennen on the road home from the Jacobsens, took him to the clinic, and forced him to open that particular file?" Madison said.

"So far, so agreed," Brown replied.

"*If* the blood matches . . . ," Sorensen added.

"It will. It's the only way that makes sense of how the killer got in—with Dennen's key—and why nothing else in the room was touched, because all he was interested in was in the clinic's server."

"Why Ty Edwards's file?" Brown said.

"I have absolutely no idea," Madison replied.

"Did he go into any other file?"

"I don't know. He could have. It's impossible to work it out without checking every single registered patient. I'd like Dr. Lynch to start on that first thing tomorrow morning. Unless . . . well, unless we can get one of *our* people to do it remotely from Seattle."

"I'm reasonably sure you're not actually talking about *hacking* into the system."

"No, more like getting in through the back door. It wouldn't be hacking if Lynch knew about it. It would be a shortcut. Getting to what we need a little faster, that's all."

"And you think he would agree to that?"

Madison rolled her tense shoulders and puffed out air from her cheeks. "Never in a million years. I'm just venting out of frustration."

Brown smiled.

"Where's the tissue?" Sorensen said.

For a moment Madison hesitated about handing her the paper bag: if she had screwed up the collection, the case would be compromised.

"Give it here," Sorensen said, took it out of Madison's hands, and undid the seal. "Why was a tissue left in the wastebasket?" she asked no one in particular as she lifted the square of paper with tweezers and unfolded it gently on a clean work surface. "I've been asking myself the question since you told me about it." She shifted her lamp. "We now know that Dennen was very probably taken there by coercion," she continued. "I'm willing to bet that the doctor realized the kidnapper wasn't going to let him go, and he wanted to leave something behind to tell anybody who might come looking that he had been there. Clever Dr. Dennen."

"He might not have realized about the blood on the window," Brown offered.

"The blood might have happened after he left the tissue, anyway," Madison said.

Sorensen examined it with her magnifying glass. "Here . . . ," she said. "It's not much, but it's the thought that counts."

Madison leaned forward; she hadn't noticed anything when she picked it up.

"A very small amount of spit, probably from a nice bit of fake coughing, enough to give us the beginning of a DNA match." Sorensen smiled, and there was little mirth in it, only the sneer of the cat who's got the canary. "It will put Dennen in the clinic *after* the cleaner, which the blood couldn't do. What about the note?"

"When you say *note*," Madison said, "you imagine pen and paper. This," Madison held up the bag that contained the scrap of cloth, "is a piece torn off somebody's shirt."

They gathered around the table. Under Sorensen's blazing lamp the fabric and its scrawled message looked pitiful. The fabric had been cut off roughly on two sides, and the other two were crudely stitched like the shirt tail of a fledgling tailor. It spoke of despair and determination, and the voice in the uncertain handwriting felt awfully, appallingly young.

Vague panic and a sense of being trapped flashed across Madison's consciousness as she studied the fabric. For a moment they all just took it in.

"A kid," Brown said.

"Looks like it," Madison replied.

"Let's keep a straight head and go over what we have, not what we *think* we have," Brown said, and he turned to Sorensen.

Madison's eyes stayed on the words scribbled in charcoal. *Help us.* What had Dennen discovered? And who wanted to shut him up?

Night had fallen—frosty and clear—and, for once, only a few windows were lit on Ludlow's Main Street. One after the other, the customers had left the diner and Joyce Cartwell had reluctantly driven back to her house, a few minutes away, and locked herself in with her drapes closed and her cell within reach.

Darryl had watched the work of the patrols on the streets from his window above the Tavern until daylight had faded away and only their footsteps crunched in the gloom.

The senior center and the police headquarters, across from each other at the end of Main Street, were the only signs of life in the empty street. The parking lot was crowded with law enforcement trucks, deputies, and state police officers in full SWAT gear, waiting for instructions.

"We can't go talk to him now, I think we can all agree on that," Sheriff Cherevka said. He was leaning against the wall of Sangster's office and his arms were crossed—an impressive task considering the breadth of his chest and the ballistic vest he was wearing.

The overheated room was thick with bodies and purpose. Brown and Madison stood to one side, watching the interplay of personalities and jurisdictions. In the outer room the telephone rang every few minutes; Polly, the chief's assistant, would answer, give the agreed reply to the inquiries, and then replace the receiver. After a minute it would ring again.

"His farm is at the end of a dirt track—ten minutes' worth of dirt track after the road runs out, actually," Chief Sangster said. "So, no, we can't go talk to him now. Not in the dark. There's little kids up there and it could get messy 'cause he's not exactly a people person. We'll go at first light, and even then I recommend a small group. He's just one man alone and I don't want him to get cranky before we've even had a chance to interview him. In the past, we haven't had the best of relationships."

"The way I understand it, there's no physical evidence to tie him to either of the crime scenes," said the captain from the state patrol.

"We're working on that," Brown replied.

"Well," the sheriff continued, "we've been through the streets and back at the hill, and everyone's locked in nice and tight. I'm going to leave a couple of patrols to keep an eye on things overnight and all you good people will be back here tomorrow at 8 a.m. to go talk to Mr. Tanner and see what he's got to say for himself." He turned to Brown and Madison with a half smile. "I bet you're real happy you put your hand up for this little experiment."

Brown pushed his glasses up on his nose and returned the smile. "We have only the beginning of a trail of evidence: it barely makes him a suspect. Tomorrow morning we're going to have to tread lightly." It was one of Brown's great gifts that he could make a warning sound like the kindest piece of advice.

"I hear you, but he's all we've got," the sheriff replied, "and I don't see anybody else in town causing upsets."

Madison wanted to say that in Seattle *causing upsets* was practically a job description for a whole group of alienated citizens who never went on to kill but who slowly, carefully self-destructed using drugs and alcohol. She didn't say it, though, feeling that any sentence that started with "in Seattle" or "in our experience" wouldn't go down too well in the room.

"You're sure you know what you're doing?" the sheriff asked Brown.

"Yes, I do," he replied.

"Hope so." He smiled. "Hope so."

The party broke up, and Brown and Madison walked back across the street, where Sorensen was at work in the back room, harnessing the might of her portable lab to find the story hidden in a few dozen specimens.

They didn't interrupt her but left a candy bar for her on the edge of her table—the owner of Ludlow Sweets down the road had delivered a bowlful to the police station after they'd closed, as a thank-you for their day's work.

It had been a mutual, if unspoken, decision between them: Brown and Madison would remain at the senior center as long as Sorensen was running her tests, and they would all leave together at the end of the day—however late that might turn out to be. It was a chance to go over notes, file reports online, or simply sit quietly and consider the extent of the mess they had walked into—while, in the next room, Sorensen's devices ticked and hummed.

Madison sent a text to her best friend, Rachel, in Seattle—who might have seen the news—to reassure her that she was okay and would call when she had a chance. Rachel was not just a friend, she was a sister in all but blood, and Madison found solace in thinking of her at home with her family, far away from a crazy man who had taken shots at a mourning crowd. The thought of Rachel and her family always had a steadying effect on Madison, and she needed it now when she found her thoughts returning to Ty Edwards. *It's okay, sweetheart.*

"You saved a person's life today," Brown said, as if he'd sensed the hue of Madison's silence.

"Doesn't really feel like it."

"What does it feel like?"

"Like I failed to help a man who was standing right next to me."

"Would it have helped if you had been shot?"

"What do you mean?"

"Would it have helped if, while you were protecting Mrs. Edwards and making sure everybody else got away safely, you were also shot? Something minor that wouldn't cause too much trouble but wouldn't make you feel like you cheated your way out of all the bullets that a maniac shot at you?"

Madison smiled. "Perhaps, a little. Then again, I don't think I was ever in any real danger—and neither was anyone else."

Brown nodded. He had used the word *maniac* but they both understood that whatever madness had sparked off the murders, there was a degree of cunning that was far from frantic or hysterical.

"He didn't hurt the dog," Madison said.

"No, he didn't. But I wouldn't let that guide our thinking in how best to find him and trap him."

Madison didn't know what kind of thinking was needed to find and trap the killer. She felt pulled in different directions, and she longed for solid, unequivocal evidence to show her the way. It was a tapestry of events that shouldn't belong together, and yet they did. *Help us.* The words flashed before her, and she only just heard Brown beginning to brief Lieutenant Fynn in Seattle about the morning plan.

Lee Edwards was born and raised a Catholic and, even though she had not been inside a Catholic church for longer than she could remember, there was a kind of genetic memory that seemed to swing into action when needed, a religious fight-or-flight gene that was lurking in her Irish background, waiting for a suitable moment to reemerge.

That night, while her girlfriend was making dinner, Lee excused herself and sat on her bed—it had been *their* bed only that morning. She would have knelt, but her knees would not allow it, and she contented herself with bowing her head and joining her hands the way she did when she was a little girl. What was she supposed to ask for now?

The words of the prayer came to her unbidden, and when she reached "forgive us our trespasses," her breath caught. She prayed for Ty's soul with words she had not used in years, and though she had known—even as a child—that some wishes would not be granted, she continued to pray until her friend knocked on the door.

Every other thought seemed to have been washed clear out of her mind. All that was left was prayer and shock and grief so profound that it felt like she would crack in two.

Angel of God, my Guardian dear . . . The words reached far back into her past, but she found no comfort there either.

Chapter 28

"It's not Dennen's blood." Sorensen emerged from her back-room lab and snapped off her latex gloves.

"The blood from the car crime scene?" Madison said.

"Yup, it's not Dennen's."

"So we have the killer's DNA," Brown said, and he was at the business end of a hard look from Sorensen.

"What we have is blood collected at the car crime scene. We don't know it was the killer's," she said.

"What are the chances that someone else was out and about?" Madison said.

"What are the chances that if I eat a blue M&M I'll turn into a Smurf?" Sorensen replied.

"Roughly the same that Jeb Tanner will say *yes* to a DNA test without a warrant," Brown said.

Alice Madison stepped out onto Main Street with Brown and Sorensen a little after midnight and lifted the collar of her coat against the chill. Her breath was puffs of white and her ungloved right hand rested on the butt of her sidearm. The evidence that should have been locked away in the police safe had been delivered to Chief Sangster, and Sorensen had just called it a day.

The road that stretched ahead of them was a line of shadows, of blacks and grays of various depths fading into the distance, and yet above them the sky was wide and full of stars, brighter than she had ever seen them, so bright and so many. It was miraculous in a place that had known such horror only twelve hours earlier. A memory tugged at Madison's sleeve, but she couldn't quite grasp it.

Their steps were soft on the icy pavement as they headed back toward the Miller house. None of them felt like talking. A couple of state police officers posted at one end of the road followed their journey and radioed their colleagues at the other end, by the Magpie Diner, that the detectives were on their way. Madison thought of Hockley and Kupitz, the young local deputies who had done so well on such a difficult day, and she hoped that they were in their beds—hopefully asleep, though in all probability awake.

"Scrambled eggs on toast?" Madison said as they walked in and Brown locked the front door behind them.

"Is this dinner or breakfast?" Sorensen replied.

"Does it matter?"

They ate quickly. And while, in any other company, it would have seemed rude to bolt down their food without chitchat, they all understood that after midnight, exhaustion wins over manners every time. Then each withdrew to their rooms, leaving the plates in the sink.

Madison put a single log on the hearth and lit a handful of kindling to get it going. She needed the flickering light almost as much as she needed the warmth.

Once she was under the covers, her head on the pillow and her eyes on the shifting flame, she dialed Nathan Quinn's number. He picked up on the first ring. He had already spoken with Lieutenant Fynn and knew what facts there were to know.

"When I was a criminal defense attorney," he said, and his voice was a low rumble in her ear, "there were at least five good, solid stressors that I could use to switch a charge from first-degree murder to a diminished responsibility plea. And any prosecutor would have had to argue their case twice as hard if I could find just one juror who could sympathize with the defendant."

"I know, and they still love you for it."

"What I mean is that, if you have a farmer trying to bring up a family in the middle of nowhere, living under all kinds of pressures until he finally snaps, some people—some jurors—might have a degree of compassion for him."

"Not in this case, I assure you. If Tanner is the killer, he murdered the beloved town doctor and a sweet guy who let him buy on credit. He *lured* the couple out of the crowd so that he could shoot the man. Not even you could make him out to be a poor, distraught farmer who snapped due to the geofinancial pressures of the modern world."

"You'd be surprised at what a determined defense lawyer will try, and what an incompetent jury will believe."

"I know," Madison said. "I've seen it."

"Eyewitnesses and a murder weapon would be nice."

"They always are," Madison said. "It's just that we don't really get many of those, do we?"

"Be careful tomorrow," Quinn said.

"I will. And I'll be sure to let you know ASAP if I get shot at."

It was a bad joke, and Madison instantly regretted it. "Tanner's got kids up there," she said. "I don't know what we're going to find. The chief told Brown that Tanner's wife divorced him years ago and left him alone with the children on the mountain. We need to get him to talk to us without it turning into an incident."

"Brown has a lot of experience diffusing that kind of situation. The chief knows Tanner, and he doesn't sound like a fool."

Madison did not reply.

"Something's troubling you, Detective," Quinn said.

"If Tanner is the shooter, why did he need the medical file?"

"Why do you read any medical file?"

"To find out something I didn't know, or to confirm something I already knew."

The silence between them was comfortable, each deep in their own thoughts. Madison could see Quinn lying on his bed, two pillows behind his head, maybe a Henry James novel open and facedown on the sheets.

"The file and the fact that Ty Edwards was killed are the only things linking the two murders," Quinn said.

"Yes," Madison conceded, and she knew what he was about to say.

"It could be a coincidence."

Madison hated the word. "I don't think so. I can't believe everything has been going along peacefully for decades and suddenly we've got two different killers on the loose."

Quinn thought it over. When he spoke, his words surprised her. "Just because the same man kills two people within two days, it doesn't mean he killed them for the same reason."

"Maybe."

Neither wished to end the conversation.

"What's the town like?" Quinn said.

She smiled. "You would go nuts here: only one restaurant open after 8 p.m., and no sushi. People's lives are stalked by the weather, and they're one bad tourist season away from serious trouble . . ."

"And yet?"

"And yet there's something about living a life so close to the wilderness that I find deeply appealing. It's harsh and unpredictable and merciless, and yet . . ."

Madison could hear Quinn's smile. "You would do just fine in the woods. It's the woods I would worry about. Diana the Huntress."

The small attic felt too quiet after they hung up, and Madison wondered how it was possible for a voice at the end of a phone to change so fundamentally the nature of a room. She closed her eyes and saw him lying on his bed.

Sleep came as she was making a plan for the following day.

Chapter 29

There would be other times in her life when Alice Madison would experience fear—many of those early in her career in the Seattle PD and some very recently, side by side with Brown. Nevertheless, by that turning in the road, when she was twelve years old, holding on to the handlebars of her red bike as if they were the only thing anchoring her to the planet, Alice felt a jolt of panic that punched right through her. What had she done? How could she have assumed . . . ? Adrenaline scrambled her thoughts, and the pit of her stomach ached with it. Every rotten notion, every frightful idea that she had been holding back since she had snuck out of her house and caught the ferry fell on her like ice.

Alice was alone in the world. She would not go back, and now she didn't even have a place where she could sit down, rest, think, sleep. Suddenly she wanted to sleep more than anything else; she wanted to fall asleep right there, standing up at the end of the dirt path.

Alice got off her bike—she was shaking, and she knew that she'd fall if she tried to pedal anywhere. *I'd get a great big concrete smooch*, she thought, as her skateboarding friends back in Friday Harbor would say.

She could walk off to the right or to the left, and it didn't seem to matter one way or the other. This simple notion was terrifying. Alice reached for any strength she could muster, turned left, and pushed her bike slowly along. Her brain had gone through some kind of short circuit and she found it difficult to get together anything resembling a coherent thought.

After a few minutes she found that she had traced her steps back to the bus stop and the center of the small town. Without any real decision to do it, Alice walked to a bench by the water and sat down. The pretty lake had a name, but she couldn't remember what the heck it was.

Great, she thought, *my life is falling apart and I'm losing my mind, piece by piece. By the end of the week I'll have forgotten my own name.*

The water was a flat sheet of blue, and above it rose a huge mountain of snow and rock. Alice sighed. *I should know the name of that.*

She sat back against the bench and dug into her pack for the ham sandwiches. She ate them both, watching the people go past, the little kids playing in the fountain, and a dog running after a Frisbee on the grass. She envied the kids, and for a brief, absurd moment she even envied the dog. She went through the bag of Cheetos too, and once she had finished she pressed her index finger into the bottom of it to catch any stray crumbs. Her chocolate milk was not fridge-cold anymore, but she didn't care—the comfort of that sweetness was all she craved.

The sun was warm on Alice's skin and, little by little, it worked like an icebreaker through her panic. Little by little, drawn in by the food and the quiet, her thinking seemed to come back to her, tentatively, testing that the ground was steady enough to bear logic. Yes, she had run away from home. Yes, the night before she had found out that her father had stolen away the last of her mother's things for a game of poker. He was a pro who had played in Vegas—but so what? Her mother had died in March, and she wouldn't buy, make, or touch anything else ever again. All they had was all there would ever be of her. For an instant, standing over him while he slept, Alice had thought that her father did not deserve to draw another breath. For an instant, she almost did something about it. Then the thought had dissipated, she had stabbed his folding knife into his bedside table—two inches deep—and left.

They had been so close when she was little. How long ago could it possibly be? The memory of holding the deck of cards in her tiny hands as he taught her to play—and her mother watched—made her eyes well up and the waterfront blur. Yes, she was sitting on the shore of a lake without a clue about what to do next.

She wiped her eyes with the cotton of her sleeve because her hands were covered in orange Cheetos powder. *Yes, sure, I'm in a little trouble. But it doesn't mean leaving was a bad idea. I just need to think this through and I can't do it sitting on this bench.*

Some weeks earlier, when she had visited with Jessica and her family, they had gone hiking in the area around the house; there were a number of trails there, and some led to very pleasant little spots where Alice could bunk down for the night and not be mistaken for the world's youngest, neatest hobo.

In a couple of hours the sky would turn violet, and while no one had noticed her sitting by herself in the middle of the day, she had no doubt that someone would see her lying down behind the carnation border at dusk. And in a couple of hours her father would realize that she was not coming back.

Alice returned to the convenience store and bought more food to take with her and—in a moment of inspiration she was particularly proud of—a flashlight. She tied the shopping bag with a bow to her handlebars and pushed off, back toward Jessica's house and beyond it.

Reaching the turnoff was a very different feeling from a few hours earlier, and Alice did not look—it would have been almost painful—she just pedaled a little faster until she arrived at the crossroads. And ten minutes after that, she was at the beginning of the trails.

A group of five people was just emerging from one of the paths—three adults, two teenagers, somebody arguing, somebody sulking—and Alice turned her face away and pretended to look into her backpack until they were gone. She waited to be sure and then she took the middle trail—smooth and even—and her bike flew on it.

I only need to work out the next thing I'm going to do, Alice told herself. *If I can do that I'll be all right.* She didn't need to decide everything that very minute, and that reassured her because, going deeper into the woods, the light had already begun to change and she had felt a whisper of the earlier panic. It was still there, it reminded her, waiting behind a locked door, pressing to get out.

When Alice reached a fork in the path, she slipped the bike behind a boulder where overhanging ferns would mask it from view and she left the trail.

It would not occur to the young girl until many hours later that, while she had been scrupulous about hiding her route and had effectively disappeared when she had stepped off the ferry, the problem with disappearing is that no one will come and rescue you when you need to be rescued.

The small clearing was surrounded by firs, pines, and spruces on all sides; Alice had reached it after a few minutes and by then the sky above her had turned into a rich, deep purple streaked with pink. She was glad to be in the open because it was becoming too dark to walk under the canopy, and tree roots had found and snagged her foot twice already. The darker it was, the more twisty they seemed to be.

She picked a corner to set up camp and unshouldered her pack. *I can do this,* she said to herself. She eyed a couple of fallen branches that carried a bounty of soft needles and dragged them to her corner. Normally there would be a fire in a camp, but

Alice paused: she was so close to the trail that if anybody saw the flames and decided to drop by and say hello, they would find her all alone and it would be impossible to explain. No, no fire tonight. If she wanted light she had the flashlight, and her food did not need reheating. She didn't dwell on the thought that she had only managed to light a fire once while camping, and it had taken three hours of humiliating effort. *Tomorrow I'll buy some matches*, she thought.

Alice surveyed her kingdom: a bed of pine needles with a thick, leafy branch leaning against a trunk for the roof, and all her worldly goods around her. *Alice's Hilton*. This time yesterday she was eating a peanut butter and jelly sandwich and watching *Quantum Leap*. She looked up: soon there would be stars; it wasn't *Quantum Leap*, but it was something.

Tiredness came suddenly and Alice crawled under the branch, over her sleeping bag. She had needed to do this one thing—find a place to spend the night—and she had done it and done it well, so that was okay. Tomorrow, she would get some proper thinking done. She fell asleep with her arms around her baseball bat and with her pack as a pillow. Somewhere in the back of her mind she was aware that there are situations you can't just *think* your way out of—she had learned the heartbreaking truth of it in the last months of her mother's illness—but that night she needed the confidence to believe that she could find a way out of the mess she was in. And that, because she had the skills to make herself a bed out of pine needles, she could fix everything else too.

Alice woke up wrapped inside a darkness deeper than she had ever felt: her eyes were open and yet she was utterly blind. The pitch black was alive with whispers. An owl hooted sharply only a few feet above her and Alice remembered where she was. She crawled out from under her makeshift roof and shivered. How late was it? She couldn't tell. She had fallen asleep in her T-shirt, and the summer warmth had held her for hours, but the night had come with a chill and it had sought out the lone girl sleeping on rough ground.

Alice turned on her flashlight, dug out her sweatshirt, and pulled it on quickly. She took two hesitant steps into the middle of the clearing, and waves of moths danced in the beam of her light. There was chirping, hooting, twittering, and wailing all around her. *I'm not afraid*, she said to herself, and to prove it she stood right in the middle of the clearing and counted up from one to sixty, until a loud rustle in the spruce behind her sent her rushing back to her den.

Nothing came for her, nothing followed her into her lair, and after a few minutes all the sounds blended into one motley rush of noise. Alice shivered inside the smooth, synthetic folds of her sleeping bag, and she told herself that it was only because she was cold. She fell asleep out of total exhaustion, thinking about the patch of open sky above her, an almost perfect circle, cut out of the forest and bright with stars.

There were no stars to follow when Alice woke up at dawn, and maybe for that reason—or maybe just because that's how the world spun that day—she missed the way back to the trail, took the wrong turn, and headed deeper into the woods, farther and farther away from the red bike, which she would never see again, and from the matches, which she would never get to buy.

John James Walker had been in the US Army all his adult life and had retired in 1991, after Desert Storm, with the rank of warrant officer. He was born in Oregon, had hated the heat of the Iraqi desert, and couldn't even bear the humidity of the US southern states. Since he'd left the army he had mostly hiked in the Rockies, living off his pension and keeping to himself. That was one way to tell the story. Another way was that he had barely escaped a charge of conduct unbecoming, couldn't stand to live anywhere near his family—or, for that matter, most human beings—and preferred being alone on a mountain with his rifle and a hunting knife. He trapped small animals for food and filled his canteen in any of the numerous streams. The rest of his days took whatever shape the weather brought in the morning. A few times—for the sheer fun of it—he had stalked groups of hikers, crept through their camp as they slept in their tents, and written his name in the smoldering ashes of their fire. They never noticed; they would emerge from their tents as sleepy and helpless as newborns and never had the slightest idea that he had been among them.

Sometimes stalking was not enough of a challenge for a man of his tastes and experience.

It was this particular set of skills that had alerted him the instant the kid had begun to follow him half an hour earlier. He was small and Walker couldn't fathom what he was doing alone so far away from anything and anyone, and yet the boy had not approached Walker straight out. He had shadowed him in an approximation of tracking that was nearly laughable; however, there was something meticulous about the boy. The mere fact that he hadn't cried out for Walker's help was interesting. It was a diversion from the routine, and John James Walker was in the mood to be diverted.

He pushed through the dense forest and into an alpine meadow. And on the edge of the tree line he spied a shadow following him. When it got dark, having tired of this game—he could have lost the little insect anytime he wished—in fact he'd had to slow down to allow him to keep up—Walker stopped, built a fire, and put on some water to boil. There were few luxuries in the life he had chosen, but coffee was one of them.

It was easy to slip away in the gloom and make a loop around the camp. He moved quietly, even if his quarry was a child, because that was how he had been taught to move.

The boy stood thirty yards away, edging toward the camp, peeking through the shrubs to see where Walker had gone. The man grabbed the kid by the scruff of his sweatshirt and lifted him clear off the ground.

"You've got to be careful sneaking around like this, boy, people will think you're up to no good," he said.

"Hey!"

"Don't you try to kick me now, son. I have the right to check out who's been stalking me."

"Put me down."

"You weigh about half a feather. If I were you, I'd use more manners and less kicking."

"Put me down. Please."

"There you go . . ." Walker dropped the kid and returned to the camp.

After a couple of minutes the child appeared in the shivering light of the fire. He was short, skinny, and filthy, and the bugs had been feasting on his pale skin. There was a rip in his jeans by the knee and he held his hands in tight little fists. A baseball cap was low over his head.

He had to hand it to him, considering that he must have been wandering in the woods alone for a while. Mostly the kid just looked pissed off because the man had grabbed him by the neck, like a kitten.

Walker poured some coffee into his spare stainless-steel mug and placed it on the ground.

"You look too young for coffee. Then again, you look too young to be out here. So we'll split the difference."

The kid approached warily, then sat down on the other side of the fire. He lifted the mug and blew on it to cool the steaming-hot drink.

"What do I call you?" Walker said.

"Adam," the boy replied after a beat.

When it became clear that no more was forthcoming, Walker said, "A man of few words, I like that in a fellow."

Alice blew on the coffee again. Holding something warm in her hands was wonderful, and though she hated coffee she took a sip. She had filled the bottle that had once contained chocolate milk with water from a stream, and it sat at the bottom of her pack. She was very hungry, but she didn't want to mention it—truth be told, she didn't know how to feel about the man she had been following through the woods.

She took a good look at him, the way her father had taught her when they were at the poker table: the man was older than her dad—maybe in his late thirties—and he hadn't shaved for a while. He was tall and wiry, his cropped hair was the color of dust, and his stubble was graying. He sat watching her without a care in the world. And even young as she was, Alice knew that most adults would have asked her about her family, where she was from, was she all right. A barrage of questions should have been coming her way. Never mind the fact that he believed she was a boy—she had slicked her hair back under her cap—this was not the behavior she had expected from a grown-up. The man studied her as if she was a puzzle to be solved.

Alice noticed the rifle by his side and the knife strapped to his thigh, the camouflage pants and the brown T-shirt stained under the arms. Was he some kind of professional hunter? Was he a soldier or a vet? In the end, with a puff of breeze, it was his scent that did it: it was something more than *unwashed*, it was almost goatish, and it set Alice on edge. She should get away from him, or just get him to take her someplace with other people. Her mind was spinning. The way he was looking at her made her nervous. Suddenly, without knowing why, she was particularly glad that he thought she was a boy, as if that made her somehow stronger, somehow less of a skinny little kid far away from home.

"Please, can you help me get to a telephone?" she said.

"How did you get lost? You hiking with your folks?"

"Yes, sir."

"Where did you start from?"

She told him the name of the place.

"How long have you been wandering around by yourself?"

"Since yesterday morning."

"What happened?"

"I was messing around, I stayed behind and took the wrong path."

"How old are you?"

Alice thought fast. "Almost twelve." There was a very small chance that she could in fact pass for an eleven-year-old boy, but no older than that.

"You don't look too bad for having been by yourself for so long. Are you hungry?"

"Yes."

"Have you ever skinned a rabbit?"

Alice blinked.

"Have you ever skinned a rabbit?" he repeated.

"No."

"Well, that's what's on the menu tonight."

"Okay," Alice said, and the nugget of fear that had told her not to approach this man hours earlier pressed against her gut. "When . . . how can I get back to my family? I want—"

"We're on the wrong side of Mount Baker, boy. There are no phones, no roads, no people. Tomorrow morning I'll see what I can do. In the meantime, you can find us some firewood."

Alice hesitated.

"Go on," the man said. "It needs to be dry—no green or wet wood. In winter I'd want to burn hardwood—oak, maple, and ash—but right now, I'm happy with softwood like cedar, pine, and spruce. Do you know the difference?"

"Not really."

"What do they teach you kids in school?"

Alice was about to answer when she understood that he didn't expect her to reply. By now, she hoped, her father would have started looking for her. He would have driven to Lime Kiln Park and seen that she was not there; he would have called her friends on the telephone and he would have been told that no one had seen Alice all day. At some point he might have ventured into her bedroom, stepping through the destruction she had inflicted with her baseball bat, and he would have seen her rage played out. Maybe he would have noticed her pack was missing, maybe not. Maybe he would have searched for her late into the night and called the police. Then again, maybe not: the switch-blade knife had been buried into his bedside table as deep as her little-girl strength had allowed.

Alice sighed. The weight of her loss pressed down on her shoulders, and fatigue almost overwhelmed her as she dragged herself to her feet. She could not count on her father to come to her rescue, and she had firewood to worry about.

The man was taking a furry, gray shape out of a canvas bag in a side pocket of his massive olive-green pack. *At least*, Alice reflected, because she needed the small joke, *I'm not the rabbit.*

That night Alice fell asleep with a full stomach and, even though she had washed her hands three times and rubbed them hard with grass, the sensation of rabbit's blood lingered on her fingers.

Skinning the rabbit had been awful and it had been made worse by the man's obvious enjoyment of her discomfort. Eating the rabbit, on the other hand, had been wonderful. Alice was a child of one of the richest countries in the world and had never gone without food for more than a few hours: it had been a shock when she finished her supplies and had nothing to eat for more than twenty-four hours. Still, in a grubby, elemental way her sated hunger had overcome her guilt.

There had been little or no conversation with the man over the evening, aside from his instructions on how to handle his knife: he had not volunteered his name, and Alice had not asked for it. She had followed his directions and proved herself surprisingly adept with the knife—a silent apprentice who had thrown up in the stream, quietly and out of sight.

Alice did not want to fall asleep; she felt more alone now than she had the previous day wandering through the deserted valley, because "The Hunter"—that's what she had decided to call him—behaved like no other adult she had ever met. Even in Vegas, two years ago, where she had been a kind of mascot to the poker pros in Joey Cavizzi's basement, where her father had played, they had treated her as the little kid she was, even if she understood the game almost as well as they did. This solitary man who had not tried to reassure or comfort her—a lost eleven-year-old boy—was an unknown quantity. Alice decided that, unless he was going to take her back someplace safe the following day, she'd get away from him somehow.

She was aware of how ridiculous that notion was, and yet she clung to it. Sleep didn't come for a long time because she waited for The Hunter, on the other side of the fire, to fall asleep first. When his breathing deepened and slowed down, she allowed herself to let go and drift into ragged, unsettling dreams. She was wrapped in her sleeping bag, her head on her pack and her arms around her baseball bat.

Chapter 30

"Can you hear me, Charlie One? Over," a man's voice whispered in his earpiece.

"I hear you just fine, Charlie Two. Over," the man said.

"Just checking," Charlie Two replied, and then added as an afterthought, "Over."

Charlie Two had checked twenty minutes earlier and no doubt he would check again soon, as he had done all night at regular intervals.

Charlie One rolled his eyes and shifted a little against the branch that was supporting his back. He had built the tree house for his boys two summers previously and they had practically lived in it ever since. The day he had finished hammering planks and nailing timbers to the spruces in his backyard, though, he would not have believed that one winter night he would use the plain wooden structure to stalk a human being.

The idea had begun in the diner that afternoon and had taken hold very fast, as most ill-advised notions seem to, when the patrols of state troopers and sheriff's deputies had spilled out onto Main Street. Ludlow was not *their* town and—as much as the efforts of the county and state law enforcement agencies were appreciated—Ludlow men were not going to sit idly by while someone else was protecting their families from a madman. Most men—and quite a few women—Charlie One knew owned a rifle, and even those who didn't hunt knew how to point and shoot the thing if necessary.

It had been decided in half whispers, and by the time everyone had returned home a plan was in place: there would be lookouts in shifts until dawn, and if any person was seen creeping through the side streets in the middle of the night during the "shelter in place" they'd better be a trooper or have a darn good reason. No more than four, maybe six, officers had been left to keep an eye on Ludlow overnight and it was an inadequate number, even with the small knot of streets that radiated from the center of town.

The "volunteers"—as they had decided to call themselves—were only doing what any person in their right mind would do in a similar situation. Some of them—like Charlie Two—had never even gone deer hunting, and yet fate had seen fit to put them on the front line of a manhunt. *That's the way it goes*, Charlie One reflected, and he rolled his shoulders to keep them from cramping in the cold. *You step up or you get stepped over.*

The wind had died down and the air was still; snow was on the way, and every breath was a frosty blade poking at his lungs. Cold nipped at his fingers, even though the man wore many layers of clothing and was wrapped in a sleeping bag, and he badly wished he could run around a little and warm up. The man had a thermos of black coffee and one of Swiss Miss hot chocolate, and he had pretty much gone through both already, which—he now realized—posed its own set of problems. He needed to wait until the next round of checks and then he would—what did his father used to say?—empty the tank.

A few minutes later his earpiece croaked to life, and one after the other, the voices of seven volunteers spread around the town confirmed that all was quiet and safe in their square of the grid. It had been George Goyer's idea—being a pilot, of course—for everyone to have code names, in case anybody was listening who shouldn't be. George lived out of town and thus was not on the volunteers' roster, but the name thing had been his contribution—and it was a good one.

The man sniffed; his breath was warm and damp in the folds of the sleeping bag he had pulled up to cover his mouth. He was supposed to be a lookout but, unless he brought the night-vision goggles to his eyes, he saw little past his own gloved hands. His backyard was as pitch-black as those on either side of it, and the road was barely lit by the pallid glow coming from Main Street and the portable lights of the state troopers.

Charlie One clicked on the goggles and the world became a vivid green screen. He was glad his wife was fast asleep and the drapes were drawn—he could *see* they were drawn—because she wouldn't have approved of what he was about to do. Call it the first line of defense, he told himself with a smirk as he rested his Ruger carbine on the floor of the tree house and gingerly stood up. He fumbled through the layers of sleeping bag and clothing and managed to unzip and relieve himself onto the ground below with a patter like rain on dry dirt. No, he thought, his wife would have definitely not approved, but it was probably the only fun he'd had in hours—being on a stakeout was not as much of a hoot as it had seemed in the diner.

Charlie One folded the sleeping bag tight around his shoulders and peered all around. It must be about three in the morning, and so far not so much as a squirrel had stirred. His neighbors' yards were quiet, and the slice of road he could see was deserted. The troopers had walked around some, and he had seen their body armor and the clear WST insignia through his goggles. They had stayed put for a while, though, and nothing and no one had crossed his line of sight. What he really needed was chocolate or a few cookies, and his thoughts turned to the abundance of both in his kitchen cupboards only yards away.

He should have thought about it before coming up, he chided himself. A lot of good they did in the cupboard. How or why he decided to move he wasn't sure, but suddenly Charlie One was shrugging the sleeping bag off his back and climbing down the tree-house ladder with the rifle hanging by a strap over his shoulder and determination in his steps.

It was easy to cross the yard quietly with his goggles on. And he decided that he wouldn't turn on the light, even when he was inside, as he wouldn't need to—and, most important, it would be kind of cool to wear the goggles indoors.

He unlocked the back door with a key and crept into the kitchen. His wife kept a drawer full of spare plastic bags, and he picked one just the right size. He tiptoed to the cabinet and found what he was looking for: food supplies for the cold and hungry. Yes, it was mostly sugar and candy, but if a man was going to freeze his ass off for a noble reason he had the right to eat what he wanted. He added a couple of cans of soda for good measure and then snuck back out of the kitchen, locked the door, and made his way back to the tree house with a bagful of goodies. The tree house was a box with three walls and one open side—useful to keep an eye on the boys—topped by a peaked roof. Each wall had a window and the open side had a small platform that jutted out of the tree and held a narrow ladder and a railing. All in all, the man was very proud of it: kids should have tree houses, they should have adventures and campouts and the chance to get a little *untamed*. Come to think of it, grown-ups should too.

Charlie One stepped onto the ladder and his goggles bumped into a rung higher up, so he pushed them off his eyes to rest on top of his head and kept climbing. Soon there would be another check and he wanted to be in position.

The man picked up the sleeping bag off the floor and settled himself in his old spot. After a few minutes the voice of Charlie Seven started the round of checks and—as expected—all was well. A bird fluttered nearby and the branches swayed in the dark.

Charlie One didn't know what to think: did he want the shooter to be hanging around town for them or the troopers to catch? Would he have preferred for the man to have left, become somebody else's problem, and possibly murder elsewhere, in another small town just like Ludlow? The man gazed above the trees and above the mountains, where the stars shone in a stream like a river of silver dust. You didn't get a sky like that in the big towns.

It wasn't a reassuring thought, but the truth was that if the man who had shot Ty Edwards was still around, they'd have a much better chance of catching him in Ludlow. At least they *knew* he was there. If he left, he could have gone anywhere and started all over again, and those poor bastards would be just as defenseless as Ty had been. Chief Sangster had kept his mouth real zipped up about the investigation, but it was fairly clear from where Charlie One stood: only a nutjob shoots into a crowd. Unless, of course, the whole thing had been political, in which case—

"I've got something," a voice hollered in his earpiece. "This is Charlie Five. I've got something."

The man stiffened. His whole focus shifted to the thin voice coming from the west of town. He clicked the goggles back into place and squinted into the green darkness. His heart started going rabbit-fast, and every detail appeared to stand out: the mulchy scent of dead leaves all around him, his own perspiration under the thermals.

"What is it?" somebody else said.

"Someone's moving, down in the street, real sneaky-like, and I could swear it was no trooper."

"Which street and which direction?" one of the Charlies asked.

Charlie Five told them.

"Can you describe him?"

"No, he was moving too fast."

"Was he armed?" Charlie One asked.

"I don't know. Could have been. Didn't see clearly enough."

"Could be coming toward you, Four."

"Don't I know it."

"Where are you?"

"Standing by in my front room. I'm peeking through the drapes, but the road is clear."

It occurred to Charlie One that most of the other volunteers were doing their volunteering from inside their warm homes, while he was out there looking over the neighborhood and peeing from a tree.

"Anything yet?" Five asked.

"Nope," Four replied. "All clear."

The man stood up and rested the butt of the rifle against his shoulder in the nook that seemed made for it.

"Got him!"

It was Four's voice and the earpiece burst into a crackle of voices. Charlie One stood stock-still, his eyes trained on the part of town where he knew Charlie Four had just spotted their target. He couldn't see him, of course. He was too far away, and yet it felt as if he could sense his movements through the dark, empty streets and across the deserted yards. He automatically cocked the bolt of the 10/22 and it sprang forward, ready to shoot.

"Where? Where is he?" Voices crossed and overlapped.

"Just cut across the alley. Running like the dickens, actually."

If this creepy-crawly was heading toward Charlie Three, it meant he was moving away from the tree house. Charlie One's heartbeat was so loud that the voices reaching him seemed to be filtered through it.

"We should call the chief," somebody said, and someone else said they'd do it.

The man breathed in and out, in and out, and he waited. He waited for someone to say something, anything. From where he stood he could spot roofs peeking out from between the tops of the trees, and some stretches of ground. The green world he could see was motionless and utterly silent. He debated whether to climb down and join the others, whether they should all go toward Charlie Three and search every street and every yard that side of town.

"I called the chief. He was napping in his office. He's on his way."

"Three, do you see him?"

"No, no one came through here."

"Shit."

"Four, was he armed?"

"Couldn't say, but I barely saw him. He sure was in a hurry."

Fuck it, Charlie One said to himself and he climbed down the ladder as quickly as he could, swearing under his breath when he bumped the goggles, slipping on the rungs, and almost losing his balance on the icy ground. He straightened and made his way to the side gate. If they were going to trap the sucker, he was going to be right there.

"The chief said for everyone to stay right where we are."

Shitshitshit. Charlie One froze with his hand on the gate. They'd gone behind the chief's back with their little neighborhood watch project; nevertheless, the man was reluctant to out-and-out disobey the chief's instructions.

"What's going on?" Charlie Two murmured, as if their target could hear them.

"Don't know. Just saw a couple of troopers running past," someone replied.

Charlie One sighed. It was the troopers' game now. Hesitant to go inside, turn on the lights, and wait to hear—like everyone else who hadn't been keeping watch half the night—Charlie One decided to go back up to his sentry post and remain there until they heard, one way or the other.

There was no talk on the earpiece, and he could imagine six other men rooted where they stood—cold and tired and, sure, a little bit nervous, but mostly, secretly, so keyed up about the hunt that they could have gone on for hours.

Charlie One reached for the plastic bag, because all that excitement needed to be crowned with a cookie, and it was only when his hand didn't find it where he had dropped it that he turned. Wearing the goggles that gave him a clear, green view of the inside of the tree house, Charlie One stared at the spot on the floor where he had left the plastic bag with its booty of candy and cookies. It wasn't there. The man touched the bare wooden plank with his gloved hand, as if the bag had somehow become invisible. It wasn't there.

What the heck? He leaned out of the platform and gaped at the ground below. Could he have accidentally pushed it off and made it fall all the way to the dirt? No, that was impossible. He would have heard it land and would have tripped on it when he had rushed down. *How . . . ?*

The man studied the floor of the tree house, as if it contained the meaning of life. And yet the one unassailable truth he found was that the bag was not there. He had left the platform for a couple of minutes, gone into his kitchen, come back, and put the bag on the floor by his feet. And now it was gone.

Something was warm and sticky on his skin under the layers and he felt a swooping in his gut, like falling off the ladder backward. He could see everything clearly with the goggles in place, like eerie daylight. *You weren't wearing the goggles when you climbed back up the ladder, remember that, brother?* He wasn't: he had pushed them up, because he kept banging them on the ladder as he climbed up. And when he had reached the top— the pitch-black top of the ladder, the deep murky gloom of the inside of the hut—he had turned with his back to the dark room and plopped himself down like a fool, and only when the alert had come through had he clicked the goggles back into place and . . . and there had been that awful smell of dead leaves and mulch and earth and sweat, and the rustle of the bird in the tree . . .

"Oh, man," Charlie One said. "Oh, man." He couldn't say any more than that. His eyes searched the floor of the tree house and right there, under the back window, he spotted two muddy footprints. He had never gone near that window that night and, for sure, they were a man's footprints, not a boy's. Just outside the window the branches met and parted and curled and plunged all the way to the ground.

"Oh, man," Charlie One repeated, and he didn't know whether to stay or to run, to throw up or be gone. He didn't know whether to tell, or to shut up about it forever. He had been looking at the stars, he had been looking at the damn stars.

Chapter 31

After the detectives had locked up the senior center for the night and gone back to the Miller house, Chief Sangster had stretched out on the sofa in his office. He lived a ten-minute drive away, but even that meager distance seemed too much when he had officers patrolling the streets. He wanted—or maybe needed—to stay where they could reach him with a holler.

The sofa was short and uncomfortable and was thus the fitting end to the most hideous day he'd had on the job since he'd moved to Ludlow. As a concession to anatomy versus gunmetal he had removed his belt—with the holster and the sidearm—and had draped it on the chair next to the sofa. He had locked his office door and lain down, still wearing his boots. Sleep found him as if it had been lying in wait for him, just around the corner, and the chief, with one foot on the ground and one arm thrown back, had fallen into a black pit without dreams.

Barely three hours later he unlocked the office door, tore through the main room, and hurried outside. The slap of icy air woke him up better than coffee. His eyes sought and found two uniformed men standing at the end of the street.

He ran toward them.

It had been a crazy idea, and yet it was exactly the kind of thing that he should have expected of his people. Chief Sangster strode toward the alley where the running man had last been seen. Every window was dark and every door was shut.

Three troopers had rushed ahead and three covered the street behind him. The alley cut through a block of houses and led straight to a patch of woods. There were no windows, side gates, or doors of any kind: if the guy had run into the alley, he must have come out at the other end where all Sangster could see was a wall of trees. If the runner had made it to the trees, they were going to need hounds and trackers more than the obliging local Special Weapons and Tactics section.

Sangster, eyes gritty and limbs stiff from his short sleep, swept the beam of his heavy flashlight across the trees. How long after the call had they made it there? How much time had the man had to disappear into the forest? Sangster wiped his clammy brow with the palm of his hand. Had there been anyone at all in the first place? What had the men really seen? A blur through cars and shrubs and shadows.

Could have been a man, could have been a deer.

He pointed the flashlight at the dirt by the end of the alley: all kinds of footprints stood out in the frozen mud, and there was no telling how old they were.

They searched the backs of the houses and a strip about a hundred feet deep into the forest, but there was no trail to follow, no prints to track.

After about an hour, the chief called the man who had woken him up from his brief sleep and politely asked him to haul his ass down to the station for a debrief. And to bring his friends with him.

Nobody had gone to bed, and a few minutes later seven men ambled up to the station.

The chief watched them arrive and suspected that each one of them had been holding on to a weapon most of the night. Thankfully, they had thought about it and left their firepower at home. Sangster believed in the right to bear arms, and yet he was also convinced that, given half a chance, some moron in the wrong place at the wrong time would have gotten shot for his sins. And one of the men in front of him would have gone to jail for it.

Sangster had made a fresh pot of coffee to show them he was not in a pissed-off mood, and once they were all settled in the main room, he spoke. His voice was croaky with tiredness but friendly enough.

"Guys, I need you to tell me exactly what you saw. Not what you think you saw, or what you perhaps could have, maybe, possibly seen. Only what you saw."

It didn't take long for the two men to brief him. The others drank their coffee and stood by in polite silence.

"Are you absolutely sure you saw a man, Billy?"

"That's what I thought, Chief," Charlie Five replied. "Hand on my heart."

"What do you think now?"

Billy gawked at Charlie Four, and his friend shrugged.

In the bright light of the police station things felt different and all the certainties they had held, watching over their homes in the middle of the night, had faded to nothing.

They had seen a fast-moving blur . . . could have been a man, could have been a deer.

"Anybody else have anything to add?" The chief looked around the room.

The seven men filed out and walked back to their houses. Charlie One, his mouth dry and his guts clenched, walked a little more quickly than the others.

Once home, he made sure he'd double-bolted the door behind him.

What should he have said? That a ghost man had stolen his candy?

It was the stupidest thing, and he was never going to tell anyone about it. The ghost man was gone. And if he'd wanted to shoot Charlie One's head off from the back of the tree house he could have done so at his leisure, anyway.

The following day, Charlie One went to the grocery store and quietly replaced the missing candy in the cupboard.

Chapter 32

Alice Madison pulled the Glock from her shoulder holster and sat on her unmade bed. It was 7 a.m. and the Miller house was creaking its way into a new day. The building's clicks and whines as the furnace came to life had become pleasantly familiar.

Madison had slept. She would not have described it as *sleeping well*. Nevertheless, her eyes had been closed and she had been unconscious—with the kind of day they were expecting, it was as much as she could hope. She hadn't gone running since Alki Beach on Thursday, and that was unusual; the brittle energy rattling around in her system made her restless and unsettled when she should have been focused and calm.

The solution, she found, lay in the piece of high-strength nylon-based polymer in her hand. Madison hadn't brought her full gun-cleaning kit, but that didn't mean she could not field-strip her piece and make sure it was ready for whatever the day would bring. It was somewhat soothing, and Madison didn't want to look too deeply into why that might be.

First, she cocked back the slide and peered inside—empty, good. Then she took out the magazine, pulled back the trigger, and gently moved the slide back one eighth of an inch. From there it was easy to draw it right out and extract the barrel with the recoil spring.

Madison was scrupulous about keeping her weapons in perfect working order—the backup piece was already in her ankle holster—and she didn't find much in the Glock that needed cleaning or oiling. If anything, it was—as always—a little odd to see the various pieces lying there quite so inertly, as if they didn't actually come together as a lethal whole.

Madison was a competition-level shooter who respected guns and understood the necessity of an armed law enforcement agency. And yet—and this was something she did not talk about with her colleagues—Madison did not believe that any Tom, Dick, or Harry should be able to walk into a sporting goods store and come out with a new tennis racket in one hand and a semi-automatic in the other. Madison reassembled her Glock with smooth, practiced gestures and returned it to its holster.

The navy-blue ballistic vest went over her fleece, and she tightened the straps on both sides. For the last two years she had worn a Tactical Unit vest with ceramic plates inserted into a soft structure. She didn't wear it every day, and in fact it was hardly ever needed—except on days with a high potential for danger. And today definitely qualified.

Madison pulled down the vest so that it sat tight around her shoulders, and when she was satisfied she slipped on her holster. She didn't check herself in the mirror; she knew what she would see.

Kevin Brown tucked the soft checked shirt into his trousers and pulled the thick sweater over his head. He hadn't shaved, and his stubble was silver against his pale skin. He checked himself in the mirror.

It would have to do.

* * *

"A deer?" Sorensen said.

"Looks like it," Chief Sangster replied.

"Well, it's the thought that counts." Sorensen poured herself some coffee.

The chief wanted a quiet word with the detectives before the day ran away from them, and he'd rather do it privately. The round clock on the wall read 7:30 a.m., and he looked like he hadn't bothered to go back to sleep at all.

"Are you sure?" Sangster asked Brown for the second time that morning.

Madison's keen eye was on her partner.

"Yes, I'm sure," he replied.

"Alrighty, then. You know what you know," the chief said. "To make things more fun, it looks like the weather is going to turn, might get a little snow in the afternoon, keep things interesting."

Madison was already wearing her parka, and Brown picked up the heavily lined coat the chief had brought for him. Neither was wearing visible Seattle Police Department or local law enforcement insignia.

"You'll be okay?" Madison asked Sorensen.

"I'll be fine: in case I get bored with the mass spectrometer, I've always got crayons and basket weaving."

They left the Ludlow Police Station in a convoy: Chief Sangster in his cruiser first, with Deputies Hockley and Kupitz, followed by Brown and Madison in Hockley's pickup, and finally a state police truck with officers in full body armor. It was the first time the deputies had worn their ballistic vests since they had joined the Ludlow police, and neither was sure what to expect—or what to wish for—from the day ahead. Kupitz rode shotgun and Hockley sat in the back, his eyes on the houses and the stores he had known all his life, which today felt a little less familiar.

Madison was glad to have some time alone with Brown on their journey to the Tanner farm. As always, even in the depths of Colville County, he was the one behind the steering wheel and Madison had the opportunity to observe him. He seemed preoccupied—well, they all were to a degree, sure—however, there was something else. She remembered the aftermath of the shooting in the square and Brown making his way into the copse of trees, chasing after the shooter.

"What's up, Sarge?" she said, and instantly regretted the blunt approach.

Brown turned. "*What's up?*"

It was impossible to lie to Brown, and on this occasion Madison would rather sound foolish than be less than truthful with him.

"Is there something on your mind?" she said. "I mean, something other than Tanner?"

"Why do you ask?"

"Seemed like there was something yesterday in the square, and maybe now."

"We got shot at in the square."

"I know, but . . ."

"No, nothing else on my mind—aside from getting Tanner to cooperate."

"Okay, sure thing."

They were leaving town and Madison concentrated on the view. If Brown didn't want to talk about whatever it was that troubled him, experience told her that the only option was for her to wait until he was ready to open up. And at some point he would, she knew he would.

The vest was tight around Madison and it felt like both a hindrance and a reassurance, while—curiously—the weight from her holster and around her ankle was unequivocally a comfort. Such an elemental notion, Madison reflected, when in fact should any of them be forced to reach for their sidearms, the whole enterprise would be doomed to failure.

They left Ludlow behind them and headed for the highway. Before the junction, Chief Sangster turned into a road that bent back toward the town but rose up into the mountain. After a handful of residences the landscape became a dense stretch of firs, unbroken on both sides, and Madison emptied her mind of every other concern except Jeb Tanner, who had a grudge against each of the dead men and might have been just angry enough to do something about it. As the ribbon of concrete road coiled around the mountain, the patches of snow became larger.

"It's called Jackknife, 'cause it's a twisty, dangerous one and it'll cut you in two if you're not careful," Sangster had told them. "Same as the old mine up near the pass. Killed enough miners in its time. Now the tourists lap it up."

Jeb Tanner's farm was on the far side of Jackknife, covering almost two thousand acres of land that spread out toward Canada. His nearest neighbors were miles away, and judging from the feeling in town, that was exactly how he liked it. Madison went over what they knew about the man: he was born in Ludlow, had left to go to college in Kansas on a sports scholarship, dropped out, apparently lived in California for a while, and when his father died had come back with his wife and taken over the family farm. Over the years, the increasing isolation had become a thick shroud around the Tanner family and some years back his wife had left. Two thousand acres was enough land to keep things private, and few people knew much about the daily life of the family.

Sangster had explained the previous night.

"Tanner's got supporters—some, at least. Others who like the way he does things. If people come to live all the way out here, it's not because they want to live like everyone else, right?"

After about half an hour, the chief's cruiser turned into a dirt road. It was narrow and almost overtaken by the trees and shrubs around it. Naked branches scraped against the sides of the cars as they made their slow progress. It said everything they needed to know about the landowner's feelings regarding visits.

"Kind of says *go away*, doesn't it?" Brown said.

". . . *and don't bother coming back*," Madison replied.

After a couple of minutes, they arrived at a wooden gate with an arch. It stood in the middle of the path and, even though there was no fencing on either side, it bore a hand-painted sign that read NO TRESPASSING, PRIVATE PROPERTY. And at the top of the arch someone had crudely carved the words JACKKNIFE FARM.

The chief pulled in on the side and got out. "From here on, it'll just be us," and he pointed at his cruiser and the pickup.

It had been agreed before they'd left that the state police truck with its Special Weapons and Tactics team would stay behind and wait. Hopefully, they'd remain where they were until it was time to turn back.

Sangster pushed open the gate and left it open after they drove through.

If Tanner was the shooter, he would have seen Madison standing next to Ty Edwards and returning fire. If Tanner was the shooter, Madison wanted to look him right in the eye when he saw her. Because there was no way that he wouldn't recognize her—wouldn't recognize the person who had emptied a full magazine in his direction not even twenty-four hours earlier.

The dirt road to the farm continued for several minutes in the same cramped, awkward manner, and Madison was becoming impatient to get there. Brown drove without conversation, in his usual steady manner, staying at a safe distance from the cruiser and missing nothing of his surroundings.

The narrow road broke out into a flat, open area. The view of the jagged peaks around them was all the more breathtaking for being unexpected. Even the sky and the streaks of cloud seemed closer than in Ludlow.

Tanner's homestead was a collection of wooden structures close to the tree line: a few barns, sheds, paddocks, and what looked like the main building—a large cabin with a porch. Smoke drifted from the chimney, and the barn doors were open because although it was early on a Sunday morning, the farm's day had already begun.

"There's no machinery," Madison said.

"And I only see the one car," Brown replied.

A red pickup truck, which was possibly older than Madison, was parked by the paddock. It was the only hint that they were not on an early twentieth-century homestead. Six horses in the main paddock twitched their ears in the direction of the approaching cars, but aside from that there was no other sign of life.

"No dogs," Brown said.

"I'd be surprised if they didn't have a couple somewhere. And no eagle bait, either."

They pulled in behind the cruiser, which had come to a stop by the red truck, and up close Madison noticed that the buildings had been badly worn by the harsh weather and what had looked pleasantly old-fashioned from afar was in fact austere and unadorned. The yard was neat and the ground was hard with frost. There was a bare and pared-down quality to the place that spoke to Madison of tough winters in a beautiful, ruthless landscape.

The car engines and slamming doors should have alerted the residents that someone had arrived, but the main cabin door remained shut and the plain drapes were drawn.

"I'm sure they're here, somewhere," Sangster said.

"He's just having a good look at us," Brown said quietly. "Give him a minute."

Hockley and Kupitz lingered by the cruiser, and Madison realized that they had never been to Jackknife Farm. They were country born, only a few miles away, and were probably counting the ways in which the place differed from their own homes.

Madison took a lungful of the chilly air: wood smoke and animal manure and something deeper—a warm, sweet scent that made her hackles rise.

The only sounds were the snickering of the horses and the jingling of a metal chain wrapped around a post. Two ravens landed on the roof of the cabin and kept a watchful eye on the visitors.

Blood, Madison thought.

The scent was fresh blood, and it was somewhere close.

Chapter 33

Samuel had woken up in the dark. His body ached from the time in the lonely place the day before, and he thought that the sooner he started his chores, the sooner he would get warm and loosen up his cramped muscles. The horses' cubicles needed mucking out and he looked forward to it; he didn't particularly enjoy shoveling dung, but working close to the large, skittish animals was pleasing and snug. Their barn was warm, even on the coldest day, and Samuel appreciated their company: they were bigger than he was, and yet he knew how to soothe their nerves; they were good listeners, and they didn't bite like the edgy mongrels his father seemed to favor. Overall, they were better company than some of his siblings.

The cabin was silent as he poured himself some fresh coffee from the urn—someone must have been up earlier than him—and snuck some sugar into the tin cup. Crossing the yard, he wrapped one gloved hand around the hot mug and covered it with the other to keep it from cooling.

The animals whickered and shifted when he stepped into the barn and closed the door behind him. He was familiar with each creature's tics and moods, and the atmosphere in the barn was usually peaceful.

"Hello," he said. He didn't expect them to answer, and yet somehow he had come to expect them to understand the spinning thoughts that made his brain hurt. If it was a contradiction, the boy didn't know or care.

Since Luke had grabbed him on his way back to the farm, Samuel had been nudging and poking the same notion. Why had Luke said that Cal was a liar? And why the ugly glint in his eyes when he had told him?

Samuel ran his hand along the strong neck of his favorite—a chestnut quarter horse called Flare. In a life where the days followed one another with hardly a ripple of change, where snippets of news from the outside world were rare and far between, the smallest detail acquired importance, and in Samuel's mind everything began to connect: Luke's words, the red plane he had spotted, and the certainty that someone was on his side, someone who had risked his father's wrath and passed him food when Samuel was in the lonely place.

Could it really be that Cal had returned?

There was a whole world out there, and he wondered if each and every person was a beggar, a killer, or a thief—as his father had always said. If that was the truth, how had his brother survived among them since he'd run away? His hand went unconsciously to the raven's feather in his inside pocket. It was not the very same one that Cal had given him when he was twelve. As the first one had come apart, it had been replaced with a new one, and a new one after that. There was a long line of tatty black feathers in Samuel's life, and he had kept each one.

The boy swept the floor of the barn and wished for a way to tell the good people from the bad, the way you can with dogs.

Amy Sorensen had been working in the senior center since the law enforcement convoy had left for the Tanner farm. The instruments in her makeshift lab clicked and buzzed—it was generally accepted in her unit that no instrument would dare malfunction on Sorensen's watch and it would wait until she was in her car on her way home to short.

The cloth that bore the scrawled message had been unfolded under a powerful lamp, and Sorensen picked up her magnifying lens.

It was cotton—thin, frayed cotton—from a shirt, maybe, or a slip dress. And the stitching . . .

Sorensen examined the stitching on the hem: there was no way that it had been done by a sewing machine—it was too irregular and crude, and it lacked the bland conformity of a mass-produced item of clothing.

Homemade.

It had to be: wherever the scrap had come from, the item had been homemade, sewn and stitched together by someone who wasn't very good at it and didn't have access to a sewing machine.

Sorensen reached for the senior center phone and the telephone number they had been left.

"Hello, dear," Polly, the chief's assistant, said when she picked up. "How can I help?"

Five minutes later, Sorensen had the name of the only store in town that sold fabric and textiles, and the owner's home phone number.

Twenty minutes later, an SUV pulled up in the police station parking lot.

Sorensen was not surprised when the owner and her husband met her in the station: in Seattle, she would have had to wait until the store's official opening hours; in Ludlow, there was an element of curiosity and the currency a juicy piece of gossip would provide anybody even marginally involved in the investigation.

"Most fabric trade is done online nowadays," the woman said as she unlocked the store's door with the sign LUDLOW OUTFITTERS. "But there's still those who want to come in and choose in person. And that's what we're here for."

She turned on the lights: the store carried clothing and footwear for tourists but also a staple stock of common brands for the residents. A corner was dedicated entirely to fabrics, sewing, and quilting.

"Do you sew?" the woman asked Sorensen.

"Not really, but my mother did. She was a quilter. Good one too."

The woman smiled. She was easily a six-footer, with blonde curls and flawless makeup. Her husband had parked himself by the door and pretended not to listen to the women's conversation. Sorensen remembered seeing them both at the vigil a day earlier.

"What exactly are you looking for?" the woman asked Sorensen.

"Cloth. Cotton. White. Bought here a while ago by someone who might have been making a shirt or a dress. Here . . ." Sorensen showed her a magnified picture of a detail of the cloth on her smartphone.

The woman examined the photograph. "Solid white. We carry three types of that specific white. Come with me."

"Do you keep records of who buys what? Would you be able to tell me?"

"We don't keep electronic records, no. Whether it's cards or cash, it just goes into the till as a receipt. We do the fabric inventory by hand—unless we run out of something, and then we order it straightaway."

No records. That would make it impossible to find out who had bought the cotton, even if they found a match.

Sorensen sighed.

"We do have our *book*, though," the woman continued as she led the way. "That's how we keep track of things. Otherwise how would you know how to match something you bought seven years ago?"

"You have a book? Like a records book?"

The woman looked at Sorensen as if she'd expected better from her. "We supply two quilters' groups, five sewing classes, the senior center sewing parties, and the Ludlow High School Young Designers project." The woman stopped in front of a rack and, with practiced hands, pulled out three rolls of white cotton fabric. "Of course we have a records book."

Chapter 34

Madison sniffed the air. The horses in the paddock behind her pawed the frosty ground—they could smell the blood as clearly as she could.

A tall man walked out of the mouth of the largest barn. In the frigid air he did not wear a coat and his white shirt, open at the neck, was spattered with red. He wore black trousers, and the outfit was stark and somewhat formal—as if he'd just dropped by on his way from a funeral. He held a small child over one hip and the boy, who was as fair as the man was dark, was barefoot. Two youths in their early twenties flanked the older man.

Early fifties, at least six feet tall, dark hair and blue eyes. Jeb Tanner's driver's license photo did not do him justice: his hair was swept back, as was the fashion in the 1940s, and his blue eyes were fringed by long lashes. His features were almost delicately drawn, and the result should have been attractive. And yet, while it had every reason to be handsome, the outcome was unpleasant.

The youths were a watered-down version of the same genetic makeup: tall and heavy, with farm toil muscle. One was almost a head taller than his father and the other seemed eerily vacant. Both carried rifles and were dressed for farm labor—layers of work shirts, jeans, and heavy boots—their hair was shoulder length, and their starter beards made them look like sullen, armed hippies. Their clothing, Madison noticed, had seen many seasons on the farmyard.

The child whimpered—how old could he be? Three, possibly four—and reached around the man's neck, hiding his face from the strangers.

The man's gaze traveled over the officers and came to rest on Madison. She looked back and stared into the void of the man's eyes. If there was any recognition that they had been shooting at each other merely hours earlier, Madison didn't see it.

"Mr. Tanner," Chief Sangster said.

"Chief," Jeb Tanner replied.

"I'd like to speak with you."

"What about?"

"It would be easier to do it in town."

"*In town* means in the police station."

"It means what it means."

"I don't think so," Tanner said. "You have anything to say, you can say it to me here, or not at all."

"It won't take long."

"I don't care how long it would take."

"We can come back with a warrant, but then you'd have wasted your time and ours."

It sounded like a conversation that had played out a number of times before.

Tanner ignored the chief and turned his attention to the two strangers in his yard—Hockley and Kupitz were also strangers, but they wore the local uniform and thus were no more significant to him than a spare tire in the chief's cruiser.

"Who are you?" Tanner addressed Brown. The tone was not hostile, it was more of a rough kind of curiosity.

"Someone who's here to make sure the chief does his job right," Brown said.

The reply seemed to amuse Tanner, because he smiled at Sangster. There was nothing pleasant about the smile.

"I can see how you'd want to check up on him," Tanner said. "Local police couldn't catch flies in a bucketful of honey."

Brown didn't exactly return the smile but bowed his head a little, as if they'd just shared a private joke. He extended his hand: "Detective Sergeant Brown, Seattle PD."

Tanner looked at the hand for a moment, then took it. His own hand was large and calloused and it gripped Brown's like a snake's coil.

"Detective Madison, Seattle PD," she said and was glad she was standing too far away to shake his hand. His touch, she had decided without knowing exactly why, would be as foul as the scent in the yard.

"Let's keep it short and to the point, Tanner," Sangster bristled. "We need you to come back with us. The sooner you come, the sooner you get back."

"We're on the man's land, Chief," Brown said. "Maybe we can show a degree of respect. What do you think?"

"I think I've just about had enough." Sangster turned to Tanner. "Do I need to get a warrant?"

"You can go to hell to get your warrant, Chief. I'm not going anywhere with you."

"It's all right, Sangster," Brown said. "Mr. Tanner here doesn't really need to come back to the station."

"The heck he doesn't."

There were the men's words, rising in pitch, and there was the pale little boy, so exposed in the icy air. Madison focused on the father but her attention kept drifting to the child's dainty foot. Was he not cold? Where were the others? And how *many* others were there?

"We can talk to him here just as well," Brown said.

"Back off, Detective," Sangster said. "You're here as a *guest* of the county."

As the exchange had become sharper, the kid had tensed up in his father's arms. He might, or might not, be cold, but he certainly was scared.

"How old is your boy?" Madison said abruptly.

"What?" The question had surprised Tanner. "Why do you care?"

"Because he shouldn't have to listen to this kind of rudeness, sir," Madison replied. "I'm sure you have plenty of better things to do but, please, let *us* do our job and we'll be out of here faster than he can go get his warrant signed." She looked at the chief. "Faster than *shit* through a goose."

"That's not—"

"The choice," Brown said, "is Mr. Tanner's."

The notion of sticking it to the chief was simply irresistible. How many times had Sangster pestered him over the years? How sweet would it be to humiliate him in front of his superiors? Tanner was going to enjoy the moment.

"Get off my land," he said. "Didn't you see the NO TRESPASSING sign? Don't you know how to read? Don't they teach you that in cop school?" He sneered at the local officer. "Get off my property, Chief. The Seattle cops can stay."

Chief Sangster's cruiser made its way back along the dirt road that led to the gate of Jackknife Farm.

When he reached the state police truck, the captain—still in the cab—met his eyes.

Sangster gave him a thumbs-up.

"Come with me," Tanner said.

How much time did they have before he tired of their company? How much time to get what they needed? Tanner's sons both carried rifles, and either could have been used in the murder of Ty Edwards. For the first time Madison made eye contact with the youths, but they quickly looked away and followed their father: they were his bodyguards. And the small boy, she sensed then, had perhaps fulfilled the same function as the ballistic vest that bound her chest—if not protection, definitely a deterrent.

The barn was dim after the wide, watery sky of the yard. In the far corner a deer hung upside down, tied by its hind legs to a joist. Their visit had interrupted the men in the middle of field-dressing the animal, and Madison blinked away the spiky scent.

A table covered with sharp tools stood in the middle of the cavernous space and a boy looked up as they entered. He was in his teens, so lean he was scrawny, and if he was ever going to go through the same growth spurt as his brothers there was no sign of it yet.

The boy stared from his father to the strangers and back to his father, as if to gauge what his own reaction to the strangers should be.

The man passed him the little boy, and he took him without words; Madison noticed his gentle handling of the child, how he tucked him under his coat.

"Take him inside and come back. Tell the others to go back to their chores," Jeb Tanner said.

The boy acknowledged the instruction with a curt nod and left. The man waved to the youths and they propped their rifles against the bales of hay stacked on one side, then started to work on the deer. Madison, who knew more than she would have liked about the subject, watched their incisions. They were fast and efficient.

There had been no question or hesitation in following the orders given, and Madison doubted there had ever been.

"What do you really want?" Tanner said after a moment. "Aside from offering me a chance to vex old Sangster, that is. And I sure thank you for it."

The question had been asked of Brown. "The chief does what he can in a situation that's less than good," he replied.

"You don't need to apologize for him. I've known him for years. Have endured him for years."

"We're here to make sure things are done right, and this particular situation is bigger than the chief can handle."

"Is it now?"

"Yes, it is."

"What are we talking about?"

"We're talking about a double murder."

Tanner stiffened. Madison glanced at the young men, and for a heartbeat their knives hung still.

"A double murder?" the man said.

"Yes."

"In Ludlow?"

"Yes."

"Well," Jeb Tanner said. "I'm very sorry to hear that. Who died?"

"You didn't hear about it on the radio?"

"We don't have a radio, or a television for that matter."

"Why not?"

"I won't let my family be corrupted by the filth and the lies they push."

"Very wise."

"Who died?"

"Dr. Robert Dennen and Mr. Ty Edwards."

Jeb Tanner's small, bright eyes shone in the gloom as he turned to the deer to check his sons' work. "What a loss for the community," he said.

"You knew them?" Madison said.

"I knew them, as the chief has no doubt told you. I go into town from time to time. Edwards owns . . . owned the only hardware store in Ludlow so, yes, I knew him."

"And the doctor?"

"I knew who he was, but I've never been to the clinic."

"Never?"

"Never needed to."

"What about your kids?"

"Never needed to."

"Fair enough."

Tanner examined the deer's empty chest cavity. "They were murdered?"

"Yes," Madison replied.

"How?"

"Mr. Edwards was shot, and we're still trying to establish the cause of Dr. Dennen's death."

"And that's why you're here?"

"We're here to ask you if you've seen anything unusual in the area recently, and whether you might know something useful to the investigation."

"Is it one investigation or two?"

"We're still working it out."

"I see."

"When was the last time you went into town?" Brown said.

"I can't remember exactly. Probably a few weeks ago."

"You sure?"

"Do you know how Ludlow started out? Whores' cabins and bars. It's moved forward, but not that much. I go only when I need to, and I come back quickly."

"You weren't in town yesterday?" Brown said.

"No, I wasn't."

"Where were you?"

Tanner snorted. "Are you asking me for an alibi, Detective?"

"Let's just get it over with, Mr. Tanner. We have to ask everybody."

"I could order you off my property, just like I did the chief."

"You could, but we know this mess has nothing to do with you. We only need to dot the *i*'s and cross the *t*'s, because the chief doesn't know his left from his right."

"What time do I need an alibi for?" Tanner said.

"About noon yesterday."

"Easy: I was with a neighbor at his farm from about ten to one o'clock. Couple of miles from here. Will Clay."

"Great, thank you. And where were you in the early hours of last Thursday morning?"

"Right here in my home, asleep. As any of my children can bear witness."

Tanner pointed. "This is Luke, my firstborn. And Jonah, my fourth son. Where was I in the early hours of Thursday morning?"

"At home," Luke spoke, and his voice had a rough quality to it. "With us."

Jonah said, "Yes," but it was so quiet Madison barely caught it.

"Where are you going to keep it?" Brown pointed at the quartered deer.

"We're going to smoke a lot of it. Keep some in a meat box—no trouble keeping things cold around here. Exchange the rest for dry goods with neighbors who don't hunt."

The dates for the deer-hunting season were well past, but a farmer could kill a single animal that was damaging his property—Tanner's kids had to be eating a lot of deer meat, whatever the season.

"You've got a big family, Mr. Tanner?" Madison said.

"Children are a blessing, Detective. Don't you think?"

"Can you see them?" The state police captain whispered into his radio.

"No," the SWAT team member replied. "They're still in the barn." The officer lay flat on the ground on the edge of the forest, his binoculars trained on Tanner's compound one hundred and fifty yards away. His partner lay three feet to his left and saw the yard through the crosshairs of his M14.

They had darted through the firs and the spruces to find a sheltered spot behind a Sitka mountain ash. The cold under the man's belly cut through the layers of his clothing—then again, maybe it was his regular nerves that reminded him to stay alert.

The captain didn't like incidents in rural areas: everybody always had more firepower than they knew what to do with, and his officers got shot at more often than in urban situations. This one was a peach—the targets were packing even as they greeted the detectives. He hated the idea that they were out of sight in the barn, but it was impossible for his men to get cover to approach any closer, and he had been asked to keep his distance. They had gotten into position as soon as Sangster had given them the signal, and now they were his eyes and ears on the farm.

"Any movement in the yard?" he asked.

"Young kid carried the child into the main cabin. After that, nothing."

"Copy that."

"Wait . . . cabin door is opening . . ."

"I don't know . . ." Jeb Tanner said. "If you hadn't come up here today I wouldn't have known about what happened, and I sure can't think of anything unusual in the woods this past week or so."

"Your neighbor, Mr. Clay, didn't he tell you about the doctor's murder when you were with him yesterday?" Madison said.

"No, must have slipped his mind—or maybe he didn't know himself."

"He doesn't have a radio either?"

"I don't know that he does. I was helping him with his truck. We didn't talk about anything else."

"What was the matter with his truck?"

"The ignition coil didn't spark," Tanner said. "As I'm sure he'll tell you when you speak with him."

"Did you manage to fix it?"

The cuts of deer meat had been lined up neatly on the table. Tanner speared a large chunk with a knife and lifted it to examine it. Luke, who had cut it and placed it there, waited for his father's judgment. The man pointed without words, and the youth hurried to correct whatever mistake he had apparently made.

"You have to be able to fix things around here," Tanner said to Madison, "because nobody'll fix them for you."

"First time I quartered a deer," Madison said, "I tried to cut the scent gland from the leg and sliced right through it.

Spoiled more meat than I took home. Your sons have done a good job."

"How old were you?"

"That time? About twelve."

"Learned your lesson the hard way, didn't you? Bet you didn't make the same mistake again."

"No, the next time I made a whole set of new ones."

Tanner smiled, but it didn't reach his eyes. "That's the way it goes," he said. "I've taught my kids to trap and hunt since they could walk. Started with squirrels, then rabbits and all the way up to wolves and bears."

"You hunt wolves and bears?"

"No, Fish and Wildlife wouldn't be so happy with us if we did, but a man has to protect his land, and from time to time things just can't be helped."

Luke and Jonah had listened to their father's every word even when they had been outwardly engrossed in their work. Whatever the man said always seemed measured and always appeared to fall on the youths like a blade from a great height. If Madison knew a better way to describe *fear* she couldn't think of it. She heard a rustle behind her and there he was, the boy who had been so tender with the little child.

How long had he been standing there?

Madison was glad to return to the yard and to the fresh air. She wanted to give Brown some room for a quiet word with Mr. Tanner, and it was a chance to look over the place without the man's sharp focus on her.

It was only when she reached the paddock and leaned against it that the word came to her. *Unforgiving*. That's how the man came across. That seemed his default state of being. She couldn't begin to imagine what it would be like to be a small person growing up within the reach of his hand.

The drapes in the cabin had been opened, and though it was impossible to see clearly inside, she noticed shadows shifting behind the panes. Were they watching her? Had one of them scrawled the appeal given to Robert Dennen? Madison had studied the shirts the brothers were wearing, but none of the fabrics matched the cloth—Tanner's white shirt looked town bought. And anyway, she doubted any garment of his would have been used to throw out into the world that desperate plea.

Somewhere nearby someone was chopping wood and the cracks echoed in the open plateau. By her reckoning the SWAT officers were going to be to her left, by the spruces, and no doubt they would be telling their captain that Brown and Madison had made it out of the barn in one piece.

One of the horses padded close as the boy appeared to Madison's side and pushed some hay, oats, and the seed head of dry grasses into a bale feeder. Some grain spilled onto the ground and Madison saw a glossy dark feather that the breeze had blown against a fence post. She bent and picked it up. It was dusty and she blew on it. It must have come from the ravens on the roof of the cabin. They had flown off but the shiny black was beautiful against the palm of her hand.

"Your horses are pretty," she said to the boy. It was a limp conversation opener, but she didn't have anything better at that moment.

He was looking at her, wide eyed, and Madison realized that it was quite possible he had never spoken to a police officer.

"I'm Alice Madison," she said, but she looked straight ahead because something told her the father wouldn't have wanted her to talk to his boy. "What's your name?"

The boy didn't answer. He just stood there, pouring the horses' feed from a bucket into the metal contraption. After a second something came over him and he climbed onto the fence and shook the grains at the bottom of the bucket into the feeder.

Madison reached out and stroked the hard place between the horse's eyes. Maybe the boy had been instructed by his father not to talk to strangers—it wouldn't surprise her one bit if that had been the case.

"Samuel," the boy said, so quietly that it could have been the breeze. "I'm Samuel."

Madison's heart sped up and she almost tripped on her racing thoughts, because there was too much she wanted to ask and no time to ask it. "Samuel," she said, and the words rushed out before she could think them through. "We're here to help you. Do you understand what I mean? We're here to help you."

Why had she just said that when in fact they were there on a murder case? When the fate of Jeb Tanner's children was not the business of the Seattle Police Department?

The boy picked up a stick from the ground and poked a knot of hay that had gotten stuck. He nodded, or maybe it was only Madison's imagination.

"Did you ask for help? Do you know if one of your brothers asked Dr. Dennen for help?" she whispered as she patted the horse's neck.

The boy shook his head.

Madison should have asked him about his father's alibi, she should have asked him about the previous day. Instead something else fluttered into her chest. "How many of you are there? How many brothers and sisters?"

Madison could hear Brown and Tanner speaking behind her by the barn door and tried to gauge their distance and whether they were coming closer. Tanner had eluded her question, he had not answered, and as Madison turned to look there were only shadows behind the cabin's windows.

It seemed as if Samuel would not, or could not, answer. And then—when Madison had lost hope and the silence between them had stretched to over a minute—the boy dragged the tip of his stick through the mud by the horse's hooves.

12

The number remained etched in the dirt for a heartbeat and then the boy scraped it away.

"How many under eighteen years old?"

It occurred to Madison then that she should stop that very instant. What would happen to the boy if the father found out he was telling her anything at all about the family?

Samuel thought about it for a while, and Madison realized that he was counting in his head. People's ages, people's names. At last, he scribbled.

6

And just as quickly that number was scraped off too.

"Thank you. How old are you, Samuel?"

15

How much time did they have? What should she ask him?

"Is there anything you'd like to tell me? Anything I could help you with?"

"There's something you should know," Brown said to Jeb Tanner as they left the barn and he paused by the door. It was a kind of confidence, not quite a secret but definitely something that should only pass between the two men.

When he had the man's attention, Brown continued and his voice was soft in the open yard. "Chief Sangster is going around telling people that you argued with both victims before they were murdered. With the doctor because he wanted you to take your kids to the clinic. And with Edwards because of I don't know what business in the man's store. Seems to me he just hates your stinking guts and is trying to find evidence against you."

Tanner blinked. "He's been saying that, has he?"

"Yes. My partner and I think we should look elsewhere, but the questions have been raised. Is it true you had a confrontation with the doctor and with Ty Edwards?"

Tanner's eyes were pinpoints of hard blue. "You live in a place long enough and you'll end up disagreeing with this person or that person, Detective. That's just human nature. The doctor was obsessed with talking to my children, with finding fault with how I'm raising my family. He's got his own ideas . . . had his own ideas about how a family should be run, and I have mine. I don't go around to his place telling him to take away his kids' computers and their televisions, and he shouldn't come to my home to tell me how to raise my flesh and blood."

Tanner shook his head. "Ty Edwards sold me a cracked tire gauge. Probably didn't realize he had. We argued about it and he wouldn't exchange it. I left. He was a decent man, and I'm sorry he's dead, but I'm not going to kill a man over a cracked tire gauge. Do you know anybody who would?"

Brown smiled: Jeb Tanner's questions were never straightforward. "You would be surprised," he said.

There was no sun in the sky but the low clouds were washed-out white and heavy, and they filled the sky from one end of the horizon to the other.

"There's something else," Brown said, "and there's not much I can do about it . . ."

Jeb Tanner's temper was a foul thing, and Brown knew that—within ten minutes of meeting the man. He had no problem nudging him into a fit, and yet he didn't want to provoke him into taking it out on his family.

"There was blood recovered at the scene of one of the murders, and it doesn't match the victim's. Chief Sangster is working on a warrant to get you tested."

Brown wanted—needed—Tanner's reaction to this more than he needed his alibi. A DNA test in court in the hands of the right prosecutor is as good as a color picture of the defendant at the crime scene.

Tanner's sleeves were rolled up and his arms were bare. He didn't appear to feel the cold at all. His skin, which was February pale, was crisscrossed by old scars. "Why are you telling me this?"

"Because you might want to get that test done and get Sang-ster off your back."

"What's it to you?"

"It's a distraction and I have a double murder to deal with. If you did the test for exclusion purposes we could all get on with our jobs, and the chief would have to stop harassing you."

Tanner bent down and picked up a handful of dry earth. He crumbled it and let it slip through his fingers. The breeze picked it up and it blew away.

"There's going to be a snowstorm, Detective. You'd better get back into town, you don't want to get stuck up here on Jackknife. People have been known to get lost in the whiteout a couple of yards from their own front doors. Never made it back."

"That's a shame," Brown said, and they both knew what he meant.

"I don't trust the chief, Detective Brown, and quite frankly I don't really know what to make of you and your partner with the knife skills. I think it would be a dangerous thing to give the chief anything that he wants, because he will try and crucify me with it, even if I'm innocent."

"You have an alibi for both murders."

"I do, but I wouldn't be the first innocent man put in jail."

"If you do the test, I'll get Sangster off your back myself."

"You'll go back to Seattle, and the chief will find a way to twist the science to fit his purpose, as most men like him do. He's a liar in a world of liars."

Brown couldn't disagree with him; today they all lived in that world.

Madison put her hand in her pocket and extracted one of her business cards—she always made sure she had some ready for that particular purpose—and then she stopped. Even if she managed to pass her card to the boy, he wouldn't have any way to call her because they didn't have a telephone; he wouldn't be able to write to her because he would have to mail the letters. Someone had already tried that—and he or she had needed to resort to cloth and charcoal.

"I'm staying in Ludlow, at the Miller house. Alice Madison." Steps were coming up behind them. "Is there anything you want to tell me?"

The boy didn't reply. The stick carved stripes and crosses in the mud, and then Brown said, "We're done here." And there was nothing else she could do.

Samuel's eyes had glazed over and he looked as hollow as his brothers had. Madison understood—it was the look of someone who doesn't want to draw any attention to himself, who wants to blend into the landscape and disappear.

"Thank you for your help, Mr. Tanner," she forced herself to say.

A single snowflake floated down between them and onto the frozen ground.

"They're coming back. They're in the car. They're leaving the yard right now."

The SWAT officers followed the pickup's journey, and as the car reached the forest they backed away from the tree line. Once far enough away from the edge, they stood and dashed back to the truck. The dirt road was so difficult to navigate that the officers were the first to arrive.

The drive was quiet. There was much to absorb, and both Brown and Madison needed the silence to metabolize what they had learned on the farm, almost as the brain needs sleep to process the memories of the day. They just exchanged one look when the pickup left the dirt path and turned into the concrete road that would take them back to Ludlow: they were leaving a fragment of the county that existed in a different time zone—and it was not about the lack of electricity or running water. Jackknife Farm lived in medieval times because of Jeb Tanner: nothing had troubled Madison as much as the lack of the unsettled energy of youth in Tanner's sons. She had seen four of them, but somewhere on the farm there were other children. Many others. If she closed her eyes she could still see the number carved in the mud. *Twelve*.

Madison knew Jeb Tanner's kind, knew what that type of man could mean in the life of a child. How easy that life could be twisted and bent out of shape by someone like him.

She needed light, she needed the memory of something good, and her thoughts went back to the boy, Samuel, holding his little brother and the feel of the horse's brow under her fingertips—the coarse, short chestnut hair. Just then, Madison reached into her coat; there was the black feather she had picked up in the farmyard. It had found its way into her pocket, and for no logical reason at all Madison was glad of it.

Chapter 35

Samuel had been the first to hear it: the sound of engines in the distance. A car, maybe two. Someone was coming. Someone had driven through the gate and onto their land. As far as he knew they were not expecting anyone, and the notion of another break in the routine almost made him dizzy with expectation.

It happened quickly. His father sent everyone inside, except for the four of them—David had been playing on the steps and his father had scooped him up before Abigail or Elisabeth could take him. Luke and Jonah had come back with their rifles and they had all waited in the barn to see who would appear on their doorstep.

"Stay here," his father had said, and Samuel had obeyed.

The voices had drifted into the barn and the boy had crept to the door, leaning against it, watching the visitors as the argument escalated. He couldn't guess what they were arguing about and there were words he didn't understand at all. He had seen one of the police officers before, but not the other ones, and the pair who were not wearing a uniform were nearly exotic to the boy for the quiet way they appeared not to be concerned by his father's temper. They stood and listened and talked back, when anyone in their right mind would have shut up or fled altogether.

Occasionally Samuel had seen women he was not related to before—acquaintances of his father who had come by the farm, like Mrs. Clay, who smelled like cookies, or Mrs. Taylor, who sold them propane—but he had never seen anyone like her. The woman in his yard looked his father in the eye and spoke to him like an equal. Samuel could read his father's mood from the angle of his shoulders and the stiffness in his back, and he didn't like what he saw.

When some of the visitors left and the others moved toward the barn, he backed away from the door. He was grateful to take David away because the boy was beginning to cry—he gave him to Abigail, ducked her questions, and returned to the barn. He was grateful that no one looked at him or spoke to him and that to them, even to the two strangers, he was no more than a bale of hay.

Samuel tried to follow the conversation, but there was too much that appeared to belong in a world he had no experience of, and all of it made him nervous.

Were they after his father? What had he done?

He considered it, and the answer was relatively simple; nevertheless, for Samuel it carried the weight of his whole world. His father could have done anything, anything at all. If laws existed that could stop him, the boy didn't know about them.

Moods ebbed and flowed. When Samuel prepared the bucket for the horses' feeder, he felt reassured that things in the barn had mellowed.

"Your horses are pretty," said the woman leaning against the paddock's rail.

Samuel was only going to finish pouring the feed into the bin and leave, he wasn't going to look at her or speak to her, except that he did look. He looked, and in the palm of her hand there was a raven feather.

He had asked for a sign. He had asked for a way to tell good people from bad people. In the palm of this woman he had never seen before, who had come to him from a world of killers, beggars, and thieves, Samuel saw what he needed to see.

Chapter 36

Brown and Madison radioed Chief Sangster, and the cruiser and pickup headed straight for the Clay residence. The SWAT truck hit the highway at full legal speed on its way out of Colville County even before the others had reached the turn of the Clays' driveway.

By the time the chief rang the doorbell the snowflakes were falling like so much shredded confetti, and it was clear that very soon no one would be going anywhere.

The Clays lived in the current time zone and whatever it was that had cemented a friendship with Jeb Tanner was not immediately visible. Their home looked like any other in Ludlow, and they certainly lived their lives with the benefits of electricity and running water. They talked in the kitchen while the deputies waited outside; a small flat-screen television sat on the counter next to the blender. The odds of the Clays not knowing about the doctor's murder when Tanner had turned up to help fix their truck were pretty much infinitesimal.

"We went to school together," Will Clay said. "Lost touch for a while but when he came back to town with his family, we picked it up again. Jeb does things his own way but that's not a crime in a free country, is it?"

Will Clay and his wife worked in Sherman Falls but had kept the family home in Ludlow. The investigators had to consider that Clay would tell Tanner of their visit and thus appearances had to be kept up: Brown and Sangster ignored each other, and Madison conducted the interview.

"No, sir, it sure isn't," she said. "Have you heard about the death of Dr. Dennen and the shooting in the square yesterday?"

"Yes, we were shocked."

Mrs. Clay looked genuinely upset; she fluttered around the modern kitchen making coffee and getting out mugs. She was willowy and blonde where her husband was stocky and brown haired.

"You didn't go to the vigil?"

"No, car broke down the night before."

"Right. And Mr. Tanner came to help you fix it."

"Right."

"How did you call him?"

"What do you mean?"

Clay knew exactly what Madison had meant. His wife had turned away to busy herself in the pantry.

"If your car broke down in the evening, how did you contact Mr. Tanner to come and help you the following morning? We understand that he doesn't own a telephone."

"He doesn't."

"Maybe he owns a cell phone for emergencies?"

"Not that I know of."

"Then how did he know to come and help you?"

"He just happened to come by. He sometimes comes over for a chat on a Saturday morning, and when he stopped by yesterday he helped me with the truck. He's very good at fixing things."

"That's what we heard," Madison said. "What time did he arrive?"

The Clays looked at each other. "About ten?" he said.

"About ten," Mrs. Clay said to Madison.

"And when did he leave?"

"Around one o'clock," Mr. Clay said.

"And you managed to fix the truck?"

"Oh yes, wouldn't want to be without it in this," and he waved at the window. The snow had begun to stick.

"Why are you asking us about Jeb?" Mrs. Clay said.

"We're trying to work out where everybody was who wasn't at the vigil," Madison replied.

"You're looking in the wrong place," she said. "It's going to be some crazy person, like the ones who shoot up the schools."

"We're keeping an open mind," Madison said in her friendliest voice. "But we have to ask questions in order to exclude people from the investigation."

"By the same account you should be asking where *we* were yesterday, shouldn't you?" Mr. Clay said.

Madison smiled as she stood to go. "You were with Mr. Tanner, weren't you?"

Deputy Hockley had been eyeballing his colleague in the rearview mirror ever since the chief had stepped on the gas at Jackknife Farm and driven back to the gate like he'd been bitten by a rabid fox. Kupitz had watched the meeting with Jeb Tanner play out, and even if he kind of knew what was going to happen he was still uneasy about the exchanges between the chief and the Seattle detectives.

"You okay, Koop?" Hockley said.

"Yes," Kupitz replied, but his eyes stayed on the falling snow. There was nothing to look at in the Clays' front yard aside from a rickety birdfeeder.

"You understand that things happened exactly the way they wanted them to happen, right? That it was a setup?"

"Uh-huh."

"What's eating you, then?"

Kupitz shrugged.

Hockley felt like he was talking to his younger brother, who was sixteen. Hell, his younger brother was more grown-up than Kupitz any day of the week, and twice on Sunday.

Still, Hockley couldn't let it go. "What, then?"

Kupitz looked like he was wrestling with ideas bigger than his brain could contain and he was on the losing side. "I know that it was a setup," he said, "but it felt like it could really be real, you know. Like they were really that nasty with the chief."

"They didn't mean it, you dope."

"Well, they could have."

"He was pleased as punch when we got out of there, didn't you see?"

"I guess."

"Koop, you slay me, man. You really do," he said, and to make his friend feel better he punched him on the arm.

"Quit it," Kupitz grumbled, but his heart wasn't in it.

"Do you think Tanner owns a cell phone?" Sangster said as they walked back to their cars.

"Yes, and I bet you anything Clay called him on it," Madison said.

"Why would he lie about it?"

"I don't know. Thing is, whether he does or he doesn't, it doesn't necessarily have an impact on the alibi. It would look shifty in court, but a good defense attorney could come up with fifty different reasons why Tanner didn't want it known he had a cell." Madison wondered what Quinn would do with a Tanner defense, and something in her hoped that Nathan Quinn would not have taken his case in the first place.

It would be an interesting conversation the next time they spoke.

They pulled out of the driveway slowly and carefully, and Brown felt the snow sticking on the road in the steering of the pickup. The sky above them was nothing but white.

* * *

Amy Sorensen looked out the window of the senior center. In her heart she knew that they were going to get snow at some point during the trip and the question was purely when and how much. She was sitting at her desk in the main room, going through the record books from Ludlow Outfitters. She wasn't looking forward to telling Brown and Madison that she had checked under the Tanner family name—they were the only Tanners in Ludlow—and there was no record of them ever buying a length of white fabric that matched the cloth of the message.

Jeb Tanner had bought patterned fabric and solid-colored fabric that could have been used for clothing or upholstery, but nothing white. And, Sorensen had noted, the last purchase had been made four years earlier by Mrs. Naomi Tanner, who must have busied herself with sewing and quilting before deciding that enough was enough and leaving her husband and children to return to California.

Sorensen didn't want to be flippant, and it wasn't in her nature to be cynical, but she had been staring at lines of numbers and cloth swatches for one hour. She would much rather have been elbow deep in garbage—someone's garbage would tell her more than a psychologist would find out in a year—or possibly tracking a questionable fingerprint that needed to be eye matched. Fabric swatches were not where her interest lay, and what she was trying to do—finding out who in town, if anyone at all, had bought the white fabric—was very likely going to be a wild-goose chase. And, she mused, she didn't like geese in the first place.

What remained of the rifle that had shot Ty Edwards a day earlier lay in the waters of the Bow River not a mile away from the square where the shooting had taken place. The owner had field-stripped it and disposed of the various pieces in the freezing, fast-running waters minutes after the shooting. Some—the lightest items—were already miles away, while other components had come to rest between and under the rocks that formed the bottom of the riverbed.

The owner had accomplished much in a short period of time because he was not the kind who would dawdle and because it wouldn't do to hesitate at such times, when the hand of fate could so easily fall this way or that.

A good winter frost would ice the top of the river, and the rifle would remain under its glassy cover. By the time anybody might recover the various pieces, everything and anything that had connected the carbine to its lawful owner would have been washed away by the river, cleansed by the rushing stream. It was good to know that the pieces were there, a few hundred yards from the police station, mocking the investigators and all their efforts. The pieces were there, but it was far too late for anyone to put them back together.

Chapter 37

"Hi," Madison said into her cell.

"Hi," Nathan Quinn said, and she could tell that he was surprised to hear her voice. "What happened? Where are you?"

"I'm stretching my legs. We had a pretty useful morning and we're about to regroup, but there's a serious snowfall on the way and the chief needed ten minutes to work out road closures and safety warnings."

"And you're stretching your legs out in the storm?"

"Yup, snow's nice and dry. I'm standing by the bridge at the end of Main Street and I can barely see the other end."

Quinn knew that Madison ran in all weathers and in all seasons. A walk in the fresh snow was not a surprise.

"Did you meet the guy?"

"Oh yes, we met the guy, and he's swell."

"Still the prime suspect?"

"You bet."

"Alibi?"

"He's got two: one for each murder."

"Doesn't that exonerate him, Detective?"

"Possibly but not definitely. I'm not convinced one hundred percent by either. The first one is supported by his kids, and they're terrified of him, and the second by an old friend who might be lying about something else, anyway . . ."

Quinn didn't jump in. He wasn't the kind of person who needed to fill in silences. She could hear indistinct sounds around him. Where was he, anyway? Madison was reluctant to ask.

"I'm having lunch with Carl," Quinn said. "I'm meeting him at the restaurant and I just got here."

There was only one restaurant that didn't need to be named—The Rock—a business that Quinn had inherited from his father and that was still trading on Alki Beach. Quinn had nothing to do with the daily running of it, but there were long-established sentimental ties that often brought him back. Carl Doyle had been Quinn's assistant, years earlier, and he now managed a different law practice with his usual combination of velvet manners and steel discipline. Madison had met him and liked him enormously.

"I'll let you go," she said, and stopped herself from saying, *Say hi to Carl from me!* Because, like the rest of the universe, Carl had no idea that Madison and Quinn were seeing each other—whatever that meant.

"No, wait, tell me about the guy," Quinn said.

"He's still the prime suspect," she said, and raised her face to the sky, where layers of white shifted and changed. "I think we have a potential child abuse situation. He's got twelve kids up at the farm and—"

"Twelve?"

"Twelve," she said. "We've met four, and they all appear to tread very lightly around him. I've seen those kinds of situations before. I know that kind of man."

"You're going to have to be—"

"I know, I *am* being careful."

"It's not what I was going to say," Quinn said quietly. "If the children are part of his alibi, if he's somehow made them accomplices in a double murder or accessories after the fact, you need to watch out for their rights versus his rights, and it could be a godforsaken mess for everybody involved."

"I have absolutely no doubt that it's going to be a mess. He's . . . he's got his hooks into those kids, I can tell." If it was strange to make such a statement about someone she had only met for a short time, neither Quinn nor Madison seemed to notice. He trusted her judgment and, as much as her judgment, he trusted her gut reaction to people. It had saved more than his life—in ways he couldn't begin to explain to her.

"I hope you're wearing your vest," he said, only half in jest.

"I am," she replied, and then her voice changed. "I've been thinking about the case, the alibis, this man's family, and I was wondering . . ." She didn't know how to ask the question, and yet she couldn't not ask. "When you were a defense attorney, did you ever turn down a case because you didn't want to represent a client?"

"What brought this on?"

"I've been thinking about what would make the prosecution's case vulnerable, and how a good attorney would exploit those weaknesses."

"I see."

It occurred to Madison then that, while other couples had to steer their new lives together around former lovers and husbands, in her relationship with Quinn they had to navigate around their respective legal, criminal, and law enforcement pasts.

"Yes and no," Quinn replied.

"Okay."

"It was a murder case. It was particularly gruesome, and I did not want the case because I didn't even want to be in the same room as the defendant. I decided that I wouldn't be an effective advocate and let someone else in my firm take it."

"Was he guilty?"

"She was. The defendant was a woman. Yes, she pleaded guilty to a lesser charge just before the jury verdict."

"You don't sound happy about how it turned out."

"I am; she'll never be free again. But I should have been able to represent her effectively, whatever the crime."

"If *you* had represented her effectively, Counselor, she would still be on the streets."

"Both flattery and censure in the same breath." Quinn was smiling.

"It was neither. I've seen you in court. I just hope Jeb Tanner won't have anyone half as good as you on his side."

"You've already decided that he's the killer."

Madison tried to stay entirely objective, and it was not easy. "He's something, Quinn. I'm not exactly sure what he is, but he is *something*."

After they hung up Madison paused for a moment by the edge of the bridge and then turned back toward the police HQ. None of the stores were open, and she couldn't see far enough to determine whether the Tavern and the Magpie Diner were in business. It was Sunday lunchtime under a moderate to heavy snowfall, and downtown Ludlow was shut down.

As she passed the radio station Ben Taylor, the DJ, waved at her from his seat by the decks, behind the window. Madison waved back. Two days in town and she was already a local.

Jeb Tanner needed to be alone and think over what had happened. Solitary work in one of the outbuildings was not going to be enough. As he had often found at times of distress—he was not distressed, he told himself, he had *concerns*—he needed to put some distance between himself and everyone else, to clear his mind and get some perspective.

He had grabbed his coat, left Luke in charge—as per usual—and had taken the path that led to the pass, with the pretext of checking on a trap before the snow set too deep.

Samuel had already led the horses back into the barn, but Tanner told Jonah to saddle his own chestnut mare and he was out and riding before there was hardly more than a dusting of fresh white on the ground. The horse's hooves on the frozen ground hushed the birds in the trees and Tanner rode into the silence.

Chief Sangster had behaved in the manner he had come to expect from him; perhaps the presence of the detectives had made him even more obtuse than normal—if that were possible. The other two were more of an unknown quantity. They were happy to throw their big-city weight around, that was clear, but they were also clever, and Tanner didn't like clever. He had played their silly game and given them the alibis they wanted; nevertheless, there was much more to them than they let on.

One thing that pleased him was that his children had learned about the death of the doctor from someone other than himself, and they could draw their own conclusions. Dennen had come onto his land more than once and had made his crazy demands, then he'd sent a lackey from County Hall and hoped to crack open his resolve. And where were they now? His children had heard what happened to those who opposed him, and that was good—they should know. They had no idea what kind of twisted, perverted world he was protecting them from. And the boundary lay just beyond their gate.

Tanner nudged the mare with his heels. The path opened to a wide view of the rolling valley: the horizon was streaked with snow, and soon the stretches of brown earth would disappear.

It took him twenty minutes to get there: a clearing with an overhanging boulder, halfway between the farm and the Jackknife mine. He led the horse to stand by a dry area under the rock and dismounted. It was a bleak little corner—hardly ever in the sun, even in the summer, because of the boulder. It was dark and humid, and the soil stayed damp with morning frost all day. The kids didn't like that spot because of an old legend that the soil was watered by the blood and the tears of the dead Jackknife miners. Tanner liked it well enough, though. And that day he needed to be there to reassure himself that all the talk of double murder would amount to nothing.

A double murder was the kind of thing a lesser cop like Sangster might think of building a career on. Jeb Tanner was not in the least intimidated by the Ludlow chief of police; however, he was keen that the chief's stupidity and greed would not lead him to his own door. The doctor got what he deserved, and the other man got what was coming to him. It was a simple lesson in life, and clearly they had to learn it the hard way. What goes around.

Tanner thought of the woman detective and her deer story. Maybe it had really happened, maybe not. There was a lesson on Jackknife for her to learn too; she just didn't know it yet.

Jeb Tanner always carried the Remington 870 he had inherited from his father when he went more than a hundred feet from the compound. It would have been foolish not to, and he was not a foolish man. For the sheer pleasure of it he pumped the action twice to slide a cartridge into the chamber. It made a *snick-snick* sound that he loved. *Some lessons*, he mused, *have to be taught—whether they want to be learned or not.*

After a few minutes in his quiet place, Tanner got back on the horse and rode home.

Everything was just as it should be.

The moment his father was out of sight of the farm, Samuel let out the breath he had been holding. He didn't know why the woman police officer had asked him those specific questions. However, her intention had been clear: she meant to help. It went against everything they had been taught. She didn't look like a killer, a beggar, or a thief—she looked ...

The boy couldn't find words to describe her. *She looked like she meant what she said* was the best he could come up with.

Samuel looked around the cabin: it had never crossed his mind to count his brothers and sisters. What an odd question that was. And how curious that the woman officer—he should call her by her name, Alice—had been interested in their ages. It had taken Samuel a little while to sort it out in his head, and he had been afraid that she would walk away from him before he had a chance to answer her question. There were twelve of them: Luke, Seth, Joshua, Jonah, Abigail, Caleb, Jesse, Samuel, Elisabeth, Ruth, Sarah, and David. Luke was twenty-five, David was four. Everyone else was in between. At present Luke was making sure the cows were settled before the storm; Seth and Joshua were feeding the pigs; Jonah and Jesse were stocking the wood stove; and Abigail was running his younger sisters ragged around the house. *And Caleb*, Samuel thought. Caleb was somewhere, somewhere nearby. The boy knew it in his heart.

Their father had been gone for half an hour and the snow had made the yard light where it had been murky, and soft where it had been stark. Jesse was pushing for a snowball fight, and Luke gave in because it was Sunday, but mostly because it made him feel superior to be able to grant something when he was still shaken about what he'd overheard in the barn.

They all spilled out of the cabin in a rush of energy. As always, Jesse was the loudest and Jonah the quietest. Ruth and Sarah, ten and six, were fast on their feet and impossible to catch. Seth and Joshua, who were not twins but might as well have been, engaged in a furious battle and rolled small, hard snowballs that flew like missiles between them.

Abigail, holding David lest he get hit by mistake, sidled up to Samuel. "Who was that woman?" she whispered.

"A police officer," he replied.

"What do they want from Papa?"

Samuel shrugged. "I don't know." It was the truth, although it was less than the full truth.

Abigail reached over and ruffled Samuel's hair with a gentle hand. "Don't make Papa punish you, Samuel," she said, her voice low and serious. "I worry about you."

"Don't, I'll be as quiet as a mouse."

She kissed the top of David's head while he was wriggling and trying to get free and into the snowball fight. "Is it true the doctor is dead?" she said.

Samuel nodded.

Abigail sighed and hugged the little boy tighter. She would soon go back inside because under her coat she was only wearing a long skirt and a shirt that she had fashioned from an old dress, as white as the flowing sky.

With remarkable timing Luke called out for everyone to get back inside just before their father turned the bend in the path. That kind of play was frivolous and, though not forbidden, it was discouraged and almost a dereliction of his supervisory duties.

Jonah was the first to obey, because he always did what he was told.

Chapter 38

Working a double murder did not release Chief Sangster from his normal duties, and after they returned from interviewing the Clays, he managed the closing of three roads and two thoroughfares that would be either completely impracticable or too dangerous to pass if the snowfall continued as predicted. Admittedly, the closing of a road only entailed Deputies Hockley or Kupitz stretching the ROAD CLOSED sign across it, but quite frankly, with everything else that was going on, working out where the signs had been stored and how to split the work between the two deputies was as much as he wanted to handle.

Any distraction from the case was to be put on the back burner. And if someone else turned up about a missing dog, he would—

Sangster stopped himself midthought: the missing dog had been taken by the killer, and Lee Edwards was at home mourning her dead husband. It occurred to him that he should go visit her—or that, at the very least, he should call her to make sure that someone was with her. It was the kind of thing Polly would have been good at. But Polly didn't work on Sundays.

"Twelve," Madison said. "And six are minors."

"It's not illegal to have a big family," Brown said.

"One of them asked the doc for help."

"Allegedly."

"There's no record of anyone in the Tanner family buying the white cloth from the outfitters," Sorensen said. "But it's definitely the same cloth. I have a sample, and they're a perfect match."

The blinds of the senior center were open because the streets were deserted, and nobody felt like entombing themselves in a lavender-scented vault.

"Does Tanner buy fabric there? I wouldn't have taken him for the quilting type," Madison said.

"He's not, but his wife was. She made a lot of stuff for the kids."

"Is it worth trying to reach her? How long ago was the divorce?"

Brown consulted his notes. "The papers were filed from California, came through about two years ago. I could find out the attorney's number and her address."

"How old was the little boy? Three, maybe four years old?"

"Yes, about four years old," Brown said.

"Whatever happened between her and Tanner must have been quite something to up and leave. She was quitting the kids, as well as the marriage."

"I've seen a mother leave a toddler in an Emergency Room and move to another state," Sorensen said. "We worked on what the child was wearing for a month to find out where he was from, and we got zip. We only caught up with the mother a year later; she was living in Indiana with her new beau."

"That's just . . ." Madison could not find the words for how depressing that story was, but Sorensen was smiling.

"What?" Madison said.

"The boy is doing great. He was fostered by the nurse who found him in the ER, who adopted him legally three years ago. He's in Little League. I still get pictures."

Madison blew out air from her cheeks.

"Tanner's ex hasn't even visited for years," Brown said. "The last person who spoke to her was the woman who owns the diner. She called from California to say she wasn't coming back. She wouldn't be able to tell us anything about what happened here four days ago."

"I concur," Sorensen said. "What's happening with the warrant for the DNA test?"

Brown and Madison had briefed Sorensen on the morning's events and the failure of getting Tanner to agree to a test. In terms of DNA the only positive news they'd had so far was that the dried blood Madison had recovered from the clinic had been a match to the doctor's.

"There was no way in hell Tanner would have agreed," Madison said. "But we had to try."

"Nothing is going to get through this today." Brown waved at the window and at the weather behind it. "Hopefully tomorrow."

"Tanner is under no doubt that the warrant is coming. It's just a question of when."

"You know," Brown said, as he leaned back in his chair, "it was clear that he wasn't going to agree to it, but it didn't feel as if he was overly worried about it. I mean, he told me that he thought the chief would try to fix it and make him look guilty when he wasn't."

Sorensen, outraged by the notion, looked up from her fabric records book. "That's not how testing works. I like the chief but he has more chance of becoming an astronaut and walking on the moon than he has of manipulating short tandem repeat sequences and *fixing* a DNA test."

Sorensen and Madison had listened to the same words, but Madison had heard something different. "You think he believes the test wouldn't be a match," she said. "You think Tanner thinks Sangster would fix it, because the test would prove the blood at the scene is not Tanner's."

Brown didn't reply straightaway. He had picked up on Madison's tone—for her, it seemed, there was only one possible result to the test. It would be a match for Tanner, and it would put him at the crime scene where Robert Dennen had died. The medical file would then link the two murders, and those would be the first nails that would pop the defense's balloon.

Brown toyed with his glasses. "I'm not so sure that, when we get him to submit to the test, we will achieve the result we desire," he said. "He wasn't happy to talk to police officers, whatever their badge or jurisdiction, but he was intrigued by us and entertained by the spat with the chief. He didn't seem particularly anxious about the murders. His game was to tell us as little as possible, and make us dance for it."

"That's not how I read it," Madison said. Then again, while Brown had been exchanging confidences with Tanner about his relationship with the victims, she had been trying to weasel information out of a boy who might—even as they were speaking, in the relative comfort and warmth of the senior center—be in terrible trouble if his father had found out.

Brown met Madison's eyes. "I'm not so sure that, when we get him to submit to the test, we should hope for one result over the other."

Over two years working Homicide side by side and he was still telling her to *keep an open mind*. At the beginning of their partnership Madison would have felt stung by his assumption that she might not, but today she checked her tongue. She knew what she knew about Jeb Tanner, and it wasn't something that she could easily share with Brown. She busied herself with making a list of things that the deputies might help them with—like identifying, for exclusion purposes, every resident caught by their cameras and the footage of the news channel taken in the square.

When Sorensen went back to her instruments in the next room, Madison took over flipping the pages of the fabric records book, looking for a purchase of white cloth. *That's what they make surrendering flags out of,* she muttered to herself.

Brown, who knew better than to press an unsolicited point with his younger partner, let her be.

The call came twenty minutes later. Madison saw the caller's ID on her cell screen and replied with a circumspect *hello*.

"Detective," the dark voice said, "It's Nathan Quinn."

Madison knew then that it would be bad news and the call was official business.

"Judge Eugene," Quinn continued, "has rejected the warrant for the DNA test. I'm sure Chief Sangster is going to be informed by my counterpart, but I thought you should also know as soon as possible."

"He what?"

"He rejected the warrant application," Quinn repeated.

About a dozen words rose to Madison's lips, but only one got through. "Why?"

"In his words, there wasn't enough for probable cause. Give him more and he might rethink."

"We gave him plenty. There's a history of conflict, there's—"

"I did not make the decision, Detective."

"This—" Madison tried to stem the flow of profanities that was threatening to spill over. "This is *really* not helpful," she said.

"Luck of the draw. Judge Eugene is tight with his warrants and a friend of the Fourth Amendment."

"So am I. I love the Fourth Amendment. It's my favorite amendment. But no DNA test also means no warrant to search the Tanner farm, right?"

"That's correct."

Madison stood, because some news is just too frustrating to hear sitting down. "We need those warrants. We can't go back there with a quip and a smile. We need legal handcuffs that will let us search Tanner's property with a very small sieve."

"I understand your frustration."

Madison was about to snap her reply, but she didn't. It wasn't Quinn's fault, and it wouldn't be professional or, more important, kind to jump up and down when he had valiantly brought her news that he knew would upset her.

"I know, I know you do," she said finally. "Thank you for calling. We'll find more, there has to be more ..."

Brown took off his glasses and rubbed his eyes with his fists, like a child. He had grasped the gist of the call.

Probable cause is the grail of warrants and searches—without it, any seizure is deemed illegal—and Madison couldn't so much as peek through the window and inside Tanner's cabin without him slapping her with a harassment suit if it pleased him. And there was no question that it would have pleased him very much indeed.

"We need a list of Tanner's gun permits," Madison said, because she needed to do something achievable, something that would help dissipate her temper. "The sons had a rifle each, and there might be more lying around the place."

Brown reached for his laptop. "I'm going to look at family connections."

The door of the senior center flew open and Chief Sangster rushed in from the road. His shoulders and the brim of his hat were white. He opened his mouth to tell them about Judge Eugene; however, one look around the room told him they already knew.

Deputy Hockley's pickup inched its way up Main Street and stopped by the Magpie Diner. A misty glow from behind the window told anyone who was foolish enough to be walking in the flurry that the diner was open for business—the combination of a Puritan work ethic and an owner who lived three minutes away. In truth, Joyce Cartwell was not in the mood to stay at home by herself. If she was going to be alone, she'd rather be in the diner, where there was at least the potential for unexpected company.

Brown and Madison covered the few steps from the car to the door, leaning against the wind.

"I'm impressed," Joyce said with a smile, keeping her place in the book she was reading with her finger. "I'd have thought you were more the phone-and-delivery types."

"We're indomitable," Brown said. "Especially when sent on the lunch run."

Madison decided to let them get on with it. She perched on a stool, took a menu from a holder, and pretended to read while Brown and Joyce Cartwell agreed that the weather was really something, wasn't it? And wouldn't you know it, just when spring was around the corner. Brown had in his pocket the lunch order for the whole Ludlow police force plus Sorensen, and he was jousting his way to it.

"What can I get you?" Joyce said. "I'm only doing cold today, but yesterday's meat loaf alone is worth the walk in the snow."

The meat loaf had been prepared by the cook in anticipation of a busy afternoon after the vigil. In the end, the diner had been full but few customers had been hungry.

Brown took out the piece of paper and flattened it on the counter with the palm of his hand.

"Here . . ." he said, and rattled off each request for food, drinks, and coffees. "There's something else," he said, and Madison looked up. "I'd like to ask you about your brother, Jeb Tanner, if it's okay."

Joyce Cartwell sighed, as if she had hoped against hope that the question wouldn't come but had always known that, ultimately, it would. "He hasn't been my brother for a long time," she said, and she began to gather what she needed to make the sandwiches.

"You're not in touch?"

"No, not for years."

"May I ask why? Since you're the only family he has in town."

Brown's questions were so calm, and his tone so gentle, that Madison made herself very still and—she hoped—invisible, because there was something there, she could tell, and for what they wanted she hoped that Joyce Cartwell hated her brother's guts.

"Jeb has never been that great with family," Joyce said.

"What do you mean?"

The woman hesitated. "Why do you want to talk about Jeb? Is he connected to what happened?"

"That's what we're trying to work out, but Mr. Tanner isn't an easy man to speak with."

Joyce smiled, and there wasn't much mirth in it. "I bet."

"People fall out for all kinds of reasons," Brown said. "And we don't want to pry into your personal business. But chances are that you're the person in Ludlow who knows him best, and it would be really useful if we could find out a little about him so that we're in a better position to get him to open up to us—to talk about what happened."

"Jeb isn't the kind of person who opens up to anyone, not really. And if he did, I'd be terrified of what I'd find inside. I don't want anything to do with him, and even talking with you about him is—"

"Dangerous?" Brown said.

"Yes."

"Has he threatened you?"

"He doesn't need to threaten me."

"Because . . ."

"We're not in each other's lives, haven't been since he came back after our father died. It suits us both."

Joyce was assembling the food as if it were her one connection to all that was safe and good. Her hands trembled a little as she pressed down on the blade.

"Have you met his wife?" Brown said.

"Ex-wife, from what I've heard. Barely. We met once by chance in a shop. Jeb was never big on get-togethers."

"So you haven't met his children."

Something flickered in the woman's face. "No, I haven't."

Brown's eyes were sharp and yet kind with it. "He has twelve children living with him on the mountain."

Joyce's breath caught. "I didn't know."

"You didn't know he had such a big family?"

She nodded.

"Should we be concerned for his children?"

"Are you asking me if he is a better father to them than he was a brother to me? I'm quite sure I don't know the answer to that question. And he wouldn't thank me for talking to you about the past."

"He doesn't have a record—not here or in California." Brown was treading very lightly. "But it doesn't mean that there isn't a history of trouble," he said. "A history of violence."

Joyce didn't look up from her work.

"Is there anything that you could tell us that would help us deal with the situation?"

For a while there was no sound except the muffled burbling of the television in the corner and the sizzling hot plate where the bread was turning golden.

"I would like to help you," Joyce said. "I really would. But whatever happened between me and Jeb happened a very long time ago. It's all in the past, and that's where I'd like it to stay. It has nothing to do with why you're here today."

"Okay," Brown said, and he smiled. He knew when to push and when to let go, and they were not done with her. They were nowhere near done.

"There is something you could do to help us," he said.

"Anything," she said.

Brown had to word it carefully. "Some blood was recovered at one of the crime scenes. It could be Jeb's. If we could run a test on a sample provided by you, it would tell us whether he was there."

Joyce stared at him, frozen, her hands in midgesture. "You can't mean . . ."

"You share part of your DNA with Jeb. It would tell us with complete certainty whether he was present at the crime scene."

"Why don't you . . . I don't know . . . why don't you get a sample from him?"

"We can't." Brown had decided that honesty was the way to go. "The judge said we didn't have enough to get a warrant."

The woman crossed her arms and leaned back against the fridge. Her eyes were wide and frightened.

"Joyce, I'm telling you this because there is no other way to prove that he was there. And because, even if you don't want to talk about it, I think you have reason to believe that Jeb is capable of violence. And you might want to help us."

The woman reached inside the fridge, pulled out a can of orange soda, opened it, and took a long sip. She pressed the chilled can against her flushed cheek. She looked from Brown to Madison and back.

"You have no idea what you're asking me," she said.

"We wouldn't ask unless we needed it. And only because I think you know that he's dangerous."

"Do you know what he would do to me if he knew that—?" The woman shook her head. "I'm still living in Ludlow because I made sure I didn't have anything to do with Jeb, and to him I don't exist. His wife called me from California to say that she was never coming back, and I wished her well. She called me because she knew I would understand why she had run. And if she had gone all the way to China to get away from him, I'd have understood . . ." Joyce paused, took another sip of sweet fizzy orange to soothe herself. "I'm sorry," she said. "I can't help you."

Madison waited; it was up to Brown how to finish it.

"Okay," he said, and he stood up. There was no animosity there, only a whispered sadness. He put some bills on the counter and picked up the bags.

"Please consider it," he said. "Think about it. Think about the fact that, whatever occurred between the two of you when you were young, he now has power over twelve young lives."

Brown and Madison went back into the swirling white.

After she heard the engine start up and go, Joyce Cartwell came out from behind the counter and slipped into one of the booths—her legs wouldn't hold her, and the scar over her ribs prickled hot.

In the car Madison turned to Brown. "You made the case against Tanner as if you really believed that he was the killer," she said. It was at odds with his *keep an open mind* attitude.

"I believe the woman is scared to death of him, and I want to find out why," he replied.

Chapter 39

Deputy Kupitz, who Madison thought had been strangely quiet since the morning visit to Jackknife Farm, seemed appeased and more like himself as he monitored the easy way the chief and Brown were comparing notes and eating the diner's lunch.

There was a large amount of footage to go through from the vigil, and the deputies dragged two chairs to a monitor in the corner of the main room in the station and proceeded to point and name. Between them they would be able to identify most of the crowd by the end of the day.

Madison's thoughts didn't stray far from the diner and Joyce Cartwell's distress. Had she really not known that her brother was holed up on Jackknife with little kids? And what about the grown-up ones? How had their hearts and their souls been molded by their father?

Madison stood and paced. The wall thermometer on the window said it was 32°F outside. What she wanted was a nice solid run to shake off the excess energy and focus her mind. What she had was the prospect of an afternoon stuck indoors, poring over paperwork, because Ludlow, the county, and apparently the entire world was in shutdown mode.

Madison turned and, on the muted television, caught herself in the square, crouching and firing rapid shots against an unseen enemy. If the killer was in the mood to settle scores, who was next on his list?

Deputy Hockley was about to say something to Madison but then thought better of it.

"I still don't understand why the shooter had to go and check old Edwards's medical file." Chief Sangster sipped the last of his diner coffee and sank the cup into the wastebasket with a perfect shot.

The issue had bothered Madison from the beginning. With Tanner as a prime suspect everything had been straightforward: motive had followed action, and the crimes had followed the motive. The file, though; the file was a splinter in her thumb, and everything she touched caught on it.

Sorensen, who had run back to the senior center to check the progress of her temporary lab, came through the door with a blast of icy air.

"We have a match for the bullet recovered from Dr. Dennen's body," she said, and the whole room stopped. The deputies paused their monitor and twisted in their chairs to hear.

Sorensen was not one for dramatics, but she seemed somewhat unhappy with the result and reluctant to share it.

"I'm running it again and I'm going to eye-match it to be one hundred percent certain," she said.

Madison did not like the sound of it one little bit.

"The bullet recovered in Dr. Dennen's body is a match to three bullets recovered from the scene of an armed robbery in a pawn shop four years ago," Sorensen said. "In Florida."

In the silence that followed her words it was Deputy Kupitz who spoke first. "But . . . but that's all the way on the other side of the country."

"I know you said you're going to countercheck but . . ." Madison said.

"I will, I absolutely will, but in the meantime you should face the numbers," Sorensen said. "In terms of my experience of the system getting it right the first time, the odds the database got it wrong are tiny."

"But—" Madison protested.

"Tiny," Sorensen interrupted her. "It would be wise to proceed with the understanding that whoever shot Dennen used a firearm that had been used in Florida four years earlier. And the cherry on the cake is that it looks like the shooter used a silencer."

How in the sweet name of everything holy did Jeb Tanner get his hands on a piece with a silencer that had been used to shoot a clerk three thousand miles away?

Madison met Brown's eyes. "Let's go over this again," she said, and he nodded.

"This time, though, let's leave the cloth out of it," he said.

"Why?"

"Let's just leave it to one side. It was found in the doctor's drawer, but that's incidental. We don't know that it played any part in what happened in the clinic the night the doctor died. What we do know is that the killer wanted to look at the medical file, that he forced the doctor to show him and, having accomplished what he set out to do, he took the doctor to another location and killed him there."

Sorensen shrugged off her coat and joined them around the table. Normally it stocked all the brochures for the local attractions; that day it was covered in the faxed pictures from Dennen's postmortem.

Madison cleared her mind and followed the evidence. She needed to think without Tanner in the picture, because whenever he was in it her logic seemed to sway under the weight of her dislike.

"Okay," she said. "So, the killer intercepts Dennen on his way home from the Jacobsens. It's the middle of the night, and there's no way the good doctor wouldn't stop for a stranded driver, whether he knows him or not."

"The killer takes him to the clinic. They get in with the doctor's key, and access the file," Brown said.

"We don't know yet if other files were accessed," Sorensen consulted her notes. "But we know the killer wanted to read whatever was on that specific set of medical records."

Brown was reading the copy of the medical examiner's report on Ty Edwards's body. "I think I know why," he said. "And it has nothing to do with his murder, which is why it wasn't brought to our attention."

"What do you mean?" Sangster said.

"Ty Edwards only had one kidney," Brown said. "He lost the other one to illness a long time ago, apparently. The ME found only one kidney, which had grown to compensate for the lack of its twin, which would indicate that Edwards had lived most of his life without it."

"It would have been in the file," Madison said.

"For sure," Brown agreed.

Sangster looked from one to the other. "Why would the shooter give a damn whether Edwards had one or two kidneys?"

"We don't know that yet," Brown replied. "But it definitely made his medical file stand out, wouldn't you think?"

"I'm calling Dr. Lynch," Madison said, and stood to grab her cell.

Sangster did not want to be the kid who kept putting his hand up. Sorensen leaned forward.

"At this point the smallest detail might tell us why the killer wanted that file and not, say, yours or somebody else's," she said. "How many people in Ludlow have only one kidney? It's a pretty good identifying characteristic, and not one that's immediately visible."

Brown's gaze traveled over the report. How much of a man's life was not immediately visible? How much was missed by reports like the one he held in his hands? Had someone sought out the old man because of that one specific characteristic?

"Edwards had only one kidney," Madison said after she hung up. "I got Lynch to admit that, yes, that was the case—not that he could deny it. The detail was in the file. He had lost the other due to a childhood illness and had suffered no consequences because of it. Aside from that, there was nothing else of any note in the file."

"So," Brown said, "what happens next?"

"The shooter kills the doc," Sangster said.

"Sure," Brown agreed. "But he doesn't shoot him in the clinic, as soon as the doctor has done his part. The shooter removes him from the office—having made certain that it didn't look like a break-in. And he takes him someplace else for what I can only consider an execution."

"Damn it," Madison said. "He could have shot him there and then, but he didn't. What he wanted was . . ."

". . . not to draw attention to the clinic and to the file," Brown concluded her thoughts.

"And we wouldn't have known it, if not for Dr. Dennen's quick thinking in leaving us a little calling card in the wastebasket with his DNA on it," Sorensen said.

Brown's voice was calm, but Madison recognized the anger under his composure. "Which means we wouldn't have known that Ty Edwards was the primary target the whole time, and Dennen was merely incidental."

"That's why he took the dog only after he was positive that he had the right man," Madison said.

"About the dog," Sorensen said. "In the combings from the fur I found a whole number of useless trace, but I've got something cooking in my special pot . . . a nice juicy handful of fibers. Man-made, ugly, and perfectly shaped for the scanning electron microscope."

"Carpet, car, a fake wig?" Madison said.

"Too short for a wig, I think. Don't break out the champagne yet—the fibers could belong to the Edwardses' home. That curly fur picked up every single bit of debris on the forest floor."

"How long before we know anything?" Brown said.

"This is not where you want to rush me," Sorensen replied, and Brown was smart enough to let her be.

With the roads as difficult as they were, Chief Sangster phoned Lee Edwards instead of dropping in on her in person.

She was fine, everything was fine. The neighbors had been visiting her and there was always someone keeping her company, bringing food, and chatting if she wanted to chat. No, she didn't need anything. No, she didn't remember Ty mentioning anything about his kidney. They had been together for near on thirty-five years and they had only spoken about it maybe three times. Did it matter?

The chief had no real answer to give her. He repeated for a third time that she should call him if she needed anything at all and then hung up.

The cloth, Madison reflected, the cloth that bore the appeal and the desperation of one of the Tanner children—and so far even that was conjecture—was not part of the narrative at all. If it had been important to the killer, if it had been in any way significant with regard to why the killer was in the clinic that night, he would have removed it. Madison didn't know what to do with that. Her thinking kept getting snagged on Tanner. They had to follow the evidence. Always follow the evidence. Where that small scrap of white would have led them, Madison didn't know.

"Do we have a list of who bought the white fabric?" she asked Sorensen.

"Yes, but Tanner's not on it, you know that," the investigator replied.

"Can I see the list?"

"I haven't been through all the records yet."

"Let me see what you have."

Sorensen flipped her notebook to the right page and passed it to Madison.

She read the lines of names and dates. "There," Madison pointed. "Five years ago Mrs. Clay bought thirty yards of it."

"And . . ."

"And if Mr. Clay is friendly enough with Tanner to give him an alibi, his wife might have given Naomi Tanner the fabric. Or maybe they swapped, I don't know." Madison reached for her cell. "He said that he barters deer meat for dry goods with his neighbors. He could have bartered deer meat for the fabric."

"They did buy from the store at different times."

"Maybe it was a particularly difficult year and they didn't have the cash for it."

Madison wanted very much to call Mrs. Clay and ask her a direct question; however, there was no doubt that anything she asked would be relayed back to Jeb Tanner—in all likelihood via the cell phone that didn't exist. Madison had to find a way of asking the question without it being obvious.

She dialed, and the woman picked up.

"Mrs. Clay, it's Detective Madison. So sorry to interrupt your Sunday again. How're you faring up there? Yes, here too. A real monster. I forgot to ask you earlier today . . . Mr. Tanner's boys were working on a deer and he told us that he sometimes barters deer meat for dry goods, tools, other materials—is that true? I'm only asking to have a general picture of the running of the farm. No, ma'am, it has nothing to do with the alibi. We're just trying to understand a little of the life here, being from the city and all."

Sorensen had never heard Madison in full *aw, shucks* mode—and it was a beauty to behold.

After a while Madison said, "Thank you very much, Mrs. Clay. Much appreciated. You take care now, ma'am."

Madison's face darkened. "Flour, sugar, tools, coffee," she said to Sorensen, "and, occasionally, fabric. When Naomi Tanner was still around she made dresses and shirts for the kids with white fabric the Clays had swapped for farm goods. Mrs. Clay uses the eggs from the farm to bake cakes. Apparently, they're much better than store-bought."

It was the first tangible link between the doctor and one of the Tanner children.

"It would be great to get some DNA trace off the cloth. Did you find anything on it? Anything at all?" Madison said to Sorensen.

"I haven't thrown the whole lab at it yet, no," Sorensen said, and almost regretfully she added, "Right now, I have to concentrate on the bullet and the fibers. As soon as I can, I'll look into the cloth."

"I understand. Of course, it makes sense."

Amy Sorensen was, at present, all the Crime Scene Unit lab they had, and Madison knew there were priorities. She didn't mention it to Brown, because she didn't want to see his eye-roll, but Jeb Tanner had lived in Kansas and in California; he had contacts in places other than Ludlow, and one of those contacts could have obtained a firearm for him. One that had been used in crimes before and would throw the scent off him.

Madison didn't say anything, because she could also imagine Sorensen's comment. *Sure, all that from a guy who doesn't even own a phone.*

The windows were swirls of white, and behind them there was only more white. A pretty close representation of her own spiraling thoughts, Madison reflected.

Brown had finished his call with Lieutenant Fynn in Seattle—if asked, they'd both concede that those twice-daily briefings had brought neither of them much joy—and he turned to the room.

"What do we know about Ty Edwards?" he said.

Chapter 40

A late February snowfall is a reminder that winter is not going to let go as easily as some might wish and often it bears down harder and longer than would seem possible. The town of Ludlow was not going anywhere: it was not on a route to some other, possibly more interesting place, and it was not itself a destination for anyone traveling on that Sunday afternoon. All that happened was that the town came to a slow, inexorable stop. People paused where they were and didn't venture more than a hundred yards from their front door; they checked their furnaces, looked in the pantry, and made sure that they had the number for the snowplows at hand for when the storm would stop. Somehow, the shooting in the square and the murder of the doctor became only another—darker—measure of the sense of being under siege by something unknown.

For Samuel Tanner it had been a day of firsts, a day when things had been shaken up and could not be unshaken. When their father told Luke to go see to the horses, Samuel stood and followed under the pretext of helping his brother and checking on Flare. If Luke was surprised, he didn't say anything; the play in the yard had left everyone giddy with delight, and the afternoon hours in the cabin had been quiet and mellow.

Samuel waited until they were alone in the barn, where the horses' scent and warmth were a comfort, and he said, "Why did you say that Caleb was a liar?"

Luke almost dropped the leather halter from his hand. "Why are you looking for trouble?" he replied.

"I'm not. But you said that he was a liar, and you must have had a reason." There was no hostility in the boy, only a steady keenness that caught his brother off balance. Luke knew how to deal with anger or deception; he could dispense with either because he was the biggest and strongest of anyone on the farm—except his father, and he would never have gone against him. Nevertheless, Samuel's manner told him that the boy was all too aware that he might receive no answer except for a slap around the head, and still he had to ask the question.

"Why do you want to know?" Luke said.

"Because Caleb isn't a liar."

"You don't know what you're talking about."

"Then you tell me. What did he lie about?"

If Luke's only power over his brother was to withhold the information he so badly wanted, then it was exactly what he would do.

"I'm not going to tell you what he lied about," he said. "But I can tell you that he was found out and he got what he deserved."

"When . . . how . . . ?"

"You don't want to ask me any more about this. It's done. It's over. Go back inside and don't even think about talking to anybody else about Caleb. Papa finds out about it and you'll be in the lonely place for a month. Papa finds out and—"

Samuel nodded and stepped backward until he bumped against the door. His cheeks felt hot in the early evening air and he busied himself with a fallen fence post before going back inside. He needed time to work out what Luke had told him and what he had meant. He had hoped to find out something about Caleb and instead he had seen fear in his brother's eyes. Hidden under his usual quarrelsome temper Samuel had seen a hint of panic, as if Luke had only just realized that he was in trouble too.

The words stayed with him all evening and all night. *He got what he deserved.* There was the lonely place in the yard—just a little shed that no stranger would look at twice—and there was his father's belt when the punishment required it. Luke had been through both, and his dread had implied that much worse was possible.

Something cold and clammy settled in the middle of Samuel's stomach: What had happened to Caleb? His mind wandered to the only safe place the boy knew. He lay on his bed, wrapped in the blankets, closed his eyes, and saw the cave's wall. He felt it, smooth and cool, as he drew a tiny shape with his fingertip. And falling asleep, he saw the pack move like rushing shadows through the forest, and Caleb was running with them.

Joyce Cartwell went home in the middle of the afternoon because it was clear that no one would be coming by the diner and, in truth, the conversation with Brown had left her so unnerved that she wanted to be in a place where she could make sure the windows and the doors were locked and she could be alone with her thoughts.

All the years that she had spent building a life of quiet contentment were balanced on a razor's edge. Jeb had left for college, she had married and started the diner with her husband. Jeb had come back and they had spoken to each other three times since: twice around the time of their father's death, and once when she had bumped into him and Naomi in a store. Then her husband had died of leukemia seven years earlier, and she had found herself running the diner alone. The thought of Jeb only a few miles away had receded into a low-level kind of alarm: he was there, but he had made no attempt to contact her or be part of her life.

The only way to cope with the unwelcome proximity was to keep away and mind her own business. Few in town remembered that Jeb was her brother, and there were long stretches—months long—when she didn't even hear a single piece of gossip about the Tanner family up on Jackknife.

Joyce had thought about it, as Brown had asked, and she had reached her conclusion: if a judge had decided that there wasn't enough cause to give them a legal way to get their test, she was not going to upend her life and get dragged into the nightmare again. If it was right that they should go after Jeb for whatever crazy thing he had done, they would find a way. It was their job, after all—not hers.

There was soup in the fridge, and a classic movie on television. Joyce curled up on her favorite chair and tried to care about the love life of an American girl in Rome in the 1950s.

While the deputies' list of local residents recognized in pictures and footage of the vigil had grown longer, Brown and Madison had looked into the dim corners of Ty Edwards's life and found nothing that they didn't already know. Nothing in the time that the man had spent on earth appeared to indicate a motive for the killing and a reason why someone would go to the length of identifying him by a medical anomaly.

"The grouping of the shots was less than accidental," Madison said to Brown.

They sat at the table with their heads together. Between them the picture of the victim taken at the scene revealed a tight cluster of gunshot wounds on the man's chest. There had been screaming, hollering, people running every which way, Madison returning fire and emptying her magazine at the sniper.

"Shooter knew what he was doing," Brown said.

They had thought *angry farmer*, but by any standards the shooter was lethally proficient.

"Are you thinking *pro*?" Madison said.

"Normally I would," he said. "The killer used a silencer—you don't pick those up for the hell of it. I just don't see any place in Edwards's life where that could have happened, though."

"If the killer was a pro who dropped by to do a job, he would have left town already."

"Maybe, but not necessarily. If someone left yesterday—out of the blue, after the shooting—people might notice."

"He's a pro *and* he's a local?"

"I don't know. The Florida lead is a mess, but we need to work it," Brown smiled. "The local law didn't make any arrest for that armed robbery, but I'm pretty sure we can solve it from here."

"There's a chance that someone went all the way to Florida to procure a dirty piece specifically to throw us off . . ." Madison saw the look in Brown's eyes. "I don't mean Tanner. Hear me out. We have someone who wants to make sure that Edwards is definitely who he says he is. Never mind that he's a man who has always lived his life in or near Ludlow and has never put a foot wrong. Our guy really wants him and doesn't want anybody to know that he got to him through the medical file. Is it so preposterous to think that he also made certain that the piece he used on Dennen had a history somewhere else? Something that was never going to be connected to him? Just to muddy the waters?"

"Edwards must have really ticked someone off."

"Why the dog?"

"The dog?"

"He wants to kill the man, he can do it anytime he wants and wherever he wants: when he goes to the store, through the kitchen window, in his garden, and while he's driving his SUV. Why did he take the dog?"

"I don't know," Brown said. "We should get a lineup together, get the dog to point out the shooter."

"Sure," Madison said. "Judge Eugene will definitely go for that."

They had more questions than answers and—unspoken, though acknowledged—the sense that the killer was not done with Ludlow yet.

*   *   *

Hours later, in her attic room, Madison lay in bed watching the fire glowing in the hearth. Hockley had dropped them off at the Miller place and they had spent a quiet evening in the rambling guesthouse. They all needed a bit of space from one another—and from the only subject of conversation of the last three days—and had retired early to their rooms.

Sometimes, Madison mused, in order to understand she needed not to think. Perhaps it was a contradiction in terms, and she wasn't even sure that it was anything more than bumper-sticker wisdom, but there it was.

The drive back had been slow and slippery, and the forecast for the following day had not brought much solace. Madison took a deep breath: the snow was pressing down on the town and every single person in it. Still, unless he had left after the shooting the previous day, the killer was still there, just as trapped as they were.

Amy Sorensen pulled one boot off, holding her cell against her shoulder. "I don't know, honey. Soon, I hope. How was your weekend?"

She pictured her daughter in her room—a room that used to be yellow and had transitioned into pale green, with posters that Sorensen privately thought looked like mug shots.

"You did?" Sorensen laughed.

Her daughter's voice traveled all the way across the state and lifted Sorensen away from the narrow marks on the gunmetal that she still saw, even when she closed her eyes.

Brown tried to focus on the book he had brought upstairs from the living room. After ten minutes he gave up, lay back on his pillow, and went over the events of the last couple of days.

The snowfall had hushed many of the sounds around the house, except for the pipes and the furnace. He heard a peal of laughter nearby. It sounded like Sorensen. They were lucky to have her there for however long it would take—possibly forever—to make sense of the case. Two stray thoughts collided and Brown made a note of something that he wanted to ask Chief Sangster the following day.

By then, Joyce Cartwell would have returned home from the diner. What did he really want from her? How far did he want her to go—for them, for him? Brown allowed himself a small success: he had not lied. At least he hadn't told her that they would protect her from her brother, when they would not and could not. He had wanted to; he had felt the need to tell her rise in his chest when she had looked so upset and so vulnerable. He had been glad Madison was there then. Her mere presence had yanked him back to the fact that, once they were on their way back to Seattle, and Polly and her volunteers had locked the Miller house after them, the town would continue as it always had. And Joyce would be left alone with the consequences of her actions.

"How is Carl?" Madison said.

"Managing Greenhut Lowell within an inch of their lives," Quinn said. "Seems happy."

Quinn had called Madison. She had briefed him about the latest developments, paltry as they were.

"You should have seen the boy, Quinn, how brave he was to speak with me."

Nathan Quinn knew something about the courage of boys in terrible circumstances.

"Can you do something for them?"

"Hope so," Madison said. "Hope so."

Madison fell asleep after his call with her cell on the pillow and her Glock within hand's reach on the floor by the bed.

She fell asleep and into a dream of deer and knives. And the black-and-white silhouette of a man trailing a child on a snowy street.

Chapter 41

John James Walker's days started early: Alice discovered that the man she had christened The Hunter would stir before dawn and expect her—or the boy he thought she was—to do the same. He spoke a great deal, although he seemingly had no wish for a two-way conversation—and that was good, because Alice was afraid of betraying herself. From the beginning he would issue an instruction and expect it to be followed; Alice wasn't sure what would have happened if she had not obeyed.

We're on the wrong side of Mount Baker, boy. There are no phones, no roads, no people. Tomorrow morning I'll see what I can do.

"Sir, can you help me get back to my family today?" Alice said as she rolled up her sleeping bag. "I would really like to go home."

It was her longest sentence so far and she had kept her voice low. She didn't like the whiny tone of it, and she certainly did not want to go *home*, but she sure wanted to get away from that man.

"I'll see what I can do," the man replied. "Now, snap to and be ready to saddle up in five minutes."

What did he mean? It was not a straight answer and all that Alice could do was get herself ready, and be prepared—for what, she didn't know.

The weather was not cooperating; the dawn drizzle had turned into heavy summer rain, and it dogged their steps all morning. They walked under the canopy of a forest of never-ending firs and tried to stay dry. Alice was disoriented: she knew that the sun rises in the east, and attempted to divine the direction of their walking; however, the tree cover and the absence of shadows were confusing. One thing was clear, though: in spite of their hiking they were no closer to any kind of trail, and Alice had spotted no other living soul in the dense woods.

The Hunter, three steps ahead of her, walked and talked.

"Do you know what's the most important thing in hunting? The single most important thing is to move through the woods like a ghost. Real hunting is done on foot, not on those so-called *stands*. You use one of those and you just end up sitting on your ass for days."

He didn't need to turn to check that she was there because Alice had not yet mastered the skill of moving like a ghost and was making as much noise as possible—in case anybody should be nearby to hear them.

"No," the man continued, "you need to stalk your prey, hunt into the wind, and shoot your target in the eye."

I need to get away.

The woods opened into a valley, and a few hundred feet away, like a mirage of normality in the sudden sunshine, Alice spotted a group of five or six hikers following a stream in the opposite direction.

The Hunter turned to the little girl and said, "I'm going to teach you how to stalk people, boy. There's no better fun, I promise you. You learn that, you can do anything. When you're done learning, I'll take you back to your family."

He wasn't asking a question, he wasn't proposing a deal. He had told Alice what would happen, and that, as far as he knew, was that.

Alice looked at the group of tourists in the distance, moving farther and farther away from her with each passing second, and she looked at the man. Whatever passed through her face must have been clear enough because he lifted her chin with one finger and said:

"Now, don't you go getting ideas about running after them and leaving me stranded here like a fool. There's no saying what can happen to a group of people who don't know the mountains and don't know how to protect themselves in the wilderness. Many dangerous animals around. People have got to be real careful where they camp at night, because they could fall asleep and never wake up. You understand me, boy?"

Alice nodded.

Alice followed the man as they tracked the group all afternoon. They stayed under the cover of the shade a few feet into the forest and matched the slow speed of their quarry, who walked in the open valley and stopped from time to time to take pictures of one another by the river, blissfully ignorant that a predator had picked up their scent.

The weather had cleared and the sun was working hard to make up for the damp morning. Alice, thirsty and hungry, felt disconnected—as if she had strayed into a weird dream, the kind you have when a fever is eating you up. The man, she observed in her haze, had never been quite as alive or as focused as he was then, keeping his eyes on the prey ahead of him and the one trailing behind him.

In spite of the long summer evenings at that time of the year the group stopped to make camp with the sun still high in the sky; they were close to the river and in a spot completely open to the elements. There were six people—Alice had had hours to observe them. Three couples in their twenties who were setting up three small tents and collecting wood for a campfire. Their voices, their laughter, drifted in the breeze up to Alice, concealed behind a clump of spruces and shrubs.

The man brought out a pair of binoculars. They had followed the group all afternoon without being spotted; surely this was enough, surely this was all he had meant. Alice shivered in the cool of the forest.

"We're going to wait until they fall asleep and then you're going to get into the camp and take something of theirs without being noticed," he whispered.

"You want me to steal?" The squeak had come out before she could stop herself.

"I'm not going to repeat myself. You heard me right the first time. What did you think was going to happen?"

He brought the binoculars to his eyes and the little girl watched him as he monitored the six tourists, evaluating their possessions and no doubt deciding what Alice's task should be.

The next few hours were excruciating. Alice wanted to run, there and then; however, the man had displayed enough of his skills that she was sure he would quickly catch up with her—and then what? There was the serious possibility that she might lose what little goodwill she had with him. There was the serious possibility, Alice considered, that he had no intention of getting her back to civilization at all. That everything he had done and said was nothing but a game to him and she was in even more trouble than she had thought. She remembered her red bicycle, hidden under the ferns, and her eyes welled up. It would slowly rust, week after week, and fall apart under the rain, and no one, no one in the whole world, would ever know that it was there.

The man gave Alice a piece of rabbit from the previous night. She hadn't asked but had guessed that they would not light a fire, because the campers might see it. She ate the meat and drank from her own canteen while her mind was racing to find a solution to a situation that didn't have one.

The moon had risen above the mountains and the air had cooled down. Alice dug into her backpack for a sweatshirt and was careful to pick the blue one and leave her pink top rolled up at the bottom. As the sky darkened her heart began to pound: what was he going to ask her to do? What would happen if she failed? Could she ask the campers for help? They looked like kids—and she understood the absurdity of a twelve-year-old thinking that—but it was the truth. Compared with the man, they just looked like little kids playing in their backyard. And he had a rifle and a hunting knife as long as her arm.

The man gave her the binoculars. "Look," he said, and she did.

The campfire was still throwing shadows around; four people had gone into their tents and two were talking and giggling close enough to the flames that she could see their faces very clearly in the dark.

"The tent on the right. Can you see? Can you see the red canteen hanging on the hook?"

Alice found it and nodded.

"When the happy couple have had enough romance in the moonlight and go into their tent, *you* go to work. Make your way down there, pick up the red canteen, and get back. Quick as you can. Your mission objective is to retrieve the canteen without being seen or heard."

"But—"

"If you run away, I'll come get you and I won't be happy about it. If you ask them to hide you, I'll come get you and I won't be happy about it. And if I have to ask them where you are, things might get a little rough, who knows? You go slow, you go quiet, and you get yourself back here. I'm teaching you important skills, son. What you learn here, you'll never learn in a schoolroom. I found that out myself the hard way."

There was nothing that Alice could say to that.

The young couple stood up and made their way into their tent, and all that was left was the last flicker of fire, more ember than flame.

"Now," the man said, and he took the binoculars from her hands, ready to follow each and every move she made.

Alice took a deep breath and stepped out from behind the spruce. She had calculated a possible way to the camp—following the line of trees to the nearest point and then rushing through the tall grass—but she had not realized just how awful she would feel doing it. Her dread was a tight knot in her chest right next to her heart: fear for herself, fear for the campers. Fear of failing, fear of succeeding.

Alice proceeded along the edge of the forest until she was fifty yards above the campsite. It was a bright, clear night and she could see every blade of grass between her and the tents. Was the man watching her? Unconsciously Alice looked back at the dark space where she had come from. Something glinted in the half gloom, or maybe it was her imagination. The girl shuddered. There was nothing else for it: she dropped low, her elbows brushing the tall grass, and she started her way down.

Keep it together, just keep it together. He's going to fall asleep at some point and you'll leave then. Just keep it together a little longer.

One thing Alice had not considered was how loud the forest was at night and what a blessing that would be in her present circumstances. Her steps—quite unlike a ghost and more like an awkward child trying to be stealthy—were mostly covered by the sound of the breeze in the trees and the world of birds and insects calling to one another in the dark. There were also the voices coming from inside the tents—the hikers still talking to one another, still laughing. *Don't you know what's going on, you morons?*

Alice reached the tents almost easily and crouched next to the closest one. The ground where they had set up was scrubby and bare, the grass short, and the dirt full of river stones. It occurred to her that out of the field of grass she was completely in the open. And at least a few of the hikers were awake enough to hear her unless she was very careful.

Go to sleep, just go to sleep.

Alice, crouching low, worked out which tent had the red canteen and made her way toward it. They had washed their dishes in the river; nevertheless, she could smell a hint of cooked food in the air, and something else—an oily herb scent that she didn't recognize.

Alice crawled around a tent and saw the red canteen hanging on the post six feet to her right, just as they had seen it from the forest. Something clicked in her mind as she realized that, behind the tent as she was, the man could not see her. In spite of his binoculars, in spite of everything he had and he knew, in that moment he could not see her.

Alice peeked at the canteen and at the pitch-black forest behind her. She could creep through the grass, keeping the tent between her and the man. She could make it to the forest and from there she could follow the valley—she had an idea that it would lead her southwest toward people and safety. Could she put enough distance between herself and the man before he understood that she had run? How long she had sat, curled in the dirt, her hands digging into the warm earth, she couldn't tell. Suddenly the flap of the tent flew open and one of the guys staggered out, stretched, and ambled toward the river. Alice skittered backward and flattened herself against the tent, her heart rising up into her mouth.

Maybe I should just let them find me, like it's an accident. He can't blame anybody if it's an accident. And yet even as the thought popped into her mind Alice knew that The Hunter would find a way to blame her and the hikers, and she did not know—because her life so far had shielded her from men like him—what he could do, only that his displeasure was a wild and dangerous thing.

The young man relieved himself in the river and then meandered back to the tent. He would have seen a little girl crouching and trying to hide if only he had walked three steps to his right, but he didn't. He stooped, went in, and zipped up the flap. Alice wiped a single tear of fear and frustration from her cheek. She glanced around the corner and the way was clear. There was nothing else to do.

The red canteen hung from a post by the front of the next tent along. Right by the entrance stood a small folding seat and right there on the seat Alice saw it: the journal one of the girls had been sketching on in the afternoon. The journal and a pen. Alice looked up. The man could not see her.

Alice stared at the journal.

Inside the tent somebody shifted and someone else whispered words she could not hear.

The journal.

John James Walker was not a patient man, and this little project was testing his limits. Why wasn't the kid back already? He wasn't going to be so stupid as to go for a walk in the middle of the night, was he? Maybe he was more foolish than he seemed.

The man peered at the campsite. The fire was all but extinguished and he couldn't even see if the red canteen was still there.

He heard the soft steps from yards away and something inside him lifted.

Alice dropped the canteen at the man's feet. She was shaking. Even in the darkness she could see that he was smiling and it was more frightening than what she had just done.

"Tomorrow," she said, and she checked her voice, kept it steady, kept it low. "Tomorrow, sir, please take me back."

The man mulled it over for a moment. Alice's hands were tight fists and she was struggling not to cry. She was relieved to have made it back; she was terrified to have made it back.

The Hunter reached into his backpack and brought something out, snapped off a piece, and offered it to her. It was chocolate. "Take it, you earned it."

Alice hesitated.

The man leaned forward. "You're not done learning, child. When you are, I'll take you back. You did good tonight but that was lesson number one. Lesson number two is how to hit the target right in the eye."

Alice knew then, if she had not known it before, that whatever this man had done in his life before they had met, he had killed people, real people. Maybe it had been in a war, maybe not, she couldn't tell. The world was spinning around and her insides felt ice cold in the August night.

She didn't take the chocolate, and the man ate it in a single bite.

"We'll see how you feel about things in the morning, boyo," he said.

Later, much later on, Alice heard his breathing deepen and slow down, and she stirred in the sleeping bag that she had left unzipped. She could make it look like she was moving in her sleep, but she was ready to make a run for it, ready to grab her pack and go.

In the darkness the man sat with his back against the trunk of a mossy tree, holding the rifle across his knees—his eyes wide open.

It had been two days since Alice and the man had first spotted the hikers, and they had never let them out of their sight for more than a few hours. The Hunter had tracked them, anticipated their route, left them for a while, and then picked them up again—as if they were a plaything he used for his own grim amusement. And all the while he had been trailed by a twelve-year-old girl who he was watching even more closely than his targets.

The Hunter had trapped rabbits and squirrels and had taught his reluctant, taciturn apprentice how to skin them, gut them, and portion them. Alice watched him—she was so far beyond fear that she felt mostly numb, with sudden moments of despair—and she waited in dread of the next lesson, the next task. The man—it seemed—never slept and his eyes never strayed too far from her. The one good thing was that he still hadn't realized that she was a girl.

"I can see something in you, boy," he said to her once. "You don't whine, you do your part. That's more than a lot of grown men do."

The dawn of the third day was pink and yellow on the jagged edge of the mountain, and Alice idly wondered whether they were still on Mount Baker. The man had been silent for a while and Alice tried to gauge his thoughts the way her father had taught her a thousand years earlier. There was the sense of a plan coming together, of potential scenarios being considered and eliminated. The Hunter glanced at the hikers' camp—half a mile away and quiet in the early morning—and he glanced at Alice.

Today is the day, she thought. She was too far out of herself to be either surprised or scared. *Today is the day he's going to tell me that I have to kill one of them.*

Chapter 42

Alice Madison woke up and wished that she was in her home in Seattle, where she would go into her kitchen in the bunny slippers that Rachel had given her for Christmas and she would make herself warm milk. She hitched herself up on her bed in the attic room: it wasn't about the darn milk, she thought, it was about being in a place where everything reminded her of the darkest time in her life and what she'd had to do to survive it.

The wind rattled the pane and the chill drove Madison back under the covers. Brave Samuel, she thought, who had gone against his father. Would twelve-year-old Alice have been as brave? Courage is an oddly shaped thing: razor-sharp on one side and blunt on the other. You push forward because you have to, and you do what you must.

After a while, in spite of the wind rattling the old house, Madison fell asleep.

No one came for her in her dreams, and she lay motionless under the blankets until dawn.

* * *

The snowplows started early on Monday morning and worked Main Street and the thoroughfare that linked Ludlow to the highway. Emergency vehicles could just about get through, if needed, but travel was discouraged: if the snow melted even a little and then froze again when the temperatures dropped, the road would become deadly.

The radio news confirmed that the schools would not open and gave a telephone number for parents to call. It was the third time it had happened that winter.

The roads off Main Street were still difficult to negotiate, and Brown, Madison, and Sorensen made their way through the snowdrift to the police station under a watery sky. The deputies had already left the office, busy trying to reach a couple of elderly residents who lived alone—to make sure they were all right.

"When we were in her home," Brown said to Chief Sangster as he was pouring himself coffee, "Mrs. Edwards said something about the town not being what it used to be. That's what she'd said the first day, when she was talking to you here about her dog. I remembered it last night. At the time I thought nothing of it, but she repeated it after the shooting. She meant something by it, didn't she?"

It took Sangster a second to register what Brown had asked him.

"It's nothing," he said after a beat.

"What's *nothing*?"

"A few months ago there was a run of break-ins and a couple of burglaries. A few cameras were stolen, some small jewelry, a couple of laptops. That's all."

"Go on."

"They were linked to three ex-cons who were trying to get to Canada. They spent a few days in town and then moved on. They were arrested in Christina Lake, across the border."

"Did they find the stolen property on them?"

"No."

"Why did you think it was them?"

"Too much of a coincidence: you've got three felons passing through with robbery convictions involving violence—parole violators on their way back to jail, if you ask me—and suddenly I get calls that people's homes have been trashed and their valuables are gone."

"Robbery is very different from a break-in or a burglary."

"These guys were in a hurry. They snatched what they could and made for the mountains."

"Was any business hit? Any store?"

"No, that would have been too dangerous. They were just trying to get some easy money. If they'd hit a business they'd have had the state police and a dozen choppers on their asses in three minutes flat."

"How many?"

"What?"

"How many break-ins and burglaries?"

Sangster sighed. "Four break-ins, three burglaries."

"Seven incidents in all."

"That's right."

Brown sat back in his chair.

"I'd like to see the list of the residences who were hit," Brown said.

"Wait a minute . . . ," Sangster replied, and then something passed across his face and the man paused.

Brown did not need to ask—but he did so, anyway. "Were the Edwardses hit?"

Sangster pressed his fingers on the bridge of his nose. The whole notion that the break-ins and the shootings could be connected was ridiculous.

"Was the residence of Lee and Ty Edwards one of the ones broken into?" Brown repeated.

"Yes, it was," the chief admitted. "And let me go on the record that I don't think it had anything to do with a nutter shooting Ty Edwards dead."

"It's on the record," Brown said. "And now, Chief, if I may, I really need to see that list."

The chief looked like he'd had a bad night. The telephone had been ringing every couple of minutes since they got in, and Polly was trying to field the calls from the locals and the media in the best way she could. The online news reports alluded to the *task force* in charge of the case; Madison wondered how many people you needed to be called a task force. As of that morning they had four full-time officers, two part-timers, and one civilian—if she counted Polly, the chief's assistant, who seemed to be doing better than they were.

Sangster was on the fifth day of his first double-homicide investigation, and he didn't look good on it. He worked at his desk for a few minutes and then produced a file. Brown and Madison read it at the table—the task force table.

When they were done, they looked at each other: Sangster's day was going from bad to worse.

"Chief," Brown said, "we think there's a pattern here."

"What do you mean?"

"See, look at the addresses . . . the perpetrators didn't stick to one area of the town. They moved around and chose mostly houses, but also one apartment. Nothing too valuable or awkward to carry was ever stolen. And, chronologically, we have the break-ins first and the burglaries later."

"You can't be serious."

"All the people whose homes were hit were above sixty and married, and the Edwardses were the last ones. What are the chances that the one common factor between all the victims is that they were couples of the same age?"

"He was looking for Edwards," Madison said.

"Guys—" The chief's patience would only stretch so far. "Are we really saying that the killer has been in town since last summer?"

"No," Madison said. "He must have arrived much earlier than that, looked around for a while, found which of Ludlow's residents fit the bill, and then begun to eliminate them from his short list until he found the person he was looking for."

"You do know this sounds like guesswork wrapped in baloney with a dash of bullshit, don't you?" Sangster said.

"Yes," Brown replied. "We get that a lot."

Sorensen had been studying a section of one of the recovered fibers in her microscope. In spite of Madison's crack she had actually considered whether the man-made fiber could possibly have come from a wig, but she had quickly crossed out that possibility. Sorensen's gut told her *car carpet*. The dog must have been transported in some kind of vehicle—and presumably the killer would have wanted him unseen during transit.

Looks like Tucker might have been put in the trunk.

There were a huge amount of variables but FACID—the Forensic Automotive Carpet Fiber Identification Database—was a useful tool. Sorensen had sliced the fiber into two sections: one half for analysis via infrared spectroscopy, the other for observation under a polarized microscope. Hopefully, it would minimize fiber distortion and give her better results.

In order to search the database Sorensen still had to ascertain color, cross-sectional type, polymer class, and presence/absence of delustrant and heavy striation—and even once she had managed to fulfill all the requirements, it might turn out to be a pointless exercise.

She stood, paced around the senior center's main room, and then returned to her desk. At least in Seattle she had her team to irk and nag for her own amusement, to keep things lively.

She made a note in her pad and her thoughts turned to powdered titanium dioxide, a common delustrant. Just then, her gaze fell on the evidence bags that contained the bullets: the killer had used two different firearms and in all likelihood had already gotten rid of both. He had also used fire to destroy the evidence at the first crime scene. He was about fire and gunmetal, about total destruction and execution.

Sorensen appraised the meager resources of her back-room lab and hoped to God that they would be enough, because there was a time line: Robert Dennen had been killed in the early hours of Thursday morning and Ty Edwards had been shot on Saturday around lunchtime. If the shooter was following a day-on/day-off schedule then Monday, Sorensen thought, as she adjusted the specimen under the lens, was a kill day.

Lee Edwards's home felt as if it was not quite hers any longer. In the rush to help and support her in her time of need—her daughter was flying in as soon as possible—friends and neighbors had almost forgotten that the widow was perfectly capable of cooking her own meals and seeing to her own needs.

It was nice to have company, and Lee appreciated everybody's efforts; however, from time to time, she just needed to go into her bedroom for a bit of solitude and a quiet weep, and possibly a nap too. When she returned to the living room, she was sure to find a couple of friends chatting away and eager to be there for her.

What had happened two days earlier had thrust her many years into the past, and it had all poured out: how she had met Ty and her early days in Ludlow, the uncomplicated ease of their life together, and the joys of living in such a remote place.

Talking, napping, and weeping seemed to be all that she was good for these days.

Somewhere in Ludlow, in a house not so different from any other on the same street—a street that had been cleared by the snowplows—a man sat on the bargain-basement sofa in his living room and stared into space. Life, he knew, was a cruel joker. And just when you thought it couldn't dump any more of the brown stuff all over you, there it was, a fresh new truckload of it coming around the corner just for you.

He had planned, he had executed, and still—still—it had not been enough. The man reached for one of the sofa cushions. He placed it flat on the dining table and then opened the cutlery drawer in his kitchenette. Once he found what he was looking for he returned to the table. It was a poor substitute for the actual target of his rage—but all things in good time. He clasped the knife tight and ripped through the fabric, over and over and over, until there was nothing but shreds. He did it without a word and, when it was done, he cleaned up and sat back on the sofa.

In front of him, on a coffee table he had bought at the Jacobsens' yard sale, lay a steel trap. Its bright metal jaws were clamped shut, but shards from a piece of kindling were visible where he had tested the mechanism a few months earlier. It was an antique—clear proof that they didn't make things how they used to, he thought.

The man had had other plans for the hunting trap. But life, in its sick and twisted way, had taught him to improvise, and he had learned his lesson well.

Chapter 43

His da had been a fisherman, and the blindfolded man had been brought up to love, respect, and fear the sea. It had taken the lives of some of his da's friends and provided the food on his table. It was somehow fitting that he would be brought there that day, for the savage sea to be his witness.

"Do you believe in God?" the man said.

"Yes," the blindfolded man replied. He did not believe, though, and had never believed, not really, not with faith and fervor and hope, as his parents had. He had shed his religion like a bad suit, as soon as he was old enough and his mother couldn't physically carry him to Mass. Was that why this was happening to him? "I believe in God," he said.

"Good. But he's not here right now, and I am."

The blindfolded man did not reply. He was exhausted, he was confused. He sat bound to a chair with heavy ropes that stank of algae, and he felt the floor of the boat under him roll with the swell. There were seagulls too—he could hear them—clamoring high above them, not understanding that this boat, these men, were not out there on the open sea to fish. There might very well be some killing, and some dying, but nothing that should concern the shoals of fish around them.

The man had woken up on the chair a while earlier and since then he had heard nothing outside the cabin but the shrieking of the gulls and the splashing of the waves against the hull. Wherever they were, they were far from the harbor, far from anybody who might perhaps hear them and come asking questions. The air was salty and sharp and it could have been a great day out. It probably was—for someone else, somewhere else.

The man found it difficult to concentrate: fear had strapped a ton of lead to the middle of his chest and it was hard to breathe, let alone think. In his fatigue he caught a draft of sea breeze, and for an instant he was on a pier with his da when he was eight, after a day at the Cape.

A squawk from a bird brought him back and he shivered, a deep shiver that had little to do with the cold: he had tried in vain to leave his wretched body on this boat and escape into the memory of a perfect day, but the ropes biting into his arms told him that he'd stay right where he was, because his da was dead and buried in St. Augustine and no one on this boat was going to buy him cotton candy.

"Tell me about it," the man said.

"I don't know anything."

"I'm going to give you a minute to gather your thoughts. Consider whether we would really go to the trouble of taking you all the way out into the blue forever if we didn't know you knew. If we didn't know for sure that you knew."

The man was not angry. His voice—pure south Boston—sounded amused, almost pleased.

"I can't," the man on the chair said.

"Because of what they'll do to you if you tell me?"

He nodded.

"What about what I'm gonna do to you now? Isn't there kind of some urgency to your situation right here and now?"

"I'm afraid of you too," he said, and to hear the other man laugh was a good thing. It pleased him, as if they were talking man-to-man. Then he felt the point of the knife in the soft spot between the collarbones and he stiffened.

"I appreciate your dilemma," the man continued. "But I really think you should look at it from my point of view. I've invested a certain amount of time in this business and I need information that you can provide. If you don't, if you decide that their threat to you is more of a problem than you being alone at sea with a man with a knife against your throat, well, that kind of makes me feel bad. Do you want me to feel bad?"

"I have a family," the man said.

Somewhere behind him someone scratched a match, and a second later the man smelled the cigarette smoke.

"We all have families. We all have jobs to do," the man in front of him said. He didn't sound amused anymore. There was something tinny in his voice that scared the man on the chair more than anything else.

It wasn't a question of loyalty—he was only a paid employee. However, he had a brother who sparred in a gym and did well in the ring. And the man knew that if he talked there would be people who would meet his brother in the alley behind the gym and break all the bones in his hands. And his children, what would they do to his wife and his children?

It happened more quickly than he could ever have imagined: the man's hand pinning his on the arm of the chair, and the metal blade against his skin. He left after that and, sure, his body was still on the boat—and would be for many hours—but he traveled through place and time, and even spoke to his father on the pier that day when he was eight. He spoke to the man who was asking him questions too—he couldn't help it, he couldn't help anything—and in the end he commended his soul and his family to God.

By the time they got back into the harbor the boat had been washed clean and they had put his body in a bag.

It would be left in the trunk of a car and found two days later.

Chapter 44

Madison had been reading the same page of notes for ten minutes. Her thoughts kept getting tangled in this or that detail and every possible permutation of the case led to more questions and impossible solutions.

If Edwards had been the primary target all along—whatever the motive—then the killer might very well be a professional engaged for the simple job of putting four bullets into the man's heart. The target would have been identified and the rate between parties agreed—a straightforward transaction for all involved.

Then again, if the killer had been in town for a while, assessing the situation and learning about the locals, it meant a much deeper engagement with the project: it was extremely rare for a hit to come into being over a number of months, and those kinds of circumstances usually had to do with organized crime and drug cartels. This was Ludlow, a town that didn't need more than two police cruisers at the height of the summer season.

Ty Edwards was the wrong kind of victim for that kind of crime: the farthest he'd ever traveled was Seattle, and all he had ever done was work hard in his store and look after his family. He was definitely the wrong kind of victim; and yet, at this point in the investigation, to consider the killing the random act of a lunatic was out of the question.

Madison went over her notes from the previous day and her conversation with Dr. Lynch.

What had Sorensen said to the chief? *How many people in Ludlow have only one kidney? It's a pretty good identifying characteristic, and not one that's immediately visible.*

"Sarge," she said.

Brown looked up from his own troubled speculations.

"Let's forget about Edwards for a minute," she said.

"He's the victim," Brown said.

"I know, just . . . let's forget about him for a minute. Let's just look at the killings without looking at the victims."

"Okay."

"We have one man killed to obtain information and all evidence destroyed by arson, and another man killed from a distance, in public and to make a point. Four in the chest. Quick and clean."

"I'd love to know where this is heading."

"Here it is . . . if we weren't in Colville County—if we were, say, in New York or Chicago or LA—what would you say we were looking at?"

Brown took off his glasses. He had shaved that morning but he looked drawn and, without glasses, oddly exposed. "Looks like an execution," he said.

Madison held his eyes. "Yes, it does, doesn't it? But sometimes killers get it wrong," she said, and she reached for her cell.

"What . . . ?"

Madison dialed a number. "Dr. Lynch," she said into the cell, "I know you're at home, but I need to ask you a question about your patients and, if you can't answer, I'll need you to go into the clinic and check on your server."

Dr. Lynch was clearly objecting, but Madison interrupted him.

"I know, sir, I do. But unless you want to keep calling the Sherman Falls ME to come pick up more dead bodies, I need you to be a little flexible. You can judge the question and make up your mind about it. Okay? Okay." Madison reached for the burglaries file. "I'm going to read you a list of names and I'd like you to tell me whether any of these men have only one kidney. Yes, sir, that's right. Just like Mr. Edwards."

The list was short, and Madison wasn't sure whether she should hope that she was right or hope that she was wrong.

"Chris DeVetta, John Griffin, Howard Wilson, Andrew Howell—"

The doctor gave her his answer.

"Thank you, Doctor."

Madison hung up and turned to Brown.

"Who the heck is Andrew Howell?" she said.

Polly had just entered the room with a plate of home-baked cookies. "He's my husband," she said.

Madison looked at the list. "The residence of Andrew and Polly Howell was broken into last summer. That was your home?"

"Polly," Brown said, "have a seat for a moment."

"Is it about the break-in? Because they caught the men who did it—"

"No, it's about something else," he said.

Through the glass partition in his office Chief Sangster saw Polly being led to a chair. He finished his call and joined them.

"Polly," Madison said when the woman was settled at the table with them, "is Andrew from Ludlow?"

"Why do you ask?"

Madison wanted to go slow because she didn't want to upset the kindly soul who had taken such good care of them. And yet she needed to press on. "Bear with me," she said, "and we'll explain in a minute. Was Andrew born here?"

"No, he's from Gloucester, Massachusetts."

"When did he move to Ludlow?"

"He was a young man. Maybe thirty years old or so."

"Why did he move from Massachusetts to Washington State?"

"He wanted a change, he liked the mountains."

"Does he work in town?"

"No, he's retired. He's worked ever since he got here at the county hall in Sherman Falls."

Madison's mind was collating information, and a job in a county hall did not look good for Mr. Howell.

"Have you met his family back home?" Brown said.

"No," the woman replied. "He lost his parents when he was a boy and had no brothers or sisters."

"No family at all?"

"No."

"Have you ever been back to visit? To see the places where he grew up?"

"No, he wasn't happy there, has never wanted to go back, and it's a shame because—"

"Any friends from back home—phone calls or letters, maybe?"

"No," Polly replied. "But if you want to know more about all that, you should talk to him—or even to Lee. Andrew and Lee arrived in Ludlow together, they're both from Gloucester. They split up after a couple of years, and then Andrew and I started dating."

"Lee? As in Lee Edwards? Your husband Andrew moved to Ludlow thirty years ago with Lee Edwards?"

"Well, she wasn't Lee Edwards then."

You bet she wasn't, Madison thought to herself. She met Brown's eyes and read the same conclusion she had reached.

"We need to talk to Andrew," Brown said. "Right now."

"But why? Is he in danger?" Polly turned from one to the other.

"He might be," Madison said. "Please call him now. Where is he?"

"He should be at home . . ." The woman was getting flustered. She stood to go to the phone and almost bumped into the chief.

"What's going on?" he said when she was out of earshot.

"Andrew lost his kidney because of a childhood illness. It would have been in his file."

"So what?"

"There is a very reasonable possibility that Andrew Howell has been in WITSEC for the last thirty years," Madison said.

"WITSEC?"

"The Federal Witness Protection Program," Brown said. "And it looks like someone found out he's here."

"Polly's Andrew?" he said. "Polly's Andrew is in the Witness Protection Program?"

"No family or friends back home, not even a postcard," Madison said. "Didn't keep in touch and has never been back. Has worked a job in a government office all his life. What do you want to bet that no one in Gloucester, Massachusetts, has ever heard of Andrew Howell?"

"We need to talk to Lee Edwards," Brown said.

"The shooter could have hit both," Madison said. "Lee was right there. And if she arrived here with Andrew, she must be in the program too."

"I guess he wasn't paid to shoot her," Brown said.

"He's not picking up." Polly's cheeks were flushed and her voice shook. "I've tried the home number and I've tried his cell, and he's not picking up."

"Where's your house?" Madison said.

Polly and Andrew Howell's home was only a few minutes away by car, beyond the stone bridge over the Bow River. The snowplows had done what they could, but the chief's cruiser had to creep forward part of the way, negotiating snowdrift and black ice.

Madison called Sorensen from the car and briefed her quickly.

"Do you need me with you?" Sorensen said.

"No, you'd better stay where you are. And make sure the door's locked and the blinds are drawn. Are you wearing your vest?"

Sorensen looked at the ballistic vest hanging on the peg next to her coat. "Yes," she said.

*   *   *

They smelled it before they saw it: acrid and pungent foulness. When the cruiser rounded a bend in the road they saw the house on fire, and Polly shrieked.

The home the Howells had lived in all their married life was a pretty wood-and-brick three-story building with a sloping roof and a small front yard. Their mailbox was the same slate blue as the house—and sometimes, on sunny days, the same blue as the sky. That day the sun was not shining, and flames were consuming the ground floor. They licked at the windows and moved through the house, they rushed up the stairs and were just beginning their eager work on the second floor. The warm glow from inside was like a candle inside a toy lantern.

For a moment everyone was too stunned to react. Then the ground floor windows blew out, and everything happened at the same time: Sangster swearing and calling the fire department, the neighbors pouring out into the street, Brown and Madison hurrying forward, and Polly screaming her husband's name, running and almost losing her balance.

Madison eyed the front door, but fire was already eating it up by the time she ran up the path. Brown grabbed her by the shoulder and pulled her back. The heat was fierce; it was a solid wall around the house and it was beating them back, step by step.

Was Andrew inside?

Of course Andrew's inside, Madison thought, *we know the killer loves fire, he's used it before.*

"We have to find another way in," Brown said.

The fire engine was already on its way. One of the neighbors had called just before the chief, and—one small blessing—the fire station was on their side of town.

"Back door," Madison said.

The fire had its own voice, and it hollered and screamed over their voices. There were crashes coming from inside and every window on the ground floor was lit with it.

Brown and Madison reached the back of the house where the flames were worse than in the front. However the man had started the fire—and not for a second did Madison believe that this was not arson—he had done a heck of a good job.

They circled the building, but there was no possible way in that Madison could see. She was so intent on finding a potential entry point that only when she turned to the street did she notice the people who had already gathered there and hear the siren of the fire department in the distance. Some locals she recognized from the vigil, others from the diner. Two women were looking after Polly, who could barely stand.

Fire is the ultimate killer: it takes everything, it eats everything. A thick, black plume of smoke reached upward into the white sky, while on the ground near the building the snow was already melting.

"Can we go in through the cellar?" Madison said to the chief.

The Howells' basement had long, narrow, horizontal windows. Were they too narrow for an adult to crawl through? There was no fire there yet; the beast was moving upward and the panes were still intact.

Madison did not look at the street. She was vaguely aware of the crowd, and of voices and people moving behind her, until a single thought skewered her where she was. She turned to Brown and said, "He could be here. He could be in the crowd."

The fire engine had arrived, honking and braking almost into a skid as close as possible to the hydrant: two men in full gear were in the truck and others—the volunteers, Madison guessed—were running forward to grab their equipment and suit up.

That would be just perfect. That would be peachy. Light a fire and then put it out.

He could have been one of the volunteers.

"Watch your back," Brown said.

Someone yelled at their side, and Madison saw that it was Hockley.

"I see him!" The deputy was pointing at a basement window. "I see him!"

They rushed and bent low—to avoid the heat from the ground-floor windows—and peered through the glass: a body lay face-down on the concrete floor. The room was dim but it was clearly a body.

"Is it Andrew?" Madison asked Hockley.

"Looks like him."

"Break the glass! We break the glass and drag him out." Was it Hockley or Kupitz? Madison couldn't be sure.

But one thing she did know: no one was going to be able to get in through those windows. They were set into the brick foundation of the building, which was solid and still cool to the touch in spite of the flames a few feet above it. Madison studied the room: the fire had not broken in yet, but there would be smoke—and smoke kills just as well as fire does.

The fire chief pushed through the crush while his men hooked up the hose and hollered to the crowd to stand back.

"We don't have much time," he yelled. "The floor could give up any moment and collapse into the cellar. You should stand back."

"Andrew Howell's in there," Sangster said. "We need to get him out."

"We've got clubs and brick hammers," he replied. "But anything that's going to take more than a few minutes is going to take too long."

Hockley stepped forward. "We could use my truck," he said.

"It will take too long to pull—" Sangster started, but Hockley cut in.

"Not to pull. To crash in. I could crash into the window," he said. "Like the Davis boys last summer, remember?"

It took a moment for Sangster to react. "Hock, this is not—"

"I can do it, Chief. Andrew is far enough away, but I need to do it now."

Sangster hesitated. If they'd sat down and examined the situation and listed exactly all of the problems that that particular course of action would present, everybody would have agreed that it was nuts and they were idiots to even think about it.

"Boss?" Hockley said, and Sangster nodded.

"I can't guarantee . . . ," the fire chief started to say.

But Hockley was already sprinting to the pavement and digging for his keys in his pocket. He passed under the arc of water that was shooting up into the air and climbed into the truck.

Sorensen had heard the fire department siren and yet she had not allowed herself to be sidetracked from the work at hand. After Madison's call she had made sure that the door of the senior center was locked and the blinds were drawn. She had slipped on her ballistic vest and tightened the straps so that it would sit snug around her shoulders and chest, and then she had returned to her instruments. Because that was how she fought the fight.

The fiber came from the carpet of a car, and Sorensen was going to identify precisely what car—even if, compared with her resources in Seattle, she was working with one arm tied behind her back.

The heavy knock on the door startled her, and she looked up from her laptop.

Chapter 45

Hockley buckled his seat belt and pulled it hard. All around him he could see scared, disbelieving faces. Darn it, *he* was scared and disbelieving, but there wasn't much else that they could do.

Keep it slow and measured and straight on, he told himself, *and aim for the window farthest away from Andrew.*

Hockley revved the engine and mounted the pavement, turning into the blazing house. His knuckles were white and his mouth set as he drove over the patchy winter lawn and the ornamental aisle—aware and sorry that he was driving over Polly's flowers.

Keep it slow, measured, and straight on. Fifteen miles per hour should give it just about enough of a knock.

There was a path clear of people and Hockley pressed his foot on the accelerator. The wall surged before him, faster than he would have expected, and he hit it squarely at thirteen miles per hour. The air bag punched him and the crash rebounded through his body. He looked up, dazed, and all he could hear were the sounds of hammers against the bricks.

Kupitz yanked the door open and dragged him out. "Hock, are you all right?"

The fire chief and two of his men were finishing the job. The crash had destroyed the window and dislodged a handful of bricks: enough for men to go through, enough to reach the motionless body on the floor.

The heat was building up and now even the second floor was eerily illuminated. Madison, half of her face hot and half cold, swept her eyes over the crowd and over the firefighters. She didn't know what she was looking for, and she hoped that she would recognize it if she saw it. If the killer was there, if he was moving among them, would he try to stop them from saving his victim? Would he reveal himself in a look?

So far, Madison thought, he had kept himself hidden: his was not an assassin's mission to immolate himself for the sake of achieving his object. He had been careful, he had been cautious.

Let him be wary a little longer, Madison prayed. *Let him be prudent and not try anything in the middle of this mess.*

The SWAT team was already on its way back to Ludlow but nobody knew how long it would take for them to get there— and, once they did, whether there would be more victims to be counted.

"Here we go . . ." The fire chief shone his heavy-duty flashlight inside the basement. "In and out, people. No lingering for mementos."

His words were still in the air when his body disappeared into the hole followed by two firefighters; a third one was left to point the flashlight inside the dim room and prevent anyone else from going in.

A puff of smoke leaked out of the opening, floating out into the air like poison. It found Madison's throat and she coughed. The firefighters had been wearing masks, but Andrew Howell had not, and he wasn't moving. Any second now, they would pull him out; any second now, he would be out. Brown and Madison kept their focus on the crowd, their hands resting on the butt of their sidearms, seeking out something—or someone—that might not be there at all.

Madison heard raised voices from inside and knew that something was wrong. There was swearing and loud exchanges muffled by the men's gear, and she tried to peek into the hole. The beam of light cut through the smoke and her eyes found the men standing around the body in the corner. Andrew Howell lay with his arms spread out and his legs bent to one side and . . .

Madison blinked.

Above her something crashed in the living room. The heat was becoming unbearable, but she couldn't move from where she was. And she couldn't look away from what she saw.

"They're going to need an ax," she said to Brown, and she ran to the fire truck.

"Give me an ax," she said to one of the firefighters. "Quickly."

The man didn't ask why—or who she was—and as Madison turned to the blazing house she saw Kupitz and Hockley disappearing into the hole. The ax was heavy in her arms, and every detail stood out in the full horror of the moment: the sheen on the steel blade and the curve of the handle, and her breath catching in her throat. They needed an ax because Andrew Howell lay in a heap on the concrete floor in the basement of his pretty wooden house, and around his right ankle the jaws of a steel trap had been snapped shut. The trap's chain was wrapped around a heavy beam, and no one in that basement was going anywhere.

"Here . . ." she said, and she passed the ax down into the gloom. If they tried to pry open the trap's jaws, it would take too long and the man might bleed out. How much time did they have? The killer didn't have to do anything. All that was left was to stand back and watch. He had already done enough, and the house would do the rest.

Colville County had decided to catch up with the rest of the world in madness and evil, and they, who had been sent to help, were failing. The glint of metal around the man's foot was the mark of their failure.

There was a sudden surge of heat as some of the upstairs windows blew out and shards of glass rained around them. A piece caught the material of Madison's coat by her shoulder. A firefighter stood before them and started to push Brown and Madison backward.

"They're still inside," Brown said to the man, but he put the flat of his gloved hands on their chests and pushed them back firmly.

The chief and the deputies were in the basement with the other firefighters, and neither Brown nor Madison were inclined to do as they were told.

Chief Sangster stared at the figure on the floor. One of the firefighters had taken off one glove and was feeling under Andrew's jaw for his pulse. It was Polly's Andrew, for Chrissakes.

"Fast and shallow. Going into shock," the man said.

Sangster wanted to cough out the taste in his mouth. The smoke was getting thicker as it seeped under the basement door, but everybody's eyes were on the thing, the dreadful thing, hanging on the man's ankle.

"Pull the chain tight," Kupitz said to Hockley, and he did.

"Ready to move him as soon as we're clear," the fire chief said.

Normally Hockley would have made a crack about Kupitz hitting his hand and not the chain, but all the jokes had gone out of him. Koop looked ready to smash his way into hell if necessary. Hockley nodded, pulled the chain tight from the end with the locked jaws, then watched his friend raise the ax high above his head and swing it down hard.

The blade hit metal a couple of inches away from the beam and split the link open.

"Let's go!"

"Take his shoulder."

"Lift the trap and keep the weight off the foot."

"On my count . . . one . . . two . . . three . . ."

* * *

Brown and Madison saw Sangster emerging from the hole.

"Back away. Give 'em room." The firefighter finally managed to get them to inch away.

Through the haze Madison saw them carry out the limp, lifeless body. They were almost completely out of the building, almost all clear and safe, when the air was torn by a crash. A wave of heat knocked into them: the ground floor had collapsed into the basement. Madison walked backward away from the house.

How many men had gone in? How many had come out?

Brown spun her around; he looked suddenly stricken. There were cheers for the firefighters, and some people were clapping. They really had no idea about what was going on.

"The killer hit Edwards by mistake," Brown said.

Madison nodded.

"How did he realize that he'd gotten the wrong guy? Why did he come for Polly's husband?"

Somewhere behind her Hockley was calling out Kupitz's name, his voice ragged and raw.

Brown eyed the crowd. "How did the killer find out that he'd gotten the wrong guy?"

Chapter 46

Lee Edwards woke up in her bed. The room was dim because her heavy drapes were drawn, and she remembered that she had gone back for a nap sometime earlier in the morning. She had hardly slept the night before. What had begun as a trickle of memories had become a flood, and it felt as if she was stuck on the *This Is Your Life* channel. Conversations of any kind had turned into a welcome distraction, and as she sat up she wondered who she would find on duty in her living room. She had left Rhonda there earlier, reading her book club paperback.

The poodle looked up when she stood but seemed perfectly content to remain at the bottom of her bed. Ty would have objected, but Lee needed the familiar warm weight of another soul lying next to her in the darkness.

She emerged into the living room and smiled: Ben Taylor was sitting on the sofa where Rhonda had been, reading one of Ty's historical mysteries.

He looked up.

"There you are," he said. "How are we feeling?"

"Better," the woman replied.

"Would you like some tea?"

"That would be lovely."

"Have a seat, let me do it."

"You're a sweetheart."

Ben busied himself in the kitchen, humming a tune, and a few minutes later he returned carrying a tray with a teapot and mugs.

"You're going to make someone a wonderful husband one day," Lee said.

Ben smiled. "Here you go . . ."

The snowfall had made every sound muted, and the neighborhood felt peaceful. They drank the tea in silence because Lee had become accustomed to not having to entertain her guests. They didn't expect her to—and in fact seemed poised to do the entertaining themselves.

"I really loved the stories you were telling us yesterday," the man said. "About how Ludlow used to be when you first arrived. I should do a program about the history of the place. What do you think?"

"Sounds good, a lot of old-timers have stories to tell."

"Maybe," the man said. "But they wouldn't be as good as yours. Coming to Ludlow all the way from Massachusetts."

"A lot of people here have come from other places."

"Still, a story is a complex thing. Everybody has a story to tell, but not everyone's story has, you know, the kind of human interest that gets people to tune in, right?"

"Sure."

"You, for example, you were born in . . . ?"

"Gloucester."

"That's right. And it's a fishing town, a real old-fashioned harbor and all . . . and here you are surrounded by mountains, nowhere near the sea. And if Ludlow is isolated now, I can't imagine what it would have been like then. No Internet, no cell phones, barely even a newspaper."

"Lord, no. We had none of that."

"Not a movie theater or a store that sold more than two brands of coffee."

Lee chuckled. "It was different, I'll give you that."

"Well," Ben Taylor said, "forgive me, but I've got to ask. Why the fuck did you come here, then?"

Lee Edwards smiled and sat forward, because obviously she hadn't really heard what she thought she'd heard.

"What?" she said.

"I just asked you," Ben Taylor said, as courteously as if he were addressing a foreign monarch, "why the fuck did you come to Ludlow?"

The profanity was a sharp slap.

"Ben—"

"I find it difficult to believe anything you say, when you already lied to me about the most basic thing."

"I don't understand."

"I'm sure you don't . . . but you will in a minute."

"I want you to leave," Lee Edwards said, and stood up.

"Where were you born?" the man said, and he took a sip of tea. "Please don't say *Gloucester* because we're way beyond that."

Lee Edwards froze.

"Sit," Ben Taylor said.

The woman hesitated.

"*Sit!*"

Lee Edwards dropped down onto the sofa. She couldn't have walked, anyway. There was a swarming in her ears and she felt icy cold, as if life had already left her.

"You were born in Boston," Ben Taylor said. "Not in Gloucester, no. I don't know if you were ever in Gloucester at all, but you had to account for your East Coast accent, right?"

Lee didn't reply.

Ben Taylor's eyes bore into hers. "You left me a note. You left me three lines to say good-bye forever, and a puppy in a box to take the sting of it away. A puppy. Do you have any idea how long it's taken me to find you?"

Lee watched him, in shock.

"Years. It's taken me years," he said.

The silence outside wasn't peaceful anymore. It was an oppressing silence that pushed down on her from all sides.

"Aidan?" The woman said finally.

"Yes," the man sighed.

"I—"

It was all she managed to say because, faster than she could move, Ben Taylor had gripped her wrist. Somehow there was a syringe in his hand and she was struggling and then falling back against the sofa and into darkness.

Ben Taylor put his arms around the woman and lifted her. He was familiar with the house and had been inside it many times since the fake burglary.

He carried Lee Edwards into the bathroom and laid her in the tub. Supporting her head with one hand, he grabbed a towel with the other and bunched it up to give her a pillow against the hard surface. There was snuffling at the door and the dog wagged his tail. Ben scratched him behind the ear and led him by his collar back into the bedroom. He closed the door and returned to the bathroom. Lee Edwards lay still, with her eyes half open.

He watched her for a moment: her chest rose and fell, her face had paled, and her hands were palms up like a bizarre Deposition of Christ, where Lee had taken Christ's place. *Once a Catholic . . .*

The song was with him again—a memory, and a light in the shadows. *Daisy, Daisy, give me your answer, do. I'm half crazy, all for the love of you.*

He went to the cabinet, still humming, and there, as he already knew, was Ty Edwards's razor. So perfect for the suicide of a widow who could not bear to live under the weight of her grief.

Daisy, Daisy . . .

Kevin Brown rang the doorbell. He could still feel the heat of the fire on his face but the fire was somewhere else, together with the noise of the crowd and the emergency vehicles. Where Brown stood there was only silence.

A tall man in jeans and a red fleece jacket opened the door.

"I'm Detective Sergeant Brown. I'd like a word with Mrs. Edwards, if she's around."

"She is, but she's having a little quiet time," the man said. "I'm Ben Taylor."

"I think we've met. You work at the radio station, right?"

"Right, your colleague recorded the appeal."

Ben Taylor had long hair in a ponytail and a crooked smile. He was holding a book in his hand, as if Brown had interrupted his midday reading.

"Yes, she did." Brown walked in. "I really need to speak with Mrs. Edwards. Is she sleeping?"

"No, she wanted to take a hot bath, to try and relax. She hasn't been sleeping at all."

"I can imagine. Would you mind knocking on the door and telling her I'm here?"

"I'd rather wait a little. She's only just gone in. Why don't you have a seat and I'll make some coffee, and in ten minutes or so I'll knock on the door and she'll come out."

"I need to see her right now, I'm afraid."

Alice Madison scanned the backyard. Every movement and every sound was significant: they needed to get Lee Edwards out of the house as soon as possible. She looked up. The sky was colorless and bright, and the snowfall had almost stopped. The firs around the house were laden with it and the branches trailed on the ground under their burden. A bird flapped its wings somewhere above her and a chunk of white spattered on the lawn.

Without looking, Madison undid the safety strap on her holster just as her cell phone vibrated in her pocket.

"Where's your partner? Has something happened?" Ben Taylor said.

His manner was pleasant, but Brown was already on edge and was looking behind the man to the bungalow's corridor, ready to go around him and get Lee Edwards out of her bath himself. The question stopped him cold.

Where's your partner?

It was an innocent question, delivered with a concerned smile.

Where's your partner?

"She's at the station," Brown replied, not missing a beat.

Taylor had already reached behind him for the revolver in his belt under the fleece.

"Good for her," he said, and the barrel of the Smith & Wesson was aimed straight at Brown's chest. His hand was steady and his voice was calm. "You got here too late, Detective. Lee Edwards has already taken her life and in due time she'll be found by a friend. Me. You, on the other hand, are going to be the Ludlow killer's next victim. But fear not, I'm sure you'll get a proper cop funeral. Everyone loves a good cop funeral."

Madison eased herself through the bedroom window. She had noticed that it was open and it had been easy to push the pane aside and slip behind the drapes. It had been too long since Brown had gone inside, and the question that had brought them there was still pecking at her.

How had the killer known?

The killer had known because he had spoken to Lee Edwards, and she had told him something that had led him to Andrew Howell.

The room Madison found herself in was a bedroom. The blankets on the bed were pulled up, though not quite straight.

Unbidden and unwanted came the memory of Robert Dennen's body on the morgue's table, and the steel jaws of the hunting trap. If the man they were after could do that, he could do anything. The adrenaline was acid in her gut and her gun hand felt clammy.

A dark shape on the bed moved, and Madison's breath caught. The dog shifted and his tail thumped once. *Good Tucker, stay where you are.*

Voices spoke harshly, somewhere nearby, and Madison listened, flat against the door. Brown's voice and another man's.

Where were they?

She peeked into the corridor: a corner hid the men from her line of sight. Across from her the bathroom door was ajar, but the light was on. Madison darted inside.

Lee Edwards was sleeping, fully dressed, in the tub, her head nestled against a towel and her arms crossed. Her breath was barely a sigh. It was not sleep, it was something else. She was holding a black-and-white photograph to her chest, and red stains were spreading on her clothes from the cuts on her wrists.

Madison felt the scream die in her throat as she seized whatever towels she could find. The woman's hands and arms were slippery and heavy; Madison wrapped them tight, without making a sound, her Glock abandoned in the middle of the bathroom floor.

She shouldn't leave the woman alone, but she couldn't stay. And she wanted to stay, but she must go.

Madison reached for her piece. If Lee was going to die because she hadn't done enough then Madison would have to live with it. She made sure the towels were as tight as they could be and she leaned close to the woman's ear.

"I beg you," she whispered. "Hang on, Lee. Just hang on."

Madison inched forward in the corridor.

When she reached the corner and peeked behind it, a man was holding a gun to Brown's head.

Fear is uglier than despair, and Brown had been afraid for a long time. For weeks—since a call for backup during a gang shootout—he had been waiting for that moment in the Edwards home. Waiting as fear had soured his every day.

Two years earlier he had been shot by a madman. Since then, he had never aimed his piece at another human being and had never looked at the business end of someone else's gun. On his way to respond to the gang shoot-out a prickling of fear had given him pause: what if his hand shook when it should be still? What if, in the instant when he should act, his mind was going to be clouded by memories of getting shot? What if he froze?

The situation had resolved itself before they'd arrived on the scene, but the fear had stayed with Brown and kept him company on every shift since. He was always first through a door, hoping to face whatever it was that was waiting for him on the other side, always going in first because the idea of letting down his partner was more than he could bear.

When the sniper shot at Madison in the square, Brown had been terrified for her and pissed off in equal measure. And now, he reflected, he finally had his answers. The timing was less than good, for sure, but there he stood, in Lee and Ty Edwards's living room, and he was still the cop he had always been.

There was fear—as there should be—but he could still think, he could still function.

Ben Taylor's gaze was like a doll's—empty and flat. Brown focused on it: he needed to warn Madison, and he needed to get to the widow.

"What the hell did you do all this for?" Brown said.

Ben Taylor was about to answer. The barrel of his revolver wavered a few inches away from Brown's head . . .

And in that instant three gunshots rang out in the enclosed room, so loud that the sound slammed into Brown's body and spun him around.

Ben Taylor was on the ground. His eyes were open and all the way gone. There was darker red pooling on his chest, and the force of the shots had sent him halfway onto the sofa.

Madison stood in the doorway. Her face was blank.

When their eyes met, she spoke.

"She's in the tub. He cut her wrists."

Chapter 47

No one had been told exactly what happened, or what kind of emergency they were dealing with, but a number of ambulances were screeching their way toward Ludlow. The fields on either side of Highway 395 were pure, unbroken white but the lanes had been almost completely cleared—hopefully, they would make it in good time.

Alice Madison's hands and arms were stained with blood from the towels, and she gazed at them as if she was not entirely sure what to do. She wanted to wash it all off, but everything was evidence. Her *hands* were evidence. Reality seemed to come in single bites: Brown was safe; Lee Edwards was on the floor; her gun had already been taken away.

Dr. Lynch and the nurses were working on Mrs. Edwards; Brown and Madison had been pushed to one side. The woman lying on the bath mat was so pale that she was almost translucent, but she was still alive.

Brown clasped Madison's elbow and guided her into the kitchen. He turned on the tap, made sure the water was warm, and put her hands under it.

"How did you know to come in?" he said as he rubbed her hands with soap.

"It was taking you too long. If everything was okay, you would have bundled her out of the house in two minutes flat."

"And Ben Taylor . . . ?"

"Sorensen matched the fibers. It was car carpet, and the only one in town who had that kind of car was the man from the radio station. She sent me a picture of his driver's license."

The warm water felt wonderful and Madison turned her wrists into the stream. She could have stayed there for hours.

"Thank you," Brown said.

Madison had been watching them, waiting for the man to move his aim even slightly off Brown so that she could shoot without risk. She had waited and taken her shot at the right moment, and Brown was still alive.

She nodded, because she didn't trust her voice.

Madison dialed the number from the backyard. When it went to voice mail she was almost relieved, because she didn't want to say *I just killed a man.*

Quinn's voice calmed her somehow.

"There's been an incident," she said into her cell. "We've got the man, but people have been injured. I'm okay. We're all okay. I'll call in a while."

Chief Sangster sat in his cruiser and held his cell. He had been put on hold.

There were so many crime scenes to process that he had simply locked up Ben Taylor's home and the Edwardses' house. Someone would get to them when they had the time. In all probability it wouldn't be Amy Sorensen, and the chief found that he was sorry about that.

The Howells' house—what remained of it after the fire—would be left for the arson investigator to pick his way through. The chief knew what had happened; he had seen Ben Taylor's body on the floor and the bloody towels in the bathroom. His brain knew, but his heart half refused to believe.

The woman from the US Marshals Service came back on the line and for the second time asked him the reason for his call. Finally, she transferred him to the right extension.

"Lee Edwards's real name is Daisy O'Brian," Chief Sangster said. "Her husband was Jimmy O'Brian, and he was Boston Mob."

The sky through the window was dark, and the chief was holding a glass with a measure of something that shone like liquid amber. Brown, Madison, and the chief were in the Miller guesthouse because it would have felt wrong to have a drink in the police station—and a drink was what they all needed. It was not the kind of party they wanted to hold in the Tavern, and not the kind of conversation Edna Miller would ever have expected of her guests.

No one had been interested in lighting the fire—that day they'd had quite enough.

"Boston Irish?" Brown said.

"Yup, and those were the hard years, the bloody years." Sangster had a sheaf of notes in his hand.

"Lee testified against him?" Madison said.

"Yes, and Sean O'Malley did too—that's Andrew's real name. Jimmy and Andrew had kidnapped a man, tortured, and murdered him for information on a shipment of diamonds. He was a messenger for one of the Winter Hill families, and Andrew always maintained that he had never even touched him. When the FBI got to Andrew, he turned on Jimmy and testified in court. What Jimmy had done to the man was savage. Jimmy O'Brian, of course, said that it had been all Andrew's doing. Anyway, Jimmy went to prison and Andrew disappeared. He had been having an affair with Jimmy's wife and, after they testified, she disappeared with him, leaving a son behind who would end up being raised by the paternal grandparents. A boy named Aidan."

"Ben Taylor."

"That's right. You can imagine what the grandparents told him about his mother. The picture Ben had put in her hands must have been taken in happier days, when the family was still together."

"How well did you know Ben Taylor?" Madison said.

Sangster took a long sip. "Ben moved to Ludlow about eighteen months ago, when the job at the radio station opened up. He got busy in the local community and he fit right in, like he'd always lived here."

"I bet he did," Brown said.

"How did he find out?" Madison asked. "WITSEC is pretty tight."

"Well, the marshals weren't overjoyed about telling me, but it seems things were not as tight thirty years ago. Some outsider found out about Andrew and Lee, and they sat on the information until they were ready to sell it. Jimmy O'Brian died in jail four years ago. Died of lung cancer, and he had never even smoked. Talk about rotten luck. Looks like his boy decided to set things right."

After the day they'd all had, Edna Miller's old-fashioned, lived-in furnishings were reassuring in a homey sort of way. It was a soft place where they could talk about and process horrible events. Sangster closed his eyes and rested his head against the back of the padded chair. He could still see Andrew's body in the cellar.

Madison shifted—one leg was over the armrest. "Do we know for sure that it was O'Brian who killed the man and not Andrew?"

"We don't know anything for sure," Sangster said, and those words had never felt truer. "Except that a deal was struck, and Jimmy got the crappy end of it."

Ben Taylor had come after the people who had betrayed his father; he had come after the mother who had abandoned him for her lover. If you squinted from far enough away, he almost had a legitimate grudge.

"Did he have a record?"

"No, never been arrested."

"The first felony he committed was the burglaries," Brown said. "Hard to believe he graduated straight to murder and arson."

"We don't know that's the case." Madison could still see the man's hand and the revolver pointing at Brown. "He could have done all kinds of things and gotten away with them, and it wouldn't show up on NCIC."

"The marshals were pretty embarrassed we didn't know about having two people in WITSEC in town, but it wasn't their fault," Sangster said. "The previous chief of police knew, but he died of a heart attack and we never had a proper changeover. For years, all that's been happening is that Andrew and Lee make one phone call every twelve months—to confirm it's all fine and dandy—and that's it."

"And now?" Madison said.

"And now," the chief replied, "the only people who know about their identities are in this room."

"I'm telling Sorensen when she gets back. She deserves to know the truth."

"No question about it. I trust her. But, as far as it goes, that's it."

"What about your deputies?"

Sangster sighed. "They went into a burning building for Andrew—whatever his name is—and I'll explain the situation. Anyone else, though—including Polly—is not my business to tell."

Sangster didn't want to burden his men with that knowledge, because there was something corrosive about it, and he knew that it would change the town around them forever. Then again, they were grown-ups who had chosen to carry a badge.

Polly Howell had gone to the hospital with her husband, and she would be coming home with someone altogether different, Madison thought. It wasn't up to the chief to tell her, but she had the right to know. And so did Betty Dennen.

"Chief," Madison said, "Mrs. Dennen has lost her husband, and she shouldn't have to live with anything less than the whole truth."

"I agree. But if she's told, then Lee and Andrew might have to relocate, create a new identity, and start over somewhere else."

"She might be willing to keep their secret."

Sangster finished his drink in one long gulp. "Looks like, soon enough, half the town is going to know, anyway."

Jay Kupitz tried to shift his body on the bed, and sudden pain reminded him that he was in the hospital. He had been asleep and was not completely awake and alert yet. Morphine had a lot to answer for, but he wasn't complaining—waiting for the ambulance had been excruciating, and painkillers were going to be his best friend for a few days. He had almost made it out of Polly's home but had been caught in the building's collapse. One broken leg and one broken wrist were small potatoes in what could have been the last shift he would ever work.

"Welcome back, Koop."

Kupitz turned to the voice.

Amy Sorensen was sitting on the chair next to his bed, her long legs stretched out and her red hair loose from its customary ponytail. "Your mom went to get herself a cup of coffee."

Kupitz frowned. Thinking was arduous with the morphine in his system: for a moment there, he thought he might be hallucinating Sorensen.

"What are you doing here?" he said.

"Hockley said that you were practically out of the building, but you went back because you said the chain might carry the killer's fingerprints."

"You said we needed his prints to nail him." It was as much as his confused brain allowed him to verbalize.

"And you went back for the chain . . ."

He nodded.

"You daring, foolish man," Sorensen said.

Then she got up, leaned forward, and kissed the top of his head—like she'd done when her kids were small.

The next time Kupitz opened his eyes, his mom was in the chair.

He didn't tell anyone about Sorensen; he didn't want to be told that it had been a dream.

In bed, with her cell phone on the pillow and her eyes closed, Madison could almost believe that Quinn was next to her. They had spoken and they had been quiet and he hadn't asked her much about the shooting. What she wanted to say, she would say. His company in the attic room was all she needed.

She fell asleep after a while and from all the way across the state Nathan Quinn listened to her breathing slow down and deepen.

Chapter 48

Today is the day, Alice thought, and she was too far out of herself
to be either surprised or scared. *Today is the day he's going to tell
me that I have to kill one of them.*

The notion didn't startle Alice, because she had been petrified
for three solid days and her system couldn't take any more. She
was there and she was elsewhere, watching herself being afraid.
There was a line, though, and the little girl could still see it, feel
it in herself like a hard ridge in her personality: she had gutted
a squirrel for him, she had stolen a silly red canteen for him, but
she would *not* shoot a person for that crazy mothertrucker—the
word was a memory from her days in Friday Harbor and it made
her smile so unexpectedly that it broke through the numbness.
Mothertrucker. That was it. That was all. *Mothertrucker.* She was
done. She was past caring, way past.

There was dew on the grass, so pretty it made her heart ache.
Her hands stroked the tips of the blades and she rubbed her
damp fingers together. What would happen if she started walking right now? If she just walked away and never looked back?

Alice placed the palm of her hand flat against the ground. How curious that, days ago, she had been afraid of being lost and now nothing would have been better than being completely alone on the mountain, meandering along the stream and lying on the warm grass with her hands behind her back, tiny under the wide blue sky.

The mountain wouldn't kill you, she said to herself. The thought had come from nowhere and there it was. *The mountain wouldn't kill you, but he will.*

What was she prepared to do? How far was she prepared to go?

The hikers were still asleep and Alice gazed at their tents, so familiar now. She believed in her bones that—if it came to it, if she tried to escape—the man would run after her and not pursue the campers. He couldn't split himself in two, and she was the one he'd go after. She knew that like she'd known a bad bluffer with a good hand at Joey Cavizzi's table in Vegas.

The mountain wouldn't kill you, the little girl repeated to herself. The man would not be happy about it, he'd made that clear enough the other night. *Well, sister, what are the alternatives?*

"The way you kill your target is just as important as making the kill in the first place," the man said. "It's got to be clean, quick, and you have to know how to dispose of it when you're done."

Alice listened to The Hunter, and as she had done every morning, she rolled up her sleeping bag and made sure her pack was zipped closed and ready for travel. It was essential, he had told her the first day, to keep a neat camp.

The hikers had left their site after a late breakfast—it looked as if they had brought with them all the food they'd ever need and were not bothered by the necessity of hunting for their meals. *Must be nice.* Alice could smell the eggs and bacon from where she was hiding.

The three couples walked off into a thicket that opened onto a trail.

"There's a waterfall about a mile that way," the man whispered. "Bet you anything that's where they're heading. We're going to cut them off where the trail forks. On your feet, boy."

This is it, Alice thought, and she shouldered her pack with her baseball bat tied to the side. She was calm all of a sudden—creepy calm, as her friend Jessica used to call it.

The weather had decided that cool rain would do better than sunshine and the wind had brought black, churning clouds. It was only drizzle so far, but you could tell that the sky was working itself up to a showstopper.

The walk, following in the man's steps, was not easy. They were striding through a sweep of roots and shrubs and low branches that whipped back against the little girl's face. Alice pushed her baseball cap down and kept on. The drizzle tapped on her visor, and raindrops found their way into the back of her neck and down her shoulder blades, but Alice kept on. When the man turned and saw how determinedly she was doing so, he grinned at her as if they were on the best of outings. Alice did not smile back.

"Look . . ." He pointed at a green shoot with oddly shaped white flowers. "Some call it *vanilla leaf*, some call it *deer's foot*—see the shape of the leaves?" An ugly glint in his eyes now. "Some people, though, call it *sweet after death*, because if you crush the leaves you can smell the sweetness."

Sweet after death. If you crush the leaves . . .

Alice looked away.

After what seemed like hours, just ahead of them, Alice saw a trail and a little farther on a fork that led south one way and east the other. The man paused and unshouldered his pack.

"This is what I want you to do—," he said, but his next words were swallowed by crashing thunder.

The rain fell in sheets over them, around them, and every which way. So heavy that it appeared to be a solid shape molding itself around everything.

A shriek nearby, and the man turned.

The deluge must have caught the hikers by surprise as well. The man squinted and, even though the trail was maybe six feet away from him, he couldn't make anything out except for the twisted forms of trees and bushes. The rain was a shroud between them and the whole world was a gray haze. The man turned back and shaded his eyes with the flat of his hand.

The kid was gone.

Alice ran flat out. It hadn't even been a decision: it was as if the thunder had been a starter gun and she was off. She was half-blind from the rain and half-deaf from the roaring of the down-pour. But so was the man, she told herself, so was the man.

She had seen the trail that led south, and that's where she was aiming. Would he guess that she would go that way? She could not stop and ponder the issue; she had hardly any advantage at all, and while the mountain wouldn't kill her it certainly expected her to be smart.

Be smart or be dead.

Alice ran—once or twice bouncing off tree trunks onto the slippery ground and straight back on her feet. She slipped and fell and kept running—and all the time the rain was a veil around the little girl, keeping her hidden, keeping her safe.

If he had called out after her she would not have heard him, and she was glad. She did not want to hear him shout after her in anger, she didn't ever want to hear his voice again.

Somehow, the relatively unobstructed progress meant that she had stumbled onto the trail. Alice followed it down the mountain, flying over the slick, stony path. With surprising clarity she managed to grasp that if she could run more easily on the path then so could he. She imagined him after her: his steps more confident than hers, and his eyes sharper—as sharp as the long hunting knife.

Alice didn't know how long she had been scampering down the mountain, and she could only hope that she was still on the trail. She had been careful, but *careful* doesn't count for much when you're running for your life.

She felt grass underfoot—soft, springy grass—she corrected her direction and felt again the slimy, reassuring feel of the path under her sneakers. The mountain was helping her, just as the rain was helping her. This simple belief brightened her little girl's heart and she pushed even harder. She let herself go with neither thought nor control: she would go wherever the mountain would take her.

When, minutes or hours later, the rain stopped—almost as suddenly as it had come—Alice found herself at the mouth of a valley so green it made her eyes hurt, and the trail—the blessed, hallowed trail—was straight ahead of her. Alice dared to look behind her for the first time. Her eyes scanned the landscape and could detect no movement aside from the tops of the trees bowing a little in the wind.

She allowed herself a single moment to catch her breath and then darted under the edge of a rocky crop from where she could follow the path without being too easily spotted from above. She couldn't run anymore but she could jog a little, walk for a minute or two, then jog again until the stitch in her side became too much.

Keep it together, keep it together just a little longer. She could hear herself huffing and puffing like some old person, but she couldn't help it. *There will be people. There will be* regular *people.*

The ground was sodden under her feet, and her sneakers flapped in the mud. Alice was soaked and exhausted and would have given anything and everything for a family in a station wagon parked by the side of a road, or maybe a ranger in one of those official vehicles. She was looking ahead so intently that she didn't hear the footsteps behind her until a hand grabbed the back of her pack and whirled her around with a yelp.

The man stood there, just as drenched as she was, the rifle hanging on his shoulder by the worn strap. His face was a blank mask and his eyes were glittering buttons of nothing.

"What do you think you're doing?" he said.

Alice did not reply.

"What do you think you're doing?"

Alice backed away from him, slowly, bumped against a tree and worked her way around it until it stood between her and the man. She had no strength to speak and no words to say what she wanted to say.

"Come here," the man said.

Alice shook her head.

"We're not done, boy. Not by any means."

Alice reached the side of her pack with shaking hands, yanked off her baseball bat and lifted it between them. It felt clumsy and ridiculous in her hands, and it trembled with each heartbeat.

"What's on your mind, son?" the man said, and he took a step forward around the edge of the path.

The rain had washed away much of the earth around the roots and what was left was slippery and wet through. The hole opened suddenly under his feet and at any other time he would have been fine, he could easily have righted himself and grabbed at the tree for support, but the heavy green backpack pulled him backward, the man lost his balance and fell into five feet of ditch full of bare roots and rotten leaves. And he fell badly.

He swore—a litany of words that Alice had never heard before. The man unshouldered his pack and with a groan threw it high above him and out of the hole. He swore again, and Alice realized that he had hurt his leg. On the edge of the hole, his rifle lay on the wet grass.

They both noticed it at the same time but the girl was closer; she dropped the bat and reached for it, pulling it out of the man's grasping hand.

Alice held it in her arms; it was an awkward, ugly thing. She brought the stock up to her shoulder as she had seen in movies and met his eyes. It was heavy and her arms were going to tire quickly. She aimed at the man's head because, at that distance, she was going to hit him no matter what.

"What's your name?" she said.

The man considered the question with his head to one side and his eyes narrowed.

"What's your name?" Alice repeated, and she could feel her arms would soon begin to shake in their effort to hold up the weapon.

"A name is a powerful thing. Why should I tell you?"

"I told you mine."

"Maybe you shouldn't have."

"What's your name?"

"You take a shot at me and the stock is going to take your shoulder right off, boy. Put it down before you hurt yourself."

"What was lesson number two?" Alice's voice cracked as she felt her emotions rise and her throat tighten.

"Lesson number two is to shoot your target right in the eye."

The girl's arm began to quiver. "Is that what you wanted me to do?"

"What do you think?"

"Tell me your name, you sonofabitch."

"Why do you want to know?"

"Because you're not going to get away with this."

"*This* . . . what? I fed you and kept you safe for three days and I was walking you back to your family."

"You know what I'm talking about."

"No, son, I don't. And I'm offended that you would think ill of me after I did my best to teach you and entertain you."

The barrel of the rifle swayed. The man reached for the thick root of a hemlock to pull himself out. It was close but his fingers couldn't quite touch it.

"Stay where you are," Alice said.

"Or what?"

It was really the only question worth answering that day, and they both understood it. *Or what?*

"Tell me your name and I'll let you go. And don't lie to me, because I'll know if you do." A bad hand in the hand of a good bluffer is still a bad hand, and Alice had been trained to spot a lie since she was five. She hoped that she was a good bluffer because she was holding a 7-2 and it was a fold 'em hold 'em hand.

For the first time the man looked at the girl with something other than disdain. "You're a little grunt, but you've got some balls on you. Put the rifle down and I'll let *you* go."

Lie or truth? Definitely lie.

What would happen if the man went on his way, free to return to his tracking and trailing? Had the hikers gone back to their camp? Would he go back to them, back to the hunt? What if he made them pay for her cheek?

The crack of thunder had gobbled up the man's words, as if they had been too repugnant for Alice to hear.

"What did you want me to do?" she said, and her voice carried the exhaustion of days.

"I wanted to teach you something that you would never, ever forget," the man replied.

Alice nodded, yes, she could see what he meant. "You have," she said. "I'll tell the rangers about you. I'll tell the police. I'll tell everybody. They'll have helicopters looking for you and for the hikers. If you hurt them, they'll know." The rifle shook with her words. "I'm going to leave now. Follow me and I'll shoot you dead."

"You're a sick puppy," the man whispered.

But Alice was already backing away from him, picking up her bat, hardly even turning to see where she was going. He tried to get himself out, but he couldn't lever his weight on the bad leg. Alice watched him until she reached a bend, then turned and sprinted down the trail.

When she was out of sight she spotted a rotten log on the ground and slipped the rifle inside it. The man would manage to get out, she was well aware of that, but he wouldn't run anywhere for a while.

Alice walked as fast as her feet would carry her. The storm had cleared and the way down lay straight in front of her.

She soon lost track of time.

She heard the voices before she saw the people. There were kids, somewhere ahead. There were kids, which meant a family, with grown-ups.

What was she going to tell them? What was she going to say? She looked down and she saw her ripped jeans and muddy T-shirt, the baseball bat still gripped in her grimy, scratched hands. What if the man caught up with her, with them?

Behind a shrub Alice took off her T-shirt, found the pink top in her pack and slipped it on. She took off her blue jeans and put on a pair of clean white ones. She rubbed some water from her canteen on her hands and face and, lastly, she pushed her baseball cap deep into her bag. As an afterthought she ran her fingers through her short hair in an attempt to primp.

When a blonde little girl walked out into the clearing where they had stopped for a snack, Mrs. Williams of Portland, Oregon, thought that her parents would be close behind her. When the girl came up to her and she saw her face she knew that something was wrong.

There were questions—more questions than Alice knew how to answer. Five adults and six kids more or less her age, all flocking around her.

To her immense relief two cars were parked next to each other by the recreation area. There were no tents. These people were going home that night.

"How long did you say you were lost?"

"How many days?"

She had to repeat it a couple of times and she was pretty sure that they didn't believe her, that they thought she might be confused. It was decided that they would take her immediately to the park rangers' station—only a few miles away—where they would try to contact her parents. Alice decided not to tell them about the man—if they hadn't believed she had been gone a week, they wouldn't have believed that she had been hunting campers with a crazy man.

The kids seemed to be particularly curious about Alice and peppered her with questions about every little detail of her life, from her name to, bizarrely, her favorite color. Alice answered easily and was glad to be with other children—it brought the world to a normal place—but she always kept an eye on the trail, because she knew that he was coming, knew that he would come after her, knew that the hole in the ground would not hold him forever, and that was a shame.

"Where do you go to school?"

"What happened to your hands?"

"Let her be, let her draw breath, for Pete's sake. Here, baby, are you thirsty?"

Alice saw the shadow approaching behind the line of firs: she recognized the slope of the shoulder and the tilt of the head. The man was studying the group and looking among them for the boy who had stolen his rifle and left him in a ditch. Alice turned sideways. The boy the man had met was gone and his ragged clothes had been left under a pile of leaves. He had never seen her without her baseball cap, never seen her smiling.

The man had his knife but she trusted that the mountain would not give him back his rifle; it would rust and fall apart, just like Alice's red bicycle.

Alice's heart beat hard as she waited to go. Her pack was already in the trunk of the car as she felt the man's eyes seeking her out, searching the busy, chattering group.

Let's go. Let's go. Let's go.

She helped fold a picnic blanket—one kid among many on a sunny day out with their families. In the gloom the shadow stirred as if to make a move toward the group.

They all clambered into the cars.

"Do you like dogs?"

"Come sit next to me, darlin'."

Alice took a shuddering breath. He hadn't seen her: the man's eyes had passed over Alice and he had only seen a little girl with a pink top. She turned back as the car sped away and the shadow was still standing by the tree. She couldn't look away and she hadn't even realized that she was crying until Mrs. Williams put her arm around her and hugged her tight.

"You're going to be all right, honey. You were so good. Your parents are going to be so proud."

The woman smelled of vanilla. *Sweet after death*, Alice thought.

Alice woke up on the narrow cot of the bare on-call room in the rangers' station. She didn't know how long she had slept. It was night and on the chair next to her were the remains of the sandwiches the rangers had given her. Alice had hardly taken a bite.

She heard her father's voice next door and another voice she didn't recognize. It was not exactly an argument but it was getting close to being one.

Alice stood up and found that every cell in her body ached, as if she had been stretched under a steam roller like Wile E. Coyote. She made it to the door and turned the handle.

"Alice . . ." The voice she hadn't recognized belonged to her grandfather. She had only met him once, at her mother's—his daughter's—funeral the previous March. His smile when he saw Alice was the sweetest thing.

Her father stood to one side. He was signing papers by the desk, and when she came in he looked up. Her grandfather hurried to put his arms around her and hug her tight. Alice found that she didn't mind at all. He felt like warm linen.

She wasn't sure what she had seen in her father's eyes and didn't know that she wanted to look at him just yet: she had left him asleep on his bed after a night of card games, after gambling and losing all that Alice had left of her mother. Before running away she had stuck his switchblade knife into his bedside table to make sure he knew how she felt about him.

Alice sighed. *I've done worse since.* At last she looked at her father.

He looked drained under his summer tan. He had not brushed his hair or shaved for days, it seemed.

"Are you all right?" he said.

"Yes," she nodded.

"Sure?"

"Uh-huh."

"You gave us a scare, sweetheart," her grandfather said. His voice was gentle, and with his arm around her he gave her a little squeeze.

"I'm sorry," she said to him, and she meant it.

"Your dad and I were thinking that maybe it would be a good idea if you came to Seattle for a while, spent some time with us. What do you think?"

"A while?"

"Yes, a few weeks, if you like. We'd love to get to know you better. What do you think?"

"Dad?"

"Your grandmother would like it very much," her father said.

"She sure would," her grandfather added with warmth.

Okay, yes, she got it then. At twelve Alice could read her father better than anyone in the world, and he had barely looked her in the eye since she'd walked into the room: he was not going to ask her to go back home with him to Friday Harbor. He wasn't going to talk to her, he wasn't going to explain what had happened. Not after the switchblade knife, not with the intricate fabric of anger and pain that lay between them.

After the last seven days Alice didn't know what she wanted anymore. And yet, maybe, exhausted as she was, it would have felt good to see her father fighting for her, just a little bit—instead of standing there like a stranger. Even the two rangers in the corner had to wonder what the heck was wrong with the girl when the dad didn't so much as give her a hug after she'd been missing for a week. Maybe he could have fought for her a little bit.

"What . . . what about the man?" Alice abruptly asked the ranger she had spoken to when she first arrived.

"What man?" her grandfather said.

"Your girl told us a story about a man in the park—"

"It's *not* a story," Alice interrupted him, and the steel in her voice startled the grown-ups around her. "I can take you back to the place where I hid his rifle. I can take you back to the place where the hikers' camp was—it's not far from the waterfall."

"A *rifle*?" her grandfather said.

Alice's father turned to the ranger. His voice was soft and each word was measured. "My daughter lost her mother five months ago. She's been going through a tough time. We all have. Sometimes she goes off into her own world. You understand?"

"I do," the ranger replied. But he was a kind man, and to Alice he said, "We'll look. I promise you that we'll look for him."

Alice could have forgiven her father for not wanting her back, but to let them believe that she was lying was more than she could bear. Tears stung her eyes.

"He has a hunting knife and he taught me how to skin a rabbit," she said through gritted teeth. "Do you want me to show you?"

Chapter 49

When Alice Madison woke up on Tuesday morning her thoughts did not tumble back to the fire or to the shooting the previous day. She gazed at the ceiling above her and thought about a skinny boy who had written in the mud with a stick because it was the only way he could communicate with her.

In spite of everything she had been ready to believe, the mosaic of truth had not delivered Jeb Tanner as the murderer and Madison couldn't ignore that. The words *evidence as truth* were coming back to mock her. And yet there was still the message—no, the appeal—that someone had given Robert Dennen on the scrap of cloth; and he must have thought that it had been sent from the Tanner children—otherwise why would he have called Children's Services?

Someone like Jeb Tanner, someone who isolates his kids, someone who teaches them how to use a knife before they know how to talk to another person . . . there had to be something that she could do to help them. Still, what Tanner was doing was not a felony, and she was a homicide detective, not a social worker.

Madison shifted on the bed and wrapped herself in the blankets. Did it matter who or what she was? For some reason Samuel had trusted her enough to speak with her.

For Madison it was enough—it was plenty.

It was barely after 7 a.m. when Kevin Brown walked into the Magpie. He settled on a stool at the counter and waited. The diner was glossy in the way that cafés can be first thing in the morning, before the day begins and customers spill drinks and drop food. At 7 a.m. the Magpie was polished and completely empty.

Joyce Cartwell appeared a moment later from the back room. She was slipping on her apron and stopped when she saw him.

"Hi," she said.

"Hi."

"I'm not going to ask you what happened yesterday. Don't worry." Joyce turned on the coffee percolator and dipped a scooper into a large can. "The chief's message on the news covered the basics. But I know you were there, and I was thinking of you. I just hoped you were okay."

"I am."

"Good."

Her smile was still a lovely thing.

"I wanted to thank you," Brown said, and he was glad that there was no one else there. How long it would be before other early birds came in for their eggs and bacon he didn't know. He had things to say, and he should speak while he could.

"You didn't have to do what you did," he said. "It took courage, and we are—I am—very grateful."

Joyce was wiping the already spotless counter because she needed to do something with herself.

"I'm not brave," she said, "but I do have a really good memory, and I remember what it was like to live with him."

"I'm sure you do."

Joyce hesitated. The words were there, and so was the recollection of the event, but she had never told anyone. She spoke quickly before she changed her mind. "When I was seventeen, Jeb and I argued about a boy that I was seeing. We were in the barn. He really lost it and he threatened me. He was holding a knife . . . and he slipped."

"He *slipped*?"

"That's what he told our father when they took me to the emergency room. Jeb was on his way to college a few weeks after that. We never spoke about what happened, and we never lived under the same roof again."

"I'm so sorry."

Joyce shook her head. "Don't be. Even our father was afraid of him. He loved him, but he was terrified of him. If that's even possible."

"I thought you were brave," Brown said, and he was about to reach for her hand, "but you're more than brave—"

Two customers blew in from the road, bringing a blast of cold air and chatter. They greeted Joyce and nodded to Brown, as if he sat on that same stool every morning.

Joyce poured him some coffee. "Oatmeal and toast?" she said. What needed to be said had been said.

"Yes, thank you," Brown replied.

He watched her as she took her customers' orders.

"You look all lit up this morning," one of them said to her.

"I have gifts for you," Sorensen said to Madison.

They had just made it to the senior center, and Sorensen had been checking on her lab's overnight progress.

"What kind of gifts?"

"The best kind. The kind that comes with bioinformatics graphics."

"My favorite."

"As you know, Joyce Cartwell came in yesterday and let me take a buccal swab."

Madison nodded. It was a bold thing for Joyce to do, and Madison was more grateful to the woman than she could say.

"I see doubt in your eyes, Detective."

"It's not doubt, Amy, it's just that Tanner isn't a suspect anymore."

"Which is why I said I brought you gifts . . . the buccal swab from Joyce was a familial match to the blood recovered at the car crime scene."

"Jeb Tanner was at the scene where Dr. Dennen died?"

"No, not Jeb Tanner. It wasn't a fifty percent result—which it would have been in a brother-sister match. We're talking about a twenty-five percent match."

Madison tried to make sense of what Sorensen was telling her.

The investigator continued. "It was the kind of match you would find between an aunt and a close relative, like a niece or a nephew. Or between grandparent and grandchild."

"If Joyce is our starting point . . ."

"Then the person who was present at the crime scene was her niece or her nephew."

It didn't make sense.

"It's really not what I expected," Madison conceded.

"And since we had her sample, I thought I'd take a good look at the cloth the message had been scribbled on. For my efforts I found something, so close to the charcoal writing that it was nearly invisible to the naked eye."

Sorensen enjoyed the moment.

"Amy?"

"Whoever was present at the car crime scene also handled the cloth and possibly wrote the message."

It was a lot to handle on a single cup of coffee, and Madison felt that she was gaping at the investigator. "One of the Tanner kids was a witness when Dennen was murdered?"

"Looks like it—since it's unlikely that Ben Taylor involved anybody else in his scheme. The blood could have come from trying to help the doctor in the burning car or from a nose bleed. I can't tell you for sure."

"And he or she handled the cloth the message was written on?"

"Yes, it doesn't mean that they wrote it—you're clear about that, right? But they definitely handled it."

Madison had trouble believing that Tanner would let one of his kids wander around anywhere alone, especially at night and anywhere near the town; nevertheless, one of them had. One of them had been reaching out. Could it have been Samuel? No, Madison had specifically asked him and he had said no. Someone else, then—and Samuel didn't know about it.

Madison reached for her notes on Tanner. Records had shown that, over the years, some in other states and some in Washington, he had registered nine children. Samuel had said there were twelve of them—three, probably the youngest, like the small blond boy, did not exist at all in the records. Three young lives did not exist at all—except in their father's kingdom. In her bones Madison knew that they needed more than Children's Services.

Samuel Tanner was on wolf duty. The day had dawned clear and cold, and the boy had left the cabin, grateful for the time alone that would allow him to put some order into his scattered thoughts. The snow crunched underfoot and the air had a bite to it. Every track—including his own steps—left a neat impression and he could read the life of the forest in each mark and in each dent.

The dread left by his conversation with Luke had stayed with him; somehow, it had infused every cell of his body. Something had happened to Caleb. Luke was big and strong: if he was that afraid, there must have been good reason for it.

Samuel couldn't quite make sense of it, because Caleb had been with him every day since he had run away—in the black raven feather and in the cave and in every thought that had warmed his heart when he'd been sure that he would see him again. How could something have happened to him and Samuel not know?

The firs opened into a view of the valley below and Jackknife Pass above. Samuel squinted in the sudden light. For a moment, in the far distance, he had seen gray dappled shapes cantering behind the trees.

Chapter 50

They left on Thursday, once the snow on the airport runway had been cleared by the plows, and the paperwork of the investigation had been written up and signed by all involved. Sorensen had packed up her mobile lab and they had each stripped their bed in the Miller guesthouse.

Polly Howell was in the hospital with her husband, who was expected to make a full recovery, but other volunteers had been ready to step in.

In the same hospital lay Lee Edwards, who was being monitored but was also expected to recover. She was too weak to be interviewed, and Chief Sangster would do the honors in a few days' time.

Deputy Jay Kupitz had been discharged and had returned home to a hero's welcome.

Hockley had driven him. Just that morning he had dreamt about seeing the house collapse on his friend and pulling him out of the smoking rubble.

George Goyer flew the red Cessna into a perfect sky, and even Brown had little to say about the flight.

Sorensen slept through it.

But Madison, as the plane soared and circled, kept her eyes on Jackknife.

Five weeks later

Chapter 51

March had been warm, and the snow that had piled up in high drifts in the yard was gone. It had left mud that seemed to dry quickly in the sun but was keen to return to soggy dampness late in the day.

Jeb Tanner had been uneasy for weeks, since the visit from Sangster and the detectives. The fact that nothing had happened could only mean that the chief had tucked his tail between his legs and gone to bother somebody else. It was a satisfying victory; however, Tanner's moods had been fickle and his temper unpredictable. The children—whatever their age—had been as wary as if a snake were living in the house among them.

Tanner walked out into the yard with his morning coffee. He heard the approaching engine sound from the dirt path and for a moment he thought it would be Clay coming with the gas tank he needed.

Alice Madison rode with Chief Sangster in his cruiser. She had been quiet since they left town, and her thumb had been rubbing the coarse navy texture of her ballistic vest. She didn't think that she would be needing it, as the county SWAT team had had Tanner in their sights since he stepped out of the house. But Tanner was not alone: in her experience it was the first time that Madison had to both protect and be protected from the same individuals.

Everything had been planned for days and there had been little chat in the car. Hockley and Brown were in the back while Kupitz, on crutches and under protest, had remained at the station.

Suddenly they were there, and the cars crowded the yard.

The brief had been simple: be safe but be careful. The Tanner children had never interacted with anyone, aside from a very small group of Tanner's friends. It was crucial that their first impression of the wider world should not be an officer pointing a firearm at their older brother or sister.

Tanner had stiffened where he was. The cars had covered the distance between the buildings and the forest too quickly for him to do anything else, and he had decided to wait. His face told them that he was as ready to chase them away as he had been the previous time.

Madison was glad to see that he was not holding a child. Her eyes searched the yard and the outbuildings for a glimpse of Samuel, but she didn't see him.

"It's your party," Sangster said when the cruiser came to a stop.

Jeb Tanner looked them all up and down: the detectives with the chief, the county deputies, the state troopers.

Madison stepped forward. "Mr. Tanner, you're under arrest," she said, and her voice was cool and measured.

"What for?" Tanner took a sip of coffee. He might have looked tough to his kids; nonetheless, there was anxiety in his meanness and it didn't escape anyone's notice that he was unarmed. Hockley and two other deputies moved to the man's side.

"You blackmailed an attorney in California to file for divorce on behalf of your wife, Naomi Tanner, when in fact he had never met her and her signature was forged on every document."

"I have no idea what you're talking about. Naomi ran out on us."

Tanner was effectively in custody and he was being interviewed. Madison read him his rights and continued.

"Reuben Martin was easy to blackmail, because you knew him and you knew his weaknesses from twenty years ago. He did what he was told."

"You can't prove it."

"He recorded you, Mr. Tanner. I met him and he's a vile piece of work, but he's not stupid. He knew that helping you would come back to bite him in the ass."

Tanner bristled.

"Where's your wife?" Madison said.

"She left."

"No," Madison replied. "She didn't. The lawyer's girlfriend called your sister Joyce from California, pretending to be Naomi, so that people would believe she had left. Joyce had met her only once and she couldn't tell the difference."

Madison was aware that a group of youths had spilled out onto the porch. She wanted to keep things as calm as possible. She glanced at them: boys and girls, the young men a little older than the girls. Some looked worried, some looked afraid—whether for themselves or for their father, Madison couldn't say. None of them was armed—thank God—but Samuel was not among them.

"Where's Samuel?" she said.

Something hideous washed over Tanner's face. "He ran away too," he said. "Two weeks ago."

A coil of ice tightened itself around Madison.

"Where's Samuel?" she repeated. She counted ten young people in total. Two were missing. "Who else is missing?"

Jeb Tanner smiled. "I want a lawyer," he said.

Madison kept herself in check. "Mr. Tanner, you help us now—before you lawyer up—and it will be taken into consideration in court. Where is Samuel? Where is your wife?"

Tanner, with his hands already in cuffs, twisted and hollered: "You're in charge, Luke. Anybody speaks to these trespassers, and when I get back there will be hell to pay. You understand me, boy?"

You understand me, boy?

A tall youth in his twenties—Madison remembered him from the barn—looked as fearful as if the cuffs had been on his own wrists.

Madison leaned forward. "I understand you better than you can ever imagine, Tanner, and I'll make it my life's mission to make sure your children are free of you. We have warrants to search your home and your land, and I've cleared my calendar for the next month."

Tanner smiled. "I'll be back home by sunset, bitch, and if I find you here—"

"You'll find me right here. And if you're back—which I doubt—we'll have us a frank and honest talk. Looking forward to it."

Hockley guided Jeb Tanner into a cruiser with the kind of manners his mother had taught him. Madison had driven the point into every single person who was taking part in the raid: whatever happened, the kids had to see their father being treated with civility.

The social worker who had visited the farm weeks earlier waited until she was given the signal that Jeb Tanner was in the cruiser and then drove in from the forest. A family law attorney, for the minors residing at the farm, sat in the passenger seat. The cars crossed on the dirt road and neither turned to meet Jeb Tanner's eyes.

Madison had learned their names over the five weeks that she'd been away. When she introduced herself, she already knew who they all were, except for Ruth, Sarah, and David—the younger ones.

"We're not talking to you," Luke said.

"I understand. I heard what your father said, and I don't blame you. We're here to look for your mother because we think that something bad happened to her, and I think that something happened to Samuel too. If you know anything, or have seen anything that might help us to find him, I hope that you'll speak with me because I want to help."

Brown and the chief were busy searching the property, but Madison stayed close to the kids.

One hour passed and no one spoke to her—even though the little ones eyed her with open curiosity.

I have waited too long. I have waited far too long.

Chapter 52

Samuel Tanner measured the streak of light that told him spring was coming. Since the cave had become his permanent home he had dragged inside short branches with soft needles for bedding and more kindling for smokeless fires.

One morning, two weeks earlier, when the hunter-and-prey game had finished with the customary gunshots, he had simply not gone back and had slept through the day curled up on the cave's floor.

The woman, Alice, had not come back, and he had never felt more alone.

One of the handprints on the wall was Caleb's, and Samuel would often find himself gazing at it. He roamed the forest and had explored the ruins of the mine. Once, he had snuck back to a spot where he could see the yard and had been glad to see Abigail playing with David. He had even seen Flare in the paddock. The mare's head had turned and the boy had backed away.

He was a ghost now.

Sometimes the boy went hungry, but not too often: he could trap his food and had even found candy that must have been dropped by summer hikers, the wrapping still intact though a little muddy.

Samuel believed that he was safer in the cave than at the farm, and from there he'd watch over the others, as Cal had watched over him.

A sudden rustle came from the entrance and the boy flattened himself against the wall. His heart raced as he got up to face whoever had found him.

There was no place to go.

Alice Madison stepped inside the wider mouth of the cave and found herself in a stone room. In the half-light she saw a dirt floor and a curved wall. The boy stood in a patch of shadows.

"Samuel," she said.

He gawked at her.

"Hello," she said.

He could not speak.

"I'm sorry that it took so long," she said.

He was grimy and as skinny as ever, but otherwise he seemed all right.

"How . . . how did you find me?"

"Your brother," she said, and she turned to the tunnel. "Come, let him see you."

For a moment something thumped in Samuel's heart, and then Jonah shuffled forward. He glanced at Samuel and then looked away.

"Jonah . . . ," Samuel said.

"We went to the farm this morning to speak to your father," Madison said. "He said that you ran away, but after he was gone Jonah told me that he knew where you were."

"You knew? About the cave?" Samuel said.

Jonah nodded.

"How long have you known?"

"Two years." Jonah's voice was barely a whisper.

Samuel thought of all the times that Jonah could have caught him but had let him be. "How did you find out?"

"I followed you once."

"Why didn't you tell anyone?"

"It was your secret."

"Why didn't you tell me?"

Jonah shrugged. "I didn't think you wanted anyone else to know."

Madison turned around in the stone room and her gaze fell on the painted figures. They shifted and danced in the dusty light.

"You did this?" she said to Samuel.

The boy nodded. It was eerie and beautiful.

Things were catching up with Samuel faster than his mind could compute them. "Jonah, was it you who gave me the bread when I was in the lonely place?"

Madison was not sure what the lonely place was, but Jonah nodded and pointed at a candy wrapper on the dirt floor. "I put the candy where I knew you would find it."

Jonah was almost as big as Luke, but he seemed to take up no space at all. His gaze had looked blank the first time Madison had seen him in the barn, only because Jonah's light came from a place very far from the surface.

"Where's Papa gone?" Samuel said to Madison.

"I'm very sorry, Samuel, but your father has been arrested. He lied about your mother running away and the divorce, and we think he hurt her."

Samuel nodded. It was a surprise, and yet it wasn't.

"I think he killed Caleb too," he said.

It took them two days. They succeeded only because of a combination of hints, clues, and scraps of memories from Seth, Joshua, and Jesse, who had seen their father return from a particular place around the time their mother had disappeared. Nobody liked to go there because the clearing was haunted by the spirits of the dead Jackknife miners.

In the soft March soil the officers from the County forensic lab found human remains—one male and one female. They would later be identified as Caleb and Naomi Tanner.

They would never know for sure, but it was possible that Caleb had confronted his father about his mother's true fate and the man had made sure he wouldn't tell anyone else.

Slowly the Tanner children had begun to talk, and they had much to say. When they finally believed that their father was not coming back—Madison explained to them that he hadn't made bail—Seth and Joshua had found two axes in the tool shed and had taken apart a small hut near the barn. Madison didn't ask them why, but it seemed to please the others.

Samuel and Jonah spent a lot of time doing farm chores together. When the social worker told them that the remains had been found, they guided the others to the cave and showed them Caleb's handprint.

There had been no crying and no immediate manifestation of grief at the news. But Madison could tell that the pain was there; they had just never been allowed to express it.

"How did you manage to get into Ludlow from here?" Madison said to Jonah one afternoon.

They were sitting on the porch as Samuel walked the little boy, sitting on the mare, around the paddock.

"There's a shortcut," Jonah said. "It takes about an hour, if you know the way."

The Tanner farm looked as austere and spartan as before, and yet there were changes in the air. Through the open doors and windows the tenderness of spring had found its way into the very building.

"Why did you visit the town?" Madison said after a while.

Jonah avoided eye contact, but his answers were always direct. "I wanted to see what the people were like."

"And your father never found out?"

"Sometimes I sleep in the barn."

"And what were the people like?"

"They didn't look like killers and thieves," Jonah said, and then added, "except for one."

Madison held up the picture from Ben Taylor's driver's license. "Do you know this man?"

Jonah nodded.

"Where do you know him from?"

"He shot the doctor and set fire to his car."

"I'm sorry you saw that, Jonah."

"I tried to help."

"I know."

It had been Jonah's blood they had found near the car.

"The doctor came here and he argued with Papa about us."

"Yes," Madison said. "You asked him for help, didn't you?"

Jonah nodded. "And he sent help," he said. "He sent you."

Madison had spent a lot of time at the farm in the last few days, but the social workers had suggested that she might need to withdraw before the children became too attached to her.

Madison had agreed.

They would stay in touch through Joyce, but it was time to go.

"I don't know why I'm so nervous," Joyce Cartwell said.

"You'll be fine. They're eager to meet you," Brown said.

They had just driven through the gate and had almost reached the clearing.

"They have a lot of catching up to do, you know," Brown continued.

"I know."

"A friend of their father faked the homeschooling records." Joyce sighed.

"And their knowledge of the wider world is extremely limited. Tanner told them that they shouldn't trust anybody. It's miraculous that they're as sane as they are."

Leaving Ludlow for the second time was different because Madison didn't know when she would come back.

Much was still uncertain: Betty Dennen had been told the name of the man who had killed her husband, but not the real reason why. She hadn't been told that two people in the Witness Protection Program had been pursued from Boston to Ludlow by a son seeking to avenge the betrayal of his father and his own abandonment.

Lee Edwards and Andrew Howell had decided to stay and keep their identities, and Andrew had told Polly the truth—or a version of it. He told her that he had testified against a brutal murderer and that's why he could never go back to Boston, and Polly had believed him. Madison, on the other hand, had read the court papers and knew that Andrew Howell might very well be the man who had killed the messenger. There was no way to know for sure.

In due time Jeb Tanner would be found guilty of two counts of murder in the first degree, and would be sentenced to life without parole. His defense attorney had tried to get him to accept a murder in the second degree charge and avoid a trial, but he was unsuccessful. The jury took three hours to return a unanimous verdict, and Joyce Cartwell was there to see it.

Robert Dennen had brought them to Ludlow and he had led them to the Tanner children. Madison didn't want to forget him in the turmoil of the Ben Taylor case: she didn't want to forget how the doctor's quick thinking, that night in the clinic, had helped them to discover the truth about those hidden lives.

Jonah, Madison knew, would not forget.

Chapter 53

Alice Madison lay on the grass in her backyard with her eyes closed. The ground was warm with April sunshine and the air smelled sweet. She had been back for a week, but her mind was full of Ludlow.

Brown was frequently in touch with Joyce, and the news was good: twenty-year-old Abigail had stepped up to lead the clan, and the others were happy to work together and stay on the farm. The only one who appeared lost was the oldest, Luke, because Jeb Tanner had gotten his talons into him the deepest.

Samuel was learning to read and write, and had spent a day in the diner with Joyce.

Baby steps.

Inside a coat pocket Madison had found the black feather from the Tanner farm, and it was still on her dresser.

Brown had seemed lighter since they returned, and that was good enough for Madison. They had not spoken at length about the shooting or the fire or anything else. They had both been there, they knew what happened. They didn't need to hash it out. Every day that she saw him across the desk, she was grateful that her hand had been steady and her aim true.

Madison fell asleep, and when she woke up the sun had dipped behind Vashon Island and Nathan Quinn was sitting next to her on the grass. He had taken off his suit jacket and his tie, and his black eyes were on the water.

"I'd like to tell you a story," she said.

"I like stories."

"You might not like this one."

"Are you in it?"

"Yes, I am."

"Then," Quinn said, "it's all I need."

Chapter 54

John James Walker managed to get himself out of the ditch because he was pissed off and determined, and no little grunt was going to get the better of him. He couldn't move very fast at first, but—having stashed his backpack in a safe place—he made his way down the trail, tracking the small footprints that would lead him straight to the boy and the rifle.

He had been worried for a second there—not that the kid would shoot him on purpose, no, but that he would blow his head off by accident. The man grinned a little . . . *that* would be lesson number three, once he'd gotten the kid back. He hadn't realized that he would enjoy the company of that little squirt as much as he did, but teaching him had been like the best times in the army.

Walker hobbled down the trail until he reached the recreation area. The boy would be looking to find other people to spill his guts to, no question about it. He heard the voices and kept himself in the shadows—far enough to be safe, close enough to see. He took out his binoculars.

Day campers, he muttered to himself, five adults and seven kids. Walker examined the children who were the right age and height. His boy was not among them, and it seemed the families were just packing up to leave. No, he was definitely not there: of the seven kids, four were girls and only three were boys—dark-haired and younger than his own recruit. Just then, one of the girls glanced in his direction, a quick glance sideways that nobody noticed. She had looked exactly at the spot where someone coming down from the trail might be stopping. A skinny blonde girl, wearing a pink top, who was laughing at something someone said.

Walker had not spent much time around kids—frankly, his sisters' bored him to tears—and he couldn't say how old this bunch was, or what grade they attended. But he did notice the little girl, and she was the exact same height and weight and coloring as *his* boy. She glanced again in his direction. Bright eyes in a sun-freckled face. *Follow me and I'll shoot you dead.*

The man studied the child. No, it wasn't possible. It was just not possible.

The sound of slamming car doors and engines starting up brought him back, but they were already driving off, already disappearing down the lane, already gone.

His bad leg faltered and Walker held on to the tree trunk for support. His anger was snake-fast and toxic. It was unlikely, but feasible, that the kid could have been picked up by another group and had been whisked off to a rangers' station or something. And *his* rifle had disappeared with the kid.

Walker counted to ten, and then to ten again, because he was angry enough to tear a chunk out of the tree with his bare hands, and anger would get him nowhere. He closed his eyes and leaned his face against the rough bark, rubbed it against the coarse texture.

It was the way things worked: the world always takes stuff away from you, if you let it. And he'd had such plans for that boy.

The hikers would still be where he'd left them, which was a comforting thought. They would be a welcome distraction from his rage; he needed to stay frosty and plan his next move. The past few days had been a revelation, and a whole new future had opened up to him: he would find another apprentice, a young one who'd do as he was told. The country was full of them, after all—lost kids who needed to learn things they didn't teach in school. And no one taught the kind of skills John James Walker taught.

The man pushed off from the tree and hobbled back toward the trail. He'd pick up his pack and try to be back to the hikers' camp by dawn. He didn't have a rifle anymore, but there was plenty a capable man—a well-trained man—could do with a sharp knife.

The morning after the missing little girl had been found by the Portland family, the ranger who had spoken to her tidied away the paperwork of the case. Whatever the father might say, it was pretty remarkable for a twelve-year-old to travel all the way from Friday Harbor to Mount Baker by herself and survive in the wilderness alone for a whole week—his own beloved daughter couldn't even make it to the mall without being dropped off with spending money and a pickup time. It seemed the kid had a temper on her as well—good luck to the grandparents, he thought.

A knot of young men and women burst in, and the ranger looked up.

"There's a man with a rifle . . ." The woman was in her twenties, sunburnt and puffing under a massive backpack, ". . . and he's going to shoot people."

They must have been running all the way.

"I need you to take a breath and tell me exactly where you've seen this man," the ranger said.

The month before, they'd had a bomb scare—an old car battery left under a fern—and the month before that, a dead body at the bottom of Riley Lake—a particularly ugly log with a shirt snagged on it.

The girl gulped a cup of water from the cooler. "We've been camping not too far from the Ridley Creek trail, and yesterday I found this in my journal . . . we got caught in the rain, and just made it back."

She pushed a battered notebook into the ranger's hand and opened it at the last page.

"I had left it out overnight, a couple of days earlier, and since then I hadn't looked at it."

The ranger's eyes traveled across the scribbled page.

"Is this true?" he asked, even though he didn't need to.

The girl nodded.

The handwriting was rushed, but perfectly legible.

A man has tracked you for two days. He has a rifle.

He watched you skinny dipping today and he said that he would like to see you try to survive on the mountain with nothing but the skin you were born with. He forced me to steal your red canteen and I'm really sorry.

Please leave as soon as you can. Please leave as soon as you read this.

I don't know his name but I think he's crazy I'm

It looked as if the writer would have added more, but had been disturbed.

The ranger reached under his desk. "Is this it?" he said, holding out a red canteen.

The girl gaped at him. "How . . . ?"

"I need to make some calls . . ."

They had little to go by, except for a sketchy physical description and the fact that the man might, or might not, limp. And might, or might not, have been a vet. In essence, they had nothing. What they did know, though, was that the man's rifle was hidden somewhere inside a rotting log—and that, everything considered, had to be the blessing of the day.

After putting out a hopeless park-wide alert, the ranger dug a piece of paper out of his pocket and called a Seattle number—the kid should know her message had been found.

Alice had never been to Seattle. The relationship between her mother and her mother's parents had been strained, for reasons that the girl knew nothing about. And yet now those reasons seemed to matter not at all as Alice—asleep in the back of her grandfather's BMW—traveled toward Elliott Bay.

Every few minutes the man's eyes strayed to the little girl lying on the back seat, as if he could not quite believe what he saw in the rearview mirror. He had called his wife from the rangers' station to tell her that they'd drive through the night to get back. He couldn't bear the thought of Alice having to bed down in some unfamiliar room in a motel along the way, not after her last week. He had called his wife to tell her that her granddaughter was coming home.

Maybe Alice would tell him why she had run away, maybe she would not. He wouldn't press her for it. The mistakes made with his own daughter were carved into his heart, and this little girl—who looked so much like her—would never again feel that she needed to cut and run.

Alice woke up and straightened up on the seat. The road was following the soft turns of a deep green hill and to their right the water of the bay was a pool of red-gold and mist. She had slept for hours and was not entirely sure that she was awake.

"Almost there," her grandfather said.

The road was empty and the neighborhood still and, for the first time since leaving the rangers' station and stealing a quick hug from her father, Alice was nervous. What if her grandparents didn't like her? What if they thought there was something wrong with her because of everything that had happened in the last seven days? And what if there really was something wrong with her?

Alice pressed her brow against the cool glass. She was tired and hungry, and her thoughts felt fuzzy. She wondered if this was the place where her mother had grown up. Her thoughts chased each other in circles until her grandfather turned right into a sloping driveway.

Alice held her breath.

The house, tucked away and invisible from the road, seemed to emerge from the very trees; it was stone, brick, and wood. Behind it the girl glimpsed a green lawn that rolled into the flat water.

"Do you like to kayak?" her grandfather said.

"Yes."

"Good, I'll find you a life jacket in the shed. Kids kayak around here all the time."

Her grandfather busied himself with her bag and unlocking the door, his hands suddenly clumsy. The inside of the house was shady, and a breeze blew through the rooms from the open French doors.

"I'll go get your grandmother."

Alice nodded.

There was a fireplace in the corner and gardening gloves on a chair. There were three trays of cookies on the kitchen counter—her grandmother must have been baking all night—and roses in a vase on the table.

Alice saw everything and touched nothing—until she saw her mother's picture in a silver frame on the bookcase. There she was, a few years older than Alice, smiling at someone Alice couldn't see. The little girl picked up the frame, with hands still a little grubby from Mount Baker's earth, and couldn't look away. There she was, younger and happier than her daughter had ever seen her, standing by the fireplace.

Alice let go of the breath she had been holding.

She gazed at the picture of her mother until she heard the voices coming up the stairs, and turned.

Acknowledgments

It is usually in these final paragraphs that I mention that occasionally—while writing about Seattle—I make up street names and addresses so that awful things would not be happening in real homes where real people live. However, in this case, things are a little different: Colville County is an entirely fictional place, and so is the town of Ludlow. Having said that, if they existed that's exactly what they would be like. I researched the climate and the properties of neighboring counties—Ferry, Stevens, and Pend Oreille—and I have borrowed the name Colville from Fort Colville near the Kettle Falls fur-trading site established in 1825.

Ludlow itself is a combination of Banff in Alberta, Canada, and Friday Harbor on San Juan Island in Washington State. I know both and it was a joy to re-create part of them on paper.

The first time I arrived in Banff the driver had to slow down on Main Street because a massive elk was crossing the road; another time we found a cougar paw print in the snow, yards away from the back of the hotel. That's the kind of place I wanted to write about.

Writing is solitary, and the people who help and support this rather odd occupation are very precious . . .

First, I'd like to thank the Seattle Police Department for giving me access to its officers and making it possible for me to watch them at work and talk without restrictions.

In particular, I would like to thank police officer Michele Vallor—only recently retired after thirty years in the SPD—who took me along on her shift and showed me what policing down-town Seattle is all about. Michele Vallor is the inspiration for Monica Vincent—Madison's field training officer—and she is everything a police officer should aim to be. Spending a day with her as she dealt with homelessness, the mentally ill, an assault, generally abusive behavior, and the constant demands of patrol—as well as keeping an eye on me—was humbling. And, as Monica Vincent did with Madison, Officer Vallor took me to Kobe Terrace to show me the cherry trees in blossom at the beginning of the shift on a bright spring morning.

Also my deepest thanks to homicide sergeant Bob Vallor for his frankness, support, and the best challenge coin I will ever have; and to homicide detective Donna Stangeland for her time and her honesty about the pressures of policing and the most important attributes of a detective.

All the officers I met were committed to their jobs and very help-ful, and all the mistakes in these pages are mine and mine alone.

My partners in crime were many, and I thank them with all my heart . . .

The Berglunds in Seattle and Mayor Nicola Smith in Lynnwood for their constant support through the years and for giving Mad-ison her home.

The Giambanco family, in Italy and in Atlanta, for their cheer-leading. And my sisters for long-distance sisterhood and up-close margaritas.

Kezia Martin, the first person ever to meet Madison years and years ago.

Anita Phillips, the oracle of all things American, brave enough to read an unedited manuscript.

Clair Chamberlain, for professional counsel and for common sense when common sense was needed.

Gerald, for large and small polar bears who guard the door while I'm writing in the cave.

And my mum, who believes in courage, always.

Blacksheep Ltd. gave the books their look and kindly allowed me to use it in other media.

My thanks to the wonderful team at Quercus USA: Nathaniel Marunas, Amelia Iuvino, Amanda Harkness, and Elyse Gregov brought Alice Madison home and managed to make sense of her British accent.

Stef Bierwerth, my editor at Quercus UK, whose passion, determination, and talent are a wonder to behold.

Teresa Chris, my agent, for cracking the whip and being a tireless supporter—her trust in my writing has been the single most important constant in a shifting world.

Valentina Giambanco was born in Italy. After receiving a degree in English and Drama at Goldsmiths, University of London, she worked for a classical music retailer and as a bookseller in her local bookshop. She started in films as an editor's apprentice in a 35 mm cutting room and since then has worked on many award-winning UK and US pictures, from small independent projects to large studio productions. Valentina lives in London.

www.valentinagiambanco.com
@vm_giambanco